CM TILLMAN

Gilded Hero

Cover by GetCovers

Editing by CC&NN

First edition

This book was professionally typeset on Reedsy.
Find out more at reedsy.com

For all the girls who were told by guys, 'Just because you can doesn't mean you should'

And to the douche canoes in my college writing class:

I could
So I did
Suck it

Foreword

Please take a moment to read the following for any content you may not vibe with:

Gore, sex, death, violence, language.

This is a work of science fiction/fantasy in the future, some things are made up entirely by the author.

Acknowledgments

Thank you for ARC reading my work!

Chapter 1

Did I just fuck a superhero?

Shit, shit, what did I do? Fucking one-night stands! I silently berate myself.

The stranger stirs next to me again as my eyes, heavy from the oncoming hangover and migraine, struggle to adjust. I can feel a throbbing behind my right temple. I swear I just saw his eyes open, and they were not human-looking.

A light jingle shatters my thoughts - the tiny screen on my wristpad, the personal device we all use, flashes, and my heart races when I see the time. I'm going to be late for work if I don't get my ass into gear.

I roll over as quietly as possible, thinking maybe I'm mistaken. He's human - he has to be. I think I would have noticed a fucking Super in a bar - it didn't matter how many drinks I'd had, there was no way I would have missed that. I find my shirt crumpled on the floor, along with my torn underwear. I pause, vaguely remembering him ripping them off in the heat of the moment.

It's not like I care. They aren't my favorite pair, but it means I will be going commando all day at work, and my uniform pants are not exactly gentle around the nether regions. I grumble and wince as my injured hand works to pull up my pants while attempting to remain silent through the searing pain. It hadn't been the first time I'd punched a guy at a bar, and as long as sleazy dirtbags were milling about, I doubted it would be the last.

I freeze when I notice the hickies trailing from my left thigh and up straight to my - I scoff, pulling the pants up as I recall the stranger being

1

particularly skilled with his tongue.

I don't mind the marks. In fact, it will be nice to have a reminder of the completely unhinged time we had, but that's just it - a fleeting reminder best left in the past.

I find my shoes, and just as I am slipping them on, I hear him. He rolls over, his dark lashes fluttering, and slowly opens his eyes to see me frozen, one foot in the air, as I struggle to get my shoe on.

"Heyyy," I say, trying to appear nonchalant. "I really have to get going, or I'm going to be late, but-" I start my usual exit line but falter when I notice his eyes. I know I'm not hallucinating it this time - his pupils aren't normal. They aren't round like a human's, but more like a plus sign.

Because he isn't human, I realize, my gut dropping as my skin grows cold.

"Fuck, you are a fucking Super!" I spit, losing my balance and falling over.

He's out of the bed before I can blink, his arm catching me before my head bashes into his wall, despite being on the other side of the room just seconds before. His hand is soft against my suddenly clammy skin, his warm breath skating over my cheek as he carefully pulls me back to my feet.

His scent hits me, a heady mixture of cedar and vetiver with a hint of fresh air. How did he smell so fresh and clean after the night we had? The thought strikes me, and my cheeks heat. I can't be thinking about his smell, not when I've just found out he isn't human!

As if his eyes weren't damning enough, his inhuman speed put the nail in the coffin. Only a Super gifted with the power of speed could do that. It's a common enough power among Supers, so it's not entirely surprising he possesses the ability, but it is jarring to see it happen in person. These assholes usually stuck to their floating city, Legion, where all the Supers who claimed to be heroes lived high above us lowly humans, flaunting their inhuman powers.

I pull away, unable to meet his amber eyes as I back up. Seeing those pupils brings up a bevy of memories and emotions that I don't expect this early in the morning, leaving me feeling off-kilter and nervous.

But mostly mad. Royally pissed off.

"Are you alright?" he asks with a voice that had made my knees weak in the bar. It was the kind of voice you let wrap around you and that you wished would whisper sinful things in your ear.

I shake my head when I recall he'd done just that the night before. I dislodge them from my mind, instead focusing on the issue at hand and not on how his voice made my knees weak.

"Fuck no, I'm not alright!" I shout as I pull away from him. "You're a fucking Super - and a liar!"

"I didn't lie," he objects, having the audacity to look hurt. "Yes, I used temporary contacts to hide my eyes, but-"

"So you lied." I finish for him, shaking my head, a feeling of shock and disgust rolling over me.

He lets out a long breath, blowing out his cheeks as he lifts a toned arm. Long, deft fingers crawl through his mass of dark hair, letting a few locks fall over his amber eyes. "Okay, I admit that wasn't the best idea. But I didn't do it intending to lie and get you in my bed. It was the opposite, in fact." His explanation rankles me, and I momentarily forget how insanely late I am about to be at work.

"You could have told me what you were at any point last night," I say, poking a finger into his firm chest. "You made the decision not to, which makes you the asshole."

His brows go up, his lips quirking slightly, even as he fights to suppress a smile.

"Could I put some pants on while we continue this conversation?" I glance down to see he is still naked. A scorching heat rolls up my spine to settle in my cheeks. I clutch my shoes close to my chest, suddenly needing to space between us.

"Nope, I am late enough for work," I say, turning on my heels and making a beeline for his front door. I blink, and he's leaning on the wall by the door, wearing a faded pair of blue sweats.

I falter, the mixture of my hangover and migraine clogging the cogs of my mind as I struggle to comprehend how fast he must be able to move if he can throw clothes on and get by me without me seeing.

"Is that your superpower?" I ask, making sure my voice is full of venom.

"Super speed?"

"One of them," he says, cracking a devilish smirk. "You got to witness some of the others last night." His gaze rakes down my body. I feel the heat settle in my core as his eyes lift to meet mine.

"Last night was a mistake." My voice is too soft, too noncommittal for him to believe me, which irritates me. I cough, clearing my throat as I force some heat back into my words. "If I had known what you were, it would have never happened."

He quirks a brow, looking genuinely curious. "That's a first."

"What, someone who respects themselves?" I shoot back.

"A human who won't jump at the opportunity to fuck one of us for a moment of fleeting fame." He says it so nonchalantly, so a matter of fact, that it's all I need to solidify an already long-held belief.

"Only it wouldn't have been, right? As much as I hate my job, it allows me to see all the popular Supers in their rise and fall. I have never seen your face, so you must not be very important. Which means you aren't remotely famous, so fucking you wouldn't get me anywhere." I watch his smirk fall as a mask of indifference covers his face.

"Ah," I say, grabbing the door handle. "Struck a sore spot, huh?" I throw him a sweet-as-sugar smile before I enter the hallway. It's a low blow, but he also struck a sore cord in me with his flippant comment.

Besides, the fucker is actively posing as a human, and I feel betrayed. It's true if I'd known what he was, I wouldn't have continued to stay in the same bar as him, let alone go home with him.

He isn't entirely wrong about humans practically foaming at the mouth for the chance to do what I had just done, though. If I was any other human, this morning would have gone an entirely different route, and for all I knew, that was his whole gimmick.

I wouldn't have been surprised if he claimed that he posed as a human, picked up girls at bars, and then took them home to surprise them the next morning with his big reveal. He probably took photos with them, and let them gush all over him before taking them to bed again.

I shiver at the idea as I make my way down the hall and to the turbo-lift.

4

I almost weep in relief when I see the Medi on the wall next to it. Already feeling the effects of a hangover remedy, I almost make it to the pad when he appears by it.

I recoil, knotting my brows in fury and confusion as he holds up his hands.

"Okay, I fucked up, I know. I just wanted to apologize to you, Lily. I didn't go to that bar with the intent of lying and taking someone home. If you recall, I was sitting in a corner alone when you approached me after knocking out that guy." My head is pounding now. I press the turbo-lift pad, deciding the Medi could wait.

"I wouldn't have if I had seen your real eyes," I say as I wait for the lift.

He sighs, a deep, defeated sound escaping his lips, and I nearly smile. "I'm just trying to say I went there to drink and to be alone."

"Why?" I ask, surprising myself. I don't mean to say it out loud, but my damned head keeps throbbing, and before I know it, the word escapes my lips. I truly don't care why - it won't make a difference in my feelings. But a Super who doesn't want to be surrounded by adoring humans?

Weird.

"I hate this holiday." He says. I look up to see him, his dark brows knotted and lips pressed tightly. I don't think he means to tell me that by the look on his face, but there it is.

"A holiday dedicated to stroke your egos? Where one of you Supes wins the popularity contest? Where humans pay thousands to buy cheap merchandise that funds your floating city? Sure, you do." I say. "Speaking of which, shouldn't you be up there with the rest of them?"

"It's true, Lily."

I rankle, sneering at him. "Lillium. My name is Lillium. Don't call me that."

He smirks, dimples appearing just as the lift dings and the doors slide open.

"That's not what you said last night."

"Like I said, it was a mistake," I say, entering the lift and saying a silent prayer that he would leave me alone. Have a great life, uh," I wave my hand around as I try to recall his name.

"Did you really forget my name?" he asks, his lips quirking.

I shrug. I'm not trying too hard to remember it. If anything, I'm trying to push it far back into the recesses of my mind and bury it beneath years of deep-seated hatred that stemmed from trauma.

"It's Athos," he says, and before I can come back with some quippy remark, he says, "You screamed it enough times last night."

My jaw drops as the lift doors slide together, cutting off his self-satisfied smirk as he watches me choke on my words. It isn't until the lift reaches the bottom floor, its cheery chime announcing my arrival, that I find my voice again.

"Asshole!" I cry out, throwing my shoes at the door. The door opens, and my shoes go flying into the lobby, where a few late-night workers move quickly to avoid being whacked.

I make a few hasty apologies just as security is called. As I rush out of the building, barefoot, I hear my wristpad ding. Taking a quick look while running down the street to the train platform, I see Libby has been messaging me nonstop for the last ten minutes.

Where the fuck are you? I just finished your section. You better be here soon or I'm going to break your knees.

Chapter 2

Vendors choke the streets in preparation for the festival. Their stands and booths burst with anything that catches customers' eye as they make their way to work.

I stand near the employee door, my head practically cracking under the constant throbbing in my temple. I slap my hand on the scanner, silently promising never to drink again.

I choke back a yelp as the door opens by itself, revealing a flower-covered head.

I almost don't recognize Libby in her festival makeup as she turns her swarmy smile to me.

"What are you wearing?" I ask, eyeing her outfit. Our usual uniform has been replaced with a dark green top and skirt, with splashes of replicated flowers.

"Sam said we could wear our festival outfits," she waves me off. "Why are you late?"

"A mistake," I grumble, finding the Medi in the employee lounge. I tap the screen to life, selecting the injection for hangovers and migraines and a painkiller for my hand.

"Late night?" Libby muses, giving me a knowing smirk.

I ignore her, inserting my hand under the scanner. A tiny needle pricks my wrist, and instant relief washes over me as the throbbing ceases.

"You good?" Libby asks. I glance over to her, seeing her holding the spare uniform I keep in my locker.

"Yeah, thanks." I grab the clothes, making my way to the bathroom where

7

I take a quick shower. I couldn't start my shift smelling like stale booze and sex. As I towel myself off, I catch a glimpse of my naked body in the mirror.

Tiny bruises have formed around my fleshiest parts. My entire face blazes hot as I recall the Super grasping me, his massive hands locking me in place while he drove himself-

"Lillium?" Libby calls, snapping me out of my daydream. Quickly, I throw on my uniform, covering the evidence. Libby is no stranger to my late nights - but those had all been humans.

How can I explain I fucked a Super to her?

I rush out of the bathroom, only to see her holding up a hot pink dress complete with a sparkly tiara.

"No," I grind out, shaking my head.

"Oh, come on, Lillium. Live a little, and lighten up. It's just for one day. Besides, you're going to be the only one wearing your uniform. And you owe me. I did your entire fucking section while you were doing what, exactly?"

"Nothing, and I appreciate you covering for me. I'll stay after closing tonight to make it up to you. But I am not putting that thing on." I shrug, putting my wet hair up into a ponytail. "I'm twenty-five, Lib, and those costumes are for kids."

"Not on Briseathe," she tuts, tossing the dress behind her.

"Especially on Briseathe." I correct.

Libby gives me a knowing look. "Because you hate the Briseathe festival? And all Supers?"

"I don't hate them-" My protest is cut short when Max yells at us from inside the store to hurry up. Libby bounces off in her skirt, and it suddenly hits me that she's dressed up like the Super Sheiba, the colors complimenting her sepia complexion. Then again, Libby looks amazing in anything.

I glance at myself in our mirror before I jog off into the store. My skin is no longer gray around my eyes, but I certainly look like I've had a wild night.

Max's costume is an eyesore. His bright yellow jumpsuit clashes with his pasty face and fiery red hair. He gives Libby a quick peck on the cheek before turning to me, smirking.

"She graces us with her presence," he says, feigning a bow.

I fail to hide a smile as I ask, "So Max, what do we have this year?"

"Vintage Jace Kace and Sheiba, obviously," he says, pulling Libby closer to him.

"I meant the merch," I sigh, but smile. They dress up as the same Supers every year.

"We have a brand new Jace Kace set." Max offers. "Even though we had one last month...."

"Well, he did just recently save all those people from that fire in the movie theater." Libby chimes.

"Oh, wait!" Max says as he pulls out a brightly wrapped box from his jumpsuit. "Happy Birthday, Lillium!"

"Sorry we couldn't make it to the bar last night," Libby says. "Though, it appears we weren't needed." She gives me a knowing wink, and I fight back against the urge to blush.

"We will all have to get together next year when Gaia is back in town," Max suggests. "I can't believe it's been four years since we've all been together."

I open the box to find a simple silver bracelet with a tiny frog charm. I smile, holding it up to the light. "It's beautiful."

"We figured it'd go great with your habitat rehab suit," Libby says, giving me a wink.

"That is, unless you've decided on something else?" Max asks.

I school my face into a mask. "I think I might actually let the state pick." They both exchange looks but say nothing. I place the bracelet back in the box, waiting.

"Makes sense," Max says finally. "That was more of Gabe's thing."

Libby shoves her elbow into his side, but I ignore them. "Thanks for this; it will look great in any of the suits they pick for me." I slide the box behind the front desk just as our manager, Sam, appears.

A click from the front catches my attention as Sam gets ready to open the doors. She throws the others a warm smile before saying, "Let's be positive today." Her gaze falls on me as her eyes tighten. I know the comment is directed at me, the only employee not wearing a costume and who looks like she crawled to work. She isn't wrong. I basically did crawl all the way here.

I watch her unlock the doors and hop off to her office, her tiny figure disappearing behind the flood of incoming customers.

The first wave comes straight for my register, and I force a smile as they surround me, praying I don't appear as tired as I feel.

"What is this year's featured Super?" A man asks. Nonchalantly, I step to the side, motioning to the giant halo-screen behind me.

"Oh, Sheiba!" A girl squeals. "She's going to win Hero of the Year for sure!"

I put on my best face and power through each transaction, trying my best to keep up with everyone's questions. It serves as a great distraction from this morning. And last night. Anytime I find my mind wandering back to him, I suddenly become the most helpful employee.

By the end of the night, I'm actually sad to close the doors for once. Working is the best distraction from my thoughts.

"Who's looking forward to restocking with all that crap in the back?" Max asks as he kicks the last of the trashed boxes into a pile.

Libby groans through her teeth, "Shut up Max. I don't want to think about that now."

"I'm just saying- it's going to have to be done." He mumbles.

"Tomorrow." I sigh. "I will come in early and do it." I owe them that much for being late.

"Thanks, Lillium." Libby yawns.

"Where are you two going again?" I ask as I close down the register. I eye the room but see no sign of Sam. She must have left early to get a good spot on the streets to watch the opening announcements before Briseathe, the annual Super holiday, got into full swing.

"Does it matter?" Libby teases.

"Not really." There are many places in the city to celebrate the festival tonight, but I'm willing to bet they have a room just for them.

I wish them a good night and finish cleaning and restocking the shelves.

10

Just before I leave for the night, I start the 3D printer so it can generate perfect replicas of whoever is announced as Hero of the Year tonight.

I take my bridge towards the train station, glancing down at the street below. It's packed with people dressed up in costumes and party clothes. Halo-screens are hovering over-head, or propped on vendor's stations showing the highlights of the past year. I pass over one vendor selling small cakes and curse to myself.

I almost forgot to get one for my dad.

I check my wristpad to see I still have time to buy one and make the last Z-train home before they all shut down for the festival. If I hurry.

I scamper down the crossway, where I have to weave my way back towards the vendor. The line is long but moves fast. While waiting, I can hear the broadcast coming from the halo-screens going over the history of the festival, which means they are getting ready to start the ceremony soon.

"Named after the first Super to appear to us during the Great War, Briseathe has always been a time to give thanks to the Supers for all they have done for us." Ugh, I think, I do not want to hear this spiel again. "After being in turmoil for nearly a decade, the world as we knew it was on the brink of total annihilation. The Great War brought humankind to our knees- and then Briseathe stepped up and showed us that there was a way to peace."

"More like he castigated them," I grumble. A lady in front of me throws me a scalding glare, and I return her look until she gets her cake and moves on.

"One deluxe royal," I say. The vendor scans my wristpad, handing me a clear box with a tiny layered cake inside. "Thanks." I hold it close in case someone bumps into me. I don't want it to get smashed. They only sell them during the festival, so it's not like I can go back tomorrow. I think they are full of too much cream, but my dad loves them. He had been invited to a coworker's in another town even further from the city, and I doubted they would have them there.

I glance down at the pretty confection as memories of him coming home with them every year run through my mind. This would have been the first year without one. I picture his surprised face when he sees the cake and I smile. It is the least I can do.

I take another crossway to the train station. Though it is further than taking the streets, it is faster since no one is on them right now. Just as I round the park for the station, I spot the last mass of people arriving for the night. I pick up my pace as I come down the crossway and bypass the crowd by dodging through the park lawn.

A countdown to the train's departure starts at three minutes just as I come up the stairs to the platform. I enter the middle doors and look around me. It is empty from the back to the front. The only sound comes from the halo-screens.

Only ten minutes on the train and my town came up. Thankfully, I don't have to make a twenty-minute commute to the middle of nowhere, like some other people. The Z-train is built like a rocket and goes over dozens of miles in an instant, but it can only go so fast.

The platform is pitch black, as usual, when I step off. My town is small, and therefore on the bottom of the list when it comes to maintenance upkeep. Honestly, it will take someone getting run over by a train to get anyone out here in a timely manner. I wait until the train takes off before considering running across the tracks instead of going over the crossway. We only have four types of trains that come into our station, and two of them only come once a week. I mentally go over the schedule of the G-train, the next one to pop in on the second pair of tracks. It shouldn't be coming in tonight, and if it does, it isn't until later, anyway. Besides, the sensors will pick up my organic read and make any train arriving come to a halt before they obliterate me.

I jump down to the tracks and pick my way through the dark. I can see the house lights on the other side of the tracks and make out the familiar sounds of the festival being broadcast. Some people have stayed in town to celebrate, apparently.

Once I reach the other end, I have to set the cake aside so I can use my hands to lift myself on the platform. Just as I push myself up some idiot sets off a firework close by. The sudden boom startles me and I lose my balance, falling down onto a track.

Laughter peals into the night followed by my curses as I roll around to get back up. Yes, how about we let off some fireworks and maybe burn the forest down around us, I think bitterly as I leap onto the platform. I grumble as I stand up, taking a look around me. It is dark still, but the lights from the town allow me to at least make out the platform. Yet, I can not find the cake I had placed at the edge of it. I walk up and down, and still nothing.

Ugh, I think, I probably knocked it down with me when I fell. I let out a mighty groan as I tap on my pad to use its dim light. I slide back down to the tracks and search around the ground. All this is for a cake I don't even like! I know I can go back into the city and get another, but I would be arriving right at the height of the celebration- the announcement of Hero of the Year. The award is given to the Super who has done the most for the world in the last year. In other words, the most popular Super at the moment.

"If I do not find this stupid cake in the next thirty seconds I-" I stop grumbling when my light runs over a very interesting sight. There, on the tracks, a fat raccoon sits, holding my cake. Our eyes meet as it freezes mid-stride.

"Do not even think about it," I warn. The raccoon takes off, and I run right after it. The box is a bit too cumbersome for it to hold in one arm, and as it shuffles down the track, it loses its grip. The box tumbles to one side, and the raccoon stops, looking like it is considering going back for it.

"Not unless you have a death wish!" I yell at it.

The little jerk picks it up again and actually hops over the tracks. For a fat rodent, it sure moves fast. As if my night wasn't horrible enough, I hear the dings of a train approaching. I had been wrong about the G-train.

I stop running and consider going back to the platform. It isn't like my dad is expecting a cake, so he won't be disappointed. Besides, he'll understand - a raccoon took his lunch once while he was waiting for a train. Come to think of it, we have had a serious problem with these things.

Just then, I hear the little guy grunting. I jog down and see that although his fat body fits into the hole he had made in the wall, the box will not.

"Ah-ha!" I shout. "I got you now!" I grab the box and try to pull it away, but he has it lodged in the hole. The dings are getting louder, and now I can see the light from the train.

"If my dad can't have it, neither can you." I huff as I try to wiggle the box out. It doesn't matter if I destroy the cake - I'm not about to let the little jerk have it.

The lights get brighter, but the box won't let up. I can jump on the platform, but I don't want to let the raccoon win. The train will stop anyway; the sensors will make it.

The whole track begins to vibrate, and the lights are blinding now. When exactly do the sensors make the trains stop? I begin to wonder.

The raccoon must have let go, allowing the box to pop out.

"Victory!" I hold the box up, only to lose it when someone grabs me from behind.

My lungs are deprived of air, my body becomes limp, and I release the box. I go from being in front of the train to above it in seconds. Then the image turns blurry, and I find myself lying on the platform.

I gasp for air as I try to sit back up.

"Sorry, sorry." Someone says next to me. I roll over to see a man standing over me, looking perplexed. "I had to move fast, or that train would have hit you."

As I gasp for air I realize who it is.

"Sometimes I forget you humans need to breathe." He laughs awkwardly.

My one-night stand. The Super, Athos.

Chapter 3

His scent hits me again, wrapping around me like a warm, silky blanket. In the dark of the night, my mind fills with the memories of his sheets and skin.

"Are you alright?" Athos asks, looming over me.

I can't decide if I am or not because my initial reaction is, "How the fuck did you find me?" I shove him off, crawling away from him as my chest tightens with anxiety. I take a quick look around the dimly lit platform for any signs of cameras. Had this been his grand scheme all along?

Maybe he wants to be a famous superhero like the others. But the platform and streets are all empty except for us, so there is no audience to witness his actions—if that is his intent. Athos sits back on his heels, watching me.

"Are you alright?" he asks again.

"I'm fine," I say, my voice hoarse.

"Are you sure?"

"Yes," I say more forcefully, ignoring his outstretched hand. Thankfully, I still have my bag, but my dad's cake is long gone.

"Why were you standing in front of that train?" he asks, head cocked to the side, as a lock of dark hair falls in front of his eyes. "You don't seem like the damsel in distress type."

"Not that it is any of your business. I was trying to get a cake back from that raccoon thief," I grumble.

He quirks a brow. "A cake?"

"Did you follow me here?" I counter. I can't recall seeing him in the city, and the train had been empty, so how did he end up in my town?

His amber eyes flash as he throws me a sly grin. "I did, yes."

I glare back at him, considering his motives. "Are you stalking me?" I question.

His eyes widen in surprise, then he tosses his head back and laughs. It's a deep, rumbly laugh that makes my core heat.

"That's absurd," he says, chuckling. "But I can if you want me to." He gives me a slow wink and I can feel my cheeks burning in the dim light.

"Why are you here?" I snap back.

He shrugs, and for the first time, I notice how old and worn his clothes appear. I try not to think back to the bar, to what he was wearing, but I fail miserably. He'd been wearing something similar then, too - a worn shirt and faded jeans, the style and material so out of date I couldn't place them. We don't use denim or cotton anymore, so where did he get them?

"I saw you in the city," he muses. "Your store isn't far from where I live, so I thought I might try to catch you when you got off to explain myself, but I chickened out. I was about to leave when I saw you get on the train by yourself, and I thought I should follow just to make sure you were alright."

My left eye twitches as I try to comprehend his logic. "I was just fine without you."

He smirks. "The train would beg to differ."

"The train has sensors that would have stopped it from flattening me. I appreciate your efforts, but your services are not needed. So please, let's just pretend none of this happened and go our separate ways."

Athos smirks, his eyes flashing as a devilish look crosses his face. "And just how much do you want to forget?"

"All of it." I snap, trying my best to ignore the way his lips curl at the edges. The more I am around him, the harder it is to pretend nothing happened between us.

He furrows his brow, the expression nearly taking my breath away. I fight back the urge to brush his hair from his eyes, to feel how warm his skin is again. Realizing I need to put some distance between us, I turn on my heel and begin the trek back home.

Who did he think he was, anyway? Following me around, picking me up from the platform? Did he think the train was going to run me over? Did he have to pin me to the ground, letting his scent swirl around me and cloud my mind with sudden need?

A blush creeps up my neck, and I try to force down some nasty thoughts, but it's hard when I am so close to him.

Without looking back, I run home. I need to put as much distance between us as fast as I can. When I reach my house, it is all I can do to stab my thumb in the keyhole and rush in as it reads my print. Only when I am safely inside do I dare to take a look down the street. I can see the area where he dropped me off, but he is gone. I take a turn around all the windows to make sure he isn't hanging around anywhere before making my way upstairs to my room.

Thankfully, my dad is still out. He would think I had lost my mind finally, seeing me smash my face into every window like that.

I rub my temples as the stress from the day starts to weigh on me. I can think about it in the morning. I said I would be in early, so I must rest before another busy day starts.

I tear off my uniform and collapse onto the bed. I am worried I won't be able to fall asleep with everything on my mind, but the instant my head hits the pillow, I am out.

When the time finally comes to catch the earliest train back to the city, I have to drag myself outside into the dim morning light. At least it is cool out while I make my way to the platform. Summer is just starting, and some mornings my walk to the train leaves me with a sweaty back. The usual early morning group is already quietly waiting for the train, probably all hungover and just as tired as I am. As I make my way onto the platform, I notice something else is going on. They are all staring bleary-eyed at the Super from last night.

He is still here.

I stop breathing momentarily while our eyes meet, and then he strides over to me. I am frozen in place, my mind reeling from shock. *How could he still be here? Why, for that matter!?*

"Good morning!" his voice is chipper for the hour. I gape back in response

17

while the others watch us. Naturally, they do not recognize this man, so they are curious. It is doubtful any of them have noticed he was a Super.

"I wasn't sure when you would be up, so I just hung around." He says.

What?

Someone chuckles from behind me, and blood rushes to my face. Everyone obviously thought we'd had a one-night stand last night. Shock and anxiety race through me - what if someone notices his eyes? Then everyone will think I'd slept with a Super.

Well, they wouldn't be wrong, but I have no intention of anyone finding out the truth.

"What are you doing here?" I say through clenched teeth, my shock evaporating as indignation fills me. "I made it very clear I want nothing to do with you."

"I understand, Lily. But I wanted to give you the chance to thank me." He counters, his toned arms crossing over his chest. He is still wearing the same faded clothes from last night.

I gape at him, realizing he really did think he'd saved me from the train. "I told you the train has sensors - there was no danger to me."

"You keep saying that, but that train wasn't stopping." His self-satisfied smirk makes my blood boil.

"It would have." I shake my head. "I was fine. I can take care of myself, and I did not need you last night."

The platform fills suddenly with his laughter, which he was bending over with; all the while, the others keep watching. I glare back at them all causing them to look away hurriedly. *Nosy bitches.* He stands back up, wiping his eyes with the back of his hand. He stands a good foot taller than me I realize.

"You humans, you'll never cease to amaze me."

"Good." I can hear the Z-train coming now, "I hope we will be endless amusement for your long, long life."

He smirks. "You honestly think that train was going to stop?"

I shrug. "It doesn't matter what I think; they are made to stop when the sensors pick up organic material. I am, in fact, organic material."

"That train was thirty feet from you when I scooped you up."

18

"And?" The train appears around the platform curve just in time.

"Even if these sensors you speak of alerted it and caused it to hit the brakes, there is no way, with how fast it was going, that it would have stopped in time to *not hit you*." He bends down to my ear just as the train stops in front of me, his breath coasting over my ear as he says, "Are you completely sure that the sensors here are working? If they are not, you would have been hit." The doors whoosh open. "And died."

A cold chill went up my spine, and it wasn't caused by his breath on my neck. I have seconds to retaliate before jumping on the train. All I can come up with is a rushed, "Of course I am sure," and then I am on the train watching as the doors close on him. Relief floods through me when we start to move away from the platform while he continues to watch me. I finally tear my eyes away from him when the train picks up speed.

There is one more stop and then I will be on my way to my normal routine, going to work with the others. I have never once looked forward to getting to the store as I did at that moment.

But what if he is still there when I come home? The thought is sobering enough to make me ignore the next stop entirely. If he is there, what can I do? Call the authorities on him? There isn't anything they can do. Contact his fellow Supers to help me out? I tried that once before, and it will never, ever happen again.

I barely notice the train starting up again, and I'm so deep in thought.

Two girls in front of me become very animated just then, breaking my train of thought. They are looking right at me, giggling at each other. I have had just about enough people staring at me today, and I am about to make some snide remark when I realize they are actually looking behind me. So I turn around and nearly scream.

What comes out of my throat was more of a gurgle than a scream. The creeper had somehow gotten on without me noticing.

"I can fly pretty fast." He smiles.

"This is stalking," I say, recovering.

"No, flying to your home and watching you through your window would be stalking."

"And have you?"

"No. Not yet." His smile widens. "Kidding. Or am I?"

It's time to change plans; I am going to have to ignore him or face possible murder charges. That is, if he can be killed.

"Just admit that you were wrong; I can settle for that much. 'Oh, I am so sorry, I was under the illusion that the sensor was working!'" I wince at his high-pitched tone.

"I will go away if you do," he says. I give him a look that means *never*. He sighs.

Maybe I can lose him in the city, I think, as we come up to it. My hopes are instantly dashed as he proceeds to casually follow me all the way to my store. I slap my hand against the pad, glaring at him as it unlocks.

"Say it, Lily. I can live with you forgetting about our little escapade if that's what you want, but I did save your life. I can't forget about that." His amber eyes are watching me, a twinge of hope in them as he sees me hesitate momentarily. A part of me wonders why he cares so much.

He could be right. Those sensors are not foolproof. But the idea of groveling at his feet and thanking him, a Super, was enough to fill my throat with bile. Besides, it clearly annoys him when I say no.

"Have a great day, Mr. Nobody," I say as I slam the door behind me.

Chapter 4

I immerse myself in work for the next few hours, frequently checking the front and expecting Athos's presence. I regret opting for the early shift today.

I fill the Hero of the Year wall with skimpy Sheiba figures. I missed the announcement last night, but the 3D printer began birthing a whole line of new figures once her name was called.

By the time Libby and Max show up, my nerves are so raw that I nearly faint from fright when they trudge in looking like ragged mutts.

"Partied a little much. But it was worth it!" Libby yawns.

"How about you, Lillium? You look like you didn't get much sleep." Max winks.

"Oh, she probably met some guy, right?" Libby teases, wiggling her brows at me.

I shoot them a withering look.

"Bad in bed, huh?" Libby sighs, shaking her head.

I kick an empty box towards them, causing them to break apart to avoid it. Libby tuts at me but smiles as she approaches her section for the day. She's been lucky when we drew sticks for sections. She gets the 'losers' section, which no one is interested in today since they only want the limited edition Hero of the Year figure.

I'm the unlucky one. I get the dreaded Hero of the Year section. Max is my lifeline, making sure the printer is popping out as many figures as it can while I try to speed through my ever-growing line.

A half-hour later, Sam breezes in, looking bright-eyed and fresh as she practically dances her way to the doors. A line has formed since I arrived, but there is still no sign of the Super when I peek around my display.

"Great job on the setup!" Sam sings out. I chance a glance at Libby, who has a fake smile plastered on her face. Her eyes convey the same thing I was thinking.

Sam is an absentee manager who waltzes in a minute before opening and leaves an hour before closing. She knows there is nothing we can do or say about it. We are only here because of the state placement program. We were placed in the service program four years ago after graduating, but we have only been in her store for about a year.

The state requires citizens to join a career faction after graduating or enter a placement program for more time and experience before choosing a lifelong job.

Now that I'm twenty-five, it means I have to choose this week. I have to pick a job or let them pick one for me.

"Are we ready?" Sam sings out again, throwing us a brilliant smile. I'm still unsure what career I want to pick, but I sure as hell know I don't want to end up like Sam - taking advantage of the program so I can slack off.

Besides, a small, withered part of me still wants to do something worthwhile. It should be easy, but when you live in a world full of Supers who take care of everything, doing something worthwhile seems to take the backseat.

Shoving the thoughts into the back of my mind, I focus on the now-open doors. Humans rush in quickly, ignoring Sam's half-assed comments to stay in the line they formed outside. A jumble of people reaches my display and I steel my heart as I watch them tear into it.

I might not like the Supes, but I am proud of how I set up the display. A voice in the back of my mind laments the destruction as I plaster a smile on my face, seeing my first customers approaching.

I help them with the digital checkout counter, keeping an eye on how many items they have. The store has AI security that will go off if someone tries to leave without paying, and regardless of the customers' intention, it will shut down the store until the authorities arrive.

It's not my lack of faith in our AI system that prompts me to double-check every transaction, but rather my lack of wanting to deal with a store during lockdown. No one will be able to leave until the authorities, usually a lower-class Super or their lackeys, arrive. Not even Sam will be able to set us free.

I lose myself to the work. At some point, I forget why I keep scanning the store and my nerves mellow out as I let the chaos and destruction lull me. Libby is frantically running around, trying her best to restock what she can, while also defusing small fights that break out when supplies grow limited. Max is punching in multiple orders for the printer while he attempts to herd some people to the ancient manual register where Sam perches, looking nonplus despite the rambunctious crowd.

As I help a withered-looking grandmother pack her items - for the grandkids she tells me with a toothy grin- I can see Sam absentmindedly scroll through her wristpad. A bored sigh escapes her lips as she sits further back in her chair, oblivious to the surrounding chaos.

Yeah, customer service is not for me, I think as I usher the old woman to the safety of the sidewalk. She is by far the oldest human in the store, and I don't put it past some of these customers to simply trample her in their effort to get their hands on the new Sheiba figure.

She talks out loud to herself as she shuffles down the walkway, something about how excited her grandkids will be. I find myself hoping the same - after all, their ancient grandmother went through a lot of time and effort to get her hands on them. I turn back to the store and whatever lightness I have in my heart dies as soon as I see the mass of humans crowded inside.

I take a deep breath, relishing the warm summer afternoon sun before I move to step back inside. The scent hits me first and suddenly my mind clouds with memories. My skin burns as it recalls his touch. I can feel phantom fingertips drawing against my skin, tracing my edges and curves as they dip to sensitive parts- I shake my head, dislodging them just as I hear the dark chuckle.

I don't need to turn to know it's him, but I still do. Athos is standing on the corner, leaning against my store with a lazy grin etched into his beautiful features. He is out of place - not just his eyes, but his air of calm. Everyone around him is rushing to get into the store, or full-on bolting out onto the walkway, items under their arms as they rush away.

His amber eyes are watching me as I falter.

"So, you're still stalking me," I say, forcing my voice to sound steady even though my heart is racing. In the afternoon sun, his ebony hair is so dark it almost appears to have violet streaks. Tall, dark, and dangerous. I vaguely remember my alcohol-laden mind thinking about it when I noticed him in the bar.

Idiot.

"I figured I'd see what all the fuss is about," he averts his eyes to the store, a smirk playing on his lips.

I quirk a brow, confused. "The same as it is every year?" I question.

He shrugs, "I haven't been around for the festival before." He chuckles at my confused look. Not around? What could he possibly mean by that? Has he been living under a rock for the past century?

For the first time, I really take in his appearance. Handsome, yes, maybe even swoon-worthy - he certainly made me swoon a few times. I push the thought down and drag my gaze to his clothes. They are retro, and not in the 'we want to be retro' way, but the legit 'these are old as fuck' way.

"Have you just stepped out of the early 2000s?" I ask.

Athos breaks into a slow, brilliant grin, making my poor pathetic heart shutter. A young woman sees him and trips over herself, rolling through the store doors. Athos is at her side in seconds, gently helping her back to her feet. His toned body is large enough to deter anyone from trampling the woman, but it's the way he holds himself that makes the flow of humans slowly part, giving him a wide girth.

I hear him ask the woman if she is alright, and I take the moment to fall into the flow and return to the store while he is distracted.

I tell myself he's only helping the woman out for clout, and maybe he'll be satisfied with the attention from it. He will forget about me and leave me alone. As I approach the checkout stations, I notice Libby has taken over for me. My feet falter when I see Sam standing behind her, her lips in

24

a tight line as she watches me.

"You left," Sam says, her voice tinged with annoyance, but her tone low enough that only I can hear her.

"I needed to help a customer outside," I explain gruffly. If she'd been paying even a micro amount of attention to us, she would have seen for herself.

"The one splayed out on the floor, blocking the rest of the customers?" She asks, sneering.

I shut my eyes and count to ten, calming my frayed nerves. I remind myself I am only here for the rest of the week. I have dealt with her for much longer than that, so I can survive a few more days.

But the thought only serves as a reminder of what comes next. I might be able to leave Sam and her store, but in return, I will need to either declare a lifelong career or let the state pick one for me.

My skin goes clammy at the thought and I suddenly feel the need to drink something cold to cool down my burning throat. I open my eyes, ignoring the look Sam is giving me, and mumble something about needing water.

Libby is smiling and chatting with the customers checking out, but she keeps one eye on me as I rush into the employee locker room. I find the water station and punch in an order. A second later a disposable bottle is printed and filled with icy cold water.

I down it, instantly feeling relief as it cools me off.

Just a few more hours, I tell myself as I go back into the store. *I can do this.*

I freeze the moment I see him. He's waiting for me outside the employee door, his amber eyes scanning the closest shelves. My eyes flick around the section for Max, who should be waiting on the off chance someone takes an interest in the older merchandise. But he's nowhere to be seen.

Athos sees me, frozen in place. I hear a crinkling noise and realize I am still clutching the disposable bottle, now crushed in my hand.

"Nervous, Lily?" Athos asks, quirking a brow.

"Annoyed." I snap back, tossing the bottle into a bin. "See anything you like? Go find the guy with red hair." I move to get around him, but his massive body is blocking me.

His scent rolls around me, curling into the darkest parts of my mind, threatening to rip up memories that I'd rather not think about in public. I feel my chest tighten as I force myself to keep those thoughts buried. I steel myself, looking up to glare at him.

Whatever smart remark I have dies on my tongue as my eyes meet his. He's smiling, a charming, safe smile that reaches his eyes. But the smoldering look he's giving me is sending my blood pressure through the roof.

It was the same look he'd given me at the bar that night, and it was that dark look in his eyes that gave me a much-needed boost of courage to approach him. Without it, I would have left him in his shadowy corner and waited until someone else approached me.

He must see the way I'm gaping at him, wide-eyed and slacked-jawed. "See something you like, Lily?" He asks, leaning closer until I can feel the heat rolling off his body. I barely reach his shoulders, so he has to hunch a bit as he bends over to my ear. "I can hear your heart beating. You better calm down, or you might have a heart attack."

I jerk back a few inches, throwing him a questioning look. *Can he really hear it?*

"Why are you so worked up? Is it just my charming personality, or maybe-?" he raises a brow, questioning. Then I see the slow, dark smile curl his lips. "Maybe you're thinking of that night, and maybe you want a redo now that you know what I am."

My neck flushes with heat that rises to my cheeks. I dip my head down, hoping to hide the blush that spreads across my face. Yes, I have been thinking of that night far too many times for my liking, but it's only because his presence reminds me of it. I can't say that out loud, though. I don't know him well, but I'm sure admitting it would bring him a ridiculous amount of satisfaction.

I also doubt I'll be able to get rid of him if I do.

"Is that it, Lily? Do you think of that night? Because I do."

"Lillium," I shoot back, trying to regain my composure. "My name is Lillium."

I don't need to look up to see the smirk on his face. I can hear it as he

26

says, "You didn't seem to mind me calling you that before."

"You mean when I thought you were human?" I snap.

"I don't think that would matter. I think if I took you back to my bed, you'd let me call you whatever I wanted." He says, surprising me. My head shoots back up so fast I nearly smack it into his chin. His amused expression tells me he's fucking with me.

That's why he's here. Maybe he genuinely thinks I should thank him, but he's also getting a kick out of annoying me in the process. Which only serves to frustrate me more.

"Let's see - you lied by omission about what you were, then you followed me home like a creep. What for? To make up a story about saving me? And now you're stalking me at work, so yeah, although I don't hate you Supers I sure do have grounds to dislike you." My words are acidic, dripping with venom as I speak.

The amusement in his eyes dims. "I'll make you a deal. If you admit I saved you, I will walk out those doors and you will never see or hear from me again."

I can't stop the bubble of laughter that erupts from me. It's a crazed, half-choking, half-wheezing laugh that carries across the store, earning us some looks from customers and Libby and Sam. Athos raises a brow, clearly surprised by my outburst.

I can't help it. It's his audacity, coupled with the asinine circumstances, that finally breaks me. There has been a perfect storm of frustration and anger swirling around inside me since that night, and it's been compounded by the stress of the day. But his assumption that he can barter with me is what sends me falling over the edge.

I've had enough of this bullshit.

"Fuck off." I laugh. "You think you're some big-shot hero? You think you're entitled to my gratitude?"

His lips twitch just as I hear someone behind me.

"Lillium, what's going on? Who is this?" Libby asks, coming up to my side.

"Nothing. A no-name Super who thinks annoying me into groveling at

27

his feet is going to shoot him into fame." I say, taking a deep breath. My sudden outburst might have made everyone close by stop and stare, but it's the mention of a Super that makes them move closer.

Even Libby looks starstruck as she looks up into his eyes. I hear her breath hitch as she notices his eyes, and at the same moment, I realize I am done.

I am done being in this store, dealing with people clamoring over limited-edition toys. Done with Sam ignoring the chaos while we work our asses off for her.

But most of all, I am done with him.

A crowd is forming around us, bodies closing in as the humans realize a real Super is among them. I slip back as they push forward just as Libby squeals something about Supers.

I see Athos's expression flicker between emotions as he's surrounded and I realize with a wave of satisfaction he's uncomfortable. It's both surprising and perfect at the same time.

Sam is calling for me at the checkout, but I ignore her. I make my way to the doors, grabbing a random figure as I speed up towards the doors. I hear the sensors chime before I see the doors begin to close, but the sheer mass of people piling into the store slows them down.

Alarms blare the moment I reach the doors and I hear the AI system scream for everyone to clear the doors before they get smashed between them. There's a moment of panic and chaos as everyone leaps away, letting the glass doors snap shut, the locks clicking into place.

But not before I manage to slide out, dropping the figure behind me.

I turn slightly, seeing Sam's seething face as she releases the doors that have been locked behind me. And they will remain that way until the authorities come to unlock them.

"I quit," I say, as Athos's bewildered face is blocked by a sea of humans.

Chapter 5

There is a picture on my desk from childhood with Gaia and I. It is a multi-photo frame that can switch through as many as a hundred photos, but I only have one. My appearance is very much the same, but Gaia looks like a completely different person; in fact, it is the only picture I have of what she naturally looks like.

For as long as I can remember Gaia has hated her appearance. Her family is affected by the 'ME' genes from the 2060s when doctors had perfected the ability to give parents the choice of what they wanted their children to look like. What started as a way to alter the appearance of their kids turned into a permanent effect on every descendant, so everyone in her family looked exactly alike.

She has self-hatred issues that seem to have come out during the last few years of school, before graduation. I did not understand it at first. I thought she was being dramatic, and I tried to get her to see how unique she is, but she felt like her body was not her own. She started changing her hair color and wearing colored eye lenses, often altering her look a few times a week.

Even as we are video chatting, I can see she has changed her hair from the last time we talked.

"What color would you call that?" I ask.

Gaia pats her curls, "Purple Peony." *Ah, well at least today she has her normal platinum eye color.*

"How long has it been since you tried your natural hair?" I ask.

"There is nothing natural about frosted blue hair, Lillium."

"Oh, but Purple Peony is totally fine, though?" She rolls her eyes.

"What I would not give to have a plain body like you!" she sighs, smiling.

"My plain body has served me well." I agree. "I am fond of my brown eyes."

"Chestnut." She corrects.

It is my turn to roll my eyes. She has a thing for elaborating features. I suppose I could see the appeal of having natural green eyes, or skin that can tan, but Gaia has her unique qualities; her skin would never burn nor blemish in the sun.

It isn't like I don't understand where she is coming from. Somewhere back in my bloodline, someone decided platinum hair was a good choice. The result was nearly everyone on my mother's side of the family has platinum hair, with a hint of black just at the roots. Sure, I'd changed my hair color a few times over the years, but never to the extent Gaia did.

Then again, my hair is the only part of my body that is altered. I might feel differently if it was nearly every aspect of my body, like Gaia.

"How is Africa?" I ask, changing the subject.

"Hot and dry. When will you come down here?" I shrug, unsure how to approach the subject.

"Lillium," I hear the warning in her tone as she squints her eyes at me. "You better not be flaking on me again. You promised you'd come out here after your birthday."

"I am!" I say, huffing. "I just... might have left the program a few days earlier than I was expecting."

She raises a plum-colored brow. "How early?"

"Yesterday," I sigh. Gaia snorts, leaning back into her chair.

"I told you that you'd be wasting your time in that program. Why don't you just declare for Eco and come work with me?"

Because that was his dream, I think but hold my tongue.

I shake my head. "As amazing as that sounds, I think I am going to go with whatever I'm assigned."

She furrows her brows. "Seriously?"

"Yeah. I don't care what they place me in." It's true. The only reason I am in the placement program at all is because I have no idea what I want to do.

I think that after four years, I would have a better idea, but the truth is I still can't see myself doing any of the jobs they have.

"So, what? You're going to let them choose for you?" Gaia asks, looking incredulous. She'd picked Eco right out of graduation, choosing to get a head start on her career while Libby, Max and I opted for more time.

"I'm out of time, Gaia. If I don't know what I want to do by now, I might as well let them choose." I pick at my nails, trying not to dwell on it. "Hey, what happened to that guy who took you out last week?"

She rolls her eyes, "He's alright. Kind of into himself, you know. But very cute."

I laugh. "Well, you should try to date him for a while. You haven't had a guy since Luke, in China."

"I liked Luke. He liked China more."

"He was stupid," I say.

"Yes. He was. He was no Gabriel."

I try not to react but fail. She notices me wince and begins to apologize. "I'm sorry, Lillium."

I shrug. "I have to get over it someday, right?"

"You need to move on, Lillium. There's a difference. There's no getting over what happened to him, but you can move on and live your life." Gaia begins to rub her fingers together, a nervous tick she's had since we were kids. "None of us have gotten over it." She confines.

"Yeah. Well, I should get going. I need to go file with the state so I can get assigned my lifetime job." Gaia waves me off but tells me to call her later. I don't mention Athos, for several reasons.

One, she already worries about my late-night escapades and it would just prove her point that I am not over Gabriel.

Two, Gaia shares my sentiments about Supers and she might have a heart attack if I told her I slept with one.

Three, I would rather die than admit I liked it.

I press the power button, and the black screen disappears to show my bedroom window. Outside is calm and quiet, with everyone being at work. I haven't seen my dad since the morning of the festival and I'm sure he's wondering where his cake is by now. I dread telling him what happened. Like Gaia, he doesn't think letting the state choose would be right for me. Secretly, I think he wishes I were more like Gaia, and had gone off on my own the second I graduated at twenty-one. She might be halfway across the world, but at least she's following her heart.

The fact is, I'm not sure what I want to do with my life, so doing this is better than not doing anything.

The sound of the front door shutting snaps me into action. I have planned on slipping into the city before going home to file with the state, but now that isn't going to be an option.

I find Dad downstairs, nursing a mug of tea.

"Oh, you're home," he says, smiling over his tea. "I thought you had work today, bug?" His nickname tugs at my heart, making me feel even worse as I lean against the doorway, preparing to tell him the news.

"I quit early," I say, fidgeting with my nails. His eyes fall to my hands and I stop. Dad knows my ticks just as well as I know Gaia's, and I see the look in his eyes as he takes a deep breath.

"You've decided to declare a career?" I shake my head slowly.

He blows on his steamy tea, brows furrowing. "Does this mean you're going to file with the state?" I nod and watch his face fall.

"Lillium, I worry about you so much. You haven't been the same since Gabriel died." I flinch but he continues, "It's a hard thing to cope with, I know, but you have to start living your own life. "

"I'm trying dad." I sigh. "I think this will be the best for me."

"I just don't want to see you get stuck wasting your time doing something you hate all because you didn't take a chance on life." I hear the unspoken thoughts. He thinks I don't take chances because of Gabe.

I sigh. It always comes down to this- Gabriel. Everyone feels like I'm making my choices based on him and his memory, like I can't have a mind of my own. Yes, much of what I'm doing is because of the plans the two of us made together before he died, but just because he is gone does not mean I can't follow through with them. Everyone else seems to think so.

"Dad, I am fine, really."

He takes a breath and sits down on the couch. "I hope you are right, after everything that has happened over the past years."

"I am," I say more sternly.

He shakes his head, taking his pad out to look at the news. I watch him for a moment, waiting to see if he is going to say anything else. My poor dad, who worries so much, that even with all that was going on with him he would think about me first. For the first time in a long while, I notice how he is changing, and getting older. His chestnut hair, as Gaia would call it, is graying around the temples and his usually smooth face has lines I haven't seen before. *When did this happen?* I think, feeling bad that I haven't noticed until now.

"We got an invitation to your cousin's birthday party again." He says suddenly.

I scoff, "That's great."

He looks over his pad at me, raises a brow, and asks, "You won't go this year either?"

I give him a knowing look to which he says, "Lillium, you are going to have to get over it, eventually. I know what your mother did was, strange…."

"Stupid." I correct.

"What she felt she had to do." He says pointedly, "I have made peace with that. So should you." I can't take it anymore. I feel like he is pressuring me to be this happy, carefree, forgiving person that I'm not, and can not be.

"Dad, you handle it your way, I will handle it mine." I take my bag and proceed to the front door. "I am going out." I say over my shoulder.

"Oh, don't be so stubborn! You will have a much happier life if you just let go-"

"Bye, Dad!" I slam the door behind me and take off down the street. It must be Tell-Lillium-How to-Live-Her-Life-Day. Everyone seems to have an opinion lately about me, and the consensus is that I'm not doing life correctly.

Libby and Max feel I am being too prejudiced against Supers. Gaia feels like I am wasting my life away. Dad also agrees with her on that, but then he has to go and mention my mother. Apparently, I am not coping very well with life.

So it's no surprise I find myself approaching my usual bar. I find a booth in the back and sink into the seat. Two drinks later I decide to suck it up and go down to the state building and file. There is no use waiting anymore, and I'm not about to be hit with the sudden urge to join one faction over another in the few days I have left to decide.

Rip the bandage off, I tell myself as I drain the last dredges of my drink and swipe my wristpad to pay.

A man in the booth next to me raises his glass as I get up. Normally I'd take his invitation and let myself be lost in the alcohol and sex that would naturally follow. But Athos has ruined one-night stands for me for the foreseeable future.

I am ignoring the man while I exit the dim bar just as I hear my wristpad chiming. I answer, seeing Libby's face popping up on the screen. She and Max have left me a few messages after my dramatic exit, but I haven't responded.

"Hey, Libs," I say as I insert my earbud.

"What the actual fuck, Lillium," Libby says, but by her tone, I can tell she's holding back laughter. "I know you don't like them, but did you have to go full psycho and get us locked up with that Super?"

"I am sure it was dreadful," I say as I board the train to the inner city.

Libby snorts, "Dreadful? Try strange. The man seemed traumatized by all the attention he was getting. I almost felt bad for him."

"Well don't, he deserved it. Besides, isn't that what all Supers want? To be fawned over by humans?" Even as I say it I can feel the doubt creep into my chest. Athos didn't look like he was enjoying the sudden attention when I left.

"Maybe, but I don't think this one was used to it. No one knew who he was, but they still asked for his autograph and pictures. He was nice, but once people started asking about the famous Supers and if he knew them, he kind of clammed up."

"Well, they have been extremely secretive since they made their little castle in the sky," I say, referring to the floating city Legion- where all the

Supers lived.

Libby hums in agreement, but I can tell she's not convinced.

"What?" I ask.

"Do you know him?" Her question surprises me. My heart thumps into my throat as I think of a response.

"Why do you ask?" I say.

"I saw you two. Standing so close together, almost like - well, like it wasn't the first time you'd seen him."

Shit. She's onto me. I don't want to lie to her, but I also can't tell her the truth. It's too embarrassing.

"Libby-" I start but she cuts me off.

"He asked Sam not to fire you, you know?" I feel my gut clench with shock. *Why would he do that?*

"I quit," I say quietly, as if that makes a difference. Sam would have fired me anyway after that stunt I pulled.

"Yeah, she said as much after he asked. But we didn't know that, and he was worried he'd upset you."

Confusion rolls through me as I hear the train chime for the inner city stop. What is his deal? Nothing he does makes sense. Supers don't care about the little humans and our mundane lives. They only care that we worship them and buy their shitty merchandise.

"It's an act," I say, unsure if I am trying to convince Libby or myself. I think of Gabriel and my heart hardens. "It's always just an act with them," I say, my voice colder, full of resolve now.

"Lillium-" Libby says softly but I don't have the heart to hear what comes next. I know that tone too well.

"I have to go. I need to file with the state." I end the call as the doors swoosh open.

Chapter 6

The state building is a large white marble structure located in the center of a vast city garden. Lush emerald lawns stretch out over gently rolling hills dotted with various fruit trees and flower beds. The networks of ponds and streams, which are fed by the river that snakes through Sun City, have gazebos and benches for visitors to enjoy.

It's warm, but not overbearing, as I make my way through the footpaths toward the building. My buzz from the drinks slowly ebbs away, and with it goes my will. I falter as the building comes into view. My feet are suddenly feeling too heavy to move.

The sun glints off the white marble, and if I stare too long, I fear I might go blind. I turn away, finding a bench close by that overlooks a fishing pond. I rush over to it, taking deep breaths as I feel my chest begin to tighten. My lungs aren't working all of a sudden, and I feel like my heart spasms.

I check my wristpad, certain it's about to alert me of a heart attack. It chimes an alert, but instead of my certain death, it tells me I am having an anxiety attack.

I shake my head, thinking it must be a mistake. Surely I'm about to die. I can feel death looming over me like a black cloud, swallowing me up as my heart and lungs struggle to keep me alive.

My neck spasms as I struggle to drag in a breath. The wristpad tells me to breathe and counts down for me, but I can't focus on it.

I tear my eyes from it, silently cursing the glitchy AI tech, certain I am within minutes of dying on a bench outside the state building.

Movement catches my attention, pulling me from my tunnel vision. A group of kids are crowding around someone wading in the fishpond.

For a split second, I wonder why someone would be wading out into the water, but then I see them disappear beneath it. The action is bizarre enough to hold my attention even as I struggle to remain alive.

A man emerges from the water, holding a fishing pole in his hands. The kids cheer, and he trudges through the murky water to hand the pole to the smallest kid, a little girl.

There's a clamor of chatter as the kids rush off in all directions. I think to myself, *what a strange thing to see right before I die.* My eyes lift slightly to see the man left behind.

My entire body freezes the moment I realize it's Athos.

He removes his soaked shirt, twisting it to wring out the water. I pray he doesn't notice me, gaping like a fish for air on this bench. A group of women squeal behind me as they take in his toned body. The noise catches his attention, and his amber eyes lift towards them.

My chest feels like it's being crushed beneath a sack of rocks as his gaze drops down on me. I shut my eyes, and press my hands against my chest as I will myself to either die or take a damn breath.

"Lily?" His voice drifts over me. I can't respond. I can barely think as I will myself to just let go and drop into the abyss.

"Lillium." His tone is sharper, deeper. My eyes flutter open to see him crouching before me, his brows knotting with concern. "Focus on me, Lillium," he says softly. Something warm wraps around my hands and it takes me a moment to realize it's his hand.

I want to pull away. I want to scream at him to leave me alone. But the dreadful dark cloud is coming down over me, drowning me as I struggle to breathe. His hands are warm, and they draw me closer to him. His scent wraps around me as he cups my chin in his free hand.

"Focus on me. I am here with you. Take a breath with me." I see him inhale deeply, but I can't communicate with him that I am unable to breathe. He must see it on my face, because he does it again, and takes a deep breath that makes his toned chest rise and fall.

"I am here with you. You aren't alone, Lillium, you got this." He lifts one of my hands and brings it to his chest. I can feel him breathing, the steady beat of his heart, and suddenly I remember how to breathe. It's shaky and ragged as I take in a gulp of air, but it's enough to alleviate some of the pressure in my chest.

"Again," he whispers, and this time I follow him as he breathes. I am not sure how many times we breathe together, or how long it takes before I feel the pressure leave my chest. When it finally does, I am left feeling hollow and tired.

"There you are," he says, his lips tugging into a gentle smile.

My wristpad chimes, informing me my anxiety attack has stopped, but I should seek out a Medi for some anxiety medicine. I ignore the alert, focusing on the Super holding my hand to his bare chest.

His skin is warm and damp from the pond. His dark hair hangs in wet locks over his brows, and I find myself curling my fingers against his chest, feeling his heartbeat.

His eyes drop to my hand, and I see the curve of his mouth tip up in amusement. It's all I need to pull away, putting some distance between us.

"Do you have anxiety attacks often?" He asks.

I shake my head. "Not in public," I mutter.

Athos raises a brow but says nothing as he stands up. The group of women behind me are still chattering, eyeing him while he drapes his wet shirt over the bench and takes a seat next to me.

I don't have the energy to protest.

"Let me guess," he muses, folding his legs while spreading his arms over the back of the bench. "You were taking a stroll through the park, and my sudden appearance made you think I was stalking you, which caused you to feel anxious."

I don't respond. Instead, I sink further back into the bench until I feel his arm behind my shoulders. He glances at me in surprise.

"I'm not stalking you, if that's what you're worried about." He mumbles.

I shut my heavy eyes, my body suddenly feeling freezing despite the warm afternoon.

"I've been here all day, watching the kids fish. You can ask them if you don't believe me. There's some big fish in there and they keep losing their poles." He explains. "How long have you been having these attacks?"

I have no response- no witty remark to barb him with. I am not conceited enough to believe his being here has something to do with me. My skepticism has also failed me here. Could he have followed me here and set this all up? Maybe, but just thinking about the time and effort it would have taken exhausts me more. I can only accept that this is a twisted, humorless case of serendipity.

I didn't believe in fate or serendipity before this moment, but I sure as shit was considering how fucked up the universe's sense of humor was.

"It's been four years," I say, surprising us both.

Athos is silent, but I can feel his arm tensing behind me. I open my eyes, focusing on the shimmering water as the kids throw out their lines.

"Four years of biding my time, hoping I would find an answer." It's half of the truth.

"To what?" he asks.

I shrug. "What do I want to do? Who I want to be." I glance over at him, to the state building that shines behind his head. "But my time is out, and I still have no idea. I was going to let the state pick for me, but that somehow seems worse than picking a career out of a hat."

Athos cocks his head to the side, looking thoughtful. "You're forced to pick a career now? What if you don't like it? Can you change it?"

I snort, then realize he is serious. "How do you not know this?" I ask. "There's no changing my career once I declare for one. With you Supers taking care of the majority of the world's needs, we humans are left with the scraps."

"What if you decide not to pick?"

I roll my eyes wearily. "They put you behind bars until you decide, or you let them."

"Well, that's shitty," he says. "No wonder you've been having anxiety attacks."

I give him a pointed look. "Have you been living under a rock?"

Athos smirks, then looks towards the pond. "I haven't been around for a while, if that's what you mean."

"Why are you here?" I ask.

"I told you, helping kids fish."

"No, I mean, why are you down here with us? Shouldn't you be up with the rest of the Supers, living like a god in Legion?"

He shrugs nonchalantly, but I can see the corner of his eyes crinkle. "Like I said, it's been a while, and the others-" he falters, failing to find the words.

I watch him closely, the way his breathing changes as he speaks about the others, the crinkle in his eyes, and the way his lips dip. Whatever confident, carefree facade he had on before is cracking before my eyes, and all I have to do is mention the Supers in Legion.

"You mentioned before you were at the bar because you wanted to avoid the Briseathe festival. Why?" I ask.

"The same reason you refuse to acknowledge I helped you," he says, side-eyeing me. I can feel my nose crinkle up as I huff in annoyance. He chuckles, his chest muscles flexing as he laughs.

I advert my eyes and blow out a breath. "Are you saying you're estranged from the others?" When he doesn't respond I chance a glance back at his face. He looks stoic, and I notice he isn't breathing. He is still as a stone. "I thought you were a tight bunch?" I say quietly.

He blinks, and suddenly his body comes back to life as he takes a breath. "It's complicated." His tone tells me that's all he's going to give me.

"I can understand that." I lean forward, resting my hands on my knees. "There was a time when it wasn't, and I was just like everyone else. I thought Supers were amazing."

"What happened?"

I shrug, "It's complicated." He smirks back at me as I side-eye him with a grin. "Thank you, by the way."

He looks mildly shocked, slapping a hand over his chest as he gasps. "Are you actually admitting I saved you?"

"No." I snap, "I mean for helping calm me down."

He sighs as his body slumps into the bench with a dramatic flair. "One day I will get you to admit I am right about the train. But until then, I am happy I was here to help you."

"I really should see someone about them," I mutter. "I think they are getting worse."

"I can always provide you with some distractions." I flick my eyes to see his smoldering grin, his dimples popping as he winks at me.

"That was a one-time thing. And it's never happening again." I say. "In fact, I think it might be healthy if I swear off one-night stands for a while."

"That's a pity," Athos says, giving me a knowing look.

I roll my eyes, "How can you go from being so nice to being a douche?"

He chuckles, "Good to know douche is still an insult." He stands, and I feel my heart flutter as I see he's about to leave. There is still time for me to go into the state building, but I rather not.

"Wait!" It comes out as a panicked plea that makes him pause.

He's staring at me, his eyes mirroring my own confusion. Why don't I want him to leave? Half an hour ago I would have been begging for him to get away from me. But something changed while we sat on that bench.

Maybe I really did have a heart attack. Maybe the loss of oxygen damaged a part of my brain - I don't want him to just disappear now.

"You look like you're about to be sick. Are you trying to ask me on a date?" He teases but takes a step back in case I hurl.

"No," I shake my head but begin to wonder if I really am going to be sick.

"Here," he leans over and taps my wristpad with his own. I hear the chime as my wristpad confirms the transfer of his contact information and my brows shoot up in surprise.

"In case you have an attack on your way home. Call me, and I will come find you. Or," he stands up, smirking, "if you ever want to have drinks again."

He takes a step back, then lifts off into the air. A few people around us begin to freak out, pointing and shouting at his disappearing figure as he glides away. I lean back onto the bench and nearly jump up in fright when I feel something cold and wet on my elbow. I scoff the moment I see his semi-dry shirt still slung over the bench.

Only then do I consider how he's flying around shirtless.

Chapter 7

Don't be a creep, I tell myself again, but deep down I know I won't be taking my own advice. I shut my eyes, as if not watching myself touch the shirt can absolve me of any guilt. Clutching the fabric, I bring it up to my face and take the tiniest, shallowest breath I can. Just enough air to get a small whiff of Athos.

I'm instantly transported back to his room, tangled in his sheets while he drives himself deep inside, his toned chest pressed against me while he picks up his pace.

I toss the shirt away, recoiling as I try to suppress the memories. But I always end up picking it back up, letting myself drift away to his room.

It's become my guilty pleasure since finding his shirt discarded in the park. It's entirely creepy, and borderline obsessive, but a part of me can't stop doing it. Everything would have been different if he'd just sucked at sex.

But he didn't.

Turning over in bed, I inhale his musky scent again and groan. I'm becoming pathetic, and the shirt needs to go. Rolling off my bed, I snatch the thing from my bed and stomp downstairs to throw it in the trash incinerator.

Ashes to ashes, I think as I tap the screen to get the fire going.

"Lillium?" Dad's voice makes me freeze. I turn to see him sitting at the breakfast table in the living room. His brow quirks as his eyes land on the very obvious men's shirt I have, but it's not his expression that makes me pause.

"Is that a Deluxe Royal cake?" I ask, seeing the half-eaten pastry on his plate. He glances down at it and nods.

"A friend of yours dropped it off this morning. He said you lost the other to a squirrel?" His lips twitch slightly and I scoff.

"Raccoon." I correct.

"What are you doing with that shirt?" He asks finally.

I blink, remembering I'm holding Athos's shirt. I lift it up, ready to toss it into the now blazing flames. But something clenches at my heart. A sneaky sensation rolls up my spine, and suddenly I know I'm feeling a little guilty about burning Athos's shirt after he bought my dad a replacement cake. It can only be him since he's the only one who knows about the damned raccoon.

"Nothing," I grumble, turning the flames off. "I need to return this."

Dad quirks a brow. "To the friend who came by?" The curiosity in his voice stops me as I head for the front door.

"Yes," I answer, wary. Then I see the twinkle in his eye, and an all too dad-like smile spreads across his face. "Stop it, it's nothing like that." I groan.

He shrugs. "He seemed nice. Nice enough to stop by with my favorite cake. Which, I wonder how he was able to get one since they only sell them during the festival?" He takes a bite, giving me a pointed look.

"He has his ways," I say, assuming he played his 'I'm a Super' card on the baker and managed to get them to make him a special cake.

"Hmm," Dad's hum of approval alerts me to the sudden smile I have.

"It's not like that," I repeat, stomping away.

"Tell him I say hello," Dad calls as I escape the house.

I take a moment to catch my breath on the front lawn, my heart pounding in such a way I find myself needing air. Slowly I fill my lungs with the crisp morning air, holding it for a few seconds before exhaling and counting to ten. My shoulders begin to relax as my racing heart calms down. Counting helps with the attacks. Usually.

Once I feel less on edge, I hold up the shirt and consider my options. I can call Athos, and let him know I have his shirt. He can fly over and get it in no time, and I will be able to thank him for getting my dad the cake.

But I have a feeling Athos will ask why I have his shirt and why it takes me a whole day to let him know. I could have called him when he flew off, or at least left a message. But I'm so drained I don't consider doing that.

Instead, I take the shirt, not wanting to leave it in the park and go home where I curl up in bed with it hanging over my chair. I lay in bed all day, too tired and anxious to get up. I only have two more days before I have to file with the state. If I fail to, they will pick for me and mandate probation for my first year of work. It isn't the worst thing that can happen to me, but it usually means getting one of the assigned jobs everyone hates.

I tell myself I need to go today and suck it up. I take a deep breath, mentally preparing myself for the trip. But first, I can make a quick detour and drop Athos's shirt off at his apartment. I know where it is, and I can just leave it at his front door. He will probably assume it is me, but at least I won't have to face him.

Besides, I can use the Medi in his hallway to get some anxiety meds before I go to the state building.

I take a tram to the city, hopping off at one of the last stops at the edge where the fancy upper class lives in high-rise apartments. Following a couple into the lift, I momentarily forget what floor he is on.

"Shit," I whisper to myself as the couple hit their floor. The man looks at me expectantly, so I punch a random floor above theirs. As the lift jets up, I rack my brain for any memory of that night.

I suggest he take me to his place, and we take a short tram ride here. I vaguely remember getting in the lift, but then - a blush creeps up my neck as the memory hits me.

His hands roam under my dress, agile fingers slipping under my panties to tease me. Heat rolls over my skin as I recall grinding against his hand with abandon, coming quicker than I expect. All I can remember is being grateful no one else gets on the lift. It can't last more than a few minutes.

The doors open and the couple leaves me shivering in the corner, trying to shake the memory from my mind. The floor I select comes up, but the hallway doesn't look familiar. I curse under my breath and let the lift take me back down. Perhaps I can leave the shirt at the front desk?

I shake off the heat blazing under my skin and move to exit when the doors open in the lobby. I pause, my foot halfway out the doors as I gape at Athos in the lobby.

A slow, sly smirk curls at his lips when he sees me. *Fuck. Fuck.*

My brain is slow to move, leaving me with no options, standing like an idiot in the lift with my foot hanging out the doors. He approaches me, quirking a brow.

"Round two?" he teases, cocking his head to the side. Then he notices his shirt in my right hand. "Oh, so you're the one who took it."

"Took it?" I snap out of my stupor, annoyance shooting through my veins. "You left it at the park."

"That was a day ago." He says, then moves closer. I have no choice but to either back up into the lift or stand inches from him. I take a step back, letting him enter. He presses floor 69, his amber eyes glittering with mirth as I roll my eyes. Of course, he lives on that floor.

"So, you've come to return my shirt. How noble of you." I huff, tossing the shirt at his face and folding my arms over my chest.

"I was on my way to the state building. I figured I'd save myself the trouble of having to call you."

He peels the shirt from his face, chuckling. "Let me guess, you forgot which floor I was on?"

"No, I decided to ride all the way up to the penthouses and back down for shits and giggles." I retort.

The lift dings and opens to his hallway. I see the Medi on the wall and my stomach turns. He must have seen my expression.

"Do you want a drink before you let them decide your fate?"

I shake my head slowly. Drinking would only lead to me putting this off for longer.

"I just need a shot for my anxiety and I will get going." He moves into the hall, giving me space to the Medi. I tap the screen and select a mild dose for anxiety. Just enough so I won't become a puddle of nerves and despair once I am there.

"Are you sure about this?" he asks, surprising me.

"I'm bound to freak out again," I say, holding my wrist out for the scanner. The Medi beeps and a tiny needle shoots out, pricking me. The knots in my stomach ease a bit, but I can still feel the fear and despair coiled deep down.

"No, I mean, are you sure about letting the state decide this for you?"

I shake my head. "What other choice do I have? Supers came up with the employment initiative to prevent unemployment. But it means I either pick a lifetime job, or they do it for me. Not choosing isn't an option. They will just saddle me with whatever job is available."

"What would you want to do?" He asks, surprising me.

I rub my thumb against the tiny prick on my wrist, shrugging. "Nothing they have."

Athos snorts, "There has to be something you want to do with your life?"

"Make a difference," I say it before I realize I thought it. I bite my lip, cursing the meds. They tend to make me loopy, which is why I rarely use them. I'm liable to say anything at this point. "It doesn't matter. I need to go." I turn to the lift, but he's there, blocking me.

His serious expression is what prevents me from trying to kick him out of the way. "Do you mean that?" He asks.

"Mean what?" I try to play dumb, but I know he heard me.

"Do you want to make a difference?"

"Of course, I would. But you Supes have made that hard for a normal, lowly human like myself. We're left with the menial jobs, the ones that don't get attention or praise while Supes take all the credit."

He raises a brow, looking thoughtful. "So you would want to do something where you get credit? Where you aren't just working in the shadows? You want to be recognized like the Supes?"

I scoff, "No. I don't want fame. I just want to be appreciated." I bite my tongue, surprising myself. Is that truly what I want? Do I feel underappreciated? I don't want fame, or attention, like the Supers had. But I want to know I matter. That my life matters.

"I can understand that." He says, and I meet his eyes. He's serious, his sly smirk gone, the laughter in his eyes nowhere to be found.

46

"Can you?" I ask, half joking, half curious. "Most Supes just want the fame and glory that comes with having superpowers and being able to move mountains." I point out.

"They didn't always." His gaze glazes over and suddenly he is very still, as if lost in a memory. He's turning to stone before me. But as quickly as it happens, he melts back to life.

"What do you mean?" I ask.

"The others used to want the same things. Before revealing who we are, they wanted to help, but they didn't want the fame. They've changed, and I haven't. I still hold out the belief we can do some good without being treated like gods." There is a hint of pain in his tone that makes me pause.

"That's why you hate the festival," I say. He doesn't answer, but I can see I'm right. Perhaps he and I agree on more than I once thought. "Thank you for bringing my dad a cake. You didn't have to do that."

He blinks as if remembering where he is. "I felt bad that you lost the other one to a raccoon."

I huff but smile. "Too bad you and I couldn't team up then and get it back."

His sly smirk is back. "We would either be a force to be reckoned with, or we'd tear each other apart."

I move to leave but stop just at the lift doors. A thought races across my mind. A stupid, silly thought, but the moment my eyes meet his, I can tell he must be thinking the same thing.

"Want to hear a crazy idea?" he says, his voice soft but filled with hope.

"Crazy like you and I should work together?" I ask, raising a brow. "Maybe actually make a difference?" It would be crazy, as it was unheard of for a human and Super to work closely together. Sure, Supers employed humans, but they never considered humans as partners. But if we did, I can get out of signing my life away to a job I would hate, and he can have the chance to one-up the other Supers.

"Exactly," Athos says, his amber eyes flashing.

"On one condition," I say, "No flirting."

Chapter 8

My computer beeps incessantly while I pack my bag. Gaia wants to get a hold of me, but I can't take her call right now. I'm also semi-avoiding her. I don't exactly want to tell her about my and Athos partnering up. She won't understand.

I figure I will call her later tonight, after Athos and I go over my plan. The truth is, I'm still skeptical of this working out. For all I know, Athos could be playing a terrible joke on me out of revenge. Or it could fall apart because, well, maybe it isn't such a great idea.

Athos had asked me to come to his house to go over our half-baked idea. And by house, he meant an actual home out in the suburbs, not his apartment. I half-gaped at him when he told me he had multiple homes across the world, and I tried not to comment on how one person shouldn't have that many homes, but kept my mouth shut.

I do keep thinking I'm crazy to try this, that I will fail, that I don't have the gumption to do it. Then there is the added layer of us having slept together.

I have to keep telling myself it is all centered around my main idea: changing the way humans worship Supes, while also keeping myself free from the state.

The moment Athos said yes, I ran down to the state building and filed a claim that I would be working PR for a Super. I spent two hours going in circles with them since PR for Supers outside of Legion wasn't an official status.

I shove my notebook in the bag and close it just as I hear the front door open. Dad's home earlier than usual.

Panic tears through my guts as I realize I will have to come up with a lie before I leave. No one knows about Athos and me, and I'm going to keep it that way for a while.

I don't think he will have an issue with me working with a Super, but I know he will have questions I don't want to answer just yet.

Until then, I will have to avoid the truth. I listen for him to start tinkering around in the kitchen before I dare to open my door. The sink is on, and I can hear him tapping on the refrigerator's screen, probably looking through the list of what we have inside.

I slink down the stairs to the bottom where I can see his back to me. I don't breathe until he moves over to the oven. I take the moment to lunge for the front door but wait until he opens the oven to sneak outside. I close the door very slowly behind me. Then the bolt slides in place, sounding like a rocket in the silent neighborhood.

"Lillium?" I hear him call.

I bolt down the walkway and sprint up the street to the corner where I turn, never stopping my pace until I hit the platform where I wait for the train.

I'm not surprised when I see he lives in an upscale, nabob area where all the homes are small castles. As I walk down the street I can see some of them hidden behind lush foliage. Some resemble cottages like mine, only grander, others look like sparkling gingerbread houses. Athos's home is at the end of the street, on a corner that turns into a cross street.

The lot is easily three or four acres with a thick forest behind the house, but the house itself is humbly small. The lawn in the front wraps around the home like an emerald sea. The only plants in the front are oak trees that line the pathway to the front door.

I can't believe he lives in such a small house in this neighborhood. It is far larger than mine, but compared to the rest of the homes here, it's minuscule.

I start up the shaded pathway and notice a driveway to my left that snakes behind the house. Did he have a car? Did he even need to drive?

To my right, where the cross street is, he has an unobstructed view of the town and the surrounding forest.

It's picturesque, with its light stone walls, charcoal trimming, and garden beds outlining the walls. Vines grow from the beds, stretching up the sides of the house. Various flowers sway in the light breeze, their delicate faces reaching out for the sun. I can distinguish some daisies and poppies among them; very common house flowers.

But there is one I can't recognize.

I reach the front door, still observing the strange flower. I rap my knuckles on the door, hoping I have the right house. A moment passes, leaving me doubting the time he'd said. I'm sure he'd said noon, but I'm late, so maybe he left already?

"There you are!" I scream, dropping my bag as I spin around. He chuckles, "Easily surprised, aren't you?"

I let my heart crawl back into my chest before I take a shaky breath. He has a clear Plexi box full of pots, each one with the odd flower. He has them on a stick, the delicate green stems tied up to them. Judging by his smeared pants, it is safe to assume he is planting them.

"How are you so damn quiet? Did you float over here?" I snap.

"I don't *float*, I *glide*." He removes one hand from the box and makes a show of gliding his fingers over the flowers. I glare back at him, reclaiming my bag.

"If we are going to work together, you need to know these things, Lily." I ignore his grin and come down to get a better view of the flowers.

"What are these?" I ask, brushing my fingertips over the velvety blue petals.

"Orchids," he says.

"I've never heard of them." Each pot has one plant, but they are all different colored flowers.

"I'm not surprised. They've been extinct for nearly a hundred years," he muses.

I gape at him. "How do you have them then?"

He bends down, his scent filling my nose as he whispers, "I know someone."

"Shieba," I scoff, but he only winks in response. I motion to my bag. "I brought some notes and questions I have for you." His face changes slightly into his statue mode. "Nothing very personal," I assure.

"Alright, let me get these kids in the ground and you can ask some."

He slides past me, and that's when I realize he has no shirt on. His bronze skin stretches across taunt muscles as he moves. I advert my eyes quickly. If this partnership is going to work at all, then we need to remain professional. And staring at his muscles is far from professional.

I follow him around the house to where the driveway ends.

Athos stops behind the house on the side of the garage, where I can see mounds of dirt. The yard behind the house is only grass with a few overgrown bushes and is just as vast as the front until it stops at the forest.

"I used to have the best garden in town." He calls from the ground. "But it died, obviously, so now I have to start over."

"How long have you had this house?" I ask as he kneels into the patch of earth.

"I have had the house for a while." He says.

Fine, keep your secrets, I think.

I sit down next to him on a bag of flower food. I pull out my mobile laptop, turn it on, and flip to the questions. "So, the first thing I want to ask before we do anything else - why do you want to do this, *exactly*?"

"Exactly?" he asks.

"Yes. Yesterday you said you wanted change, but you also said a lot about being famous, and being remembered by humans."

"That's a part of it." He glances over at me. "Who wouldn't want their name remembered for ages?"

"You're a Super. Don't you live for ages?"

He grins devilishly, "You said nothing too personal."

"It was rhetorical." I tilt my head, tapping my pen on the pad. "So? Anything outside of fame?"

"Why?" he asks. He's carefully placing his flowers into the soil, and I can't help but admire how delicate he is with them. I'm still not sure what he's capable of, powers-wise, but something tells me he is stronger than he lets on.

I sigh. "If we are going to do this, I want it to be for the right reasons. I don't want to create a monster." A deep belly laugh rumbles from him.

"I understand. Fame is a part of it, albeit a personal part." I raise a brow, "I feel a certain…need for revenge on my fellow Supers." *Now this is interesting.* I'm shocked Athos feels animosity towards them.

"For what?" I ask softly. Athos turns from me to attack the earth. He scoops soil out with his bare hands and mixes in flower food. I watch his muscular back ripple as he tears up the earth. The sweet scent of fresh soil hits me, calming my nerves, and his as well. He relaxes his shoulders a bit and I wonder what kind of inner turmoil went through him.

Do Supes have a secrecy pact against humans? Or was this a trust issue? "You don't have to tell me." I assure him, "I'm sorry I asked. This is going to be more difficult than I thought."

"No, don't apologize. It's a personal issue between me and my kind. Simply put, I feel they have changed into bullish, egotistical beings." I hold back my need to agree.

"And you want to do what?" I ask instead.

He turns to me, his face grim, "I want to show them how obtuse they are. They need to be taken off their pedestals and shown a hard reality." His tone is harsh, but his words wrap around me like melted chocolate. I shiver, despite the warm sun on me.

"Which is?" I ask, my voice thick. I am trying to hide how much this excites me, but I'm having a hard time.

"Humans are fickle." He says, teasing. But his amber eyes are boring into me as if he can sense how excited I am.

"Good. I like that reason." I say, clearing my throat. *Get a fucking grip*, I tell myself. It's great he agrees with my sentiments, but I can't afford to let that seep into my heart. Clearly, we still both feel a sexual attraction to each other.

"It's satisfactory?" he asks, pulling me from my thoughts.

"Yes." I force a smile back at him as I write down his answer with relief. If he'd kept with just fame as a reason, I didn't think I would have been able to go on. "I don't expect a problem with having clients. People will want the chance to meet you, so it's going to be a matter of distinguishing the real clients from the fakes."

"How will you do that?" he asks.

"We will have to use our best judgment until I get the web page up," I say.

"What will the hours be?"

"Whatever you want, that's up to you. Emergencies should come first, of course. But we will have to establish that you are not *the* law. You can't be sent out to beat someone up because they stole something, or murdered someone. You bring those people to the authorities." I muse.

"So, I will be catching criminals?" he asks.

"Sure." I shrug.

"What about saving people?"

I tap my pen again. "That one is a bit more tricky. Say someone is about to fall off a building. It's not like they can just call you right then and ask for help. Ideally, we will get to a point where people will have this number to call for emergencies like that; or we may have some other way to contact you."

"Perhaps we will give the authorities a way to do it. Regular people might be tempted to make false reports." He suggests.

"Yes, that's true. That's why we will have a disclosure about you crushing them if they do." I throw him a wicked smile.

He quirks a brow. "I hope you're kidding."

"Maybe," I say.

He shakes his head as he pats down the earth. I scratch down his concerns and mine about being contacted; we have to go over specifics later when we are set up, but I have a feeling that we will be improvising most of it.

"Will you be in charge of my schedule?"

"Yes, it will be on a first come first served basis, with imperative emergencies taking precedence. Since you can fly and move very fast, you should be able to do multiple jobs in a small amount of time."

Athos smacks the soil off his hands, then lies on his back and looks up at me. "Alright. I will be doing jobs that the rest of us Supers do not bother with; the specifics will be worked out later, but we already know we will not be handling cases of investigating murder, robberies, theft, and so on."

"We are not investigators. I suppose if a robbery is going on, and you are called and the criminal can be identified, you will be able to apprehend them. But you won't be searching high and low for a cold case. That would take too much time. Unless you have a special ability that allows you to do just that." I quirk a brow. He just shakes his head.

"Now, I expect there to be an influx of calls that will have to be handled once people learn about it," I say.

"How will you be handling it?"

"I have the number set up to take messages when I can not. The first week or so, if I can, I will be taking every call and hopefully, they will be genuine calls. I'm expecting people to be questioning the authenticity of the business, but it will pass once we do a few jobs. I have also set up this number." I pull a card out of the pad, "This will be your number. I will transfer emergencies to this one."

"You will be the only one with it?"

"Yes. I won't be giving it out. So when it rings, you will know it's an emergency. This way, I won't have to call you myself with the details and have to stop taking other calls. All you have to do is enter it in your computer, or your phone, and wherever you are, you will be able to get the call."

He nods, "That's reasonable. What will we be doing to start?"

"Old fashion posters. They will be low-cost and more personal. We will start around the towns, posting them at the parks. My next idea would be to make cards that we can send to the houses so people have the number."

"I can deliver the cards to the houses. It won't take too long. Which towns do you have in mind?" he asks.

"I don't. Not yet, at least. We will have to go over that." I shake my head.

"Alright, and after the posters?"

"I hope that the word will get out fast enough just by those towns, and then expand to other towns close by. Phase two starts then. We will have to get you coverage, not by pop media, but by someone else. Someone smaller, but with just as much standing as the media."

"News?" he quirks a brow.

"No. We won't do interviews with the news until later, and until that time we will only be giving information to be contacted."

"Ah, I see. The mystery and suspense will make it even bigger, right?" he chuckles.

"Yes." I smile at the thought of news and media foaming at the mouth for interviews. "We will give interviews to smaller companies, smaller people."

"Giving them the chance to shine, and have it be on a personal level as well."

"The world news and media are for the faux-heroes. You won't be like that." Athos looks up at me, his amber eyes shining with mischief.

"This will annoy the others. I will rise from the back roads of society and rip the red carpet right from under their feet."

"They won't know what hit them." I grin back. "Once you have coverage, we will need other means of taking care of requests. I'm thinking of a web page as well as more numbers, each being a specific type. You know, one number for local help, one for national, and one for international."

"International? You think it will get to that?" he asks softly.

"Oh yes, I expect it to. But we will deal with that when it comes." I narrow my eyes at him. "How many languages do you speak, by the way?"

He smiles, "Many. Languages won't be a problem for me. You can send them to me if it will be easier."

"Perhaps," I grumble. Can I ever get him to give me a straight answer?

"Your job sounds more like a secretary than a publicity representative."

I shrug. "Someone has to do it, and it makes sense for it to be me. Once we have jobs, you will be busy working them, while I will be sitting around."

"Is that what you will be doing? I thought you'd be coming with me."

I blink in surprise; he thinks I will be going with him to jobs? "Why would I?"

"As my PR, you are obligated to make sure I don't do anything wrong. Right?"

"Wrong?" I laugh, "Like what?"

"Like seducing a customer," he wiggles his brows at me.

I kick some dirt towards him, rolling my eyes.

"I would like you to be there to reassure the humans," he says, brushing the dirt off his bare chest.

"How would I reassure people? Reassure them of *what*?"

"By being there. People will see you and I interact, and they will be assured of my stance on equality. I won't be treating you like a lesser being, and you will be speaking to me like…well, like a person."

A soft hum escapes me as I think. He is right, if we are seen together interacting like equals, others will be more comfortable with him. They won't see him as a god, but as a *person* they can approach, and that is exactly what I want.

"It *would* be beneficial…" I write it down quickly as I speak. "All you have to do is fly around and help some people." I look at him through hooded eyes. He has his hands on his bare chest, face turned to the sun, smirking. Seeing the sun reflect off his tan skin reminds me I'm sweating in the summer heat.

"About the posters…" I begin, wiping some sweat from my brow.

"Let's eat." He cuts me off, standing behind me suddenly with his hands on his hips. "I want to see what you think of my cooking."

"Whoa-kay…" I breathe out. Every time he does that stunt, I feel shocked to pieces. I pick up my things and follow him to a door by the garage. Despite being dirty, he doesn't bother to knock his pants clean. Thus, when he gets inside, a trail of soil follows him.

Athos follows the hall and goes left, or so the trail of dirt I follow suggests. I come into a kitchen easily three times the size of mine. He is at the refrigerator, scrolling through the list until he comes to a picture of a green bowl. He selects it and the machine hums while he opens it to reveal the levers rotating the food inside. He grabs the green one and turns to me.

"This way." He gestures to the other side of the kitchen. We come out to a dining area with massive windows that overlook the side of his house where the two streets meet.

"You not only have the newest refrigerator, but a nice view of the town," I remark.

"It used to be better. The view, I mean. Once those houses over there," he points to a cluster of homes to our right, "went up, half my view was obscured."

"Seeing as you can fly..." I shrug, and he chuckles.

"Regardless of where I live, I always have the best views in the end." He sits down at the table, a very large piece of work piled with plates of aromatic foods. There isn't much space for his bowl, so he shoves some plates down the table to make some. "Sit." He waves at the seat across from him.

I sit and ogle the feast before me. Fresh fruits round a pie of sorts, a mound of rice ladled with vegetable gravy, two loaves of strange-looking bread, multiple mini-pies, custard, vegetables, and a steaming plate of roasted mushrooms.

He opens the bowl to reveal a whipped chocolate mousse that he places on top of petite sugar cakes.

"This looks amazing," I say tightly, thinking back to the sad little casserole I'd made. "You just have to one-up everyone, don't you?"

His amber eyes grow dark with mischief as he smirks.

"Uh, this is all modern, right? Fake meat and all?"

He laughs, "Right. I was never much of a meat eater anyway."

I attack the fruit pies ruthlessly, picking through the vegetables, slicing open the main pie- which turns out to be some kind of meat and gravy- and pour myself some pink bubbly liquid I see.

Unfortunately, everything is excellent.

I eat with such abandon that I almost don't have enough room for the delicate cakes with mousse.

Almost. They taste so light it's hard to think they hold any kind of substance. My stomach bulges in protest, punishing my mind and tongue for being so greedy.

I have to stop or face my tummy exploding. Athos continues until all the food is gone. I sit back and watch him down everything in a very calm manner. He isn't stuffing his face, but it doesn't seem like he chews either. *Does he do everything at such a fast pace?* I wonder. He stacks his plates and then stands up, stretching.

"Come on, before you slip into a food coma," he says, motioning for me to follow him.

I force myself up and follow him into a sunny room full of bookshelves that line the walls. As I collapse into a chair, I see the stacks of books are very old.

"Satisfactory?" Athos asks, leaning against one of the shelves. My eyes are beginning to feel heavy after the hot afternoon sun and food, but he looks wide awake.

"I feel like I just gained ten pounds. How are you not stuffed after all that? Don't you gain weight?" I ask.

"No," he answers, giving me an irritating grin.

"So you can eat all you want, whatever you want?" I ask, incredulous.

"Yes," his smile widens, "Before fat pills came along, it was a very unique quality. But nowadays it is hard to get overweight, right?"

I shrug. "Unless you are willing to pay for the extremely unhealthy processed foods. You've had years of practice in the art of cooking, I assume." He nods. "So you know how to make the best possible dishes, and the most addictive. I'm going to have to limit the amount of times I let you cook." I sigh.

He laughs again, "So the posters, I was thinking of a simple 'Hero for Hire' line, some information and the number. Nothing too extravagant. No pictures."

"Are you sure?" I ask, losing the fight to keep my eyes open.

"Yes. Let people call and see what happens. We don't want to appear too eager for jobs."

"Alright. I'll make some today." I yawn.

"I'll pick them up tonight then, and put them up. What towns were you thinking of?"

"Here, Fantom, Naptow, and Silverfish. The towns closest to us, and each other."

"Perfect, I expect a job tomorrow." He says, but I barely hear him as I drift off into a food coma.

Chapter 9

"My philandering sister spent all our inheritance," Jude explains, "not to mention the amount of our mother's money when she was alive. She's always had a way of getting what she wanted from our parents, who were very, very wealthy. This is their house. My mother left it to me when she died." She sniffs as she eats yet another piece of fizzed fruit. "Are you sure you don't want any?" I shake my head again, "The fizz makes them extra nutritious, and they keep you looking years younger. I swear by it!"

I've only been in her company for an hour, but she has shown me dozens of different ways to stay young-looking. None of which I'm interested in doing.

She wears high-end clothing two sizes too big that I suspect her mom left to her as well. She's an obvious user of mineral blasts - the process of blasting old skin off to make for newer, softer skin. No one has natural buttery skin like hers, not even Gaia with her selected genes.

"I planned on living out my life by going to performances, fundraisers, and social events. I hadn't planned on getting a job in Sun City as a marketer. All I have now is this house and my ridiculous sister. And to top it off, she goes and pulls this stunt, making me go all the way to Liptum just to drive that ancient relic back here to Silverfish so she can sell it and make some money! And you would think she would tell me that this car was known to have engine troubles, but no! She let me drive off with it and it breaks down in the middle of nowhere! I still cannot believe your Super is willing to go all the way there just to bring it back to me."

"Well, he can fly, so-" I'm cut off by a snort.

"And to think he is doing it for free! I cannot wait to meet this man!" She tosses another fruit in her mouth and chomps down, making it pop loudly.

"I am sure he will be just as excited to meet-" Jude ignores me like she has the last hour.

"Does he do pictures? I would love to get a photo to remember this. I won't show my lousy sister, though. She would think it was all her doing and gloat-" I tune her out, looking out the window again for any sign of Athos. Jude's nice, but damn can she talk. I'd expected some questions about Athos and what we were doing, but so far her sister is the only subject she brings up.

To be honest, I was relieved when she called this morning. So far, the only calls I have been getting were from people who wanted to know if Athos was a Supe. I was beginning to wonder if anyone was going to take us seriously.

After the third day, I began to wonder if I was making a huge mistake. Even if someone calls, and we did make this work, would I be able to handle it? Could we even make a difference?

It doesn't seem to make a difference to Jude, I think as I gaze back at her. She's around my mother's age, but with all the procedures she's had, it's impossible to tell her exact age.

Athos talked me into staying with her while he flew off to find the car. He said he has faith in me, and that I could wow her with my shining personality while he's gone. Stupid, stubborn Super.

"Oh dear, you shouldn't scrunch your brow like that. It will make your eyes sag."

My head snaps back to her, a smile plastered to my face, "Sorry, I was looking for Athos. He should be here soon." I say a silent prayer it's true.

"Oh, I am so excited to finally meet one of them! I put on my best outfit. Do you like it?"

"Uh, it's very-"

"My sister has one just like it though, so I had considered another...." She plucks at the frizzy top. "Oh, I do hope the house looks alright." She mutters. "My sister has such a nice house, but then she has money!"

I glance around the house, thinking it looks like every other human dwelling I'd been to.

"Money isn't everything. I'm sure your sister is sitting in her kitchen lamenting about something you have that she wants." I say, trying to be genial.

Jude's fake eyebrows shoot up further than any I have seen, and she lets out the most horrific laugh, like a monkey chattering.

"Oh, you are too funny Lillium!" She cackles. "That was kind to say, but it's not true. She is the most self-absorbed person in the world." I cough back a laugh. "She only cares about the money and the things it can buy her. You will learn when you and that Super become famous - the money will change you.

I am certain Athos is already very wealthy. I have no intentions of earning much from this but experience. So I only reply with, "I have seen what money does to a person, but fame has the same effect."

"Too true, dear, too true." She nods sagely.

In truth, I have no idea what kind of person Athos is. Outside of him being stubborn, kind, and all-around annoying, all I know for sure is that he wants to change the dynamic between his people and mine, just as I do. But is that enough?

"That reminds me about this one time, my sister-" *Oh for the love of all that is good and holy*, I think, slumping into my chair.

A movement out the window catches my attention. I almost cry when I see Athos gliding down the road. The car held above his head with one hand.

Jude stops mid-sentence to scream a shrill tune that almost causes my eardrum to shatter. I watch incredulously as she rushes out the front door, jabbering incoherently. I start to doubt if I want to continue with this idea, if I am going to have to deal with people like this.

It takes all types; I think as I make my way to the open door frame. Athos stops in front of the house and lands gingerly by Jude.

"You're a Super! A real live Super!" She screeches. Athos cracks a dimpled smile and holds one hand out.

"I'm Athos." She takes it, oblivious to him still holding her car above his head.

Jude pumps it up and down while jabbering, "I can't believe it! I had thought this was some kind of joke by my sister! I really did!"

"That would be one elaborate joke," I comment as I slide by her to face Athos. His odd eyes twinkle at me as I ask, "Where would you like it?" I ignore his obvious flirting. We'd agreed to keep things professional- and never, ever mention the one-night stand.

"Oh! Right here on the road is fine. Just fine." She wrings her hands like a gleeful child as he sets it down. He walks around it, eyeing the gadgets and wheels.

"I believe it's in the same condition as it was on the road." He proudly announces.

"Do not worry about that!" Jude flaps her hands wildly around her so I have to move to the side to avoid being smacked. "I wouldn't care if you brought *half* of it back. You're a Super." She nudges me, "A good-looking one. Nothing like that Super Slone." She blanches, "Now he's a bit rough looking, but I'm sure you're a different kind of rough."

I can tell Athos is staring at me as I turn away from her to hide the look on my face. Jude has no idea how true that statement is. The bruises and marks I have from that night had just started to fade, thankfully. Without them as a constant reminder, I could finally start forgetting we'd slept together.

"If you need any more help, just let us know." He says.

"Oh, well… do you know anyone who can fix cars?"She asks.

"I already took care of that. It had a crack in the engine; a simple fix. That's why it took so long."

Jude and I share a moment of stunned silence. I'm so shocked I didn't even notice she stopped talking until she lets out a cry that rings up and down her street. She starts jumping up and down with abandon and screaming 'thank you' over and over. A few of her neighbors poke their heads through windows but turn back once they see her. I am willing to bet they are used to this.

She tackles Athos, planting wet kisses all over his face. He only smiles and assures her it is nothing. Once her outburst subsides, she insists that she pay us.

"I don't have any money, but I would like to give you something."

"No, no, that's not necessary," I say.

"The poster said no payment." Athos chimes.

"I know, but I can't let you leave without something!"

"All we ask is-" Jude speeds off into the house before I can finish. "Alright...
"

Athos laughs. "She's a bit eccentric."

I turn my gaze slowly to him. "You have no idea. None." A slow, sly smirk curls at his lips and I have to advert my gaze from him. "Stop doing that."

"Doing what?" He asks.

A crash followed by a screech brought Jude streaming back outside. She holds a small green box in her hands and stretches it out to me.

"This was my mother's. I would like you to have it."

My mouth opened and closed noiselessly. I'm shocked that she's giving something up of her mother's. After all, she'd complained about her sister doing it.

"It was given to her as a gift in India, where she spent a few years studying. It is supposed to bring luck to her, and in my eyes it does." She opens it to reveal a gemstone the size of my thumbnail. It is blue, but the way it catches the light makes it look milky.

"It's a Cat's Eye stone." She says as she places it in my hand. It is cool to the touch. I can see it is shaped like a teardrop. "She became very wealthy later and had this stone set in a pure gold ring. I had to sell the setting." She sighs sadly, "I think it has to be passed on as a gift for the luck to work. When she died she hadn't said who would get it, so I took it before my sister could. I can't sell it, it's too important. And it's not worth much anyways."

My shock turns to muted dismay. So it brings her bad luck, and she is trying to pawn it off to me? I don't think so. "I really can't," I hold out my hand, but Athos seizes it and closes my fingers over the gem.

"Thank you, Jude." He carefully places my hand back to my side and smiles down at me. "We will take the gem for you, and hopefully your luck can return. In the meantime, would you mind giving these out to your friends and neighbors and telling them about your experience?" He pulls out a small stack of cards. I notice they have the number and our names on them. I hadn't known he made them yet.

"Of course! I will tell absolutely everyone I know! Including my sister." She winks at me. I force a smile.

"Thank you. If you need anything else, just call us." Athos takes her hand and shakes it again. I thank her and turn to follow him.

"Wait! Athos, can I have your autograph?" She asks.

"Of course, though I doubt it will ever be worth anything."

"I think it will. And when it is, I will say I have one, and that I won't accept any price for it!" She holds out one of the posters I had made. Athos takes a pen from her and scrawls his signature over the title.

"Lillium, take a photo will you?" She thrusts her pad into my arms. I snap a few shots as she poses next to him.

She thanks Athos profusely then dials her sister as we walk towards the platform to leave. I can hear her saying something about meeting a famous Super. Would he be? She hasn't asked for my autograph, which stands to say that if he does become famous, I won't. That will be the way of it. I assume it will turn out that way, me being the person behind the scenes while he gets all the attention.

Attention is not what you want I tell myself. I open my palm to see the glittering stone. It's very pretty and will make a nice necklace.

"She needed to give it away, Lilly." I raise a brow as he says, "It meant a lot to her that you would take it. Perhaps she feels it only brings her bad luck. That's part of the job, right? Helping people."

"I didn't realize she needed help getting rid of it," I say softly. Athos hums. "I was so frustrated with the thought that she meant to give us a back luck gem to better herself that I wanted to throw it back at her."

"That's what helping is, Lily. We have to help the people who need it, whether we like it or not. It was a small task, to take the gem, but she will be forever grateful."

"And, if she ever wants it back she will know where to get it." I smile.

"I do not think she will want it back, ever."

"Perhaps her sister will contact us for it?" I laugh.

"If she does, you can take it to her."

I scoff. "Don't you dare tease me like that. You're the hero, that's *your* job."

He chuckles, "I guess I am now."

"How did it feel, actually being thanked this time?"

"Nice." I start to feel guilty as I realize he must have felt nervous about doing this. Being a Supe only gets you so far, I have seen some try and fail to gain popularity, so there is a chance that he can be rejected. Like I had done to him.

"You were good." I find myself patting him on the shoulder causing him to raise a brow. I stop, awkwardly faltering in my steps. "What?"

"I would not have taken you for the caring type."

"I am not heartless." I grumble, *of course I care*, "I will call you when we get another job." I wave dismissively.

"Why do you want to do this?"

"Uh, this is the only way home?"

"No, no, why are you doing this?" He points to us.

"Oh," I think back to all the conversations we had had, thinking I must have told him. He notices my hesitation.

"I know you are not fond of us, that we let you down when you needed us, and that you feel like your people are content with us running things. What I do not know is why you would want to help me become famous. Are you not afraid that I could turn into one of them?"

"Of course, I am naturally pessimistic. But in the end, you are the only one who can do it." I say flippantly. A slow dimpled smile spreads across his face. I can see the heat in his eyes, and I try to ignore it.

"My people do not want a human hero right now. They want one of you, someone who is more than human." He slumps his shoulders a bit for the first time. I have never seen him anything but unconcerned. Though now, at the mention of him being able to be something more than the rest of his people, he became unnerved. Did Athos doubt his abilities?

"Well, if Jace Kace can garner hundreds of screaming fans just by changing the size of his arm, you certainly can."

That gets him to chuckle. "The bar is set high."

"So high." His shoulders relax, and his ease returns.

"Are you sure you won't let me fly you back? It will be faster."

I scrunch up my face. "So I can suffocate halfway there while my skin is torn from my bones? Nope. Besides, if anyone saw you drop me off, I would have to explain it."

"You still have not told anyone?" He gives me his lazy smile. "Am I a dark secret in your life?"

"The darkest." I snip. I see the train turn the corner as we share a smile.

"Are you saying you would deny knowing me if that friend from work saw us?"

"Libby? Yes!"

He laughs, "Have fun trying," winking he takes off with a whoosh. I jump back, cursing as the few people on the platform yell in surprise.

"Stop doing that!" I cry, holding my heart.

"Sorry." I spin around to see him standing on top of the train as it comes to a stop. That lazy grin is back.

"Is that a Super?" someone asks.

I roll my eyes, causing me to miss him taking off again. The platform erupts into chaos as people scramble to take photos while the passengers come off the train. I ignore everyone, taking a seat instead.

The whole ride home I hear everyone talking about how they saw a Super flying circles over them; some even say they thought it was Mathis. No one had noticed him talking to me, or even standing right by me. Athos is wrong. I don't have to pretend like I don't know him to keep my secret.

Next to him, no one knows I exist.

Chapter 10

I officially launch the website that night and by the next morning, Jude left a very lengthy review, mostly to do with her sister. The rest is about how attractive Athos is.

It's a start.

Another few days pass, each with a false alarm or two. I try to use the time to figure out how to tell everyone what I'm doing. If this goes the way I'm hoping it will, we could be flooded with calls soon, and then it will only be a matter of time before Athos gets media coverage.

The real challenge would be breaking it to Gaia. I spent the entire morning staring at her number, not having the courage to call it. Thankfully, the phone rings, giving me an actual excuse to procrastinate.

"This is Hero for Hire?" A gruff voice asks.

"Yes," I answer warily, fully expecting the next question.

There is a pause before he asks, "A real one?"

I choke back a groan. "He is. Are you calling about a job or some help?"

"I do need help." My eye twitches slightly in anticipation. Could this be a real job?

I change my tone completely, "Well then, what is it you need?"

"I work on an animal conservation site, and we need help to put up fencing and building shelters. We have seven square miles of land that we estimate will take us a year to cover." He explains.

"That long?" I ask, incredulously.

"Yes, I work for Sheiba's conservation program. She doesn't have the time to help us, and the other Supers can't be bothered with this. Which is why I

67

can't believe there is one out there who will."

"Athos isn't like the others," I say with more confidence than I feel.

"Well, I sure hope he can help." The voice grumbles. I feel a kinship with the man instantly.

"Oh, I guarantee it. When do you need him?"

"Truthfully, tomorrow would be great, but... whenever he can make it."

A quick look on the internet tells me it's very recently established and still in the development stages. It doesn't surprise me that Sheiba left them on their own when she has bigger and better projects to do that will get her more air time. Though, when it's finally open, she will most certainly be there to take all the credit for it.

"What is your name?" I ask.

"Oh, I'm Guinn." I write down his name and location in the scheduling program.

"We can be there tomorrow afternoon, Guinn. I cannot give you an exact time frame in which the work will be done just yet, but I can assure you that it won't take a year." Or even a month by what I have witnessed Athos accomplish lately.

"Any help is much appreciated." His tone is still gruff, but I can hear the relief in his words, "Thank you."

Athos is not surprised either when I tell him. If anything, he knows way more about the project and Sheiba than Guinn seems to know.

"Sheiba has other interests right now in Australia and the waterways. She's helping reshape the war-ripped valleys back to their original state so that the rivers and wells can run again."

"Waterways? Doesn't she normally just grow some crazy-looking plants and cover a field in flowers?" I ask.

He laughs. "She can do more than grow crops and flowers. There is no way she'd pass this up now. It's too high profile."

I scoff, shaking my head.

Athos says it shouldn't take him more than a day or two to finish the project, depending on exactly what they need and how the weather is.

"I can move as fast as I want, but I can not stop a rain or snowstorm from happening."

I cringe at the mention of snow. They are so far north that there is bound to be some snow even this time of year. I come clad in my winter best to meet him at my platform. Athos, on the other hand, wears his usual jeans and shirt.

"It's not the Arctic, Lily." He snorts, but I roll my eyes.

"Unlike you, I am susceptible to sickness." I sniff, attempting to cross my arms over my chest. My puffy jacket holds my arms back, so I let them hang lamely by my sides as I ignore the look he gives me.

A crowd of people slowly forms around us as we wait for the train. Athos glances around the platform, looking curious.

"What did Fantom used to be?" He asks, surprising me.

"Before the War?" I ask and he nods, "Uh, part of Mexico, I think. I know it was considered a desert, and after the War, it was transformed into a wooded area. Where we are going was part of Canada." *I wonder how much Athos doesn't know about this age*, I think as the train pulls up.

"That sounds a bit outside of the areas we advertised." He quips.

"He lives in Silverfish, but works out there." I retort, "Are you sure you want to ride the train? Like a normal person?"

He rolls his eyes and takes a seat. "I don't fly everywhere all the time."

"What? Too many birds up there hogging the airspace?" I tease.

"Not enough pretty girls," he retorts, giving me a look. I scrunch my nose at him and pull out my wristpad, focusing on anything but his body next to mine. We sit in a surprisingly comfortable silence the entire ride.

"How many people do you think live there?" Athos asks after some time, making me look up. I can just barely see the town before us, but he must be able to make it out clearly.

"Not many." I explain, "There was very little information when I looked it up. It's mostly farmers out here."

"Cows?" I scrunch my face up in disgust and shake my head.

"We don't farm animals, Athos. That's barbaric."

"Interesting," he muses.

The platform we stop at is half the size of Fantom's, and I never thought my hometown to be big. At first glance, we can see that all the houses clustered around it, and then nothing but forest surrounding them.

"I count twenty buildings, you?" Athos asks as we leave the train. We are the only passengers who disembark at the stop.

"This place is perfect for a conservation," I remark. "There's no one around."

Athos chuckles and steps off the protected platform into the frost-covered street. Ice flurries blow around him as he walks around, taking in the small structures, hands in his pockets. I don't want to leave the walls of the platform but have no choice once he starts to disappear behind buildings.

"Athos!" I call as I reluctantly leap off the platform. The frost crunches beneath my feet as I trot over to the building he went behind. But he isn't there.

"Where the fu-" I begin to grumble just as I hear a peal of laughter above me. He's crouching on the roof of the building, smirking down at me.

"Did you think I left you?" He asks.

"No. I thought you might pop into the local bar and seduce some other hapless human," I snap sarcastically. "We have to get going. It's ten miles to the conservation, and we said we'd be there by noon."

"Don't have kittens, Lily." I gape as he leaps off the roof to stand next to me. "You will give yourself a heart attack if you don't develop a sense of humor."

"I have a great sense of humor. It is just very dry, and we have great medical advances to avoid heart attacks. Thank you." I retort.

"Right. Anyway, while I was up there, I could see a small storm coming in." I scoff. Is he serious? "So we'd better get there before it does."

"Well, Guinn hadn't said anything about sending a car for us, so I guess we have to walk." I pull my hat down further to cover my ears, bracing myself for the weather.

Athos grins at me, a very sly look coming up in his eyes. "You don't have to walk, but I do," I say, thinking he was coming up with a joke about being able to fly or run fast.

"Not true." He smiles wide, his dimples popping in such a way I nearly lost my breath. I shut my eyes, telling myself it's unprofessional to be drooling over him.

Before I can process a thought, he has me in his arms. "Hold on." He says, and then he is up in the cold air. The sensation of not being able to breathe hits me like before, and I gasp for air. He stops suddenly, hovering over the town below. I cling to his neck, taking a deep breath, inhaling his scent as I press my body into his.

"Not so-" I'm cut off by a jerking motion as we go flying. This time he isn't moving *as* fast, so I'm able to catch my breath.

The cold air is full of frosty bits that slam into my face like daggers. I have to shove my face into his chest to avoid being blinded by it. It is chilly up in the air, and being pummeled by wet flakes isn't helping the matter, but his unnaturally warm body keeps me from shivering. I can see just under his arm where the forest is flying by in a blur. Then there is the moment of landing. He falls from the sky, knocking the air from me again, and places me back on my feet.

It all takes two minutes, maximum.

"You alright?" He asks, straightening my hat. I bat his hands away with a groan.

"You can't just go flying up in the air like that- I can't breathe when you do it so suddenly," I say, patting my chest as if my lungs had been ripped out. I've only been on a roller coaster once before, and flying around with him was like that only twenty times faster.

Athos sighs, running his fingers through his dark hair until a few locks drop dramatically over his eyes. "Maybe I just like to take your breath away."

"Smooth." I wipe the frost from my face to take a look around us. Athos placed us right in front of a small fort with a large sign that read, 'Sheiba's Northern Conservation'.

The front door busts open and a burly man comes running out. He is followed by a few other men, and a woman, who all wear looks of utter surprise. The man runs right at us so fast I think he's going to bowl me over. He stops just short of Athos and lets out a deep laugh.

"A Super!" He cries. "By gods, I never thought I'd live to see one!" He continues laughing and looking over his shoulder at the others, "He's real!"

They all exchange looks of disbelief but move closer to inspect him.

"Uh, hello." I pipe up. The man ignores me while he continues to look Athos over.

"You look so human!" He says in awe.

Athos smirks, "Thank you. This is Lillium." He pushes me in front of him, forcing me to smile awkwardly.

"Oh! I'm Guinn. We spoke on the phone!" Guinn takes my hand, nearly crushing it with his grip. I hold it as he continues to spout his disbelief. "I just can't believe he's here!"

Athos gracefully slips my hand out of Guinn's grip, replacing it with his own hand. "There's a storm coming in. It's not big, but I would like to get started before it hits. And get Lillium out of the cold." He adds with a wink. I am wedged between the two men, my back pressed up against Athos's chest, so thankfully he cannot see me blush when I dip my face down.

Damn Super.

"Guinn!" The woman comes up to us. She's just as big as Guinn and is the only one who wears winter apparel. Everyone seems to have run out without a jacket. "Guinn, it's rude to leave them out here in the cold." She eyes Athos in his short-sleeved shirt.

"Oh! Yes, I'm sorry. Come in, come in, Athos." Guinn takes him by the arm and leads him to the fort, leaving me with the woman. She gestures for the others to follow, and they all file in, with me being the last. I'm forgotten, in the corner of the large room, while everyone circles Athos in awe.

Guinn takes him to a heavy-looking wooden table in the center of the room and has him sit while another man is ordered to get him food. The whole place is one open room with a few halls that must lead to bedrooms. It has high, open rafters with wooden beams crossing the tops. There were even fake animals lining the fireplace.

"Here, this is a map of the area." Guinn pulls out a halo tile and connects it to the table. A larger halo screen appears in the middle of the table, showing a map of the forest. I can't see over the crowd of guys and don't feel like shoving my way through to Athos, so I stroll over to the fireplace to take a closer look at the animals. They have mineral logs burning, giving off a sweet fragrance.

I sense the woman next to me before I see her. "These aren't real, right?" I ask, motioning to the animals.

"Some are." I turn to her with a horrified look, "Not recently killed, though. They are old, very old. Been in my family for generations."

"Hunting is illegal up here still?" I ask.

"Yes. This one," she points to the large gray wolf I'm eyeing, "died a few years ago outside of town. He'd been living here with his pack for ten years, and we think he died of old age. I liked him and decided to have him stuffed."

"Oh," I gaze at the amber eyes of the wolf and shake my head, "I can't imagine killing anything, especially something that can't defend itself against weapons."

"We were a different race of people back then, killing and destroying our world."

I meet her eyes and smirk. "Are we so different now?"

She smiles back at me. "I don't think so. Do you?" I shrug, glancing back to Athos, who's now handing out autographs.

"Too early to tell."

"I'm Sarah, Guinn's wife." She says as she waves down a man with a tray of soup.

"Lillium. Athos's... PR." The man sets the soup down at a table for us, then rushes back to Athos.

"It's very kind of Athos to do this for us, and for free." She mentions sitting.

I nod. "We only want the word spread in return. And a review on the webpage." I take a bite of the stew, sighing as it warms me to my bones.

"We were surprised when Sheiba asked us to head the new conservation here in the North. We'd always known she'd make one, but we never fathomed she'd ask *us*." Sarah shakes her head in disbelief. It's a normal reaction, as no human expects to encounter a Super let alone work with

73

them.

"How long have you lived here?" I ask.

"My entire life. Our normal jobs are mountain tours, and collecting information for the forest registrar." I quirk a brow. "It's a comprehensive list of plants and wildlife that are currently thriving in our area. We compare it to the original plants and wildlife that grew around here and see how the place has changed."

"Oh, you are a scientist?"

"No." She laughs, "Not a certified one. I'm part of the Wild North Niche. We consist of people who have lived all their lives in the wild forest and are dedicated to helping return it to a state closest to the condition it was in before humans impacted it."

"Really? As in, what, prehistoric times?" I ask.

"Close to it, yes. We are working on getting rid of plants and animals that aren't originally from here and harm the area. We place them back where they should be, on their respective conservation."

"Oh. So, will you be working the entire conservation?" I ask, impressed.

"I will be overseeing the wildlife. Guinn is the plant expert."

"What kind of fences are you putting in?"

"Hilo fences." She smiles.

"Seriously? That's amazing." I look back at Athos and wonder how long it will take him to put it up. Hilo fences are the most high-tech systems we have; essentially, an invisible screen that solidifies when they detect objects that weren't allowed to pass through. I have never seen one before in person, so I seriously doubt Athos had either.

"So, humans will be locked out?" I ask.

"Yes, and no. If you get a pass chip, you can pass through the fence, but if you don't, it will bar you from entering. All animals are allowed in, of course, and non-bio-materials will be completely shut out and reported."

"Will it be a projecting fence?" I ask, intrigued.

"Yes. We will be able to access any post from right here and see what's going on, along with being able to project a video of us from here to there in cases of stray humans who may be lost."

"Whoa. It sounds like Sheiba has everything set." Everything but the will to see it through.

"Everything but the manpower to set it up in a reasonable time." She nods, voicing my thoughts.

"Well, there is that. Did she not give you funds for workers?"

"No, she did, but only a limited amount." Sarah gestures to the men around Athos.

"Just that many?" Sheiba sure was skimping.

"Yes. Twelve workers in all, fourteen if you count Guinn and I. It would take a year to get the fence up with just us."

"Couldn't you ask her for more?" *She's rich enough,* I think.

"We did, but we haven't received a response from her for over a month. She didn't even come down here herself. She sent us a message asking if we wanted the job, and when we accepted, she had all the materials and funds sent down here."

"Oh, so you haven't even seen her at all?"

"No. Athos is the first Super we've ever seen outside of the broadcasts." She smiles at him and shakes her head. "Guinn will be boasting about this for the rest of his life." I overhear Athos mentioning how many posts he can carry and even I have to do a double-take.

"It depends on how well they are secured together. I fly very fast, and they could get damaged. We don't want that happening." He says as we all gape at him.

The men laugh, even though he isn't joking. I feel Sarah's eyes on me and meet her smiling gaze. "Why aren't you over there with the rest of them?" I ask. "It's a once-in-a-lifetime chance to see a Supe in person."

"Supe?" She laughs at my slang, "He doesn't mind being called that?"

"Not that I know of." I shrug nonchalantly. I haven't considered his feelings about it before, since he never reacts to my using the slang. Though, in truth, I have no idea if Supers mind being called Supes.

She sits back and crosses her arms, her gaze quizzical. "I'm more interested in you. A human working directly with a Super? That's unheard of."

"Yeah, well, I expect it to go wholly unnoticed. I'm more of the behind-the-curtain person. I'm only here because he feels that other humans would feel more comfortable when they see us interact." I stick my thumb at the group without looking, "As you can see, I am not needed for that."

She raises a brow. "Oh, I thought you two might be a couple."

I snort, gaping back at her.

"No, it's nothing like that," I gasp out.

She hummed, "Well, maybe it is something else."

Before I have a chance to ask her what she means, I hear Athos behind me, "Lily?" I nearly jump out of my seat with fright.

"Sneaking." I hiss low enough so only he can hear me. He smiles at Sarah and shakes her hand.

"I believe I can get this job done by tomorrow afternoon if the weather permits." Sarah's jaw almost drops to the ground. Athos sits next to me and pulls up Guinn's halo tile with the map. "I will start by the entrance and move west. The only assistance I need is the posts. They need to be bundled for me to grab and fly. The men can do that easily, and we can have it up and working by tomorrow."

"Do you have a system ready for it?" I ask.

"Yes." Sarah clears her throat, shock wearing off. "Yes, we already have one that Sheiba sent."

"Then it should be easy enough for me to do." I raise a brow at him, but he ignores me. Do the Supes use the same technological systems? He seems confident that anything she's using could work, but he yet he has no idea that we have sensors in our trains.

"This is amazing!" Guinn exclaims.

"When can you start?" Sarah asks.

"Right now."

Chapter 11

The scent of coffee stirs me from my bed. I turn over, seeing the twin bed across the room is still empty. We are given the only spare room they have, with two separate beds. At first, I am concerned about Athos sleeping in the same room, just mere inches from me. Not that I think we might end up the same way we met - but the fear is still there.

Clearly, my worries have been unfounded, as Athos spent the whole night setting up the fence.

"He's quite a sight," Guinn remarks as I sit down to a steaming plate of beans and eggs. "He makes it look like they are feathers- not three hundred pound posts."

"How did you sleep?" My answer is interrupted by a commotion outside.

"He's almost done!" Sarah breathes as she breezes into the room. "The poles are almost gone, and he says it will only take a few more hours." She smiles at me as she sits at my table. "There was a small storm last night, but it wasn't very bad. But a bigger one is due for this afternoon. I hope we will have the system working by then. That way, he won't have to go trekking through a blizzard to fix any problems."

Sarah and Guinn beam at each other. Guinn looks younger- like a weight has been lifted off his shoulders. "I've already left a review on your webpage," Sarah says suddenly, and I cough down my eggs in surprise.

"Really? He isn't done yet." I say, glancing between them.

Sara waves me off. "It doesn't matter. I know it will be done, and it will be *amazing*." I laugh. Everyone certainly is excited to see the fences up and working.

"I had better get ready to go then, he will be done before we know it." Sarah is reminding me that I need to check with the outside world. I still have to check any messages or even call my dad. He wouldn't worry too much until later today if he doesn't hear from me, so I have time. Surprisingly, the phone has no messages, but the webpage does. When I read them, my heart skips a beat. They are both legitimate requests - two in one day.

I quickly message them both - Athos has time to get them done this afternoon if he gets the fence working as quickly as I think he can. We are well on our way towards getting more jobs and, eventually, an interview. I haphazardly pack my things up, when a sobering thought hits me.

It's high time I tell everyone what I'm up to before I get too busy. It'll be really bad if they find out from outside sources. I sit down on my borrowed bed and wonder just how to word it, 'Hey guys, you know how I detest Supes? I am working with one now,' just didn't seem right. Libby will be the easiest to tell, plus she already met Athos, however briefly.

I know I can get away with just sending her a message about it. She'll be fine with talking face-to-face later, but my dad and Gaia will be a different story.

I will, of course, leave out the fact that we slept together.

I'm just finishing my message when Sarah announces that Athos is done. I slip into my heavy clothes and trudge outside to see Guinn holding his halo-tile while the others crowd around him.

"Once the last posts are in, Athos will activate them, and they should come up on the screen. When we know that they are all working, his job will be complete." Sarah comes up behind me, sipping something hot.

"I can't believe he did it this fast," I comment.

"None of us can. We've seen Supers do amazing things over the past century- but when it happens right in front of you, it's entirely different."

"Especially when it has a direct effect on you." I muse.

"Exactly." She smiles at me. About ten minutes later, I hear a boom to my right followed by Athos landing in the fresh snow with a pop. Sarah and I are covered in a curtain of snow.

I wipe away the slush from my eyes to see him standing bare-chested in front of us, holding a look of embarrassment.

"Do you ever keep a shirt on?" I snap. A slow smile creeps up the corners of his mouth, but he stops just as I fling some snow off my shoulders.

"Didn't want to ruin it." He retorts.

"It's alright hun, no harm in a little snow." Sarah laughs. I shake the rest off my head and feel a chill run deep through me.

"It's up!" Guinn screams. A cheer erupts from the group of men as they break out in applause and praises. Athos is engulfed with handshakes and shoulder pats; Sarah and I are pushed back towards the fort. She gives me a look of endearment as Guinn boisterously thanks Athos over and over, telling him he was forever in debt and such.

As a group, we walk to the nearest fence line and take turns passing through it with a chip and watching one without one get stopped. Guinn begins playing with the cameras, projecting himself on a fence and pulling up other areas to look at.

This goes on for a good while before I clear my throat for attention. I know the men wouldn't hear me, or just ignore me, but Athos can certainly hear me. He cocks his head in my direction and I tap my pad, indicating we need to get moving.

"Thank you, Guinn. We need to leave now before the train does. It doesn't run all day for us in Fantom." He laughs and moves to me.

"Of course. Thank you so much, Athos, and Lillium. Please come back when you can. You are always welcome." Sarah hugs me and kisses Athos on the cheek. "I would love to see the expression on Sheiba's face when we tell her it is all done now." She laughs. A flicker of emotion crosses his eyes but passes quickly. Is he irritated that even now, after all he'd done, Sheiba is still being brought up? Or is he excited that she'd learn he'd taken some glory from her?

Athos takes my arm and positions me in front of him. "Remember, *slowly,*" I say. He nods and gives everyone a wave before wrapping his arm around my waist. I gasp when I feel my feet lift off the ground suddenly. Unlike before, this time I can take a few breaths to calm myself as he suspends us over the trees.

It is cold, but thankfully there is no wind, and the sky is crystal clear. I press my face into his shoulder to shield it from the icy air as he moves towards the platform.

"Better?" He asks, his voice muffled by the flight.

"Yeah!" I yell back. I feel him laughing, his chest moving against mine, and remember he probably could hear me very well despite flying.

"How well can you hear? It would be nice to know that. It might be useful later." He says something, but I can't understand him. "What?"

He brings his lips down to my ear and says, "Wait a moment. Hold on." I feel my stomach lurch as he descends to the ground. We land right on the empty platform. Well, he does anyway. I'm still being held by his arms so he has to set me down once he is steady.

"I can hear you while flying." He explains.

"How far away can you hear me from?"

He smirks, "It would depend on many things, such as if we were in an understandably loud city. I would be able to hear you maybe a mile away- if I was concentrating. Out here in the wilderness? The distance would be three times that, as long as the weather is clear."

"So, your power is certainly not sonic hearing," I smirk.

"No. That would not be me."

"Oh, so there is someone who-" I stop myself and shake my head, "That would be too personal."

"No. It wouldn't. There is someone who has sonic hearing. But I won't tell you their name." He nods towards the tracks. "The train will be here in a few minutes."

"Oh!" I grab him by the arm. "We got two requests today!" I had forgotten about it until now. "Let me see if they messaged back!"

"More than one finally, huh?"

I quirk a brow. "Be careful; it could always get out of hand."

"That's true. It's my biggest fear out of this whole...escapade."

"Really? That's the only thing you're apprehensive about?"

"Letting people down, it's scary to me." I blink in surprise; I had no idea he had any misgivings about this. "You're surprised."

"Well...I guess I thought being a Supe, you wouldn't be afraid of anything."

He chuckles as he runs a hand through his hair. "It sounds very human. But we do have emotions, you know. Just like you."

"Sure, but aren't you indestructible?" I swat at his arm.

He patted me on the head in a very patronizing manner, "Indestructible doesn't mean unemotional, Lily." He nods to my pad, "What did they say?"

I blush as I look back at it, having once again forgotten about it.

They both responded, "The first is a man in Silverfish who needs help to move furniture out of his house. The other is a girl asking you to help find her dog that ran away."

"Let's do the dog first. Where is it?"

"Naptow, close to Fantom."

"Shouldn't take long, I will meet you there. What does the dog look like?"

I show him the picture and off he goes, straight into the sky. I watch him until he is nothing but a dot.

It takes no more than twenty minutes to get there, so I'm bewildered to see him waiting for me, holding the dog.

"This is Snaggle." He says, smiling as the fuzzball wiggled happily in his arms.

I pat her, but she ignores me. "She likes you."

"I found her at the other end of town, rolling around in a field."

"Allison will be thrilled. How did you know where to look?"

He shrugs and starts to move off the platform. "I didn't. I just flew around and around until I spotted her. She'd only been gone a few hours, and since she's so small, I knew she could not have gone far."

Well, that just means we can do the next job just as fast. I break out into a smile as I think hopefully of all the jobs we can get done in a day.

Allison turns out to be a seven-year-old, to our surprise. Athos asks her how she knows about us. She says her family has a flyer, but didn't think it was real. Snaggle is not too happy to leave Athos. Apparently, the dog has become attached to him. Athos assures her that he has that effect on animals, and it has nothing to do with Snaggle not wanting to be home, as big tears form in her eyes at being rejected by her dog.

The old man is our first silent client. He never gives us his name and speaks only to tell us where to move things. Athos spends a good hour moving out old furniture to a donation center while the man and I sit in comfortable silence. He isn't for small talk, and I like that. I use my time to read Libby's response, and thankfully she is just as understanding as I had hoped, as well as excited. She and Max want his autograph, of course.

That is one weight off my shoulders. Now all I have to do is get the courage to tell Dad and Gaia.

When Athos comes back, the man gives him a handshake and pats my hand in thanks.

"Well, that was an eventful day, to say the least," Athos says as he walks me to the platform.

"Yeah, I am looking forward to passing out for a while."

"Are we sure that we want more jobs?" He teases.

"Oh yes, but there will be sometimes when I cannot go with you, you know. It wouldn't be practical."

"We will cross that bridge when we can." He says.

It comes sooner than we had thought. Over the next week, I start to get at least two calls a day and a few requests on the webpage which has Athos doing three to four jobs in a day. All the while, I tag along managing the other appointments.

The jobs all range from helping people move large items out of their houses to rebuilding homes, remodeling houses, renovating buildings for new employers, and cleaning up areas for buildings. They are all easy tasks for Athos to do, and nothing that a normal Supe would go out of their way to do since there are no cameras around. He makes it all look so menial as he zooms back and forth, barely a blur, and at the end of each job, he signs autographs and shakes hands with everyone.

We are getting more and more calls out of the four towns where he puts the posters up until we are crisscrossing around the northwest and southwest of America. Within another week it gets to the point where I can't possibly be able to meet him in time by taking the trains.

"We can schedule the jobs so you can make it to them all."

"No, Athos, that wouldn't be right. I do not want to put myself first. Not only that but what about when we get more than three a day? What about seven? Would we have to schedule them all out further in the week just so I can be there?" I point out as I map his day's schedule out for him. We have fallen into a routine where I come by every morning to his home and give him his jobs for the day, and while he is out, I take care of the increasing volume of requests.

"This is a partnership, Lily. I would like you to be there." He sighs as he rubs his fingers over his eyes. "But you are right."

"Besides, ninety percent of the time, no one pays me any attention."

He looks up and narrows his eyes. "That's not true."

"Yes, it is. How many autographs did you sign last week?"

"I do not count. Do you?"

"Yes. Seventy-two." I smirk. "Twice as many photographs were taken of you with people, and probably much more of you running around doing the jobs."

"I see the people talking to you."

"No. You see the people asking me about *you*." I point out. "Now, I want to please people just as much as you do, and if we start making mistakes this early, we will never achieve what we want later."

"You are right, Lily."

I groan. "Why do you call me that?"

"What? Lily? That's your name."

"No. It's Lillium."

"Which is the scientific name for a Lily." I quirk a brow in question. "You did not know that?"

"No…what is a Lily?"

"A flower."

"Oh. It must be-"

"Extinct." He finishes for me.

"Huh." I sit back, chewing on my nails in thought. "I never knew that…"

"Promise to come to the important jobs, then, the big ones."

"No, I promise to come to the smallest ones you have that I can make in time."

My days are filled with work now, so much so that I have completely forgotten to tell my dad and Gaia what is happening. It is going to have to change though. I know that I can't keep wandering home at odd hours without an excuse anymore. I'm supposed to be getting a new job, and my dad by now has to have noticed I'm not exactly working.

I decide to tell them at the end of the week. I will work double time to make Athos his schedule and leave myself a day to just get it over with. So I go to his house earlier than usual the day before I plan to tell them.

"This is unprecedented! Completely uncalled for!" I freeze at the unfamiliar voice. Athos hadn't said anything about having company besides me. We never speak of the other Supes, and he's never mentioned anything about human friends.

"Don't get your panties in a twist, love." Athos snaps and I can't help but smile.

"Do *not* condescend me! What the hell are you doing?!"

"Why do you care?" Athos sounds exasperated.

"The hell do you think!?" The voice is clearly a female's, and very pitchy as she starts yelling.

"This has nothing to do with *you*." Athos growls.

"It has everything to do with us!" she screams.

I feel that now is the time to make myself known. I'm confident Athos already knows I'm here, but whomever he was arguing with doesn't. I shut the door with enough force to make it bang through the house.

Silence follows, so I take a deep breath and walk down the hall to the kitchen where I'd heard them. I enter with a smile and a prepared, "Oh, hello," but never get the chance to do either.

Instead, I gape at the well-known figure of an angry Sheiba, glaring daggers at me.

Chapter 12

"This!?" She cries pointing at me. *"This* is her!?"

I'm frozen and utterly stupefied; Sheiba is yelling at me. The top female Super, one of the most well-known in the world is yelling at me, in Athos's kitchen. I had not expected this.

Hordes of humans chasing after us for his autograph? Millions of calls a day? I'd thought of all the human issues that would come with this, but not the Supe ones. Never in my wildest scenarios did I ever fathom that I would be met with an angry Supe because of this.

Athos is by my side in a split second, but I barely notice. She is still pointing her finger at me in an accusing way. She looks just like she did on TV, sans the crazy eyes, just as gorgeous. Her knee-length hair swings in its braid as she moves her petite body to the counter. Her sepia skin is completely flawless, glowing in the morning light. I watch, mesmerized as she eyes Athos angrily.

I notice she is a few feet shorter than me- she'd always seemed so tall on screen. "Leave her out of this," Athos says.

Sheiba contorts her pretty face, "It was not me who brought her into this."

"I have done nothing wrong, Sheiba." He spits, "So do not act like you have a right to belittle me."

"Belittle!? You took a job from me!" she snaps.

With a jolt, I snap out of my shock. "Job?" I ask softly, looking up at him, "The fence job?"

"Yes, *human*, that job." She sneers.

Athos takes in a deep breath, hissing, "Do not call her that."

"But Sarah told us you didn't have time to help. They couldn't handle it taking a full year." I say, quirking a brow.

She twitches, "Excuse me? I didn't have time?"

"She could not get a hold of you, and you had that other project going on-"

"Humans!" she scoffs.

"Oh please, you clearly had little interest in the project, otherwise you would have been there yourself. Or were there not enough cameras in Australia?" I ask dryly, the shock of seeing her fully wearing off. Annoyance is creeping into its place as I realize she's pissed Athos is getting credit for a job she should have done.

A dark look creeps over her face. She's not accustomed to being spoken to this way. I can feel Athos tensing next to me, causing a jolt of fear to hit my spine. Even though Athos is ridiculously strong and could drop me from the sky at any time, I never once felt afraid of him. Sheiba on the other hand, can create a man-eating plant right now and as she strides up to me, I'm sure she's contemplating doing it.

It feels slightly ridiculous; her being so much shorter and smaller than me, but the look on her face is frightening. Obviously, she's perfected the look of intimidation.

"It was my job. My area. Not his." She says, her tone threatening. Anger laces through me but is quickly followed by a punch of anxiety. Memories and feelings I've long since beaten down are threatening to come up.

"You don't own the Earth." I hiss, my breath hitching as I struggle to keep my focus on her.

"Right. And your kind has done such a wonderful job at keeping it well." She smirks. My heart thunders as my wristpad beeps an alert- I don't need to look at it to know another anxiety attack is coming on.

"Enough." Athos takes my arm and pulls me away from the kitchen entrance. "You need to leave now, Sheiba."

"Oh, time to go to work, huh? With your human?" She rolls her eyes.

"It doesn't concern you," Athos says.

She nods, glaring at him and then at me. "Athos, you should be *careful.*"

86

"Is that a threat?" I ask, anger finally taking over as I push back against the stone wall that is his body.

"I wasn't speaking to you, human." She sneers. She starts to leave, but stops just in the hall, looking back at Athos. The look on her face is indescribable, unreadable to me, but I'm certain Athos understands. She shakes her head slowly and leaves. I wait until I hear the door shut before I glance up at him. He stands perfectly still for a moment more, possibly listening to make sure she is gone, then sighs.

"So. Sheiba, huh? Lovers quarrel?" I say, breathless. The moment she's gone, I can feel the tightness in my chest easing.

"Not in many years." I twitch slightly. *So they had been together at some point? Interesting.*

"Is this something I should worry about?" I ask.

He appears in a chair a second later, drumming his fingers against the table. A slow smile spreads over his face. "Worry? Are you jealous?"

I snort, deciding not to dignify that with an answer.

"I'm not sure what you heard, but I distinctly made out a threat there." I point to the door. "Is this something I need to worry about?" I ask again, firmly.

"No." He shakes his head.

"No? No, I shouldn't worry about a Supe appearing in my house? No, I shouldn't worry about Sheiba turning my yard into a mass jungle of man-eating plants? I need to know Athos, is this," I gesture between us, "something that I should worry about?"

"No, Lily, you do *not* need to worry about anything but what we have already been doing. This is between *us*." He lays his hand on his chest.

I cross my arms, huffing. "She seemed very irritated."

"She is."

"Why?" Athos locks eyes with me, and I know I've gone over the personal line. "I am involved now; clearly, she thinks so."

"That is it. She thinks you have been let in." He says.

"In? As in your guy's secret circle?" I quirk a brow.

"Yes."

87

"So, no human before has been? Not in the many years that you've been here, in hiding?" I ask, shocked.

"No, some have. In cases of... relationships."

"*What?*" I breathe.

"Don't act daft, Lily. You are a smart girl; how else would we fit in? We have emotions like you, and some of us had relationships with humans outside of one-night stands."

I sit down across from him in shock. Sure, this has been speculated on for many years, but the idea wasn't new. But he was actually *telling me* this. This has never happened before- or it has, but only to those that were close to Supes.

"So. There have been humans that were told the truth about you." He nods. "And since you weren't known widely about until Briseathe, I'm going to assume these humans never told anyone else?"

His eyes flash a bit, then he turns away from me. "Some never got the chance."

"They were... what, killed?" I ask.

"No!" He turns back to me, glaring, "No, we never killed anyone. Damn Lillium, we can erase memories."

"Oh." Of course they do. "Will my memories..."

"No. There is no need to do that now. It was only done in rare cases of human defecting. Sometimes, humans would turn against us and threaten to tell, or just go off and *did* tell. We had to intervene and erase the memories of those people. It is how we were able to stay hidden for so long." He says it like it's so commonplace, and nothing for me to worry about.

"What about your eyes?" I ask, mentally filing away the brain-wiping powers for another time.

"Eyes?" He asks, his brows furrowing.

"Yeah, the way the pupils are. How did you hide that? I've always wondered." I figure I can ask now, while the door to his life seems open.

"Oh, we never hid them," He smiles, "If I told you this was a birth defect, would you believe me? Without any prior knowledge of us? You would never assume I wasn't human."

I sigh, "You're right, it would be very easy to explain."

"Very."

"Sheiba thinks you're telling me secrets, huh? Why would that matter if other humans have already been told?"

"They were told enough to satisfy them. Not everything."

"Then why all the drama about me?"

"Truthfully, I'm not entirely sure why she is being so awry." He sighs, "It must be several things, from stepping all over 'her job', trying to make a name for myself, and working with you. I imagine it burns her deeply that I've teamed up with a human."

"It's never been done before." Not even in the beginning did humans and Supes work together like this. It has always been them taking control of the situation and us sitting back and watching.

"Right. Therefore, I am a threat to her and the others in terms of more than fame."

"Ah, so it's not about me, per se."

"No. It is. In all our history, the only humans we have shared anything with have always been partners, spouses, not friends. It was necessary to tell your partner what you were, especially if you were expecting a child."

"Whoa, what!? Children?" Now this was never speculated on.

"Yes. Spouses and children, no friends. But sometimes, even that was difficult. In the early days, we thought it was best to erase the memories of spouses or partners, but soon it became apparent that that was uncalled for."

"Creepy."

"Indeed. It was also unnecessary, since there were only a few us who sought human comfort and companionship. Some never liked the idea."

"Ah, purists."

"Yes. There were, and still are, purists amongst us. They felt human companionship was wrong, and hybrid children even more so."

"How do you keep track of them?"

Athos shook his head, smiling, "That is the exact information Sheiba is worried I will give out."

"Oh. Sorry."

"No, it's not your fault."

I drum my fingers against my thigh, thinking about what he is telling me. It is far more than I would have ever expected to learn from him- so far I had assumed I would never learn anything.

I can understand the need to tell spouses you were immortal, but that didn't explain why Sheiba is so angry about me. Just because I'm a friend doesn't make it any different. Does it?

Unless somehow she knows about how Athos and I met. He did say they were together in the past- maybe she harbors some feelings for him?

"Why tell me any of this?" I ask.

He shrugs. "To get back at her?" I roll my eyes at his rueful smile. "To prove her wrong? Because I can? It stands to reason I would eventually have to tell you something. If we are in this for the proverbial long run, things are going to come up that you will want explained.

"Right now you might be fine with none, but there will come a day when you will *demand* explanations. It is only in your nature."

I want to protest that I'm not like that. I can stand the 'not knowing' and live with it. But deep, *deep* down, I know he is right. One day, if we continue to work together, I will break, and I will want some kind of revelation.

"I also believe you deserve some kind of form of it."

"Really?" I perk up a bit.

"Yes," he laughs, "it's only a small piece of us, but after that tryst with Sheiba you deserve some reward."

I groan, "She's very scary, you know? I always thought she was classy and sexy, but she's a real hardass."

"Yes, she is. Always has been that way, I'm afraid." He winks at me, "Time doesn't change everything."

"Anyway...hybrids, huh?" I smirk, "Anyone I know?"

He laughs and gets up. "Perhaps." I watch him strut to the kitchen and pick up two plates of food. My mouth instantly starts to water as the smell hits me when he walks by.

"Do you have any kids?" I ask gingerly as I take my plate from him. His eyes lock with mine, and for a moment I think I've gone too far, but all I see is mirth in them.

"No." He retorts.

"Really…. So, you and Sheiba, huh? What was that like?"

He shakes his head and eats, ignoring me. I'm starting to wonder if this is a good idea or not. I don't want to wake up one morning with Sheiba in my kitchen, a horde of plants at the ready to attack me.

"I am going to tell my dad about you tomorrow," I say.

"Oh, finally." He says through a mouthful of food.

I stab my fork into what looks like an egg. "And my friend Gaia…" He raises a brow, "I haven't told you about her because she, like me, isn't too fond of you guys. Actually, she is worse. She works for HFHH."

"What?" He quirks a brow.

"Humans For Helping Humans. It's a group that believes humans should not rely on you guys to reform the Earth. They go to war-torn areas of the world where people still live without modern advances and help them renovate and rebuild. No Supes allowed."

"Smart. But I bet they don't get any air time for doing it?"

"None," I smirk.

"You are worried she will not approve of me?" He laughs.

"That is an understatement. I think she might disown me."

"If she is really your friend she will stand by you no matter what. You said you are telling your dad. What about your mom? Do you have one?"

I scoff and turn to my food. I attack it as he gets up and ignore his laughter. "Let's forget about that for now. What does this week look like?"

I shrug, "Fine. You have three jobs so far, two for tomorrow, Monday, and one for Thursday."

"Thursday? Why so late in the week?"

"It's a demolition job. Well, partly," I tap my wristpad showing him a photo of the site, "It used to be a factory in the early 2000s, then changed to a warehouse by the time the war came around. It has been abandoned since Briseathe, and half of it is already gone."

"A clean-up project." He says.

"Essentially."

He chews his lip before asking, "Tell me about these clean-up projects. Gaia works for a company that does it just with humans, and there are other companies who do it with or without my kind's help. Why are there still so many areas that need help?"

There it is again, his lack of knowledge about the War and current affairs. It's at the tip of my tongue to ask why he knows so little about these things, yet I don't want to prove him right in thinking I can't live without answers.

"After Briseathe, clean-up projects and programs became very prominent. Many towns had been laid to waste in the war - even whole cities were abandoned and left to rot. Habitable cities were the first to get spruced up, then work was put on the empty ones. Since the population at that time was nearly seventy-five percent of what it had been, the abandoned cities and towns stayed abandoned and run down, without the manpower to help. Sheiba and Mathis came in and started to clear up some, removing all the man-made materials and putting it back to it's original, or near original state before human interference.

"Today we have whole valleys and fields that used to be gigantic concrete jungles or towns, and then places like where this building was. Not much attention was given to smaller areas, while there were so many other places in the world that needed the help of Sheiba and Mathis. So they were left alone until they could be dealt with.

"This one is a part of the MFCC."

"The what?" he quirks a brow.

"Mass Factory and Chemical Condition. They are a faction of Sheiba and Mathis's World Order project; they broke off of it a few decades ago. They felt that they could help out by cleaning areas themselves, and not having to wait for a Supe to get the time to do it." I explain.

"How is it you know so much about this organization?"

"Everyone knows about them. At least more than you do." I jab my finger at his chest, "Also, my dad works for them."

He looks at me over the pad with surprise. "Seriously?"

"Yes."

"Your dad...works for Sheiba?"

"No!" I scoff. "I just told you they are a faction from her program. He does not work for her, but she gets the credit in the end, anyway."

"Interesting. Why would they ask for help from a Supe?"

"Why not? It's just like with Sarah and Guinn. They had a task given to them by a Supe, who could not help. They need the help of another one, and here you are."

"Very interesting."

"Not really." I push my plate away, the food now cold.

"I find it to be. I wonder," he snickers, "if your dad is involved with this."

I shrug, "Possibly. I am sure he would hear of it eventually, I mean, asking a Supe-" I nearly choke on my words as I sputter, "Oh shit!"

Athos bursts into laughter as I jump up, gathering my things hurriedly.

"I'm going to assume you gave the person who called your whole name?" He laughs.

"Yes!" I cry, throwing my things in my bag. I toss a folder at him, "These are for today. I will have to figure out tomorrow later!"

"How did you not know?" He mocks, leaning back and watching me panic.

"Shut yourself!" I snap, "I had no idea what organization it was until this morning when I confirmed the appointment!"

"And when you learned about it, still it did not register?"

"I've had a lot on my mind! Now I need to leave. Have a *fantastic* day!" I spit.

I have to run to the platform to make the next train. How can I be so stupid?! I just hope no one has called him yet to ask if the Super they just hired was working with the same Lillium that happens to be his kid.

This is exactly what I didn't want to happen!

I press my face against the cool window, glaring in the direction of Fantom. Urging the train to go faster. I would have considered Athos flying me there and almost suffocating for lack of air if I'd thought it would have made a difference.

It seems to crawl to a stop, making me hop on my feet in agitation before

I lunge off and sprint down my street. I keep gasping, "Please don't know, please, please don't know," over and over like a personal mantra until I reach my yard. I have to stop and take deep breaths to calm myself before I can get a chance to listen for any signs of life inside my home. It's his day off. He usually spends it working in the yard or has some people over for brunch.

But all is quiet. I let out a quaky breath, assuming he is still asleep.

I tentatively press my thumb into the lock, letting it read my print before it clicks open. I hold on to the door as I enter. The house is silent but for my soft footfalls as I come into the hall, closing the door.

I thank my lucky cosmos. I still have time to intercept the knowledge, or at the very least, tell him myself.

"Lillium?" I hear my dad call from the living room.

"Yes?" I freeze, cursing my luck. I sulk into the room and find him with his pad on his knees. A program paused on the halo-vision.

All I need to see is his expression to know I'm too late. I curse under my breath.

"Lillium, I got a very interesting message from Wanda at work. Apparently, there is some girl with your exact name working with a Super," He smirks, "And they've been hired by our company today." I feel my dad's eyes on me, waiting for a response. There is a moment of complete, awkward silence while I try desperately to think of something to say.

He waits, expecting *something*, but smiling like nothing is out of the ordinary.

"I'm technically not working for them. Athos is." That is all I can come up with. It's a simple confirmation, yet slightly snarky and nonchalant. I watch as his eyes glaze over in shock. "I just do secretarial work. Scheduling. And...such." I cough. I can't take the silence.

"So..." my dad finally starts, "So...Wanda was telling the truth?"

"Yes." I smile. *Play this very cool and he might just let you off without a scene,* I think. "I was going to tell you- when I was sure this wasn't going to be a temporary...thing."

"Temporary?" he says, the glazed look slowly receding.

94

"As in, not working out. I wasn't sure it would. But now it seems like it will."

"And this Super..." he stops, puzzled.

"Athos."

"Athos..." he tries the name out slowly, "He's really a Super? Why haven't we heard of him?"

"There's a lot of Supes we've never heard of before."

"Right, but...why are you working with *him*?"

I toss my bag by a seat and slide into it, picking my words carefully. I can't tell him about Athos's wanting revenge, or me either, for that matter, it won't go over well and I'd be betraying his trust.

"We are friends," I say, trying to sound nonchalant.

His face contorts—a mixture of needing to sneeze and smelling something terrible.

"Is there something wrong with us being friends?" I ask. I'm growing weary now.

"No, Lillium." He holds up his hand in defense. "It's only strange that you are suddenly involved with a Super. I thought you hated them."

"Athos is different." I retort stiffly.

"Well, good for you. When is he coming for brunch?" I can't help but laugh.

"I think he'd like it if you came for brunch. He is a fantastic cook."

"Is that one of his superpowers?" My dad quirks a brow teasingly.

"Possibly."

"Good to know. I will tell Wanda she is not mistaken. My daughter has taken up with a Super. Be prepared for the endless calls we are about to get." He sighs.

"Oh, Dad, you have no idea." I chuckle.

Chapter 13

From the very beginning, Korra St. Cloud is my first choice for Athos's media debut, especially since she isn't the media at all. She is a lone streamer who funds herself with what she makes from her casts, makes her own sets and costumes, and has a healthy animosity towards the pop media. In the end, though, Athos has to sign off on her before I can do anything. So I make him watch a view of her casts and tell me what he thinks. It only takes one before he turns to me and asks if I am serious.

"Completely. Korra is the best person for this." I say.

"I get that she is… eccentric. But Lily, shouldn't we be getting someone a little more professional?" Athos asks.

I laugh. "If we were looking for just professionalism we should stick with the pop media. The whole reason she fits is because she isn't like them. And because she isn't like them, she has never had the chance to interview one of you."

"Anyone would jump at the chance though," he points.

"True, but they would all be the same. Korra has never had a chance to interview you guys because the pop media won't let her in, and no Supe has accepted any invitation because she is shunned by the others. So she might have a chip on her shoulder because of it."

"You think that is good?" He asks incredulously.

"I do. She will be able to come into the interview from a very down-to-earth angle. She won't see you as a superstar who needs to be fawned over. Trust me, Athos, she will take this very seriously."

"Alright," he sighs as he flips through some photos of her, "I trust you."

That catches me off guard. I am not sure how to respond so I continue to watch him study her, possibly wondering what he can get away with saying on her cast. So he trusts my judgment? Can I say the same for him? Thinking about it now, this is going to either make or break everything we are doing. Korra might not be as powerful as the pop media, but she has just as many viewers who watch her cast religiously.

This is also the first time he gets air time, his main goal as Supes. Athos trusts me, but do I trust him to stay on the same path? If the incident with Sheiba teaches me anything, it is that he truly has a strained relationship with his people. Whatever happened to make him distance himself from them is enough to make him want to get under their skin. Sheiba proves that it is working.

"Well, I have seen enough." He says interrupting my thoughts. "Are we going to meet her today, or sit here and watch videos all day?" I roll my eyes and get up. Korra agreed to meet us this afternoon and do the interview at her home.

"So you are alright with this?" I ask as we leave his home. He nods as he shuts his door. I notice he never locks it. Then again, anyone dumb enough to try to rob him would be in for the worst time of their life.

"Like I said, I trust you. If you think this is the right person, then I will go along with it. You said she lives in Los Angeles?"

"Yup."

He shakes his head. "Figures that city gets to keep its name after the War." I laugh.

"Considering it is one of the three biggest in our region. Second only to New Hope. You know, where Legion is, your people's floating city?" I ask cuttingly.

"Yeah, they are very proud of that." He replies darkly. Oh, so that is a sore spot. *Let's not mention that again,* I think.

From Fantom, we take two other trains to get to her home. Of course, Athos could fly us there in a matter of minutes. I don't have a face when we land, though. So two hours later, we arrive in her neighborhood.

Korra's house sits on a stately hill. It isn't a stone-built structure but rather a metal one. They usually look very industrial and cold, but not hers.

True to Korra fashion, she has her metal walls dyed neon colors as backdrops to an overgrown garden surrounding the house. Giant spheres stick out from the roof in what could be antennas- or some form of art.

Athos and I arrive slightly early at the bottom of her hill. A rickety gate greets us, and Athos can't help but smile. "Very unique," he mutters. The gate creaks so loud that Korra hears us from her third story. She pops her purple head out of the window and screams, "The door is open!" then she jumps back, disappearing.

We navigate the overgrown plants to find the door. Before we open it I say, "Don't be nervous. You will do great." Compared to the outside, the inside is very clean and organized, though the furniture is the ugliest I've seen by far, it is a mixture of flora patterns that do not match at all. Plants seem to grow in every corner of the room, coupled with various knick-knacks and real paper photos in frames.

"I see a lot of antiques in here," Athos comments. *I see a lot of junk* I think as she appears at the top of the stairs.

She breezes down wearing a thin silvery dress that clings to her lower body but puffs out at the top. She has a pearl necklace of every color known to man and a pearl tiara that sits upon her strikingly short purple hair.

She beams at us, bouncing up and down to make her short electric purple hair sway. Korra is like Gaia, a product of gene manipulation, but unlike Gaia she doesn't hate her body, she adores it. She has spliced eyes, half green half pink, and a perfectly petite face and features with always rosy cheeks. She is slightly shorter than me with the daintiest body I've ever seen on a grown woman.

"Lillium." She giggles, biting her lower lip, "And Athos. Welcome, welcome."

Athos holds a hand out, but she shoves it aside and throws her frail arms around him. "I am so, so happy to have you here!" She pushes off him and goes for me. I almost duck under his arms to get away, but he places his shoulder right behind me so I am trapped. I awkwardly pat her on her back as she hugs me.

"We are very glad you had time to do this." He says. I can hear the mirth in his voice and want nothing more than to break another Sheiba figure across his face.

"Are you kidding?! I would give my left foot for this! Cookies?" She pulls a plate out from behind a plant.

We both take one. "What else do you have hiding behind those plants?" I ask. She busts up laughing.

"Nickels." She says, tapping her nose. "Come on up to the studio." She leads the way up, and as I pass the bottom steps, I notice a black cat glaring at us from behind a bush. Nickles?

I follow them up to the third story. "The second floor is my room and creative space, the top is workspace. Have to keep the two separate!" She sings down to us. The walls in her home have hand-painted murals of fantastical scenes in bright colors. The door that leads into her studio at the top of the stairs is a work in progress, with only a quarter of it painted.

"I repaint the house once a year." She explains, tapping the bottom of the door with her foot. It slides up into the ceiling silently, revealing a darkened room. As soon as we pile in, lights erupt from the floor to show her studio. Half the room is sectioned off with colorful streamers and ribbons hanging from the ceiling, small gaps reveal shapes of electronics.

"This is the 'Scenes' area." She gestures to the left side of the room where two sets sit, unlit. "That's the control area to our right. I go over the footage there and add sound. Conduct my research too," she grabs a pad from behind the curtain. "Which set would you like?" She taps the pad, and both sets lit up.

The one closest to us is a large couch that looks like it is a long-haired animal. Glossy tan-colored hair cascades over the edges of it to pool on the floor. I half expect it to come alive. The background for it is a field of large hand-painted sunflowers. I can feel Athos looking at me then, and I turn to Korra, who laughs.

"It's not real hair. I made it to look like that with fine fabricated silk." She explains.

"I think I will take the pink chairs." He says over my head.

"Nice." Korra hits another button, causing a camera to pop up from the ground in front of the two neon pink chairs at the far end of the room. "Take a seat."

Athos takes his seat, then glances at me in surprise. "You are sitting over there?" He asks as I take a seat by Korra.

"Where do you want me to sit?" I ask, smirking.

"With me?" I shake my head.

"Yes! Why not both of you?" Korra smiles over her pad.

"No, thank you. This is about him, not me. Maybe another time."

She smiles, then rapidly taps on her pad again. The control room behind her whirs to life and something moves around behind the curtain. A table pops up from the ground in front of Athos, and suddenly a large metal contraption bursts through the streamers. I gasp when I realize it is an 'Oid Bot, carrying a platter of pastries and tiny sandwiches.

"This is Ofla. This is Ofla. She used to function as an 'Oid Bot, but since those are outlawed, I repurposed her as a personal maid."

Athos laughs as the bot bends over and places the platter before him. "She certainly looks different from 'Oid Bots." He replies, eyeing her inner exposed inner workings.

All I know about 'Oid Bots is that they replaced humans in battle or events of direct conflict that could prove fatal or harmful for a human. They were outlawed after the war, now deemed unnecessary to our world peace.

"She has the main body, but I used different parts and software to make her less..." She shrugs and then turns back to her control room. Ofla hovers in front of us for a second more before gliding back behind the curtain. "So..." Korra hums, "What are the guidelines for today?"

"Guidelines?" I ask.

"Boundaries," Athos says softly.

"Oh, that's up to him."

"Athos, what can't I ask you?"

"Nothing." This takes us both by surprise. I'd expected him to give her the same 'nothing too personal' line I usually get. I feel snubbed.

Korra stops her incessant tapping long enough to give him a long look.

100

"Are you sure?"

"Yes. You may ask me anything you want." His dimples pop as he smiles, irking me even more. Not that I think I am special by any means, but damn.

I watch her smile, slyly, "And you will answer them if you want, yeah?" I narrow my eyes as I see the gears shifting in her mind. Maybe this was a mistake.

"Yes." He nods, his amber gaze flicking to me momentarily. He sees the guarded look I have, but smiles wider.

Ah, so he's only letting her ask. He won't tell. Sneaky little Supe. I can see him watching me from the corner of his eye, so I turn my face completely away so that Korra cannot see the way my face changes. I might not know Supes well, but I am beginning to understand the games they play.

"Then let's get this going!" She tosses her pad on the table, barely missing the platter of food, and takes her seat in the other pink chair. "We are going to tape this first- no live feed at all."

Athos nods, and she drums her fingers on her chair's arm, causing a halo-screen to appear by her hand. "Alright Athos, here we go." Korra kicks the bottom of the table and lights flicker on. She turns her head to the camera. "Korra St. Cloud here, with a *special* person." I can see a screen appear under the table for them to see- it was the camera angle, which now turns to Athos.

"His name is Athos, and he's a bona fide Super! Very up and moving." Athos gives the camera a warm smile.

"Thank you for having me, Korra." He says, using his silky smooth voice that causes me to involuntarily shiver. I notice how Korra sits up straighter - his voice must have the same effect on her. I envision thousands of human women having the same reaction while watching him and a twinge of jealous pricks at my heart.

"It's not every day that a Super asks to be interviewed by a regular person!" I smile as they laugh together. "Athos has many super abilities. One of which is staying in the shadows for so long. He has been going around helping those in need in secret. So much so that you single-handedly built a new plant and wildlife conservation center up north, just a few weeks ago, and there was no media coverage of it."

"I helped build it, yes. I put up the fencing and helped them install the system for the fence. It would have taken them a year by themselves, but I helped them do it in a day."

"A day? That's impressive. From what I read in their review of you, on your webpage, was that it is an extensive area. I assume you move *super* fast?" She wiggles her brows to the camera.

"I can fly, and move in such a way that you would think I teleported," Athos says plainly.

"And you are a new Super, never before been on the market?"

"No, this is my first time working in the Super trade." He admits, his eyes crinkling just slightly at the sides.

"You don't charge fees, is that right?" She muses.

"No fees. I work for free."

"*Any* job?" She asks, brows raised.

"Any job within the confines of the law, yes." He smiles.

Korra tuts, "So you're saying we can't expect to see you flying off to avenge someone's honor, or find a killer and give the people's justice?"

"If I could help them find the person who has legitimately wronged them, I will. But I am not a law figure. I can not conduct an investigation and dole out vigilante justice."

"Do you believe in vigilante justice?" I narrow my eyes at the question, but Athos doesn't miss a beat.

"I have lived long enough to see that it has some merit. But it is not for me to decide if it is right or wrong." He is casual but firm, almost like he's done this before. For a brief moment, I wonder if he had been a politician in the past.

"So, you work within the lines of the law; we cannot hire you to beat up our neighbors, and it's all free? What have you done so far?"

"I've had many simple jobs over the past month. I've helped people move, rebuild homes, demolish homes, build new homes or buildings, find pets, and I've assisted in cleanup programs."

Korra raises a brow and shakes her head, "Very small-time jobs there, buddio. No wonder you don't have a fan site yet." I stiffen, suddenly feeling very protective of our work. Our accomplishments are not small, and I am beginning to take her jabs to heart.

Athos laughs and shakes his head. I watch in amazement as he turns his amber eyes to the camera and gives it his most sincere look. "I don't do it for the fame, or money. I do it because good people need help, and I am capable of giving it to them."

"No perks?" She asks innocently.

"The only perk to it is being able to meet new people and help them when no one else can."

"Is this a new road we can expect to see the others follow suit?"

"The others?" He looks thoughtful for a moment, his handsome face relaxing. "I am not sure about them." He finally says, slowly. "We do not talk."

"You don't talk? Why not? Aren't you all a part of some secret organization?"

He laughs. "No. Korra, have you spoken to every human being on Earth, outside of you Vblogcasts?"

She chuckles. "Alas, that is my life's goal, but I have not achieved it yet. Are you saying there's a lot of you?"

"I'm saying we are not much different from you. We don't have a secret society outside of yours. We just are. I'm an individual and I have chosen to do this. If the others want to follow, they can." I catch the way his eyes harden as he speaks.

"Do you think they should?" She asks.

"They seem to be doing just fine the way they are now. I don't see why they would change so suddenly." He smirks, and I realize he's goading them.

Athos is calling them out, but not only that, he is daring them to try to copy him. If they suddenly did low-profile jobs such as he is, their actions would be deemed insincere, and they will be seen as the fame-hungry snobs they were. I knew he wanted revenge on them by taking their spotlight, but I didn't think it would go as far as openly challenging them.

"I agree." Korra takes a pastry from the platter and nibbles it. "You've only been in this field of work for about a month, right? So why haven't you appeared on our screens? Besides taking small jobs."

"We started out very small with our demographic."

"We?" She quirks a brow.

"Lily and I. My partner." My heart leaps at the word. Does he really see us as partners? Equals?

"Your *human* partner?" She giggles.

"Yes. She handles all the hard work, in my opinion. Scheduling, taking calls, handling media. The only thing I have to do is show up." My cheeks warm at the compliment, but I have to tell myself he is playing to the cameras.

"This is the first I've ever heard of a human and a Super working together like this. Or even at all." Korra glances toward me.

"That's true. Even on projects such as cleaning in, say, Africa, Supers and humans never worked directly side by side. We have always worked towards the same goals, but never with each other like this. She can't fly, so it makes it a bit harder for her to get around." He turns his head slightly to me, and I can see the mirth in his eyes. So he has been doing some research since the conservation, good for him.

"My, you are an interesting…guy." She smiles, shrugging, "Even though you don't speak to the others now, how do you think they will feel, considering all this?"

"I do not know, Korra. But I hope it is nothing less than the same best wishes I have given them." It's a bald-faced lie. Athos knows exactly what they will think. Sheiba's proof enough.

"What are your plans for the future?"

"Right now we hope that this interview will get out to a bigger demographic of people we could not reach." A pipe dream, but one I hope we can make.

"Oh, so where have you worked so far?"

"Just the Americas." Korra and I exchange glances. No one has called it that in a long while.

"And you will go to other countries?"

"Of course." He nods.

"Anyone can get a hold of you, from either your web page or the number posted there?"

"Yes. We also have references from our customers on our webpage and a page on Kidgets." He explains.

"Kidgets? The *human* personality rating site?" Kidgets is used mostly as a social rating system that employers could use.

"It's a rating site that is used *by* humans, mostly." He chuckles, "It doesn't say it is just for them."

"Sure, but why not Super-Vendo? Is that where all the Supers go to get rated?" She asks.

"That is more of a popularity rating than a professional or even personal one. People who rate those pages base it on what they have seen from a screen, or in the rare case of a human being saved or meeting one of us, a brief few moments that cannot merit a real grasp of their person. I want to be rated on my achievements and interactions with people, not my abs." I stifle a cough. Korra looks him up and down, clearly admiring him.

"Well, you'd win that rating hands down." She smiles sweetly.

"Thank you Korra," he laughs, "I secretly do want to beat out Mathis as this year's most-watched man."

"Oh, I don't think that will be a problem. I can see already men and women alike will drool you over." She bites her lip coyly. Athos returns her look of admiration.

A moment of silence comes where I feel myself blush at their blatant flirtation, though I am not surprised. Athos liked to lean into his looks - I'd seen it firsthand. So why do I have this nagging feeling in my heart when I watch him look at Korra like that?

"There it is," she says, her tone husky. "Athos the humanitarian Super." And with that, the camera cuts off. "Was that adequate?" She asks, her voice normal and the smoldering look in her eyes gone.

"It was perfect." He smiles politely. I do a double take, feeling like I've just watched two actors on set. Was that all really just an act for the cameras?

We can leave shortly after that, Athos with his seductive smile, Korra waving us off, and me, trying to act like nothing awkward had just happened. I vaguely wonder if she will put that part into the cast. Needless to say, Athos is in a great mood as we walk back to find the first train back home.

"That went well," I comment lightly as we find a bench in the warm sun on the platform.

"We'll see. She could always make it into what she wants." He shrugs.

I scoff. "It seemed pretty clear what she wanted. I don't think we have to worry about her spinning it into anything other than what it was." My tone is a bit too gruff and he notices.

"Is that a hint of jealousy I detect?" He asks, batting his eyes at me.

I glare back at him. "I have no idea what you mean."

"Oh, Lily. You know I only have eyes for you," he cooes and I have to physically restrain myself from rolling my eyes into the back of my head.

"Will the others take it well?" I say, changing the subject.

"No." I hear the mirth leaving his tone.

I sigh. "Should I expect them to turn up at my door?"

"No." He pats me on the head and I feel patronized. "Is your dad still on for brunch tomorrow?"

"Uh, yeah. Of course." I swat his hand away, smoothing out my hair with a huff.

"Does he know everything?" he asks.

I scoff, "Does he know we had a drunken one-night stand? No."

Athos chuckles.

Dad had come with half his office to see Athos tear down the warehouse they hired him for. I'd been surprised to see the two hit it off right away. I had expected my dad to be a little apprehensive, but he took Athos under his arm and they went off to talk about how warehouses may come back into use in a few years.

"Good, I have a few things I wanted to show him." He says.

"I am not even going to ask." I breathe. "I just have to tell Gaia now. Maybe I will wait until the holidays."

"Don't wait too long, she will think you thought you were doing something wrong," He smirks, turning his head toward the train. He hears it coming a few minutes before it shows up. We stand and wait until it stops and opens up. "Unless you think you are." He nudges me to go ahead, so I step onto the train, only to find him still standing on the platform.

"Athos?" I question.

"Oh, I have somewhere to be. I will see you later." His dimples pop as he smiles, waving me off.

"What?" I scoff. "Hey, I didn't even pay attention to what exact trains we took."

"You're a big girl. You will figure it out."

"Oh, right. Knight in shining armor, aren't you? Such a great big hero my-" The doors slide shut, cutting off my words, but I know he can still hear me. The train moves away from his laughing figure. I wait until I see him fly off before I turn to find a seat.

"Hey sweetie, you can sit by me." I raise my brow at a young man patting the seat next to him. I physically cringe away from him and find an empty seat in the back, where I begin to look for my way home.

Chapter 14

The interview is up and running on Korra's page the day after our brunch and by the morning I'm swamped with requests. Thankfully, I have enough insight to get an automatic response system that filters the calls and messages into different categories for me. That, plus my new catch system that records the exact times they are received, allows me to respond efficiently within a time limit I set for myself. Everything is under control, no thanks to Mr. Supetastic.

Athos doesn't call me after the interview goes up, which is odd since he has been the most worried about it. Korra didn't alter his answers or her questions. The last part, with their flirtation, has romantic music playing in the background and little cartoon hearts pop up and burst just as the interview ends.

He's ignoring all my calls and messages, which both irirrates and worries me especially since he specifically bought phones for us to use for this very reason.

I try the day after with the same result. The only explanation I can think of is that he has left me. Why else would he leave me hanging now that we have more jobs to do? Either he can't take the pressure or he has decided to go solo. I have been wrong about him. In hindsight, it is a good thing I never told Gaia.

The idea that I've been ghosted by him is unnerving. I try to push the thought from my mind and focus on moving around the schedule. But a tiny voice keeps telling me he's done exactly what I've feared and left me. And if he did, and I no longer have proof with the state that I have employment, it means I will be at their mercy.

I will have no choice but to file with them.

My chest begins to tighten at the thought, so I abandon my computer. I consider going to a bar like I normally do when I start to feel anxious. Since teaming up with Athos, I've stopped going.

But right now, a few drinks and some casual sex with a stranger is starting to sound better than staying home alone again with my thoughts.

One look at my clock and all thoughts of the bar die. It's late, and in my experience, the later I go to the bars, the less chance I have of scoring a decent lay. I groan, throwing my body over my bed in annoyance.

Perhaps it's a blessing in disguise. I agreed with myself to stop drinking and having casual sex. It isn't serving me anymore.

I roll over, gazing up at my ceiling. I may have stayed home, but the thought of casual sex has started an itch deep inside me. It's growing now, and I realize how long I've gone without having an orgasm.

It's a depressing thought.

I lean over my bed, finding my vibrator in my drawers. Curling under my blankets, I spread my legs and shut my eyes as I pull my panties to the side, my pussy already wet.

I groan lightly as I brush my fingers over my clit, swollen with the prospect of an orgasm just a moment away. It's been a while, I think, dipping my fingers into the wetness there. I slide my fingers over my clit, coating it with the wetness.

Working with Athos has taken over my life in such a short time. I barely have a moment to myself since we started. It's about time I relieve some of that stress.

I flip the vibrator on, rolling the pulsing head over my clit, making my thighs shiver as bolts of pleasure shoot through my legs. My clit is so swollen I know I will only last a minute or two, and the thought both excites and confuses me. Was my lack of sex the reason? Or was there something else?

I rock my hips against the vibrator, my lips parting as I press my clit harder into the head. My mind runs through my normal stock of images that get me where I want. A few favorite scenes from some porn, some of my own secret desires, and finally a mental replay of some one-night stands.

I find myself going back to one mind-blowing night with some random woman I met at the bar. I usually end with this one when I'm masturbating - since she was my first experience with a vibrator. I replay her hand working the vibrator on my clit while her free fingers dive to the knuckles in my pussy.

I groan, arching my back against the vibrator just like I did with her, feeling the build of pleasure deep in my core. The heat there is molten, scorching through my veins as my mind pleads for release.

I'm close, so close I can feel my legs shaking with the oncoming orgasm.

Then the image changes and I'm up against a wall. Warm, rough hands are around my neck, squeezing my air off with a delicious slowness. I can feel the wetness between my legs, my clit aching as a knee forces my legs apart.

Yes, I think, pushing my neck harder against the hands. Athos chuckles darkly in my ear, but he releases my throat. I groan in protest, but I am silenced the moment I feel his hard cock slide against my clit.

"Do you think you can take it, Lily?" He asks.

I gasp, rocking my hips against his cock in my mind, while also rocking them harder against my vibrator in reality. I barely have time to register that I'm replaying that night in my mind. If I did, I might stop what I'm doing long enough to be mortified.

But instead, I roll with it, letting myself fall back into his bed, his hands roaming over my breasts while he takes me from behind. I'd never arched my back so much for a man before, but his cock felt so good I couldn't help myself. With every thrust, he forced my face deeper into the sheets, my arms barely strong enough to hold him and me up as he pounded into me.

Then I felt it, his fingers gliding over my clit with expert movement, making tiny motions that sent me right over the edge and screaming into the sheets.

I broke into a thousand tiny fractured pieces in my mind just as I did in reality, my hips bucking against my vibrator with complete abandon.

I collapse back onto the bed, my legs and arms shaking with the orgasm, the memories of that night drifting over me.

My breath is erratic as I toss the vibrator to the side, rolling over to face my window.

Fuck, I think just as I close my eyes and drift away.

A tap on my window wakes me. I blink my eyes open, looking around in confusion. The clock reads only a half hour after I'd last checked. Another tap gets me to look out my window. Athos's face is floating outside.

I shriek, sitting up quickly, then realize I have no pants on.

"Lily!" He waves so fast that his hand becomes a blur. I pull the sheet over me, then waddle to the window. I push it open, glaring back at him as he floats above the ground.

"I know we are coworkers now, but Athos, I have a front door. And a phone." He grins like a fool. "What happened to yours, by the way? I've called you all weekend." I sneer.

"Oh that. Lost it." He shrugs.

"You did *what*!?" I move to grab his shirt but he floats away.

"Clam down, don't bust a lung. Let me in and I will explain." He moves to push the window open more, but I hold it firm.

"Front. Door." I say between clenched teeth.

He chuckles, "Fine, fine."

I slam the window shut, grabbing a pair of pants before heading downstairs. My dad is up late, working in the living room, when I stomp down and throw open the front door.

"I'm going to either make business hours for myself, or you are going to have to learn to use a phone. Without losing it." I snap.

"Most women would swoon at the idea of a Supe at their window." He bats his eyes at me.

"Most women are romantic fools." I breathe.

He tsks as he moves past me to the hall. "Me thinks the-"

"I swear," I hiss, "if you say *anything* remotely like that, I will *find* something that will hurt you when I smack you with it."

"Lillium!" I spin in astonishment to see my dad staring at us. I forgot about him. "That is *no* way to speak to a guest."

"Oh, he's heard it all before." I throw my hands up and march up the stairs.

"Hey, Mr. Jones! Business." Athos laughs as he follows. I collapse on my bed and check my phone for new messages. I have two already.

"Busy?" I shoot him a glare.

"Yes. I have had to reschedule some jobs since I couldn't get a hold of you to confirm."

"So…I have tomorrow off?" He teases.

"Yes," I say bitterly. "It does not seem very professional for us to be rescheduling, you know. I didn't have a good reason for it- thankfully everyone seems to not care, as long as you show up."

"I'm sorry about that. I know it is very flaky for me to disappear like that, but it was very important."

He sets a cloth-wrapped package on my stomach, stopping me from asking what was so damn important. As I narrow my eyes at the object, I think it is some Supe stuff.

"Please tell me this isn't some kind of body part…" He rolls his eyes. With a sigh, I gingerly unwrap the cloth to find it's a lovely cream-colored fabric with gold trimming. I sit up to lay it out and find it to be a suit of sorts, with a headpiece.

"Is this the new fashion? Or are we making a statement?" I quirk a brow.

"No, it's an aerodynamic thermal suit." He explains, looking pleased with himself.

"Oh." I nod, and add thoughtfully, "I hadn't even thought of an outfit yet. Good choice. I like the colors."

"It's not for me. You."

"What?" I bark.

"Put that on, and I can fly high and fast with you."

For a moment, I'm speechless. Why would he care to fly me around? Is he that adamant about having me around jobs?

"It is made from a special new material that insulates you from the icy winds by holding your body heat, along with adding to it if need be. It can detect when you get too cold or hot, and it will adjust to your liking…" I notice he is fidgeting.

"It's very nice, but now that we have so much more to do, I don't think I will make many job appearances, even with this."

"Oh, it's not for that." He waves off my anxious expression. "You could use it for that if you wanted to, but I got it for you and I to able to go to a certain place tomorrow."

I hesitate, then ask, "Where?"

He gives me a small smile and turns away from me. "I can't tell you right now. But I would like to leave in the morning."

"When?"

"Eight." He shrugs. "Or whenever you are up."

"And you want me to wear this…" I motion to the suit.

"Yes. We can get there faster." He keeps his face from me, but I have spent enough time with him to know when he is being secretive, especially about the others.

"This place is not accessible by any other means, is it?" I ask blandly.

"Not really."

"And it's private." I sigh.

"Sure…" He's still not looking at me, which tells me I am on the right track.

I sigh loudly to express my agitation at his flippant, nonchalant manner. But inside I feel excitement swell through me like never before. This has something to do with the Supes, that's much is clear, but something tells me it's a lot more than that.

"This…It's important, right?" I pry.

He finally turns back to me, his expression serious for once. "To me." I nod, feeling my stomach leap at the possibilities. I finger the suit and ask him about air.

"The headpiece might look fragile, but do not let it fool you." I pick it up to see that it has a gossamer face mesh that looks like it could keep flies out but will be useless for air. "That part catches air in microscopic holes for you to breathe in while also keeping a shield against too much air coming in. It won't trap the air you breathe out, so every breath you take will be nothing but fresh air. It holds more than enough for you to take in, so don't worry about hyperventilating or anything."

I throw him a saccharine smile. "And who made this wonderful suit?"

He smirks back as he picks up the wrappings and starts to walk away. "You will see."

"Eight then," I say, accepting I will have to wait to find out.

"Eight." He replies. I can see the apprehension he feels all over his face. "Lily, I hope you will come...and understand..." He stops, lost for words or unable to say it. I know he wants to confide something in me, and can't bring himself to do it. What the hell makes these Supes so ensconced?

"It's alright Athos. You don't have to tell or show me anything that you don't want to or can't." *But please do!* "I knew what I was getting into."

"I know, Lily." His lazy smile returns.

"Eight then. Good night." He moves to leave, pausing just at the door. I think he might say something more, but instead, his eyes flick to my bed. I follow his gaze, seeing the vibrator still on top of the sheets. Heat burns up my neck, but I look back at him, daring him to say something.

But he's gone.

I can hear my dad and him downstairs for a while, then all goes silent. I lay back in my bed, still holding the suit to me. *Tomorrow will either change everything or nothing,* I think as I drift off to sleep.

Chapter 15

I meet him in the front yard early enough to see him fly down from the sky. Wisps of vapor stir around us as I greet him.

"Warm enough?" He asks.

"Yes. It's comfortable. Surprisingly." I keep my eyes downcast, afraid he will bring up what he saw on my bed. A girl has needs, and I'm prepared to defend those needs if he brings it up.

"Good. Ready?"

I take a deep breath and nod. He steps in front of me, ready to take me in his arms. I try to calm myself by staring at his plain clothes. "No suit for you?" I laugh ruefully.

"Not yet." He picks me up and holds me close. I can feel his warmth for a moment through the suit. "I'll go slow at first, then speed up once you're comfortable. If, for whatever reason, you want me to stop, just say so. If you can't say it, tap me on the neck." He gives me a knowing look, and I resist the urge to punch him in the face. He places my hands around his neck, his amber eyes daring me to say something. "Are you ready?" He asks softly.

Our eyes are locked for a moment, and I feel the electric pulse between us. I don't have to ask him what he's thinking - his eyes tell me as I press my body firmly against his.

"Sure," I say. My voice is soft.

He lifts off very slowly at first, allowing me to get my bearings. I can't help but revel in the experience this time, since every other time he's taken me on a flight, it's been fast and scary. Once we get over my house, he speeds up. We are going straight up, faster and faster. I wait for the biting cold to hit me, or my lungs to scream for air, but it never happens.

Then I feel a hitch in my stomach and know we are heading in a different direction, and fast. I can hear the air rushing by, but it isn't deafening. He holds me under him slightly, so I have to look over his shoulder to see the passing ground, way beneath us. I watch as we pass over the lush, mountainous valleys of our town.

"I am going to go fast now." I already thought this was fast. My stomach lurches again and the valley under us becomes a blur. Now the air rushing past me becomes very loud, and I have to close my eyes to keep myself from freaking out. I half expect my body to be crushed by the sheer force of the air pressure, but the suit either absorbs it or cuts through it somehow.

I have no idea how long it will take for us to get where he wants, but thankfully I have enough air and am warm enough to be comfortable. So comfortable, in fact, that I drift off to sleep, only to wake when I feel us drop suddenly. It's such a shock I let go of his neck and he stops mid-air.

"Lily?" He holds me out in front of him, his voice full of worry.

"Oh!" I gasp. "I'm fine. It just startled me. I think I fell asleep…"

He looks at me with disbelief, then laughs. "For a moment there, I thought the suit had failed."

"It's fine. Let's keep going."

I wrap my arms around his neck again and he speeds off to the ground. We land so fast that I have to keep my eyes shut for a moment to avoid motion sickness.

"We are here." I allow myself to gain my footage, making sure I'm steady before I open my eyes. He's smiling at me as I unwrap my arms from him. I take off my headpiece to get a better look at where we are. Certainly not in the South West.

We were standing on a coastline, atop a cliff that looks over the vast ocean. With my headpiece off, I can feel the chill damp against my face. I take a deep breath of the refreshing surf and smile into the morning sun.

"Where are we?" I ask.

"This is the North Coast."

"You won't tell me exactly where, huh?" His smile tells me no.

I walk from him to the edge of the cliff, admiring the sheer drop to the waters. I have to be nearly a thousand feet up; the land expanding behind me, forming rolling green hills and trees.

"I've never been to the North Coast. It's beautiful." I shield my eyes from the sun to see him. "Was this what you wanted to show me?" I tease.

"Partly." He holds out his hand. "Just one more flight."

"Seriously?" I groan.

"Just down there." He motions beneath us, to the bottom of the cliff.

"We are going down there? To the ocean?" I ask, dubious.

"You will see." He smirks, his dimples popping as he still holds his hand to me.

I take it as we walk to the very edge of the cliff. He places me in front of him and then takes me by my hips. "Here we go." He whispers into the shell of my ear.

Goosebumps cover my arms when we jump off. We float down to the rocky cliff bottom, where he lands on top of one rock. He holds onto my hips with one hand, keeping me from slipping while pointing to a spot obscured by all the rock formations. It takes a moment for me to realize he is showing me a cave. It's rather small, and from the watermarks on the cliff wall, I can tell that at high tide it will be completely underwater. As of now, it's not.

"I am going to take you in there." He says, a wide grin spreading across his face.

Nervous laughter erupts from me. "What? Why the hell would you?" I eye the dark hole and feel my body bend away.

"It's what I want to show you." I cut him a look.

"A cave? An ocean cave?" I ask incredulously.

"More than just a cave, Lily. Trust me. You will be just fine."

I try to argue, but he takes off again. We float over quickly before the waves break over the rock again and drench us. The cave is enclosed in a ring of rocks that keep the biggest waves out, so it's calm but freezing.

Athos flies into the darkness, hitting me with the sheer icy air and the sour smell of ocean foam and seaweed. I can't see anything around us, but he must know where he's going since I am soon placed on solid ground. Or rather, a solid mound of seaweed and sand. I can feel my feet sink with a squish that sends shivers up my legs.

"Wait, a moment." I feel him move away and then hear a mixture of taps and raps.

Suddenly, I'm hit with a blinding light that comes from a growing opening. Once my eyes adjust, I can see the opening is a type of metal door sliding back into the cave wall. Athos is standing by the door, his hand against the cave wall. At a closer look, I realize his hand is on a keypad.

"What…" I gasp, confused. How the hell did a keypad get in this cave?

"Come in." He takes my arm and leads me into the light. My feet feel like lead, and suddenly I'm doubting if I want to know what this is about. I have always assumed the Supes lived among us, carrying out lives much like our own. But this is a secret lair on a cliff-side. This screams of a secret society. All at once, I think of Gaia, and how she's right; they have secrets for a reason. Do I want to know what it is? What if it's some plot against humans? Does he think I will join?

He drags me through the doorway. I have a whirl of possible happenings run across my mind; a jumble of world domination, human enslavement, and more. I'm expecting a dank underground lair, not the gigantic bright underground home I find myself in. The giant wall of glass to our left shows me that we are not completely underground. The glass overlooks the ocean as well as under it, where I can see fish that swim around the rocks at the bottom of the cliff.

"Uh…" I want to say it's gorgeous, it's amazing, and what the hell am I doing here? But my tongue is numb.

Athos hits a pad on the wall, making the cave door close. He takes my hand with a reassuring smile that does nothing at all to calm me.

"It's a house…." I say stupidly.

"Guess you can say so. It has everything a home would, and more." He leans me over to the glass where it overlooks a large living room. The area we are in is so vast that the glass reaches up to fifty feet and spans more than a hundred. Everything is made of polished metal but for the furniture.

"How…." I gesture lamely to the glass.

"From the outside, it looks like a rock. But it's a new type of glass that can be formed to take the shape and appearance of something while giving you a flat clear view out." He taps it with his knuckles, "It's a bitch to clean, though."

"That's why we have the fish." A voice muses.

I nearly jump out of my skin at the new voice behind us. I spin around to see a young man standing behind the sunken living room, hands on the back of a very long couch. He looks no more than sixteen and has a shock of golden hair. It's apparent he's shorter than me by his stocky legs, but very muscular by the way his arms bulge to get out of his long-sleeved shirt. He's smiling at me, amusement gleaming in his eyes.

"Hi!" He waves energetically. I slowly looked over at Athos.

"Lillium," he says, "this is Briseathe." I stop breathing. Briseathe? *The* Briseathe? No, there's no possible way. "Lily?" He nudges me.

I blink from him to the short one. "But…he's…*blue*."

The supposed Briseathe laughs out loud. "It's more of a powder-blue, but yes, my skin differs from when I last appeared in public."

"You were…." I try to find the words.

"Tanner, at the time, I change my appearance every so often. I get bored with one look for too long." He juts his chin to Athos. "Pretty boy over there has to keep the same face and body forever. I don't envy him at all."

"You can change…." I must seem like some blathering idiot, but I'm trying to grasp the severity of the situation. Athos brought me to see Briseathe, the most famous of all Supes. And now he's blue.

"Yup." He rubs his hands down his broad chest. "This is a creation of my own. I once tried pink and found it to be too much. Not nearly as much as orange." He groans, "I had the worst headaches of my life with that one!"

"Briseathe." Athos interrupts, "Is breakfast ready?"

"Uh, yes, it is." He rolls his eyes. "I don't have the luxury of choosing to eat or not." Briseathe turns on his heels and makes his way to the kitchen behind him. "I hope you like sea-grown vegetables. That's all I eat." I watch, mesmerized, as he pulls up his left sleeve to reveal a pad fused to his *wrist*. He waves his other hand over it, prompting a screen to fly up in front of him.

"I'm sending the food up." He explains as he taps the floating screen.

"Up?" I squeak, looking around the room. There was a down?

"To the top floor, where we will have breakfast!" He chatters.

"Ah, Athos, what is going on? Breakfast?" As if this is a small thing, having breakfast with a person who has a holiday named after them. It's normal.

"Just relax Lily. Everything will be fine." He pats me on the head, making me feel like some reluctant pet.

"To the cave-avator!" Briseathe dashes off to the far end of the room, where the wall moves to reveal a glass elevator. "In we go!" He sings, hopping into it. I have to be led by Athos. Once the doors slide shut, we take off up a dark tunnel where the elevator is lit up only by small strips above us. I can see the look of elation on Briseathe's blue face.

He looks nothing like the man I've seen in my school books or every year on the screens, looping his first speech to us. For one, the guy in front of me is much younger than he had been then, but he also has a completely different face. It's very wide now, with big eyes and a big mouth, along with a round nose. In all the pictures I've seen of him from before, his features are tighter, more scrunched.

Right now, with his shock of gold hair and blue skin, he looks like some kind of childlike alien. He must feel my eyes on him because he turns and smiles at me.

"Almost there!" A second later, the elevator stops, and we step out into a bright room. The same glass is to our right overlooking the ocean, and as I step out, I notice it is the same view from the top of the cliff.

"We were just up there. Right above where our heads are." I exclaim.

"Yes." I can see from the corner of my eye that Athos is watching me, trying to gauge my emotions and response. Truly, I have no idea what I'm feeling other than surprise.

I look over at the table before us. The room is much smaller than the one below us, with the table being the only furniture.

I take a seat between the boys, who are both already digging into their dishes.

I mechanically eat my food, barely tasting it, and instead trying to think about what I am going to say to them. There's a reason besides eating breakfast that Athos brought me. Then it dawns on me that he is going to do what Sheiba feared. He's going to tell me the secrets of his people.

So I finish first, deliberately.

I wait until Athos finishes off the rest of the food. For a guy who doesn't need to eat to live, he sure can put it away.

"So..." I begin.

"Yes! So!" Briseathe smacks his hands together, startling me. "May I?" He's looking directly at Athos, who quickly glances at me before nodding.

"I know you're wondering what the hell you're doing in this amazing place!" Briseathe arcs his arms over his head dramatically.

"Yeah...." I drawl, earning a laugh from him.

"No, you're wondering what the hell is going on. Well, I'm Briseathe." He holds out his hand to me as if we didn't just make introductions before. I take it and shake it, puzzled.

"You're Lillium, Athos's human partner in crime. Or, non-crime. Whatever. You work with him." He waves his hand around. "This has never been done before. You know about us and humans eloping, but that was for emotional and physical reasons." Athos shifts in his chair, causing Briseathe to glance his way.

"So naturally," he continues, "you are of great interest to us." I think of Sheiba and twitch. "Don't worry about us causing trouble. The most any of us will do is gripe and moan at Athos here. Which I hear has already happened." I nod.

"Sheiba's a witch." I stifle a laugh. "No, really, she is. Or she was considered one at least, at some point. We have never let her forget it." He grins.

"She has always been difficult," Athos adds.

"Then why did you date her?" I ask, forcing a smile.

Briseathe bursts out laughing, smacking the table with his hands. "I like her. She has spunk."

"I did not *date* her." He grumbles.

"No, you just lived with her for nearly fifty years." Briseathe deadpans.

My mouth drops. "Really?" Athos glares at him and looks away from me so I can't see his expression. Conflicting emotions battle in my core as I try to figure out why he doesn't want me to know, and why the hell I care.

"So?" He mutters.

"Whoa. For a human that would be, you know, serious." I say.

"Not for us." Briseathe shakes his head. "But regardless of what happened with them, he now has her drooling for more."

"Enough about that." Athos snaps, "We aren't here to talk about past relations. Unless you want to." He gives Briseathe a cool smile, and I watch as he pales to a lighter blue.

"No, that's fine." He clears his throat. "Anyway, don't worry about her. People like her have a hard time with us." I raise a brow. "I'm half human." He explains.

My mind goes blank suddenly. Half human? Briseathe, the most revered Supe, is half human? I suddenly start laughing, hysterically, until tears run down my cheeks.

"I broke her." Briseathe shakes his head sadly.

"No," I gasp, "it's too ironic!"

"Ironic?" Athos asks.

"Of course." Briseathe chuckles, "I am the most famous, beloved Super there is. Humans hold us up so high in regard *because* we are different. I'm half human, therefore it is ironic that I should be the one they hold as the most famous."

"Ironic. They love you the most, and you are half of what they are. They adore the only one who is half-human!" I say.

"Oh, I'm not the only one."

I think back to what had been said about Supe and humans coupling. "No, you wouldn't be. Are there a lot of hybrid Supes?"

"Very few." Athos sighs.

"Very, *very* few." Briseathe intones.

"Why don't they like you? The others, I mean?" I ask.

"Because I'm part human, of course. They are all elitists, you know, purity of the oh-so-precious blood." He sticks out his tongue.

Athos coughs a warning.

"Oh, come on! She's going to have to find out sooner or later. You owe her that much." Briseathe scoffs.

"He doesn't-" I begin, but he cuts me off.

"Oh yes, he does! Athos here has his issues with the others, and himself." Briseathe narrows his eyes pointedly at him. "If you are going to work with him, he should have the decency to tell you *some* things. That is why you brought her here, right?"

"That was what Sheiba was afraid of." I sigh.

"Sheiba, like I said, is a witch. Who cares what Sheiba wants? She is one of those elitists. They freak out when we mingle with the common crowd, so to speak. They put up fights every single time one of us gets involved with a human." He leans forward and whispers, "Hybrids don't normally live past age one."

"Briseathe..." Athos sighs, looking tired.

"Oh, come on, I don't see what harm will come from saying that we originate from a mysterious island that was destroyed thousands of years ago-"

"Briseathe!" Athos gasps, shocked.

"-or that our powers come from a Source that was on that island, now lost to us forever."

"*Briseathe!*" Athos grinds his teeth together.

"We don't even have a name for it. It was lost to us, and the location of it." He says flippantly, smiling.

Athos groans and sits back in his chair, glaring at him.

"Then again, I never set foot on it, so I personally don't care about anyone finding out. You see, that's what everyone is so afraid of when it comes to you. They fear you will interfere with it." Briseathe wiggles his brows at me.

"You come from an island?" I ask Athos incredulously.

Athos rubs his temples. "I wanted to ease you into this, Lily. Not drop it all on your lap. You've been away from society for too long. You have forgotten protocol." Athos shakes his head at Briseathe.

Briseathe scoffs, "Me? I've been gone too long? What about you? You ran off for *years*."

My eyes widen. I assumption was right. "That's why you keep asking questions about the War!" I smirk.

"Yes." He says shortly.

"Why?" I ask, leaning closer to him.

"He couldn't take the way you humans were destroying the world. He didn't understand why we wouldn't get involved. So he left." I see something pass between the two of them by the gleam in their eyes.

"So, Athos was not there when you came out?" I ask.

"No. He was bunking up with some monks. Or living in ruined cities." Briseathe shrugs.

I turn to Athos. "Why did you come back now? Why not when he and the others came out?"

Athos finally tears his gaze from Briseathe. He looks drained now. "I didn't leave on good terms with the others. I told them that they were cowards, living in the dark and trying to 'preserve' our race. They didn't want a war to erupt between us and you. So I left. *Not* to live with some monks, though." He glares back at Briseathe. "I traveled elsewhere."

"Where?" I ask, intrigued. Where could he possibly travel to that resulted in him being so out of touch with the modern world?

Briseathe's head swivels between us. "Go on, tell her. I thought the mountain range sounded better."

"Space." Athos spits out sourly.

"*Space*?! As in the moon and Venus?" I breathe.

"Yeah, he went to sulk around the Milky Way!" Briseathe snorts.

Chapter 16

"Why would you go to space? How are you even alive?!" I cry. "Wait- don't answer that! This is too much." I rub my temples.

There is too much information flying around the breakfast table, and I can't digest it.

"I went to look for people like us," Athos says softly, "I thought there had to be others like us, or maybe even another Source somewhere. But I never found it."

"No one knows where the Source comes from," Briseathe explains. "All we know for sure is that this Source calls to some people."

I raise a brow. "It does what now?"

"It calls some people to it. It attracts people from all over the world to its location." Briseathe says.

"On an island?" I ask.

"Yes." He nods.

"You are playing a joke on me, aren't you, Athos?" I ask darkly. He shakes his head.

"It's no joke. The people converged on it, and it gave them all extraordinary powers. From then on, our people lived under its protection." Athos explains.

"Until the island blew up?" I ask.

Briseathe nods toward Athos, who says, "Not really. No one knows what happens exactly. One day, the entire island just erupts into chaos. The ground split open and breathed fire everywhere; all the buildings crumbled or were washed away in a tidal wave. We tried to stop it, but no one could.

We evacuated those of us that were left." I watch him slip into his statue mode. *Is that where he goes when he does this? I think, Is he recalling this horrific event?*

I lean over to him and place my hand on his. With a deep breath, he comes back, blinking.

"You were there," I say. He nods.

"Many perished, and those of us left had nowhere to go. Our leaders had forbidden anyone from leaving the island; they told us without the Source, we would die. Our home had just disappeared, so we all scattered and tried to find some place safe.

"Imagine our surprise when we first meet humans," he smirks. "We have always known there are other beings out in the world, but we have never come across any."

Briseathe shakes his head. "For all their talk of being different, we are very much the same. There are three types of us: like Athos here, who cannot be harmed and do not age; ones who do not age but can be harmed, and ones who age and die."

I can't believe what I'm hearing. Some Supes can age and die? "Like me?" I ask.

"Just like you, in fact. Those tend not to have any powers whatsoever." Briseathe says.

"How? How can that be?" I ask.

"The Source. It is what gave us our abilities. Tell her." Briseathe motions to Athos eagerly.

Athos looks away from me, to the ocean. "When we were born, our parents would take us to the Source. As a child, I witnessed it only once when my cousin was brought to it. It was always a grand ceremony for everyone. They take the baby to a pedestal under our Source. I remember it as a great orb of light, dancing around us as it bathed the baby with its gleam. We believe that this is when we acquire our abilities."

I watch the way his face turns into stone as he recalls the memory. Sometimes, I forget how old Athos is, but when he stands still like this, I can see it etched into his face—timeless.

"You see," he turns back to me, "since then any child born, whether half human or not, does not live past their first year. Those like him," he gestures to Briseathe, "are one in a billion."

"It is a painful process," Briseathe flinches as he speaks. "Growing up, I thought I could die at any time. I was always so sick and weak. If it wasn't for my father, who could heal, I might have died. When I was older, I figured out ways to fix myself."

"Yourself?" I ask, doubtful.

"Why yes, haven't you noticed? That suit you are wearing is mine. This house was my creation, dammit. I am responsible for every major technology since the twenty-first century! I might be half human, but I was graced with the ability of genius!"

"Wait, how? Without the Source-" He cuts me off again.

"We believe the Source is the reason for our abilities, and they can be passed down by blood. But something about that, it giving us these abilities, doesn't work unless we are in its presence after birth. Only three known half-humans are living right now, including me. There are a few dozen more pure-blood Supes born outside of the Source.

"This means that a full-blood Supe could live outside of the Source- but these are always born mortal, and usually did not age. There is one half-human who is mortal, but does not age."

"So, you age? How can you...." I wave at his body.

"Lillium, I have just told you. I am a genius. I clone myself, of course." I look from him to Athos, dumbstruck. "I have a stock hold of clones, at different ages and looks, so when the time comes for this body to go, I switch to another."

"How?" I ask.

"Every day I upload personal videos and data to my special 'MeM' unit, and it installs those into the memories and minds of my clones. I choose which one will be next, and bam! I'm back in action." He rubs his hands down his body with a loving expression.

Clones, magical sources, and exploding islands. I expected maybe some secrets, but nothing like this. Half humans, purebloods, internal affairs, and struggles. What is next?

"Lily, I know this is *a lot*," Athos intones, "so don't worry about under-standing it all right now. I was planning on letting you know little by little." He glares at Briseathe.

"Paw!" Briseathe groans. "Baby steps are overrated. She's a big girl, she can take it."

"To sum it all up, you guys come from an island where a blob of light gave you power, then blew up. Now, without the light, you can not procreate as much." I deadpan.

"Pretty straightforward, huh?" Briseathe smirks.

"There is slightly more than that…." Athos mutters. "The source is still out there, somewhere."

"Seriously? Where?" I ask.

"No one knows," Briseathe says eerily, wiggling his fingers. I raise a brow at his antics. "No, really. We don't know. I personally think it is hiding."

"Hiding from the very people it made?" I quirk a brow.

"Yes. We can feel it," Athos says gravely.

"As in sense it," Briseathe says. "Yup. We are all connected to it, and each other through it. I think it has something to do with when one's like Athos here were connected with it as a baby."

"The light I saw would come down and disappear completely in the baby." Athos explains.

"Those of us born since then, who have never connected with it, have weaker connections with the others. Being half-human I naturally have a very weak connection; I can only feel that the others are alive. Athos here can feel exactly where they are in the world."

"Everyone has their own frequency, so to say." Athos shrugs.

"So…how many of there are you?" I ask.

The guys instantly lock eyes, and I feel something pass between them. *Wrong thing to say,* I think bitterly.

"I don't know," Briseathe says finally as he flicks his wrist at Athos, who shakes his head slightly.

"Not as many as you might think." He says slowly, "More than half our population was wiped out by the destruction of our home. Then more died of disease, infections, mishaps, and old age within the first decade of being in the new lands.

"Many of us were separated on different lands. In the first fifty years we only had two successful births from pure-bloods. Some had thought that it would be different with humans, so many took up human companions. But once that proved even more inefficient, most of us deemed humans inferior and left them. Only those who truly wanted to be with a human stayed with them while the rest of us regrouped and left.

"It soon became apparent that we could not live separately from humans for very long."

He smirks at me. "You were always starting wars, finding new land, and procreating at the speed of rabbits. We tried to make our own home and start over again, but since most of our elders were dead by this time, we didn't have what it took to reign over ourselves. It was madness. We were all divided about what to do. Some wanted total control over humans. They thought we could have taken over the entire world. We had realized that we had been kept on our lands by the elders and the Source, for whatever reasons, and now we were free.

"Many didn't agree with domination. First off, we were outnumbered in this new terrible world, where strange things could take down the strongest of us."

"Enervations." Briseathe breathes. So, Supes had weaknesses, huh?

"Yes. It was discovered that while some of us were invulnerable in our homeland, there were dangers here that could be fatal." Athos says.

"Like what?" I ask.

"Anything. One smell of a new flower we'd never seen before could cause instant death, a tasty fruit that others ate could now be fatal to one person. Many of us died in what we now call allergic reactions." He explains.

"But it was only one person at a time." Briseathe says, "It would never be an entire group of even just two people who had bad reactions to something."

"We concluded that each of us was susceptible to at least one thing from this new world. For some, it was something as simple as a flower, or food, but for others, it was as obscure as a mineral or animal." Athos says.

"So you all have a weakness? Every one of you?" I ask.

Athos nods. "Yes, even mortals have one. The only ones without a weakness are half-breeds."

Supes *can* be defeated. This, out of everything they have told me so far, is the most significant. These people that we have all thought immortal can die. I have a feeling this is part of the reason Sheiba's afraid of me working with Athos.

"This isn't something you tell everyone, is it?" I ask. Briseathe smirks, and I know I'm right.

"Lillium, Athos wants to change the way things are. He believed the only way to do that would be to be completely honest with you when it comes to our history and our people. This information is not something that any of us have disclosed to any human ever."

"I think that needs to change." Athos nods. At that moment, I know he's telling me he trusts me completely. If I ask him right then what his weakness is, he will tell me. We lock eyes and I know he's thinking the same thing. That kind of information will leave him bare, and if it falls into the wrong hands, it could mean his death. So I don't ask. It's not my place to ask or to know.

"What era did your homeland self-destruct?" I ask instead. The relief in his eyes is evident. He hoped I wouldn't ask him about his weakness.

"Sometime around the medieval ages, we presume. No one knows for sure. Too many of us were scattered around the world, and we had never kept track of time like you do." He says.

"You're...ancient...literally." I whisper, awed.

Briseathe rolls his eyes. "Yeah, but they still are none too bright. You would think that with that many years on this earth, with so much information available to them, they would be the smartest, most well-rounded people ever."

"Nope." Athos sighs.

"Not even close," I smirk.

"I have come to realize that even though some may not age, their mental age has stayed the same for years. That's why they seek me out and hate me at the same time." Briseathe laments.

I watch as Athos smirks. "We have only had one genius in the entire history of our people, before him. She was an elder and died of old age. Apparently, brains only come to those who are mortals."

Briseathe scoffs. "They are jealous of me and hate that it happened to be a half-breed. I have to live here, in this cave, and put up deflector systems just to keep them away."

"Deflector?" I ask.

He waves his hand. "I figured out how to hide my very weak connection with a deflector system. It only works for half-breeds, though. Athos here? He'll forever be on their radars, so he only visits when others aren't around."

"What do they want from you?" I ask.

"They think I can find where the Source is." He rolls his eyes.

"You said earlier that is what Sheiba was mad about, as well. She thinks I will stop you?" I ask.

"No, she thinks that you will become close with Athos here, who will let you meet me, who will then show you where the Source is. Which, out of human spite, we will both use to our advantage to overthrow them. Or just keep to ourselves and laugh in my dark lair." He laughs darkly, cupping his hands together with a mischievous grin.

Briseathe has a flare for the dramatics, but I can tell he's being genuine. "That's insane! Are all Supes that paranoid?"

"No more than the amount of humans who think we mean to take over the world." Athos points. *Fair enough,* I think, shrugging.

"I ended up going into hiding after coming out to humans because my people would not let up on me. It did not help that pretty boy over here ran off into space around the same time." Athos rolls his eyes. "Everyone thought we were in cahoots, that I had found it and he was trying to bring it to me or something. When I told them my honest opinion was that it was hiding from us for a reason, they all went bonkers!"

"Wait, are you saying that it is conscious?" I gape.

"Sure as hell." He nods.

Athos grunts, "Briseathe has a theory that the Source is the reason our homeland was destroyed. It tried to self-destruct or something."

"You don't believe that?" I ask. It seems possible, considering how my day is going. I wouldn't be surprised if Briseathe had a giant sea monster living in the cove at this point.

"No!" He says vehemently, "It would never do that to us."

"See what I mean?" Briseathe stands up and skips behind me. "Don't listen to him. They all have some God-loving complex when it comes to the Source. It can do no evil and all."

"You guys don't have another name for it?" I ask.

"Nope. They are not very creative. Ingeniously dull." Briseathe spits his tongue at Athos.

"We had one in our language, and it translates to 'source.'" Athos grunts.

"You had a language?" I ask.

"Yeah, and they forgot it." Athos winces then reverts back to his statue mode.

I take the moment to look him over, with fresh eyes now, and see that though he looks like he was in his early twenties, this man is thousands of years old. I figured he's old, but not that *old*. He has never treated me like a child, like he knew far more than I, though at times he has a look in his eyes that says 'I know things you will never fathom'.

Plus, he's been in space! He's been there since well before the war, getting away from everyone and trying to find another like himself. Maybe even another life, or another Source. He must not have found anything of significance since he's here now.

I am starting to understand why he feels so differently than the others. They cower in the dark for years when he felt they should be helping the world. So he leaves and comes back to find they are now all famous and beloved. They have changed from cowering children to high-profile celebrities, who are full of greed and power.

What a kick to the groin that must have been.

Briseathe pats me on the shoulder. "Well, enough about the old times. How would you like to see my clones?"

Chapter 17

"This way, Lillium." Briseathe takes my arm and leads the way back to the elevator. He calls over his shoulder to Athos, "We will be right back."

I wait for him to protest, or at least follow us, but he only continues to sit and mope as he watches the waves. I won't lie, a tiny part of me hopes he will join us, but I refuse to let him see it in my face. I school my expression into muted interest as we wait for the elevator.

Briseathe, though, can see through my mask. "Let him mope for a while." He gives my hand a small squeeze before dropping it. The elevator opens for us silently. I slide in next to him and wait as the doors close. Through the glass doors, I can see Athos in his statue mode.

"How does he do that?" I ask, tilting my head. The elevator moves down and Athos disappears.

"Go robot on us? I dunno. The ones who do not need to breathe to live can do it, I've found." Briseathe explains with a bored look.

"Where does his mind go?"

"Wherever it can, I imagine." He smiles grimly, "I was told once that look means they are connecting with their inner string, the part of them that is twined with everyone else. The part that is the source of their power."

"But only the ones who are immortal can do that though, right?" I ask and he raises his shoulders and shakes his head.

"Believe it or not, we do not know everything. At times, we are just as lost as you." The elevator comes to a smooth stop. Outside the glass doors all I see is darkness. They open to the void and a cool pocket of air rushes in.

"Where are we?" I ask, my voice echoing into the black abyss.

"Under the sea level floor." We step out onto bright white tiles that light up once our feet touch them. "Energy-saving tiles," he explains as we walk on. From the tiles' illumination, I can see that we are walking down a long narrow hall that eventually ends at a steel door.

"In case of flooding." He smiles. He lays his palm flat against the middle of the door and for a moment, nothing happens. Briseathe throws his head back with a groan, ripping his hand from the metal.

"Stupid thermals. Hold still, please." He frantically rubs his hand on my arm, "Hand's not warm enough to register that I'm living." Living? Would something dead want to get back there? I glance around, wondering if he has some kind of dead sea creature haunting the halls.

He quickly transfers his hand to the door again and this time it hums to life. Lines of pale green light etch out all over the door in lithe symbols from the center of his palm. The lines of light, once they take over the whole door, grow brighter until I hear a soft crack followed by a click and Briseathe's yelp of pain.

He takes his hand back, rubbing the palm. I can see a smudge of blood in the center of his palm. "Never get used to it," he mutters darkly. He leads the way to another darkened room, only this time, once we are in and the door closes behind us, it lights up.

It is vast, which is expected, but I had not expected the amount of floating spheres full of human bodies. Naked human bodies. We are standing in what I can only imagine is his laboratory, a platform with computers and gadgets that hang over a giant room full of clones. The spheres climb to the ceiling above, and span to many many floors below us. The same pale green light from the door that runs from each sphere lit them up, making them look like a chain of sleeping people. The light here pulses slowly, like a heartbeat.

"How many do you have?" I whisper in awe.

"Right now, I have over three hundred." My jaw drops open, amusing him. "That might seem like a lot to you, but it isn't. Many of these end up defecting after some time, not to mention how many end up failing from the beginning. Rarely do I get a body that I can have for over ten years."

"Really? Even so, you have a lot-"

He cuts me off. "Yes, but they take a long time to make on top of it. Just a year ago, I lost one."

I pace in front of him, eyeing the spheres. "Why?"

"It has to do with the genetics of them being half human and half Supe. My original body would not have lasted if it hadn't been for my dad healing me constantly. It kept trying to self-destruct. The human cells could not support the Supe ones." he shrugs, "I found a cure for it, but it only applies to me, no other Halfling. And as I go on making clones, sometimes the cells defect again, and it dies." He takes a few steps toward the computers.

"I could just make multiple copies of my first body, and that would be less time consuming, but not as much fun." He takes a seat in a weird-looking pod by the computers and gestures for me to come over. I sit next to him and watch as he opens a picture of a gorgeous man with perfectly tanned skin and bright blonde hair on a screen.

A ghost of a smile plays on his lips. "That's me. The first me."

"Seriously?" I try to keep the smile off my face, but fail. "Why the hell would you go from that to this?" I poke his blue arm.

"Because I don't have to stay with the old one. I can always go back to it if I want." Then he hits a button on the screen that causes the platform to buck up and go flying. I scream in terror, groping for the back of his seat as the sea of bodies rushes past us while we gain speed.

"Hold on." He laughs madly, ignoring my screaming mere inches from his head.

My stomach rockets into my throat as we dip down, hurtling into the dark depths below. Just as I'm about to lose my breakfast, the platform comes to a screeching halt, bringing me to my knees.

"Aha! Here we are!" Briseathe sings from his seat.

I have to yank myself up using the back of his chair. My legs are like noodles, shaking and unsteady as I try to keep myself upright. "Are you insane?!" I try to yell but my voice comes out hoarse.

He rolls his eyes, ignoring me and instead pointing straight in front of us. I glance up, gasping. It's his old body, hanging in a sphere of pale green light. He has a perfectly sculpted body and a shock of blonde hair, like in the picture. I feel a lick of heat roll up my neck at the stark nakedness. I'm no stranger to it, but it's an odd sensation when you're standing next to the person and staring at their naked clone.

"That's…nice." I try to clear my throat while averting my eyes. He doesn't seem to notice or care I'm in front of his former self, naked.

"Whenever I feel nostalgic, I can go back to my roots. I've done it a few times, but I always end up wanting to be something different for the next time." He shrugs. "I guess I am a wandering soul, forever cursed to change bodies. I tried a girl once," he spits his tongue out, "not for me. Too much going on in the plumbing system, if you get my drift."

I shoot him a bemused look. I suppose if I could hop between bodies, I'd try the same out of pure curiosity.

My gaze settles on a body next to his old one. This one is tan as well, but it has a thicker torso and dark black hair. I step closer, eager to see what his other creation looked like. I eye it, feeling like I've seen it before.

"What is this?" My tone borders on horror as it clicks in my mind that I have seen this body before.

"Oh, that. I was wondering when you were going to see that." He giggles, "That's Athos's genetic body."

I turn my face slowly to him. "Why do you have Athos's body?"

He leans closer and whispers, "That's pure, one hundred percent what he looks like under all those clothes." He wiggles his brows in such a way that I can't tell if he's joking, or he knows I've seen it before. "To freak the others out. I've done it before, it's so much fun! I have a few of the others for when I get bored."

"Do they have the same abilities?" I ask.

He smirks. "No, I took all of those out. They only look like them."

"You really have been in this cave for too long," I mutter. "Also, you're missing a mole on his left hip." He laughs, and the pod shoots off again back to the lab.

We find Athos back in thesea-levell room, watching the news.

136

"You know he likes to impersonate people, right?" I ask, crossing my arms.

"Oh, that." Athos grins, "He tried that on me once, running around in my body. It wasn't the smartest thing to do, trying to piss off Mathis. He ended up changing the body's molecules into dirt."

"That would have never worked on the real you, and he knew that! He knew it was me, and just wanted to mess up my clone." Briseathe huffs.

Athos's eyes glimmer as he smirks. "Regardless, it didn't last very long."

Briseathe rolls his eyes, "Whatever. Lillium, it was such a thrill to have Athos finally bring a girl home! I loved meeting you, and I hope you will come back."

"Home? You live here too?" I ask Athos.

"Every now and then, you know siblings. They love to crash at your place when they are bored!" My mouth pops open in shock. I look from Briseathe to Athos, my brain automatically trying to see the similarities but then freezing when I remember this isn't his original body.

"Oh, she didn't know." Briseathe gives Athos a reproachful look, shaking his head..

"Alright, time to go." Athos is up and by my side in a matter of seconds, ushering me out of the room. Briseathe waves energetically as we leave.

My shock wears off as soon as we are in the cave. "Lillium, as much as I enjoy delving into Supe history, I think it is time for us to get back to work." He says, hurrying me towards the cave opening.

"He's your *brother*!?" I cry out, my voice echoing in the cave.

"Too much for one day?" He gives me his sly smile, and I try hard not to focus on his dimples.

"You think?" I shove my headpiece on and take hold of him, thankful that I will soon have a few minutes of silence to digest everything.

When we land in his front yard, I see immediately that he's added a ton of newly raised garden beds. I suspect Korra's unkempt jungle has inspired him. I have many questions still floating around my mind, but mostly I'm tired. Before I even think to say anything, Athos tells me to stay silent.

I bristle, but the moment I see the look on his face all fight leaves my body.

His features are strained and his body is rigid. If I didn't know any better, I would think he's afraid.

He walks past me and slowly enters his house, gesturing for me to follow behind him. As we enter the house, I can only think of one thing that would put him on edge. Sure enough, once we get into the foyer, we come across two men. One is none other than Mathis, Mr. Hot and Popular himself. The other is someone I'd never seen before.

"Mathis. Harold." Athos greets them, coolly.

Harold? What kind of Supe name was that? Mathis smiles warmly at us, making his perfectly pale features brighten, and suddenly I can understand how my sex would swoon at the sight of him. Harold, on the other hand, is staring at us stoically with the most unpleasant look on his face.

I look over the three Supes and wonder how the hell the Source got so many types of people together. Mathis is so pale I can see the tiny blue veins running along his arms. Harold's much taller than the others, with bright blue eyes and an umber complexion. These guys are easily thousands of years old and somehow have managed to mix cultures before anyone else. On a secluded island, no less.

"It's good to see you, Athos," Harold says, his voice like soft silk, deep and comforting. Even though he looks bemused, and down right imposing, I can see how his eyes soften when they land on Athos. Maybe he's a nice guy. Deep down.

"Yes, you've been away too long." Mathis nods. I know his voice from the many interviews he'd given; forced to sound husky and masculine. His looks have always been lost on me since I have had the distinct impression he's acting all the time. Apparently, I've been right as even now, with two other Supes around, he's putting on an act.

Athos remains silent, but I can tell he's trying to figure out what they want. Finally, he says flatly, "What do you want?" Mathis's golden eyes slide to Harold momentarily. "Sheiba already expressed concerns. I don't see why everyone should show up at my home to tell me their feelings."

Harold's hearty laugh startles me. He breaks out in a wide genuine grin, "This is all ridiculous, I agree." He drops the mask of bemusement and suddenly becomes the warmest person in the room as his entire body relaxes.

"Harold." Mathis's tone changes, warning.

"Oh, shut up. Do we really care what he does? He's not subject to any of us. No one is." Harold glares back.

Mathis turns his gaze to me then, stunning me with its intensity. His cross-like pupils narrow to small slits of black, giving me the impression of a great feline.

Athos sidesteps partly in front of me. "If you have nothing of importance to say, I would like to get back to work."

"We have a lot to do today." I agree from behind him. It isn't a lie at all. We do since Athos decided to go off and frolic with Briseathe over the weekend.

Mathis looks us over slowly before rising. He makes his way over to a bookshelf with little crystals and rocks. He plucks a red rock from the shelf and palms it.

"I do not have a problem with you fucking a human, Athos. I'm more worried about what you and," he glances up to me, eyes roaming over my suit, "*she* are planning."

"That is none of your concern," Athos growls, but I'm unsure what he's referring to. The fucking or the planning?

"Who cares?" Harold scoffs, "Briseathe has been gone for a long ass time, and he'll come back when he wants. Athos isn't going to drag him out to us, and she has no effect!" I try to keep my face neutral when he mentions Briseathe. I consider acting dumb and pretending not to know anything about Briseathe, but the look Athos has tells me otherwise.

"She might," Mathis says softly. The rock in his palm changes. It floats up and changes into a dark brown mass, particles of it drift back down to his hand. He's changed it from a solid rock into dirt. "She could influence him. He's different, after all." The dirt sucks back into itself and changes into a bright silver ball.

"I'm allowed to make my own choices," Athos says as the silver ball transforms into a bright blue feather.

Mathis drops the feather back onto the shelf. "He is." He turns to us, freezing me with his icy expression, "But we don't want a human transforming our future."

"I don't want Supes controlling mine." I snap back, earning a laugh from Harold, who approaches us and gives me a soft slap on the back.

"She's fun. You'll do alright." He pats my shoulder, causing Mathis to look annoyed. "Come on, you've said what you wanted." Harold gives Athos a meaningful look.

Mathis passes by me, his feline expression locking with my eyes, and smiles. But it isn't the usual heart-melting smile he uses in interviews. It's cold and calculated.

I watch from the window as Harold takes Mathis by the arm, and they vanish.

"He teleports." I breathe, impressed.

"He needs to mind his own damn business." Athos intones.

Again, I wonder about my safety when it comes to his people. Will they truly end up on my doorstep and threaten me? What can I do about it? Nothing really, outside of running crying to Athos.

"Do not worry about them." Athos says, reading my face, "They want to come off threatening, but my people do not believe in violence. In our homeland, it was very much frowned upon and our morals from there have followed us since."

"Well, that is comforting," I say, smirking. I plop onto the couch with a sigh, completely drained. I barely glance at my wristpad to see a few messages, then jump up suddenly when I come across one. From my mother.

Athos takes a seat in the other chair, eyeing me. I know why she's suddenly reaching out to me after so many years. "My cousin, Candice, is having a birthday party tomorrow. I think I might go."

"That's nice. Do you want me to go with you?" He asks.

I shake my head. "It's complicated. I wasn't going to go at all, but now, I don't know."

"What changed?" He quirks a brow.

"You." I look up at him. "My uncle is very wealthy. Each year he throws a huge party for her and all his high-profile friends come."

Athos laughs, "I am sure they would be a big help in getting our business known."

"Yes. It would mean national coverage. They come from all over the world to see him." I bite my lip. "There is just one problem."

Athos stretches out his arms with a yawn. "What is that?"

"My mother is his wife."

Chapter 18

Despite my uncle being my dad's twin, our two families are never very close. My uncle is the head of one of the largest companies to work with Supes in clean-up projects, and it has made him very wealthy. My aunt is equally wealthy when they marry, and much like my uncle, she lets it run her life.

"Money holds no power over me," my dad says at the few family functions we have with them. His brother laughs and continues to berate him for not going into business with him. Growing up, I learn to tolerate them, until my aunt dies and my mother leaves my family to marry my uncle.

"I had always known her to be selfish," I explain while searching my closet for something to pack. "I had even accepted it in my teenage years. That's who she was. There's no changing it. Then she went and left my dad for his rich brother- that I couldn't understand. The worst part is how tone-deaf she is."

Our relationship has always been strained, full of personality differences marked by our basic morals. The difference is that I have some, and she doesn't.

"You mean how she invites you to your cousin's birthday party?" Athos asks from my desk. He's fidgeting with my journals and travel pad while I frantically search through my clothes.

"Yes!" He's been listening to me since yesterday talk about her, and I have to admit it feels superb to have someone to talk to again. Libby and Max know all about it. They have been here for it, but they, like Dad, have their own opinions. "It's been two years, and each year I get invited to her birthday, but do you think she comes up here for mine? No!" I toss a shirt in my bag angrily. "She hasn't even invited me to come down there for it. I get a card, that is all."

Athos busies himself with a piece of paper, folding it over. "So, you don't speak to her then?"

"No, my dad does now and then. I refuse to." My dad has been angry, of course, but unlike me, he's able to move on. I refuse to let her off so easily.

"He's going with you, right?" Athos eyes my bag uneasily and I realize he's worrying about how I will react when I get there. I don't blame him. He watched me lock down an entire storm in a fit of rage.

"No, he's working. It will be the first time I have seen any of them since she left." I smirk, "Don't worry, I won't overreact."

"I still think I should go, for moral support." He gives me his sly grin. "Besides, shouldn't I be meeting your family?" He wiggles his brows and I frown.

"Yeah, no. You, sir, took a long enough break from work. You need to catch up." I wag my finger at him. "Also, Candice would take all the credit for having a Supe at her party, and I cannot have that," I grumble."

He holds a hand over his heart, feigning hurt. "You mean you don't want them to know we've slept together? But wouldn't that be a nice jab at them? Look at me mom, I fucked a Super." He grins at my glare.

"I thought we agreed to never bring that up," I say.

He raises his brows. "We said no flirting. It was a one-time thing, never to happen again, according to you. You never said I couldn't bring it up."

"It was implied," I snap, rubbing my temples.

"Oh, well then I need to imply to a few people I was joking," he muses. My head shoots up as my pulse spikes. My wristpad blares a warning - calm down or face another attack.

"Oh shit," Athos is by my side in the blink of an eye. "I was only kidding, Lily." He places a hand on my shoulder, his amber eyes full of concern.

I shrug him off. "I'm fine." I breathe.

"No, you're not." He grumbles, taking my hand and placing it over his chest. "Just breathe. I promise I won't joke about it again."

My eyes flutter to meet his. He sees the doubt there and I watch as his face crumples a bit.

"I'm sorry. It was a terrible joke and in poor taste. I understand why you don't want anyone to know, and I promise I won't be the one to tell." He's smiling, but it's not reaching his eyes. I can see the hurt there - does he understand? Or does he think I'm embarrassed? We never speak about it, but it's there, this overhanging thing that sucks the air out of the room sometimes when silence falls between us.

We should talk about it, but I keep trying to ignore it. I bury it, deep down with the rest of the bullshit that clouds my mind.

"Lily, are you sure you want to do this alone?" he asks. I realize my wristpad isn't blaring a warning anymore. The anxiety attack has been avoided, for now.

"Yes," I breathe, withdrawing my hand from his chest. "It's unpleasant, but I've dealt with my family's particular brand of unpleasant my whole life. This, I can deal with." I say, my tone firm. I know I can do this.

"As hard as it is to believe, I understand how you feel," He says, surprising me. "When I came back and found that everything had changed, including my people, I felt very betrayed. I still do...." for a moment he slips into statue mode, then says, "I know you are going because there are many people there who can spread the word about me, but Lily, if you start to feel like it is not worth it, leave." He pats my shoulder. "Don't be nervous. Remember who you are and what you have done, and you will see that no matter what, you are in control."

"Is that what you tell yourself?" I ask, forcing a smile.

"Always," he grins back. He leaves shortly after so I can finish packing, but his absence is more noticeable than I care to admit.

He's right, though, I'm nervous, and it only gets worse when I get to the station in Rio. I swore never to talk to my mother again after she left and here I am, going to celebrate my cousin's birthday. Or step-sister cousin. Whatever, the dynamic is weird.

It's for Athos, I tell myself again and again as I pick my way through the streets. I can just as easily not go, and in time we will get the coverage we needed. Korra's cast helped us, but people are attending the party that can

144

spread the word faster and more in areas that we need. It will be worth it, I hope.

My uncle lives in the only gaudy home in the city, a huge mansion atop a hill complete with fountains and pillars galore. I seriously doubt he has been in every room. I'm sure there are areas he has never laid eyes on before.

My heart's racing as I approach the front door, sliding my invitation into the key slot until it dings and opens.

"Welcome, Lillium Jones." The door announces. I slip in quickly, ready to get this over with. I notice that the inside is much the same as I remember, with perhaps a few more items added to the vast walls.

"Lillium?" A bloated version of my dad appears from one of the rooms. "We didn't think you were coming!" My uncle ropes me into a hug as I struggle to think of something to say.

Did you gain a few pounds? Thank you for destroying my life?

"Your mom is going to be so happy to see you!" I flinch and pull away with a strained smile.

"I am only staying the night-"

He ignores me. "Did you bring your Super along?" I lose the smile and shake my head. Well, that was quick, and right to the point. I'm not surprised, but damn, it still stings being so easily overlooked.

"He is busy." I deadpan.

My uncle shakes his head sadly, his jowls swaying with the motion. "Really? She's going to be so disappointed!"

My mom. Of course, she will be. That's the only reason she wants me here, after all, further proving my point I was right not to bring him. "Hm, so sorry to upset her. Which room is mine?" I ask, forcing a nonchalant smile.

By the way he's staring off behind my head, I know he hasn't heard a word I said. "Ah, once she heard about you two, she got so excited! You know, we have never met one, which has always annoyed me. I know the right people, you know."

"A pity. Which room is mine?" I ask again. We've played this game my entire life, and eventually, he will hear me.

"The usual one." My heart stops at my mom's voice. She's standing at the top of the stairs, smiling down at us. She looks just like she did when she walked out on us, sans the expensive rocks around her neck and designer dress.

I can't help the way my lips dip into a sneer as my blood begins to pound in my ears. So, she's acting like nothing has happened still; like we are all friends here. I don't think so. All my feelings from the past two years rush to me at that moment, and I want to fall into a rage.

"You look so grown up Lillium! You finally lost all your baby fat." She and my uncle share a laugh and my vision goes red. "Where is your friend, Athos?" She asks as she comes down to us.

I instantly see him in my mind back home, telling me to keep calm. *That's right,* I think, *stay calm. This is all for a better cause.* His lazy smile flickers in my vision as she comes up to me and I feel steel run down my back. No matter what happens, or has happened, I will come out of this on top with him.

"Working," I say, trying to sound nonplussed.

She shakes her head. "When I heard about you two, I did not believe it. I told my friends you would have said something to me!" She laughs her fake laugh. I hold back my response, giving her a blank look.

"It is so good to see my little girl!" She wraps her arms around me gingerly, as if she's debating to or not. I awkwardly pat her back.

"He is welcome anytime, of course." My uncle says, "You should bring him over for the holidays! How does that sound, love?"

My mother laughs, "Oh, that sounds perfect! We will have everyone over to meet him. Doesn't that sound fun?"

"Yeah. I think I am going to go get ready if you don't mind." I slip past them as they continue to talk. Two steps away and I am already forgotten as they begin to make fantasy plans for Athos.

The worst-case scenario will be me burning the place to the ground, so I'm doing pretty well. They are the same people they have always been, self-absorbed and tone-deaf. *Don't fool yourself into expecting a heartwarming welcome*, I think. I'd be lying though if I say I'm not hoping, deep down, to have some sort of closure. *That's Athos talking!* I shake my head. We've spent so much time together lately that he'd in my head. Who would have thought?

Every year, they use the acres of gardens they own to hold my cousin's party and accommodate the number of guests they have. She probably knows about a quarter of them herself. The rest are here to network like I am. I throw my things in the room I always stay in and pull out my pad to find the list of people I want to talk to tonight. There will be a few who work for businesses overseas that can use Athos's help and just one job with them will solidify our brand there. But before I find it, I notice a message from Athos.

No smacking anyone tonight, it reads. I burst into laughter, surprising myself.

"No promises," I whisper to myself.

I throw on my dress and head down to the gardens where a large group of guests have already converged. I scan the faces, trying to see if I recognize anyone from my list, but have no luck. If I get desperate enough, I can ask my uncle to introduce me, I think, eyeing the tables of food. Deciding to grab a plate, I read the plaques carefully as my uncle loves to import real meat to feed to his guests.

"You still won't try an animal?" I cringe inwardly at the unmistakable voice of my cousin. It's been too much to hope I can avoid her all night.

"I still don't see the point in it," I respond lightly without looking at her.

Her voice changes instantly from the light, airy tone she forces to her real one. "Well, I don't see the point in working with a Super and not bringing them to a party full of potential customers."

Empty plate in hand, I turn to see her in all her party glory, a perky brow raised. "You changed your face," I reply dryly, noting the new nose and higher cheekbones.

She purses her pouty lip. "You didn't bring him to spite me. You only want to ruin my day, like all the other times."

Distinct memories flash before me- the year I kicked her into the bushes,

147

only for her to come crawling back out, her hair full of leaves and an empty bird nest. Then the year I threw cake in her face for calling my dad a loser. That had been a fun year. She must be thinking the same thing as she suddenly takes a step back, eyeing me.

"Some people have to work." I spoon some food on my plate, keeping my eyes on her.

She scoffs. "This is just like you Lillium, you are so, so….MEAN!" I roll my eyes. "You ignore us for two years and suddenly pop up here? Why? To gloat?"

"Don't flatter yourself. I really couldn't care any less what you think. It just happens that your dad's well-connected, that is all." I continue to move down the table, hoping she'll give up soon. She sure knows how to push my buttons and I don't want to start the night off like this.

"I see." She leans up against the table with a rueful look. "All it takes to bring you out of hiding is the possibility of becoming famous." My hand freezes mid-spooning. "I must admit Lillium, you hide it well."

She's baiting me. I know this. She knows this. Still, I can't help the venom in my tone as I ask, "Hide what?"

Her lips turn into a sneer. "How much like your mother you are." My face burns with indignation as she continues, "I just assumed she got bored with you guys, but now that I see you like this, I know it's not that. She cares about money and fame, just like you."

In another world, we could have been close. We would have bonded over the joint betrayal we felt from our parents. Her mother was barely cold when mine snuck into her father's bed. She hates my mom. She doesn't hide it, but her father is the shield against her rage. So instead of becoming allies against them, she's picked me as her enemy, since I have no one to shield me.

In a flash, I drop my plate and spin to face her, seeing the fear register in her eyes, but the quirk on her lips makes me stop cold. This is what she wants, but is it worth it?

I think of Athos and how much faith he's put in me in such a short time. From bringing me to Briseathe and confessing his people's most precious secrets to the hopes it will bring us closer as partners. No, at this moment, throwing Candice into her birthday cake is not worth it if it means I can lose the potential customers we need.

"I guess the casserole is a no?" A man laughs as he comes between us. Candice's expression softens instantly, her features melting into the sweet, girly facade she puts on for the public.

"Brogan! I thought you couldn't make it tonight?" She says, her voice pitched.

"Well, I felt so bad, thinking of you dancing all by yourself that I had to come." He winks at her, and she swoons. She physically swoons in front of him. I decide to use the distraction to make my escape.

"Is this your cousin?" He asks suddenly, stopping me in my tracks. "You're the one who works with Supers, right?" I turn to face him, forcing myself to meet his eyes and see his face fully. He's strikingly handsome. I get Candice's swooning - he'd be my first pick if we met in a bar. Blonde, curly hair frames his high cheekbones, and he towers over us both in his slim-fitting suit.

"Just Athos," I reply, eyeing his suit and fighting the urge to imagine it off him.

He quirks a brow, a slow smile playing on his lips. "How did that happen?"

"I locked him in my store," I say without missing a beat. His brows shoot up in surprise, then he bursts out laughing.

"Lillium has always been a bit of a detergent," Candice chimes, earning looks from both of us. "She used to throw me into the ponds and bushes when we were little."

The silence that ensues stretches for a moment, causing her smile to falter.

"You mean degenerate," I say slowly.

"Are you sure you're not a laundry soap?" Brogan asks, smirking.

I give him my best smile and say, "Throw some water on me and find out." I hear Candice's scoff of indignation but I ignore her - Brogan's honey-colored eyes are turning molten gold and I suddenly feel like I'm playing with fire.

"I suppose you are here to network?" He asks, still holding my gaze. I nod. "Good. Who is it you want to be introduced to?" I blink in surprise. Is he offering to help me? Who is this guy?

Candice steps forward, nearly coming between us. I can see her cheeks turning pink as she stutters, "Brogan, don't you want to talk to Daddy first?"

"No." He sidesteps her and saunters over to me, smoothing his blonde curls back. Now it's my turn to swoon. "I work for your uncle," he explains, "So anyone on your list I know. Would you like me to help?"

The cautious side of me questions his motives, which is probably because I know a Supe. But the look on my cousin's face is priceless, and I'm not about to give up the opportunity to annoy her and get to meet these people in the process.

So I break out in a genuine smile and dip my chin, letting him take my arm and lead me away from her. I don't look back; I don't need to, I can hear Candice throwing a fit as we walk away.

"So you work for my uncle?" I ask as he leads me further into the gardens. He nods. "Yes, for a few years now."

"I should let you know Athos isn't coming tonight, if that is what you are after," I say, quirking a brow. "Better you know now than in an hour and feel you wasted your time."

He chuckles. "I don't care to meet him. I felt like I should take you away from Candice before something happened."

I laugh. "Was it that obvious?"

"You looked very scary. I would have been afraid if I were her," he throws me a wide grin. "I also didn't want to get stuck with her all night, so I am really helping myself out in the end."

My mouth pops open, shocked by his honesty. Most people suck up to my uncle, which means they suck up to his family just for the chance of working with him. "How selfish," I say cautiously, unsure why this stranger would confide in me so quickly.

"Who is first?" He asks, motioning to the grand expanse of garden before us littered with humans dressed in their finest.

It doesn't take long for word to get around that I am the one working with a Supe, and pretty quickly I don't need Brogan to help me pick out the people I want to speak with. They end up coming to me. However, he stays with me for the next few hours, introducing me to whoever comes over and even offering his opinions on people who can help. Working for my uncle has given him a vast range of connections, and I soon realized he is the person to be with if I want to stay connected.

I can't believe my luck, that this guy just appears out of nowhere and has all the ins that I need. I barely even have to talk, which is great since I am nowhere near as good at it as Athos is. Brogan gives me advice on how to talk to some of them, or who to trust, and though I remain guarded, I take his advice to heart.

"How do you know so much?" Night has fallen by this point and I'm sure we have found everyone on my list and then some. "I am tempted to ask Athos to hire you." I laugh, half joking. His connections and skills will be beneficial in the long run.

He shrugs, running his hand through his hair. "I have always been able to read people."

"I wish I could. That would make things so much easier." I muse.

He raises a brow. "You can, I have seen you."

I give him a questioning look. "Not sure when you've seen that, but I doubt it's the same. It's almost as if you can read their minds." I laugh and point toward the last person we spoke to at another table. "I would have never guessed that she was already trying to set up a business like ours. You knew all about it!"

Brogan smirks, "When you have been in my position for as long as I have been, you find things out."

"I can't believe you work for my uncle! You could get a job with another company so easily!"

He sighs. "I have worked for all the companies. I stayed with your uncle because the work isn't as tedious."

"All of them, huh? How old are you? You can't be too much older than I am. When did you start, when you were ten?" I laugh.

He smiles slyly and says nothing. I say something, but stop when I notice my mother and cousin standing close by. I nearly forgot about them since

Brogan came into the picture.

My smile fades as I watch my mother hug Candice and kiss her forehead before walking her over to a group of people. She says something that makes them all applaud my cousin. I find my heart sinking at the sight and a long-forgotten feeling comes up that I've tried for the past two years to hide.

"They deserve each other." I snap back to reality and blink at him as he says, "Your mom and cousin deserve each other. Two of the most self-absorbed people if I have ever seen one."

"Yet you come to her party." I tease, forcing my feelings back down into that dark, deep void in the pitch of my chest. I can already feel my pulse beating erratically and I pray my wristpad doesn't start blaring an alert soon.

"I came to meet you." My heart leaps in my throat, and my face burns with embarrassment.

"What? I didn't even know I was coming until yesterday." I laugh, confused.

"I took my chances." He pins with his honey eyes and I feel my legs go weak beneath his gaze. If he's hitting on me, I am powerless to resist him.

"Now why would you do that?" I ask, my voice husky.

Brogan only smiles, and it's then that I notice his eyes are just the perfect shade of honey. Almost too perfect. I lean in closer and see the telltale line of pigments, the same Athos used at the bar. Since his little revelation, I've been more keen about people's eyes.

My blood runs cold and I feel my pulse spike just as my wristpad beeps a warning. "You're a Supe." I croak, my throat suddenly dry.

He rests his chin on his hands and nods. "I am."

"Are you here to threaten me like the others?" I spit. "Do you all like to wear false eyes to fit in?"

"No, Lillium, not at all." He dares to appear hurt that I would suggest such a thing.

"Then Athos sent you!" I scoff.

"He doesn't know either." He laughs. "Believe it or not, I came here just

152

to meet you. Nothing else."

I don't believe him. This is exactly like the bar with Athos - Brogan tried to appear like a human, so I would let my guard down. He was fucking with me. My wristpad blares the warning now as I hear the blood rushing in my ears. My breaths come quick and shallow as I struggle to remember to breathe.

"Shit," Brogan reaches out to me, but I pull away.

"You're all the same," I gasp out as I fumble with my wristpad. I hit the side button and a pill pocket slips out, holding an anti-anxiety dose. I shove it in my mouth, dry swallowing quickly.

"Please don't feel like I have lied to you. That wasn't my intention. I only wanted to see the kind of person you were," He says quickly. "I was curious what kind of person it took for the famous Athos to crumble and break all protocol. You know, in all our history, he's never confined to a human?"

"You could have just read my mind. Or asked." I grumble, trying to block any thoughts out that I don't want him to see as I focus on my breathing. It feels like mental gymnastics.

"Oh, I can't read minds." I look at him in shock. "Well, not always, I should say. Mostly I get impressions from people. They aren't clear thoughts, but I have learned to understand them. Other times I barely get those, just basic feelings. Like right now, for instance, you have a powerful feeling of betrayal underlined with anger and it's giving you a lot of anxiety."

"No shit," I snap. So he can't read my mind. At least that's good. I don't have to worry about not thinking about Briseathe around him.

"But you can sometimes?" I ask.

"Some people, like your cousin and mother over there, give out clear thoughts and intentions. All the time. It comes down to how open a person is. You, for example, are very closed off normally, so I cannot get into your mind. They are desperate for people to see them, so they are open to my abilities." He explains.

"Which would be?"

"Mind control." He says.

My jaw nearly drops. He can control people?

"You can make people do what you want?" I ask, dumbstruck.

"Some, if I want to." He laughs nonchalantly. "It's a very boring ability. But it comes in handy with work. Not that I control people by any means. That takes a lot of effort that I don't care to put in these days. I mean the being able to judge people and their intentions." He says quickly. He looks a bit flustered as I weigh my options.

"I guess it would be useful," I say carefully.

"I didn't mean to con you, Lillium. I just wanted to see for myself why Athos chose to work with you."

"I keep hearing that from you guys," I grumble, unconvinced.

He chuckles. "I wouldn't know about that. I am one of the few who stays in the shadows, away from my kind." I raise a brow. So there are Supes who prefer to stay unknown? It makes sense. Harold didn't strike me as the camera-loving type, and neither did Brogan.

"Then why care about us?" I ask.

"The last time I saw Athos, he was trying to get us to rally together and intervene in your war. He felt like humans were on the brink of destroying everything. I find it interesting he's working with one now." He waits for my response, but I give him none. I'm still uncertain about his motives, and Briseathe did warn me the others were hellbent on finding him.

"Curious to know my verdict?" He asks.

"Not really." I shrug.

"Thought so." He nods with an air of approval that irks me.

"Thank you for helping me," I say, ready to take my leave.

"Anytime. Like I said, I prefer it to having to hang around her." He nods to Candice.

"She has no idea who you are, does she?" I smirk.

"No one does," he winks. "Our little secret." I blush despite myself. Then I mentally slap myself as I realize he probably knows what I'm feeling at the moment.

"I will say she is very jealous of you right now." He says in a conspiring tone as he throws me a mischievous smile. If he thinks talking shit about my cousin will get me to hang around a little longer, then he's entirely correct.

"Good." I laugh dryly.

"Try not to slap her." I turn to him, confused, until I notice she is walking our way.

I may not be a mind reader but I can see the intent clear on her face. She is ready to push my buttons again.

"Dance with me," Brogan whispers in my ear, taking my hand. We stand up swiftly and move before she reaches the table. I see the rage register in her eyes before he leads me over to a dance floor. He stops in front of me, waiting.

"I probably should have said I don't know how to dance," I say awkwardly. He raises a brow, then bursts out laughing. "It's not that funny." I sigh.

"No, no, it was just unexpected." He takes my hand and places his free one behind my back. "You see, Athos loves to dance. I just assumed you two had."

"It's not like that." I roll my eyes.

He gives me a sly smile. "Interesting. Just focus on my eyes." I look up and catch his gaze. Even with the pigments, they are intense, and I almost look away as I feel the heat rise to my face.

Get a grip! He's just a guy! You hang around Athos all day and he looks just as good as this one! Oh great, now I'm thinking about Athos's good looks too.

"Just relax and focus on my eyes." His voice is warm and mellow. I take a breath and clear my thoughts of everything but his eyes. Soon I find my feet moving, but I don't look down, I don't think about it.

I vaguely wonder if they are his real eye color. It's such a nice shade of honey. Pale, but bright. They are like deep pools, and the longer I stare into them, the less I notice around me. Right up until we stop moving and he lets me go. I blink a few times, jolting myself back into my body as I realize people are clapping.

I gaze around us to see we are the only ones left on the floor, and everyone is staring at us, including my cousin and mother. My mother's clapping along with everyone else, but my cousin has a murderous look in her eyes. I might not have shoved her into a bush, or smashed her face with cake this year, but I still upstaged her.

"Uh, what?" I stammer.

"You dance just fine." Brogan takes my hand and gives everyone a wave before leading us back to the table. I pass by a few people who praise me, oddly enough.

"Brogan, what happened?" I ask, feeling on edge with all the sudden attention.

"You danced." He says softly, looking down at me with a look of pride.

"You mind-controlled me, you mean?" I snap.

"No, not at all." He laughs. "I only threw a suggestion at you, and since you were focused on my eyes, you did it. If it was something you truly did not want to do, we would still be standing there."

"I have no memory of it," I say.

"Don't worry, I am sure your cousin will tell you all about it." I have just enough time to see her storming over from behind him before I sit down.

"If you are done, Lillium, I would like to take Brogan to *my* table to see my father on *my* birthday." A million retorts flash through my mind, but I know none will be as good as this moment is. There my cousin is, totally flustered and annoyed while my mother stands off to the side waving over at me to come sit with them.

I get the closure I want, though it might not be in words or as nice as I hope. I don't need them to say anything or do anything to make me feel better. Athos is right, I am doing just fine where I am, and I have him and my work to go back to.

"I am sure Brogan will be thrilled to spend some time with you," I say as I get up. He gives me a questioning look, clearly not understanding my vibes if he's reading them. "I hope you have a great night, but I need to get back to Athos." I lean over, take his face in my hands, and kiss him. Right in front of her and everyone who is watching.

"You know how to get a hold of me," I say huskily as I stand up. Brogan breaks out into a silly grin as my cousin nearly faints.

"Send Athos my regards," Brogan calls, laughing as I walk away to gather my things. I've gotten what I came for. There's nothing else for me here now.

Chapter 19

I feel a light tap on my nose, and then the familiar scent of sugary citrus fills my senses. "Wake up, gorgeous!" I shoot straight up in a panic.

"Gaia!?" I croak, half asleep.

"Wake up. It's almost noon." she tusks haughtily. "I took a flight, and a train all day just to come see your lovely bones sleeping?"

"Wha-, what are you doing here?" Panic tinges my voice as I realize she's here, in my home, and the only person I haven't told about Athos. I meant to tell her after my dad found out, but then we got so busy that I kept putting it off. *This is bad,* I think. *If anyone lets it slip before I do, she's going to be livid!*

She tosses herself over my bed, laughing, "I am going to spend Rapport with you!"

"Both weeks?" I cough. Images of her glaring daggers at Athos over dinner fill my head. Then those daggers become real as she plunges them into his chest. *Shit.*

"Yes! My parents were going on tour, and I didn't want to. Besides, I haven't been home for over a year, so two weeks here with you and Libby and Max sounds amazing!" *Crap,* I think, *there would be no way around this then.* I have been able to get away with keeping her in the dark for far too long. It's time to pay for it now.

Gaia cocks her head to the side, her brows furrowed. "I had thought you would be happy to see me." She says, looking confused.

"Of course I am!" I throw my arms around her, pulling her to me so fast she squeals. I have to tell her. She's come all this way to spend the holiday with me, and besides that, Athos was also spending the holidays with me. I

157

can't keep them separate forever.

I squeeze her harder, breathing in the familiar smell of her lavender and basil shampoo. She's my best friend - she's always been my best friend. I need to trust her to understand.

"With thanks and love," Gaia slips out of my iron grasp, pushing a parchment into my lap.

"You know you are lucky that I procrastinate and haven't mailed your gift, right?" I laugh.

"Naturally." She dips her chin. "That's why I came today. I know you."

A few knick-knacks fall out of the parchment as I unravel a shirt. I my blood runs cold when I recognize the backward S as the logo for Supitude, the notorious anti-Supe cult. "Where did you get this?" I ask dryly.

"At one of their meetings, of course," she laughs, "What? You don't like it?"

"You did what?" I ask incredulously. My fears of her understanding dry up instantly. If she's going to any of their meetings, she's bound to be sympathetic to their ideals, which are very anti-Supe.

"Oh, don't go getting all paranoid Lillium, I only went to see what they were doing. It isn't like I have much else to do." She's being very flippant, which only means she's lying to me. She begins to tap at her fingers, telling me she's nervous, and I realize she expected this to go a different way.

"You are lying," I say flatly.

She stops her fidgeting and frowns. "Lillium, so what if I went to one of their meetings? It's not like I joined them or anything! I was not interested in what they had to say. The truth is, I am bored with what I do." She throws herself next to me and lets out a dramatic sigh that could rival Briseathe's. "I need a change."

I swallow back my frustration. If anyone understands the need for change, I sure do. "I thought you loved the organization?" I ask.

She shrugs, twirling a lock of her hair around a finger. "I do, but there is only so much I can do. I feel like I can do more, but they have their limits."

I blow out a breath. All these years apart must have made us terrible communicators. We feel the same way - the need to do something, to add something to society, but powerless to do so.

"I worry about you, is all," I say finally, getting up to find her gift.

"With thanks and love." I press the small box to her stomach. She opens it and laughs when she finds the Cat's eye.

"A client told me it was good luck. So far, it seems to have given me some, and I thought you could use it." I take a deep breath. I can either tell her now or let her find out when Athos appears for dinner. "Gaia, there is something I have to tell you-"

"I thought I heard you!" We both jump in surprise as my dad comes in and takes her up in a hug. "I was wondering when you were going to grace us with your presence," he laughs.

"I hit up all the other important people and thought I'd give you a try," she says as he lets her go.

"Are you staying long?" Dad asks.

"Both weeks," Gaia says, beaming.

Dad looks pleased. "Long enough for you to tell us all about your adventures!"

She scrunches up her face, "Oh yeah, cleaning up the aftermath of the War. It's been a dream come true."

"Well, you can relax with us now. We have nothing planned. I don't at least. Lillium here may be booked depending on Athos." My pulse quickens when he asks, "Have you met him yet?"

Gaia raises a brow, faking a shocked look. "Athos? No, is he a new man you're seeing?" She asks.

The world spins rapidly around me, rushing by as I slowly sink to the floor, my knees weak with fear, while they stare at me expectantly. Then I see my dad's brows rise as he realizes I haven't told Gaia yet.

"I am just going to check on, uh, the food. For this week." He shuffles out the door, leaving me on my floor, gaping up at Gaia.

"What?" Gaia asks, looking mildly concerned.

"I work with him," I say finally. She motions for me to tell her more, so I say, "Athos and I."

Her face falls. "So you did it? You filed with the state?"

"Well, that's the thing. I've been putting off telling you about him because it's kind of hard to explain. I also know what you are going to say, so please Gaia, just hear me out first." I plead.

"Goodness Lillium, just tell me!" She beams down at me, giving me hope that this will end better than I thought. At the very least, she's in a good mood.

"Gaia, Athos is a Super," I say it so fast I'm sure I have said it at all.

Her facial expression tightens with confusion, then she breaks into laughter. I let her go on, keeping my face deadpan as she realizes I'm not joking. Her laughter dies down, replaced with deep exhalations of breath as she struggles to say something.

Before she can find her words, I say, "I came up with this crazy idea to work together. I thought if we gave the people a different Supe to look up to, they might see how absurd the others were."

Her features turn blank, unreadable to me. I wait for her to react, my heart racing. After what seems like an eternity, she turns to look out the window and asks, "Is he coming here?"

"Yes. For dinner. Libby and Max haven't met him yet, so they will come by too." I say softly.

She maintains her steady stare out the window, unnerving me. Maybe she's in shock?

"I wish you had told me sooner." She says softly, almost sadly. Before I can respond, she turns back around, a smirk on her face, "I guess I would have thought the same thing and held off saying anything until I knew it would be worth it. For all you knew, it could have failed miserably and I would have had a blast throwing it back at your face for the rest of of lives." She laughs at my expression. "I know you too well." She isn't wrong. Even so, her words sting.

She rubs her fingers over the Cat's eye gem absentmindedly as she says, "Meeting a real Supe, I never thought it would happen. At least Libby and Max will be there if I find him boring." She flashes me one of her sunny smiles, trying to reassure me.

"So you are alright with meeting him?" She nods. "And you will not seek

160

some kind of revenge for me waiting this long to tell you?"

She rolls her eyes. "No Lillium, I understand why you waited and why you are doing it." She looks back at the window with an expression I'd never seen before. With a knowing tone, she says, "I will not fault or judge you for doing something I would do a thousand times over." A shiver runs up my spine as I look back at the shirt she gifted me. I had no choice now but to believe her when she said she'd be alright with Athos, but I knew better than to tell her I'd slept with him.

"You want to work with a Supe that bad, huh?" I joke as I get up to dress. "You might find him more bearable than I do."

"We will find out," she muses. "Does he know?"

I pause, a cold sweat running down my back. "No," I utter softly.

Gaia doesn't push the subject. I spend the afternoon telling her about my work with Athos while we wait for everyone to arrive.

Libby and Max come early to help my dad with the food while I finish with the small load of work I have. Gaia usually takes hours to get ready for anything, so when I'm done I go downstairs to find everyone watching the broadcasts for the seasonal awards given out to Supes.

"Who do you think will win the most this year?" Max asks from the kitchen.

"Probably Sheiba. She's been working in the big cities this year," I say.

"Yeah, but the small towns give out their own too, usually to the most popular Super who helped them this year," Libby says.

I shrug. "Sure, but they rarely report those, and none of the Supes go to receive their awards from the small towns. I suspect Sheiba will win New Hope, and it being so close to Legion will be the only one she goes to accept."

"You're on!" Max hollers just as I hear a knock at the door.

My heart speeds up as I lunge for the door before Libby can. At that moment, I realize how much I have been looking forward to seeing Athos again, despite what I've told Gaia. We haven't seen each other since after my cousin's birthday. He's been so swamped with jobs.

He's dressed more formally than his usual pants and shirt, and for the first time since meeting him, he's in modern clothes.

"Hello, Lily." He says, giving me his lazy grin.

"You look nice," I reply, letting him in. His scent hits me and I stomp down the memories that it stirs. *Not now, not tonight,* I think.

"I thought my closet needed an update. How have you been?" His amber eyes roam over my silver dress. Only now do I notice how tight and short it is and rethink my choice of clothes.

I squirm under his gaze - did a few days apart really make me forget that look he gives? "Fine, not as busy. How was Briseathe and his giant squid?"

"Talkative. He needs to get out more." He holds up a large bag. "I brought presents."

"Athos! You didn't need to!" I sputter, momentarily forgetting his heated gaze and how he smells.

He shrugs. "I have to make a good impression, no?" I shake my head.

"Don't worry about that. You will be fine. People love you." I mumble.

He leans over, smiling as he asks, "Jealous?"

"Hardly." I retort, but I can't seem to find the will to muster my usual venom.

He raises a brow but says, "A lot of it is from Briseathe anyway, some of his newer inventions that he wants you to try."

Before I can respond, I hear someone shouting. "WHY HELLO!" Libby cries out.

"Good to see you again, Libby." He says as she speeds over to him. She's practically drooling by the time she gets to him, causing me to groan.

"Libby!" I swat her hands away when she tries to touch his chest.

Ignoring me, she says, "Athos, you are in great shape! It's no wonder you can lift a car over your head." She gives him a dreamy look.

He chuckles as she continues to fawn over him. Max pops up on his other side, grasping his hand and shaking it vigorously. "I'm Max, it's great to meet you - well, formally anway. I don't count the hour we were stuck in the store together as 'official.'"

"Lillium has always been a bit dramatic," Libby says, throwing me a look.

"Max!" I snap finally, "Stop shaking his hand! And quit touching his hair,

Libby! Give him some space, you spazzes!" I push my way between them, causing Athos to laugh.

"It's alright Lily," he places his hand on my shoulder, "They are just excited. How about we sit down to eat and I can answer any questions you have? I smell something great."

"Oh, that would be my cooking," Libby says, biting her bottom lip.

"Her casserole is to die for," Max says, nodding as Athos takes Libby by the arm and leads them both back to the kitchen.

I hear my dad erupt in greetings as he hoists the gift bag over my shoulder. Just before I go to follow them, I notice Gaia sitting cross-legged, looking down from the banister. Once again, she has gone and changed her hair, but her eyes are her true color for the first time in years. She is staring after Athos and the others; her gaze is hard and cold and her face is stony. She doesn't see me notice her until I say, "Dinner should be ready."

She flicks her gaze at me momentarily before she gets up and walks back to my room.

"And now we begin." I sigh.

Athos hands out his gifts to everyone while we wait for Gaia to come down. He gets Libby and Max both autographs from Mathis and Sheiba, and my dad one of Briseathe's new personal pads. I am just about to hand him my gift when Gaia comes into the room.

To my shock and horror, she is wearing a silver version of the shirt she bought me. I know my face says it all, as she locks eyes with me just before everyone turns to see her. She smirks.

"Oh, Gaia..." Libby hesitates.

"Athos, this is Gaia." I say, mentally counting to ten in my head as I feel my pulse racing. My wristpad beeps, but I try to ignore it.

"Hello, Gaia." Athos holds out his hand to her. She raises a brow, but takes it.

"Hi." She smirks in a way that tells me she thinks he has no idea what the S is for. She might be right.

In one quick motion, Athos places a gift in her outstretched hand. "With thanks and love." he sings before setting the rest of the gifts on the table.

163

I slide over to her and hiss, "Be nice." She keeps her eyes on Athos, but her lips twitch in response. I grab my gift for Athos off the table and hand it to him, glancing at my wristpad to check my stats.

"Thank you." he smiles as he opens it. I watch his face freeze as he pulls the outfit out.

"It is a uniform." My father says in awe.

"Yes, I designed you an official uniform. If you want it, that is." I say.

His strange amber eyes find mine. "Yes, of course I do. Thank you." He holds my gaze and once again, I am struck by the oddest sensation. I think I miss him.

"Try it on," Gaia says, breaking our trance. I cut her a look, but Athos nods in agreement.

"He doesn't have to now. He can wear it on a job." I say, feeling oddly defensive. I shouldn't feel so protective of him, especially with Gaia. She's my best friend, and he and I, well, we're barely friends.

Right?

"Oh, please try it on!" Max begs and Libby voices her agreement. Athos obliges the room and leaves to change in the spare bathroom while I continue to pin Gaia with a disapproving look.

"What?" she asks snidely as she collapses into a chair. I rankle at her tone.

"Gaia," it's a warning, and she knows it. She rolls her eyes as she examines the envelope he has given her.

Libby's squeal makes me turn to her. "That looks fantastic, Athos!"

Athos is standing still as she circles him like a hawk, commenting on how nicely it fits. It does, maybe too well. I can see every chiseled part of his body and it only serves to transport me back to that night. My cheeks heat as I look him up and down, recalling how he looks underneath.

"Playing up on the sex I see," Gaia snickers behind me.

I didn't mean to make it look like *that* on him. It's a sleeveless shirt that zips up the front, and loose-fitting pants, with simple boots. I made it the same gold and white as the suit Briseathe made me, and it complimented his tan skin. But the sleeveless shirt's a bit too short, so it shows an inch of his midriff.

"Uh, I can fix that," I say. He gives me a lazy smile, his amber eyes twinkling and I know what he's thinking. He thinks I'm fucking with him. "No really, I can! I just went off what I thought your dimensions were-"

"She's always been a bad judge of character." Gaia snorts, interrupting me.

"I think it's wonderful!" Libby chides. "Athos, you look amazing. You could give Jace a run for his title this year." He thanks her, but his eyes are on me. *Shit,* I think, *he totally thinks I'm flirting with him now. First the skimpy dress, and now this.*

"You don't have to wear it!" I call as he leaves to change back into his clothes.

"What did he get you, Gaia?" My dad asks. Gaia turns the envelope over and rips it open. She unfolds the paper and reads it silently. Athos is at my side suddenly. I'd forgotten how fast he can change. I can feel the heat of his body next to me as he scoots closer to see Gaia reading the card. His fingers brush against mine, sending waves of electric heat up my arm.

He definitely thinks I'm flirting with him.

"I don't understand…is this, real?" Gaia asks.

"Yes," he replies, stepping in front of me. His absence leaves a gaping hole next to me. "It's the deed to some land I own in Africa." I raise a brow as he glances back at me. "When I heard her company was working on a conservation by it, I knew it would serve them better than myself."

"You never told me that, Gaia," I say, unable to mask the hurt I feel.

"I know." She looks at me, guilty. "It's a conservation for humans."

The silence is deafening. Everyone but Athos is looking at her with shock.

"Since when has your organization started condoning human-only conservations?" I ask and he drops her eyes from me, shaking her head slightly. "They don't. Do they?" I conclude. Her silence is my answer.

"Damn it Gaia!" I erupt. "You did join that cult, didn't you!?"

"It is not a cult, and they do not hate Supes!" She counters.

"Listen to what you are saying!" I move towards her, only to be stopped by Athos's hand on my shoulder.

"Lily, calm down. She hasn't done anything wrong," he says.

165

Shocked, I turn to face him. "Wrong!? Do you know what they stand for!?"

"I actually agree with a lot of what Supitude and some other anti-Super groups stand for." I gape at him, stunned. "And so do you," he says softly.

I gape at him, then at her, completely and utterly confused and hurt. Confused that Athos, a Super, agreed with Gaia's anti-Supe cult, and hurt that she never told me about it. My brain is malfunctioning, trying to compute what just happened and how to respond. I plop down into a chair when I realize there's really nothing to say to them.

"They haven't brainwashed me, if that is what you are worried about," Gaia mutters.

"I am. I am just...worried about you. Down there all by yourself- and after what happened with-" I trail off, shutting my eyes.

"Don't." She snaps. "Do not use him to justify your paranoia." I scoff, throwing my hands up in defeat. "Lillium, it is my choice. I choose this. Freely. It is who I am."

She leans forward and stares me straight in the eyes. "If you can not be at peace with it, then perhaps I am better off down there, all by myself."

"No," my dad interjects. "No, no Gaia." she continues to glare at me while he protests. "Lillium is just being overprotective."

I hate how they all exchange glances as a silent conversation happens between them all. Only Athos is left out, looking confused when Gaia scoffs, and then looks away.

"I think it is almost time for the awards!" Libby says suddenly. "I have all the food ready!"

"Yes, come on Lily, let's go watch." Athos takes me by my arm and leads me into the living room. "You two can talk it out later." He whispers in my ear.

Everyone takes their seats, Libby and Max together on one side, me in the middle by myself, and surprisingly, Gaia and Athos together while Dad takes his plush chair.

We are just in time to see the overall awards that are going to be handed out over the next week. Sheiba wins the most awards this year, Jace is close

166

behind her.

"Figures." I sigh. "Like I said, when New Hope has their festival, she will be there for it to accept her award."

"Ssh!" Libby hisses.

"Lastly, we have Sun City, who will be giving their award this year to a very new face, Athos." The announcer pulls up a clip from the Korra interview. "Athos came into the light this year by appearing on St. Cloud's program, and has been winning the hearts of all the small towns outside of Sun City. So much so that they all demanded he be given the peace award this year. As you all know, never had an unknown Supe been given a peace award." I tune out the yammering from there to stare at Athos.

"You won." I mouth, unable to find my voice.

Libby lets out an ear-bleeding squeal and tackles Athos where he sits. Gaia's watching the rest of the cast, with a bored expression, and my father is clapping in the corner.

"Congratulations Athos!" Dad hoots. "You deserve it."

"Yes, yes!" Max's jumping up and down. "And now everyone around the world knows who you are!"

Athos is smiling nervously at them, and nodding as Max goes on and on about how famous he is going to be. All I can do is stare at them all in complete shock. Not once did it ever cross my mind he would win the award for a major city - the small towns we help, yes, but not a major city. Now he has to accept his award, and there will be press, and people, so many people. My mind is about to go into overload when I hear Gaia say, "Well, I guess you two will be very busy from now on."

I watch as my oldest friend gets up and walks slowly out of the room, never once looking at me. I want to go to her. It is obvious something is going on in her life that she needs to talk to me about, but just then my phone goes off like it never has before. In a matter of seconds, I have over fifty messages from the press, potential customers, and random people all wanting to get in touch with Athos.

"Who is this Athos?" The announcer asks, "And where can I see him in action?"

167

"Look at that face! He has the makings of the next star! Perhaps even next year's!" Another claims.

And with that, Athos explodes from the obscure Supe no one knows into a household name.

Chapter 20

"Please, for the love of all that is good, turn your stupid pad off!" Gaia growls from my bed.

"Sorry, I just need to run this through one more round of checks and I will be done," I say wearily.

"No, you need to stop," she snaps. I roll my eyes as I flip the pad Briseathe gave me off and turn to her. She glares at me from my bed, her bags packed and ready to go on the floor.

"Gaia, I don't want to fight again," I say, exhaustion marring my words. It's all we've done since dinner with Athos, and now it appears she wants to pick another one.

"I am not fighting with you," she growls. "All I ask is that you pay attention to me. All you have been doing this whole time is talking with people who want Athos, talking to Athos, talking about Athos. Athos, Athos, Athos!" she spits. "And do not even get me started on that stupid award ceremony!"

I stare at her with muted annoyance since I've been very careful not to bring him up in front of her, or to her. "Gaia, you're being dramatic. I've been working, yes, but I've been here with you this entire time and I do not bring him up to you."

"No, I'm not, you're just too dumb to it all!" she sits up and swings her legs to the ground, "You should have been given something, anything too! You should have been allowed up there with him at the least! He should have mentioned your existence!"

I frown, confused by her sudden change of topic. "What are you yapping about? You think I should have my own interview with Korra?" I chuckle.

"Yes, it's all about the Supe! It always is!" She huffs.

We have been like this since she met him, even though he has been nothing but nice to her and they have only seen each other that one day. My hopes that she would be fine with what I'm doing are completely dashed after Sun City's festival. Athos accepted his award on stage in the middle of the city and graciously thanked them all. True, I wasn't up there with him, but it wasn't about me. What I haven't told her is that he has asked me to be with him when he accepts it, and just like with Korra's interview, I told him no.

"Gaia, he is different. We are trying to do something different-"

"He is not different Lillium. The second he gets the chance, he will turn on you and leave you in the dust." She spat venomously.

I am taken aback by her venom. "What?" I sputter.

"Once he gets to the level of Sheiba and Mathis, he will no longer need you." She hisses, "He's using you to get what he wants. Fame. That's why he never mentions you when he gets his award. That's why he's alright with you standing in the crowd like the rest of the humans. Because that is where you belong."

"Gaia, what is wrong with you? Stop-"

"No! You need to hear the truth, you idiot!" Well, at least we are back to familiar territory. "Supes are not like us, and they never will be. They only care about their own kind, and honey, you are not it!"

"Stop it!" I scream. "You have no idea what you are talking about!"

She stands up, "Yes I do!"

"Just because you are a part of some stupid Supe hating group doesn't make you an expert on them!"

"Oh, and sleeping with one does?" The hate in her voice brings tears to my eyes. She's never spoken to me like this before, we've never fought like this.

"How can you say that? That's not-"

"Don't you dare, Lillium. I know you too damn well, so don't you dare lie to my face and tell me you didn't."

I shake my head in disbelief. I have been so careful, how did she know?

"It was one time, and I didn't know what he was. It's not like that, we're-"

"What? Friends? Business partners? Let's not forget how you kept him a secret from me! I saw the way you looked at him, and how you treated him. It wasn't anything like Libby or Max! What the hell are you two?!"

"That is not the point! You are wrong about him, you think you know, but you don't!"

"And you do?" She scoffs, "Yeah, he just went and told you all about him and his people." I sit there, fuming, as she stares me down.

Her face changes a bit as she looks at me, "Has he?" she asks.

"Why are you being so malicious?" I counter, "You said you understood why I was doing this!"

"I lied!" I wince at the venom in which she says it.

"Why?! You know I care about what you think!"

"Why?" Her laugh is maniacal. "Because you lied to me? Because I feel like I have to?" Her voice grows colder with each word. "Because they have won you over, you, the one person in this world who I thought would never, ever love them! Not after Gabriel!"

"Do not dare bring him into this," I hiss.

She moves over to face me, slowly, her eyes full of rage, her face contorting to the point where I don't recognize her. She stops inches from my face.

"Everything you are doing is an insult to his memory."

All the fight in me is leached out with those words. I feel my legs go weak, forcing me to stumble into my chair.

"What happened to you?" I say, tears forming in my eyes. "What happened to my friend?" For a moment, she looks like she is about to cry, too. She lets her guard down for just a second and I see the girl I know. But it passes, and this stranger she is becoming comes back.

"She died a long time ago. And you replaced her with a Supe." I feel my heart break.

"Gaia-"

"I am done, Lillium." She picks up her bags, flings her hair over her shoulders, and walks out of my room without a backward glance. I am so shaken by her words I can't even get up to run after her.

When did she make this change? Did she hate the Supes more than I did this whole time, or is this the work of that crazy group? Sure, I am far more busy since Athos won his award, and yes the job takes a lot of my time, but I spend every moment I can with her while she is here.

No matter what, we will end up fighting over it, and she always starts it! 'What do you mean, he doesn't pay you? How do you expect to make a living? You do all the work!' Then she tells me she has been reading about us online, that I am mentioned as his Public Relations person but that I have never been interviewed and not much is known about me.

"Some people think he is just using you as a gimmick!" She says.

"And some think I am the one pulling the strings, so what? I don't want the coverage and I don't care about what people think of me."

But she keeps at it incessantly until today. No matter her feelings, no matter the reason, she shouldn't have said that, I tell myself. But it doesn't stop the flood of tears that come, or the wracking guilt I feel. Perhaps she is right, and I am doing the wrong thing. Maybe Gabriel would have sided with her.

Maybe I should have gone with her when she joined her organization. I might have been able to stop her from joining Supetitude.

Or maybe I would be right there with her now.

Chapter 21

I wallow in my misery for weeks, curled up in my bed with my personal pad and wristpad as my only companions. Since winning his award Athos has been on jobs daily all around the world. He wants me to go with him but the logistics don't make sense - I'm far too busy figuring out his schedule and handling the requests to even think of going with him.

The work keeps me from going insane as I wait for a response from Gaia, hoping she will respond to all my messages and videos begging her to talk to me. As far as I can tell, she hasn't even opened them.

Briseathe is my only contact with the outside world besides my dad. Part of him giving me the personal pad as a gift is so that he can video chat with me when he's bored. At first, his calls are a welcome distraction. After some time though, I start to look forward to our talks. He is even working on creating some programs and gadgets to help lessen my workload. He keeps telling me to get out more, have Athos take me on a job, and see the world.

I tell him I'm too busy, which isn't a lie, but I have no motivation to leave my room.

"It will all pander out," he tells me nonchalantly, his blue head bobbing on my screen.

He has some goggles on and is typing away furiously on his computer while he speaks, "Once everyone and their cat have requested him to wash their feet, the novelty of it all will wear off and everything will be back to normal."

"Whatever normal was." I sigh. "How can you keep typing like that? I had to start using the voice system to compose my stuff."

"I am old fashioned. I could always send you a few clones to distract you." His blue brows wiggle behind his goggles suggestively.

"Oh, go feed your giant squid." I bark.

"You could always come here and stay a few days," he offers.

"Thank you, but that would require Athos to fly me. We do not have time for that right now." Again, not really a lie, but the idea of leaving my cocoon of blankets and emotional support snacks makes my heart race.

I haven't seen him for weeks. We only speak through messages on our pads, and as the New Year closes in I realize I miss him. I miss his barbs and his antics, the way he knows just how to push my buttons until I right on the edge only to bring me back down. I even miss our flights, how he holds me close to him while we glide over the earth below, his warm body pressed against me, his scent filling my senses.

I shake my head, trying to dislodge the thoughts before they go into pathetic territory. I cannot do this - I can't go down that road. We are coworkers, that's all.

But even as I try to convince myself, I know it's not true. No matter how hard I try to deny it, I know in my heart we've somehow traveled into friend territory. Which isn't the end of the world, I know, but it's dangerously close to, well, more.

Sure, when we started out we agreed on the basis of being coworkers, but we never said we couldn't be friends. I just never thought we would. It scares me. It means I am getting attached to the fool.

Gaia's words haunt me at night after I spend the whole day setting up schedules and rescheduling jobs; will he really just leave me? After all this, will he just forget about me?

I fall asleep dreading to wake up and find a message from him telling me he no longer needs me. Then what will I do? Move on with my life. I think. Hell, after this I will have some popularity.

Being a Supes' associate can do wonders for my career, whatever that may be. Plus, Athos will never do that to me. He is too good.

"Well, suit yourself. I would rather see the Northern Lights than stare at a screen for hours." Briseathe says from the screen, pulling my attention

CHAPTER 21

back to him.

"Please, staring at a screen is all you do," I laugh ruefully.

"To his credit, he goes scuba diving now and then." I spin around so fast that I almost fall off my bed. My eyes are so tired that Athos appears fuzzy, but it's him nonetheless.

"What the hell are you doing here?" I glance around my room in a panic. So messy. So, so messy.

"Did you think I would leave my friend to spend New Year's Eve on a computer?" He asks, leaning against the doorframe. I didn't hear him come in, let alone open the door.

But it doesn't matter. I blink at him slowly, trying to register what he said. "It's what now?" Is it New Year's Eve? I glance down at my wristpad seeing he's right. How did I forget? I've been staring at dates for too long.

"Here, get this on." He tosses me my suit from nowhere. "We are leaving as soon as you are ready."

"But, I have messages…."

"Shut up, girl, and go!" Briseathe snaps from my screen. "You can take a day off! He has the emergency line on him in case. And let's be real here. He's still not on the level of being called to take on robbers or crime bosses."

"Not that I couldn't." He grumbles.

"Athos, we have so many requests-" I protest

He waves me off. "Let Briseathe take care of them."

"What!?" something crashes off-screen as Briseathe tears off his goggles. "That wasn't our agreement!"

"It is now." Athos appears by my bed and shuts off the pad before Briseathe can spit out a response. "Are you ready yet?"

He smiles as he glides out of the room. I am too tired to argue further, so I take a shower and get dressed before meeting him outside.

"Where are we going?" I ask, eyeing the clear sky.

"You will see." He takes my arm and up we go, fast and high. It isn't until we are somewhere over the ocean that I realize he has called me his friend. I feel all warm and bubbly at the idea.

So it must be true, we are friends, I think as we fly. It feels nice to be outside, doing something other than sitting in my room working. I didn't realize how much I needed to get out until I feel my feet hit the ground when we stop.

We have landed on top of a hill overlooking a familiar scene below. "Paris." I say breathlessly.

"Yes, I had a job here earlier, remember?"

"Changing over a field for a new vineyard, yes!" I laugh, giddy with excitement, "I have only seen pictures of Paris! I have always wanted to come and see it!"

He smiles. "The last time I was here it was war-torn. Very little still remains of what it used to be, but it still has the same charm. I thought you would enjoy the celebration in the city tonight, Briseathe tells me it is one of the best places to celebrate New Year's."

"Yes!" I squeal, and then I grab his arm in a panic. "But I didn't bring any clothes."

He smirks and takes me by the shoulders, pointing me to the city. "One thing that still remains true about this city is that it is a great place to shop."

"I don't have-"

He places a finger over my lips, hushing me. "Do not worry. It's on me."

"No!" I grumble around his finger.

"Yes! Come on, Lily. Live a little tonight." He takes my hand and leads me down the hill. Dizzy with excitement, I stop protesting and let him show me to the shops. I feel so light-hearted as we move through the crowds, taking in the sights of the city.

It is true that the city was almost completely destroyed in the War, so many monuments that have stood for hundreds of years are now gone. We make our way over to the Arc De Triomphe, one of those few that has made it through the war. It is only mid-afternoon but the streets are already packed with people ready to celebrate the night. Vendors are set up, all the stores are open.

We stop for a moment to take in the sight of the Arc, and that is when I notice how people are staring.

"You are now in the leagues of Supes who are recognizable," I note as we move through the crowds. Many people stop in their tracks to do a double-take as Athos passes them.

"Come on Lily, let's go over here." We are constantly moving so as to avoid people. It strikes me that one day, we won't even be able to do that.

"Tonight is about us enjoying ourselves. Nothing else matters." I eat till I feel like I will be sick. I let him buy me a ridiculous dress and wear it, changing in an alleyway while he stands watch, and I force him to wear a knock off of Mathis's skin-tight suit.

I forget about Gaia and her words, and let the world melt away as we run all over the city, or occasionally fly when the crowds are too much. By the end of the night, I am laughing hysterically while he flies me to the top of the Eiffel Tower to watch the fireworks.

We ignore the people below us pointing and taking photos and watching the city ignite itself.

"Want to see something cool?" He takes to the air and flies just to the clouds above the exploding fireworks. We hang there in the air until the show dies down, and the party below hits an all-time frenzy.

Soon I am dancing in circles with a guy covered from head to toe in bubbles and sparkles without knowing how or why. I can make out Athos dancing with a wisp of a girl, laughing hysterically. The music gets faster and louder, and I can't keep up with Bubbles, who is by all accounts a very good dancer. I feel myself lose my footing and I break off from him to spin into Athos.

He catches me and spins me around, faster and faster, until I can do nothing but laugh and hold on. When the music stops, I am left clinging to him with tears streaming down my cheeks.

"Again," I croak. And so we go again, dancing into the night, on rooftops, up alleyways, laughing the entire time.

I wake up the next morning in a strange room, in strange clothes, but I am not worried. I find Athos out on a balcony, watching people clean up the streets.

"How do you feel?" He asks, smiling as I rub the sleep from my eyes.

"Sore. I don't dance, ever," I yawn.

"Really? You're pretty good at it," he laughs.

I shrug as I take a seat next to him, "The people at my cousin's birthday party would agree with you, but I think that has more to do with Brogan than my skills." He raises a brow, confused all of a sudden.

"Brogan? You mean, one of my kind, Brogan?"

"Oh, yeah, I did not mention him, did I?" I groan, "I meant to, but after the party we were so busy that I must have forgotten."

He reverts into his statue mode, causing me to roll my eyes. It is too early for this.

"He works for my uncle," I explain, "He helped me find all the people I wanted to connect with, and then he helped me get on my cousin's nerves." I smile, remembering the look on her face when I kissed him.

"I haven't seen him for years," he says, coming out of his state. He gives me his lazy grin, "How is he?"

"Fine, I guess." I shrug.

"He's always been a bit of a loner, but we got along well. I should go visit him," he says thoughtfully.

"He was only interested in meeting me to see why you would associate yourself with me," I say, feeling like I need to make sure he doesn't think Brogan had acted anyway like Sheiba or Mathis.

He laughs, "That sounds like Brogan." He stands up, stretching, "Are you hungry?"

"Sure." I yawn, "We can eat, but I need to get back to real life afterward. So do you."

"As you wish." He winks as I get up.

"By the way, where are we?"

"Oh, this is an apartment Sheiba owns." I stop in my tracks, mouth agape. "What!?"

He chuckles, "Don't worry, she won't ever find out."

I don't want to ask how he knows this, so instead I gather my things and follow him out into the streets. We find a cafe by the Eiffel Tower where the river used to run before the war. We sit outside and watch the people make their way languidly around the streets, hung over from the night before and clearly under-slept.

"The last time I was here, the river was here, and there was a brothel over there." He points to what is now a personal appearance modification business.

I raise a brow, "Oh?"

"Shut up. I don't mean it that way."

"Uh huh, whatever you say." I smirk as I look over the menu. My pad beeps to tell me that it is full. I glance over it to see if anything is from Gaia before shutting it off.

"Oh, look there. Lily just shut off her pad." He teases.

"I can take a day off to eat in Paris with my friend, can't I?" I snap back, smiling.

"Sure you can." He looks off towards the tower for a second, "I am glad you came with me."

"Did I really have a choice?" I grumble.

"Of course you did. You could have come with me, or I could have abducted you."

I sigh, "Such the charmer. It's hard to believe you are single." I look up from the menu. "You are, right?"

"Why? Looking for a new angle?" A slow, sly smile appears on his lips.

"No." I snap my menu down, "It just seems like you and Sheiba have something going on."

"We did. About five hundred years ago." I almost ask if that's how he knows about the apartment, but bite my tongue. Just because we are friends doesn't mean I have to know that much about him.

"Hmm, well Supe relationships aren't ever in the media. It's almost like we think you guys are a bunch of monks running around scantily clad," I say and he huffs, but doesn't say anything. He's looking at the tower again.

"I guess we are kind of playing that card anyway with your suit. Which you didn't wear last night." I say.

"Huh?" He looks back at me. "Oh, yeah, sorry about that. It wasn't a party outfit." He smirks and looks back at the tower.

"Either way, it wouldn't hurt your image. But all jokes aside, I am glad I came with you. I was wasting away at home obsessing over this fight I had with Gaia, which was about you, naturally." I wait for him to respond, but he's gone into his statue mode. "Alrighty then." I sigh and look around for the waiter. Supes are so odd.

I feel a tremor beneath the table and hear the silverware clinking suddenly. I look down at it and see that his hand, placed on the top of the table, is shaking so violently it's causing the table to tremble.

"Athos?" I ask. His glassy eyes still stare at the tower. I grab his hand, but it only gets worse, and his whole body is shaking.

"Athos!?" I stand up, knocking over our table. The entire cafe is staring at us now, and the waiter is soon by my side asking what is wrong.

"Athos!" I yell at him and try to shake his shoulder. Tears are rolling down his cheeks. I start to scream at him, not knowing what else to do. Then, just as suddenly as it starts, it stops. His whole body goes rigid, shocking me to the point that I pull away from him. I watch him blink the tears away and slowly look up at me.

"Athos?" I ask softly. A thunderous boom causes the people around us to scream. Athos keeps staring at me like he is in a trance.

"Look!" someone shouts. I look up just in time to see the Eiffel Tower collapse. Everything goes quiet as we all gape at the spot where the tower was just seconds ago.

The silence is broken as we feel a rush of air blow through the street causing such a commotion I barely hear it coming, but Athos does. Just as I look down the street to see a wall of water come rushing at us, he takes my arm and moves so fast that the air is knocked from my lungs. I find myself standing with him on top of a building across from the cafe, now underwater.

I gaze down in shock at the flooded streets, looking everywhere for the source. Suddenly, it dawns on me that the tower is completely gone.

"Did the tower just-"

"Get turned into water? Yes." He finishes, grimly.

Chapter 22

"Athos, you have to-"

He zips down, nearly causing me to fall, and dives into the water. I watch him burst out with drenched people and place them on rooftops up and down the street.

The flow of the water is calming down, but it is still very high. He speeds up as he dips in and out and pulls more and more people out, but he is getting further and further from me, and I want to help somehow.

The water is all but a stream now, and I can see the street below it. Thinking it is safe to go down, I start to look for a way to get off the rooftop. I have to get down and help in some way, I think. I can hear the screams and shouts from people all around. The least I can do would be to comfort someone. Or find out why the hell the tower turns into a flood of water.

"What shall I do now, little flower?" The hairs on my neck stand up. There is only one person who can change matter and turn a whole tower into water. I slowly turn to see Mathis standing adjacent to me on a rooftop, a few soggy people sitting behind him. He is shirtless, sporting baggy pants and a creepy, crazy smile.

"You! What the hell is wrong with you?!" I scream.

"Aw, Lillium dear. Do not be cross because I have turned these streets into my personal rivers."

"There were people in these streets! They could still be trapped inside these buildings!"

"Oh," he throws his hands up dismissively, "who cares?"

"I do! You have gone insane! Athos is going to tear you into tiny little

181

pieces!"

"Oh? I doubt that. He hasn't told you about our little law, not to kill one of our own kind?" he laughs.

"I don't give a damn you psycho!" My mind is reeling. How can he be doing this? He is a Supe! He is supposed to be helping the world and saving people, not destroying it and killing us! Even in my darkest thoughts, I have never considered a Supe a threat like this before.

"He might not be able to tear me into tiny pieces, but that does not mean I cannot rip you to shreds." His lips curl into a toothy sneer. *Damn,* I think. He laughs again as his body shivers and shifts. He turns himself into water and is now making his way down the roof towards me.

In a flash, he climbs up the building to me and reassembles himself. *Double damn.* I have no idea he can do that.

"Shit..." I breathe.

"Most certainly," his cat-like eyes bore into me with such malice that I know for certain he means to kill me. I take a step back, but I know full well I stand no chance against him. A shrill noise coming from behind us causes him to momentarily glance away. In a flash, he disappears into a wispy vapor, just as Athos's figure whirls before me.

Athos means to capture him but flies right through him instead. By the look on his face, I'd wager he doesn't know Mathis can do that either. The wisps glide down to the water below, where they change back into Mathis.

"Do not look so perplexed, old boy," Mathis laughs.

"Mathis, what the fuck?" Athos pants.

"I wonder," he smirks, ignoring the question. "how does it feel to be severed from me?"

"You did that willingly? How!?" Athos cries, the pain in his voice makes my heart hurt.

"Who cares about that?! He's attacking the city!" I snap.

Mathis snickers. "You had better listen to your little lady there."

"Mathis, whatever has happened, we can fix it." Athos pleads.

"Fix it!?" I scream, hysterical. What was there to fix? The psycho just killed a bunch of humans.

"Lillium. Shut. Up." Athos says between clenched teeth. My mouth hangs in shock. I've never seen him like this before.

"Yes, little flower dear, shut up." Mathis bends down and scoops some water into his hands. I watch him change it into sand, his eyes ablaze with a truly terrifying look of glee.

"You have declared war on the humans," Athos states.

"No! I have declared our dominance as the super-species in this world!" He glares up at me. "The world is no longer yours." He lets the sand slip through his fingers.

"It doesn't belong to anyone you psycho!"

"No?" He turns back into vapor. In a second he is on me, but Athos is faster. He picks me up and shoots off in a random direction far and fast and he can without killing me. We land just before I pass out from lack of air, right where the tower had stood moments before.

"How dare you tell me to shut up!" I shove him away, tears in my eyes.

"Shut up, Lily! This is serious!"

"No shit! Quit telling me to shut up!" I scream back.

"You!" someone yells.

A boy is kneeling over a body, his face contorted in rage as he stands up to point at us. "You Supers are to blame! Why would he do this!?" he screams.

A group of people with him try to calm him down, but he shoves them all away.

"Hey, that's Mathis, not him!" I snap back.

"He's gone insane!" the boy pushes his way through the group and starts to stomp over to us, clearly looking to take matters into his own hands.

"Time to leave," Athos says. I grab him by the arm, ready to take off, but a sudden shimmer in front of the boy makes me stop.

"No!" I scream. Mathis solidifies and grasps him by his hair. He screams in terror as Mathis spins him around to face us. Athos stiffens next to me as Mathis runs a finger up and down his cheek.

"There's something about a scream out of fear. It's so much more potent than one out of admiration." The boy whimpers as I try to push Athos away, but he holds my arm in his grip, his face grim.

183

"Let the kid go." His voice is low, but I can hear the rumble of a threat in it. The boy trembles violently when Mathis laughs next to his ear.

"What are you going to do if I don't?" Mathis taunts.

Athos pulls me back when I take a step to respond and replies in the same tone, "Mathis, whatever it is you are trying to do, or prove you have done it. That's enough now."

"Oh Athos, you truly are the people's hero. Even when you know you cannot win, you still try." He turns his feline eyes to me. "I haven't even begun to make my point yet."

I break out in a cold sweat as I get the feeling of being caught in a predator's gaze again.

"I will turn my mortal over if you will give me the same courtesy." My heart nearly stops beating.

"Or?" Athos hisses.

"Or we will have a new landmark here, the first-ever human turned into metal by a Super." Mathis grips the boy behind his neck, shaking him back and forth. "How about it?"

"Stop it!" I try to move but Athos stops me. "Let me go!" I snarl.

"Yes, Athos, let her go. Does her life mean more to you than this boy's?" Mathis chuckles.

"Lily, we can't win this." His voice is hollow when he says it, and I know he is right. There is no way we are going to be able to end this without more people getting hurt. If we flee, he will continue his rampage. If we stay, there is no guarantee he will give the boy up in my place. My mind races with possible options, but there are none.

I can't see a way out of this, and it makes me so mad that I finally say, "Why are you so obsessed with me?!"

"Such a human thing to think that it is all about you. I hate all of your kind, little flower."

"Then go live somewhere else! No one is making you live with us. Go find your island!" The curve in his lips drops when I mention the island. He flicks his gaze at Athos and I silently curse myself for saying it. If Mathis has any doubts about what I knew, they are all dashed now.

"Have you grown so weary of the attention that you seek another form of it?" Athos asks.

Mathis smirks, and in response slides his hand down the boy's arm. He grabs it by the wrist and thrusts it out, making the kid yelp.

"Tick Tock, little flower." He locks eyes with me, making sure I am watching as he slowly turns the hand into sand. The boy's screams are soul-piercing as we all watch in horror as his hand disintegrates before us.

"Stop it! You can have me!" I cry. "Let me go Athos, I can't bear it!"

I've never seen him look so defeated than the moment he releases my arm.

"You cannot save them all, hero," Mathis sings gleefully. "The second you can, you put a stop to him."

I breathe before I take a shaky step forward. "Not one move, hero," Mathis warns, pulling the boy close to him. The kid has nearly passed out from the pain. He sags against Mathis, who has to hold him up.

"Let him go, you idiot. Your stint is up." My voice shakes even as I try to sound brave.

"Oh, hardly, my flower. I am only getting started."

"Do you really think the others will let you get away with this?"

His smile unnerves me, "Do you?" he counters.

"Of course not!" I scoff.

"Are you sure?" he hisses. I am only a few feet away now, just another step or two, and he can have me, and there is nothing Athos can do about it.

Ignoring his answer, I say, "You can have me. You won't need him anymore."

He taps the side of his head and smiles, "Very logical, flower. But you forgot one thing." He flings the boy's entire arm to his side.

"I am flamboyant, and there are no cameras right now." I watch in horror as the stub that was once his hand turns into solid metal. He screams as the material spreads up to his elbow.

"Stay right there, Athos!" he shouts. "Or I will turn the rest of him into it as well," he continues to scream as he lets the arm go. It falls heavily against his side, and the rest of his body goes with it.

Mathis has to pick him up just to keep the boy at his side. "Does it hurt a bit?" he chuckles. I feel sick. My stomach churns at the sight of his arm gleaming in the sun.

"What more do you want?! You can have me!" I scream.

"Good," he sneers.

"Lillium!" Athos croaks.

"You let him go," I say.

"Sure," he smirks. "If you come and take his place now." He chuckles. "I want to make your skin glow." I shudder involuntarily.

He is going to kill me, after certainly torturing me, that is for sure, but really, what choice do I have? So I take a shaky step towards him, and another.

"I will change places with him," I whisper, accepting my fate. *Gaia and I have been right,* I muse. Supes are dangerous, capable of taking down a whole country in the blink of an eye. They can take over the world in an instant if the idea piques their fancy. Mathis has caused such chaos in a matter of moments. I can only imagine what harm he could do in a day. Probably more than the entire war has.

Who can stop him? Athos? Sure, if I am not between the two of them right now. So removing myself would be a blessing to them all, as Athos wouldn't have to worry about me anymore. He could take Mathis out without a second thought. Or would he? The thought creeps up and I feel a deep sense of dread at the realization that maybe Athos wouldn't. Not because he physically couldn't, but because Mathis is one of his own.

"Stop." Mathis's bark stops me cold. I feel a chill while he takes a deep breath of the kid's hair, smiling. "I think you are being a little too willing to martyr yourself."

"Just shut up and let him go!" I say hoarsely. "It is me you want to torture, not him. I saw it in your eyes at Athos's house. It's me you hate."

He locks eyes with me. "You are right. I want to torture you." I see it in the way he smiles at me before it happens.

It only takes a second, in reality, but to me, it feels like an eternity. In one swift movement, he grips the kid by his head with both hands, holding the body up in front of him. The kid's eyes are barely open, then a tremor goes through his body and they shoot wide open. The air around him shimmers, contorting what I can see, but then my eyes adjust and make out the indescribable shapes of flowers. He changes the boy's entire body into flowers that correspond with his natural colors. Everything from his jet-black pants to his blonde hair is a bunch of tiny flowers bound together.

And then Mathis takes a step back and blows on the back of his head. It explodes, and the entire image falls apart. Blossoms dance around Mathis, his face plastered with pure joy, his eyes filled with rage. The roar of my blood rushing out of my face fills my ears as I open my mouth to scream, but I never get the chance.

Athos is on me in a matter of seconds, lifting me and taking off fast and high. I can see the crowd around Mathis making a mad dash to get away from him while he dances in the floating flowers.

Athos is right, there is no way to win that battle. Mathis wants blood, he wants chaos; he needs to release the rage held in his eyes. How long has he been able to stave it off?

How long has he wanted to wrap his fingers around my people's throats and watch the life drain out of them?

But by far the most terrifying thought ever is how long Mathis's people have known this.

I am choking, gasping for air, for a breath, but I can't get a lungful, and I can't take the air pressure around me. I try to hide my face in Athos's shoulder, but I can't move my body. It is being crushed by his arms.

Without my suit, I can't breathe, and in a matter of seconds, I watch my blurry vision being eaten away by blackness as I pass out in his arms.

Chapter 23

As you clearly can see, Jace Kace is vigorously trying to evacuate the area. As you clearly can see, Jace Kace is vigorously trying to evacuate the area while half the valley turns into a swamp-like wasteland, sucking hundreds of homes and humans into its depth.

Jace has managed to make himself large enough to dam up the mud, letting the humans in the city below him have time to escape.

This is the third attack on a human town by Mathis in the past week. The death toll amounts so far to nearly one hundred, with countless injuries. Backlash for the Super community has been rampant these last few days, with new organizations popping up supporting groups like Supitude and- Oh my, it's Mathis!

He's made his way to Jace!

The camera swerves closer to reveal a miniature Mathis morphing into mud, mixing with the swampy substance, and disappearing. Jace shudders violently, but does not budge from his place.

This could be the first open confrontation between two Supers since the Paris incident, the announcer says.

Supers have been, so far, very closed off about their opinion of Mathis going rogue, and have not established if there are others who plan to do the same, says another.

Jace seems to shiver violently for a moment. There's a stunned silence as the mucky swamp behind him morphs into solid stone.

Mathis has just - the first announcer gasps as the form of Jace shakes. He's trying to free himself from the stone that now held him in place. *Jace is trapped! He is trying to free himself now, perhaps by shifting into a smaller form, but it seems-* the announcer is cut off by an all too familiar blood-chilling scream from Jace.

He is being turned into stone! The other screams. *Mathis is turning Jace Kace into stone!*

He continues to cry in pain as his body slowly changes, foot to head, to stone. The cameras are on him like flies, swarming around his head and torso, getting shots of the morph. It seems like an eternity until the stone overtakes his face, and the screams finally stop. His face is contorted in pain.

Movement to the left of the stone head catches the camera's attention. Mathis is standing there, on the shoulder, and bows to the cameras. I take a deep breath, hissing, and then Briseathe turns off the halo-vision. We both sit in silence on his couch, listening to the waves lap against the window. I am still staring silently, fuming, at the spot where Mathis's face had been when Briseathe adjusts himself.

"Well," he says finally. "This changes things."

I can hear the pain in his voice. Even though Briseathe actively shuns the others, they are all still connected on some level. "I hope Athos is alright." Is all that I can muster.

"Yes. It will be far worse for the others. They feel it more than I do...." He trails off, his face unreadable.

"I am sorry, Briseathe," I whisper.

He shakes his head. "I am too." He stands and slumps away, his blue shoulders sagging. I am sad to see him leave. These past few weeks he has been my only companion since Athos dumped me here from Paris. He abandoned me here to deal with the others.

Three days after Paris, Mathis took out two more cities with waves of destruction. There is nothing Athos or the others can do. Once news gets out, Mathis is long gone before they can get there.

Briseathe is uncharacteristically quiet about the entire ordeal. He barely answers my questions and spends most of his time down in the depths of his lab with his clones. I am left by myself unable to leave, unable to contact anyone, unable to do anything but watch the destruction play out on the news, and think.

Briseathe has my dad moved somewhere even I don't know about, just in case Mathis decides to take another swing at me. I haven't been in contact with him, other than to say I am fine, and that we need to stay low.

That goes for Gaia as well. I can only assume what is going through her mind now that groups like Supitude are gaining popularity due to the media frenzy.

Now and then the news interviews one group or another and asks their opinions on Supes, and the group boasts about the new recruits they are getting in by the handfuls. I know it is mainly due to fear. Those people don't really agree with Supitudes views on Supes, they are just scared.

In my seemingly infinite spare time, I am thinking about what this means for Athos and, subsequently, me. Can we still continue? Should we even? Does he still want to? Briseathe is being very candid about his feelings, and whenever I mention the others or Athos, he leaves.

I have to keep telling myself to wait for Athos. He will come back soon, hopefully, and then I can get my answers. Everything depends on whether he still wants to go on or not. Only then will I let myself even think about what we are going to do.

The halo-vision beeps, alerting me that something is going on. I turn it back on to see a figure standing in the rubble.

"....down!" I recognize Korra's voice. A building in the distance crumbles.

"Where the hell is this now?" I snap. Mathis comes into view seconds later, holding the rubble in his hands and laughing at the cameras.

"Mathis is now attacking Tokyo! Mathis is now attacking Tokyo!" she screams.

Well, thank you for that information, I think bitterly. We can't afford to freak out just now; she needs to get a hold of herself. A blur comes into view and then crashes behind Mathis. I watch as the dust settles, and Athos appears.

"Shit, Athos is in Tokyo! Athos is in Tokyo!" I scream along with Korra. Mathis laughs at him tauntingly, turning into dust just before Athos can grab him by his neck. He pops back into form a yard away, with a bloody

190

nose.

"Athos can hurt him...." Korra says breathlessly.

For the first time, Mathis is not smiling. Athos comes at him again, but this time he turns into water, covering him. Athos tries to brush it off, but it turns into a silver metal, constricting him.

I curse as Mathis laughs, a very metallic sound that seems to come from everywhere. *Come on Athos, don't let him get you!* Is he the only Supe in the area that can stop Mathis? Is he the only one that can?

Or does he even? So far, he is the only one of his kind who keeps confronting Mathis at every turn. Everyone has gone into hiding, it seems, none of them will openly condone Mathis for his actions, or even mention him to the media. Jace Kace has only come out to help that town, after Mathis has caused his destruction.

Perhaps now the Supes will respond to the threat Mathis poses.

Do you think he will forsake our one rule? Mathis's words ring in my head. Murder of your own kind, that is the Supes only rule, it is forbidden.

Athos stops brushing himself off and shakes so fast he becomes a blur. The metal falls off like silk, forming into sand before it is blown down to become Mathis. Athos flies at him, but even he cannot catch and hold sand.

"Is there no one else to help Athos?" Korra says grimly. "No, who would help him? He's already killed Jace, and Supes can't do that. Who would risk it?"

Athos is indestructible so the risk to him is very minute, and that makes him the only Supe likely enough to beat him. But only if he can catch him. Sand Mathis blows completely away in all directions, forcing Athos to stop his pursuit. A few minutes crawl by before he disappears completely.

Over the next few hours, several stations have heated debates over what needs to be done. *Kill him? How? Athos seems capable. What if others defect? What if the others turn on us completely? Why is Athos the only one not harmed?* And on and on. Briseathe remains in his clone cave all day and night. When I get up the next morning there is breakfast, but he is gone, as usual.

Just as I sit down to eat, the elevator dings and Athos steps out. He stops just at the edge of the table, and we stare at each other as I plate some food.

It's slightly awkward. I'm not sure what to say to him now that he's in front of me. There are many things I want to say, but none of them sound right.

I swallow hard and finally come up with, "Are you alright?" Stupid, I realize just after saying it.

Of course, he isn't. He only stares at me in his statue mode. Which only makes things more awkward.

"I know you aren't," I grumble, feeling slightly annoyed at his demeanor all of a sudden. Many things come to my mind then, and I want so many answers.

Why did he leave me like that? What does this mean for us? If there is even an 'us' anymore.

But all I can do is stare at him while he remains in statue mode. I have no idea what to do or say. For all I know, he could be falling to pieces right in front of me. Or seething in rage.

"Athos…." I finally manage. He doesn't move.

"Athos?" I try again. This time when he still doesn't move, I stand up. "Athos!" I take his hand in mine, and he finally blinks.

"Tired," he mumbles. He gently places my hand on the table and goes back to disappear in the elevator.

Apparently, he needs space. I know he doesn't sleep, so perhaps this is a mental tiredness. I eat by myself, again, and hang around in hopes that the guys will find their way up to me. But after night falls, and there is no sign of either of them, I go to bed with a heavy heart.

It is not until then that I truly realize I consider Athos a friend, and even Briseathe too. I really don't want to lose them. I wake up the next morning feeling even more downtrodden than before. I prepare myself for a lonely day again and go up for breakfast. Sure enough, the table is laid out spectacularly, but no one is sitting there.

"How are you?" I jump and turn to see Athos leaning against the glass wall. I hadn't noticed him there.

"Fine," I say finally. He has been looking out the glass, but now cocks his head to look at me.

"And you?" I counter.

"Confused." he sighs. "Hurt. Angry. But most of all, confused. I am sure you are as well."

I snort in response and throw myself on the couch. "What does this all mean?"

"I do not know. No one does."

"The others?"

He scoffs. "They are acting like poultry with their heads cut off."

"What?" I ask. "Why would they do that? Why would anyone cut the head off of poultry?"

"Never mind." He sighs. "There is a lot we do not know. But if there are others out there, like Mathis, they do not want to be found. Otherwis,e they would have made themselves known by now.

"But the fact that there are those of us who wish to defect..." he turns away from me. I awkwardly place my hand on his shoulder, unsure of what to do.

"I can not fathom the depth of what you are feeling, Athos. Humans are not connected as a whole." I think of Gaia, "But those that we are connected to- it hurts, when they leave or betray you. So I am very sorry..." *You handled that nicely.* I think bleakly.

He places his hand over mine. "Thank you, Lily. It is odd how things work out. Here I was trying to get back at them and show them how infantile they were being. But really, Mathis beat me to it. And now they are distrusting of each other, and wary of the humans and what they will do next." He chuckles. "Bad timing, I guess, to be famous."

"Or perfect..." I murmur as a thought strikes me. He cocks his head. "This is probably not what you want to hear. But I think it needs to be said soon." I withdraw from him, biting my lip. "You just said you are the only one who can stand against those who defect, without risking bodily harm."

"Yes?" He raises a brow.

"And you already have, on the news, for everyone to see..."

"Yes..."

"I think that you should continue to fight the others that defect." I blurt out.

193

He stares at me, quizzically.

"Look, you will be the only one doing it, and it is the most high-profile of duties, so you will get serious coverage from all over the world. There is no way that you can go unnoticed. And people will see you as a real Superhero, like in the comics! You will fight Super Villains - I mean, this is perfect for you! It's like you were born for it!" *Ok I'm being a bit too enthusiastic. People have died, for heaven's sake! Chill out.*

"Lily, of course, I am going to continue to fight them. But I never thought of it as a way to get to our goal of changing the world. It has already been changed." He says blandly.

"Yes, and it still is. We can go two ways now, Athos, war, or come together as one."

He shakes his head, smiling. "You always have a plan, don't you? Here I was thinking you were going to ask me to send you off to your dad's, and for me to stay out of your life."

"Why the hell would I do that?" I snap.

"Because of Mathis." I feel my heart skip as I recall the boy's face in Paris. I don't notice him take my hand. "Lily, no one would blame you for wanting to stay as far away from us as possible after that."

I shake my head. "Mathis is crazy, Athos. He needs to be stopped."

"You could get hurt." He warns.

I squeeze his hand. "It would be worth it."

"Does this mean you are going to do it?" We both turn to see Briseathe standing by the elevator, arms crossed. "If you make things worse, if you fail to capture and hold Mathis and whomever else that defects, then all the world will turn on you and you will turn on each other. Fast."

We let our hands drop. "Thank you for the vote of confidence." I sigh.

"He is right, though," Athos says and I roll my eyes.

"Yes, he is. But the risk of not acting at all is the same outcome, but for sure. Athos, not only can you stop a full-out war between us, you can unite our kinds as equals."

"Equals? When he is the one fighting?" Briseathe scoffs.

"Yes, when he appears humble and human, he can." I say.

"And when I have a mortal by my side as my equal." Athose smiles at me.

"As an equal, yes, but I cannot be seen as helping you the way I am. People will think I am a puppet master of sorts." I say.

"So she must be an adviser?" Briseathe asks.

"Yes," I say. "I can be his adviser-"

"A friend," Athos interrupts.

"That too." I smirk. "We will show we are close, but that you are making choices of your own."

"Seeing you two together like that will make most of the humans a little more comfortable They will see that there are still some of us that wish to keep the peace." Briseathe says.

"There are some who have turned against us," Athos says.

"And some will come back to you after seeing you fight for them. Besides, those Supe hate groups are still minuscule in number." I say.

"Do not underestimate them Lillium. Hate groups have a way of creeping up when you least expect it." Briseathe warns.

"Our main focus has been, and should still be, those who need help. And everyone is in desperate need now." Athos says. I nod in agreement.

"Sure, yeah. But you two are forgetting about one thing. Even if Athos manages to capture Mathis, he cannot be held. Is he going to hold onto him for the rest of their lives?" Briseathe groans.

"If I get him," Athos says gloomily.

"You can. And you will." I say with the utmost confidence.

"He is slippery though, literally. Briseathe is right. No place could hold him." Athos says.

"You could always fly him to the moon and leave him there." Both men stare at me in shock. "Or not. He'd probably just turn into a hunk of gold and fly into the earth, anyway."

"I can not kill him, Lily. It is against our beliefs, no matter what he has done." Athos says softly.

"I know." I sigh, but how much easier that will make things. "But this would require you to fight your own people Athos. People you have known your whole life. You do not have to do this, if you do not want to."

"I need to, though." He says.

"You can always fly away." Briseathe snickers.

"I already did that once." he looks at me then, intent on doing this.

"Alright. We will do this." I say, breathless.

He takes my hand. "Yes. We will."

"You know what this means, right?" I smirk at Briseathe. "Another interview."

Chapter 24

Two more Supes defect after Jace is killed, which means Athos is completely outnumbered right now. He is also the only Supe who seems to be capable of doing something about the destruction they are causing.

Which, after just a few days, is a lot. The timing seems to be on our side now, and the fact that people are crying out for answers. Which means Korra, of course.

"We have to do this fast and clean. Straight to the point. People want the fundamental questions answered - mainly they want to be assured something is being done and they do not need to worry."

"Just a spokesperson," Athos says dully.

"No, not a spokesperson." I correct. "You need to show them you care, that you are on their side. Show them that, and you will win them.

Korra nods. "She is right. Just think of this as a message to us- and Mathis."

He narrows his eyes, full of heat, and goes into statue mode. Korra quirks a brow at me, and I only shake my head. He's been doing it a lot more lately but I still hesitate to ask him where the heck his mind goes when he does.

"Alright... let us get started." Korra chooses a plain setting this time with no backgrounds and no chairs.

Standing face to face, both wearing somber-looking clothes, Korra and Athos wait for the machine's cue. It beeps, and Korra turns her face slightly to one camera.

"Korra St. Cloud here with Athos, the moderately known Super." I roll my eyes. "In light of these dark events, Athos here has decided to speak out to us, and offer his hand."

She turns her gaze to him. "Athos, thank you for coming here again. I have heard many great things about your business so far. And you won an award this year!" Her smile turns. "But the last time I saw you, you were fighting off Mathis and newly defected Snare in the Southern Americas, saving the city of Rio from sure destruction. The event concerning Jace Kace shows that you Supers are not immune to each other's abilities, and can actually die. But after seeing the way you handled Mathis and Snare, I believe it is safe to say you are, in fact, immune. And also against what Mathis is doing, so on our side to boot. You have come here today to give the people a message- do you speak for all the Supers, or just yourself? "

Athos looks directly into the camera, his eyes serious as he says, "I speak for those of us who are for liberty and freedom from tyranny. As you have probably guessed, we as a whole were taken by surprise when Mathis defected, and even more so by Snare. As of this moment we do not know who is truly for or against these acts. For all we know more could defect tomorrow." Korra straightens in her seat. It's an uncomfortable thought that the entire world shares, and a Supe just admitted it can happen.

It's not lost on me - history is being made at this moment, and it's a heavy, suffocating feeling that wraps around me. My palms sweat as I take deep breaths of air, willing myself to remain calm.

I will not freak out now, I can't. I've been on edge for weeks but never fell into a full-on attack, and I wasn't about to start now when Athos was making history happen.

"But that is not to say that there are none of us who stand against this. Many do, especially after Jace. This rogue group of Supers stands alone in their actions." He says.

Korra clears her throat. "So we should not expect all Supers to act like this?"

"No, not at all." He deadpans.

For once, she appears unsettled. "But you do not know for sure who is or is not against us?"

"No." He admits.

She flicks her gaze at me, but my face offers nothing. I hope she didn't assume he'd come on her show to pander to the people. "I imagine that has caused some strife in your group." She says.

"It has been a blow to us, for certain. We are second-guessing each other." Athos is airing out all the Supers' dirty laundry. I can see the cogs working in Korra's mind and how she can spin this in her favor.

"Not much is known about you as a whole, but it seems you were a close group before?" She says finally, quirking a brow.

"Yes. And as such, we thought we knew what to expect from each other. But not this. Never this." He shakes his head.

She taps a finger on her chin, looking thoughtful, but I know she's stalling for the audience, milking it. Finally, she raises her brow, as if a thought just struck her. "So Mathis was never openly hostile towards humans?"

"He never gave any indication he felt this way about you." I can't help but twitch at the lie. *They had to have known something*, I think. There's no way that Mathis harbored such feelings of ill will against humans and never once mentioned it to someone of his own kind.

"Have others?" She asks.

"No. There have been those of us who were wary to come out in the very beginning, but not since Briseathe has anyone given any indication they wanted anything but to cohabit with humans."

Korra glances at the camera. "Should we expect more to defect?"

Athos doesn't hesitate and doesn't sugarcoat his answer. "Possibly."

"What can we do to protect ourselves," she breathes it as a statement as there's no question at all - humans are powerless against Supers. We can't protect ourselves. It's a dark, unsettling truth that many of us have refused to even examine since Supers came into the picture.

Maybe we should have been more cautious of power-wielding immortals.

"Do not engage Mathis, or whomever chooses to follow him. I am going to be frank: there is nothing you can do to stop him." Athos warns.

"But you can." She says bluntly.

Athos flicks his eyes at me momentarily.

"I can." He breathes. "I can stop him, and any who would choose to break the peace. I will take on all who oppose the great work we have taken so long to achieve after the war."

He looks directly at the camera closest to him. "You cannot hurt me. You cannot defeat me. I will hunt you wherever you go, and I will find you. I choose to protect the people of this world, and I will be their champion when they need me. Take heed, Mathis. We will get you."

Korra glances at me, but I know he is talking about Briseathe, and whoever else wants to help them. He is letting Mathis know that he has to deal with both of them now. The brawn of Athos, and the genius of the millennia.

"Can we expect others to join you?"

Athos shrugs. "Maybe not in battle with Mathis, but when they can, yes. Whatever it takes to bring Mathis down." He's all but told the others Briseathe is working with him at this point. He's stirring the pot, but it has to be done.

"What about Legion?" Korra asks.

"I intend to go to Legion, to the council, and to help them in whatever way I can. We plan to use Legion as our base for now."

"We?" Korra asks.

"My partner, Lillium, and I." My pulse quickens when his amber eyes slide to mine.

Korra's brows shoot up in surprise. We didn't mention this in the briefing. "The human you have been working with?"

"Yes, she is here now, and I would like to get her to say a few words before we leave." He waves me over.

My jaw drops. We haven't planned this, I have no desire to say anything!

"Lillium, would you please join us?" Korra smiles.

I glare at her, willing her body to spontaneously explode. What the hell am I going to say? Who cares anyway? They only want to listen to a Supe. I take a shaky step onto the stage floor and am met with a floating camera. I know I have to look ridiculous.

"Oh...." I clear my throat. Korra motions for me to stand by Athos.

She smiles at the camera. "So you two are a team now?"

"We have always been a team. Lillium is camera shy, though," Athos says.

I can only plaster my best fake customer-service smile on as I internally wither inside. The idea that hundreds if not thousands of people seeing me makes me want to puke.

"So you will be going with Athos to Legion then?"

"Yes," he answers for me, surprising me. He never mentioned this.

"No human has ever been to Legion since its breaking from the ground. You will be the first. How does that make you feel?" Korra asks.

I look at Athos, feeling helpless. "I... I guess I am excited," I say. Korra nods, encouraging me. "But I am not going there for autographs."

Athos chuckles. "We will be there to work."

"Interesting. I think you two will be the first human Super-duo so far. Is it also your goal to stop Mathis, Lillium?"

I stutter. "Yes. I think the best way to beat him is to collaborate with the Supe-rs." I correct myself quickly.

"Well, I wish you both the best of luck, and I hope to see you again, in happier times. Korra St. Cloud, out."

The cameras go out as the lights dim. Have I just been seen by hundreds of people? It sure doesn't feel like it.

"What the hell is that!?" I snap at Athos.

"That, is perfect," Korra giggles.

"What?" The two of them are grinning at each other like idiots.

"Sorry Lily, Korra thought of it as the last moment and we don't have time to run it by you."

I scoff. "That she was going to make me look like an imbecile?"

"No, like a perfect human companion. You are the assurance Lillium. You want humans to be assured that he is genuine in his endeavor, but until they see you act with him, they will only see you as a shadow." Korra says.

"Yes, but the Supes will see it as the opposite," I say.

"Which is why I am taking you to Legion, where they will see you for what you are. My friend." Athos smiles, making his dimples deepen.

"Well, good luck to you two." Korra grabs Athos's hand, "You get him," she says, staring into his eyes.

"I promise." He says. She pats him on his chest and winks at me as she walks away.

"Legion," I say flatly.

"Right into the snake pit." Athos sighs. "It has to be done, and fast."

"What? My death?" I throw my hands up.

"No, my people have to choose. They have to make a choice to side with me now, or Mathis. And they need to do it before the humans decide for them. So far, there hasn't been any kind of major backlash against us."

"They are too afraid of that," I say, shaking my head.

"For now they are. But when they decide to get even with us, any of us, they will, and then there will be war."

I sigh. He is right. But I am not so sure about going there.

"We could shake them up, Athos. I can make it worse and cause others to defect with just my presence."

"It will happen eventually. It is better if it is on our terms." His amber eyes sparkle at me. Not a note of deception in them. He does want me to go with him for all the right reasons.

"Plus, you will have a few of Briseathe's gadgets to help you out." He smirks.

"Oh, yay." I rub my forehead.

"Well, when do we leave?" I mumble, earning a grin from him.

"So you will go?"

"Yes." I smile, "Of course I will." Even if it means I might get a lick or two from some Supes.

"Good. We leave tomorrow."

Everyone sees the interview, far more than I had even hoped. It is broadcast by many other groups until the whole world sees it. And it is mulled over by all. By the next day, everyone is talking about Athos and his declaration. And me.

Athos takes me home for a moment to get my things, and I am confronted by many neighbors and calls all at once to ask me so many questions. I barely have time to tell Max and Libby goodbye and to see that Gaia has still not contacted me. Athos takes us to his home, where he takes a few last rounds to check on everything.

"I thought you said you have a house in Legion?" I ask, sitting outside in his garden. I tug at my suit. No matter how many times I use it, it is always so very constricting.

"I have many homes, in many places." He laughs. "I like them all, and I would like to make sure they all stay in good condition."

He stops by a flower bed, frowning. "I do not know if these will make it through to Spring without me…"

"I could always have Libby come by," I suggest then chuckle when I envision her and Max fan-girling over his home.

"No, no. I can always replant." He disappears in a flash.

I pick at my suit again, trying to conceal my excitement. I have never traveled to another continent and have wondered if I will ever. Just to think that a few months ago I was walking around in a fog of a life, with no real purpose or drive.

Here I am now, going to Legion where no human has been before. I am friends with a Supe- no, if I am being honest we are best friends now.

How can I think anything else? He saves me, and I trust him, and he trusts me. Athos zips up to another bed, muttering to himself. I feel bad that his plants will die after he spends so much time making them grow.

Then again, I wonder just how many plants he watches die in his long lifetime. Does it get easier? At the thought of death, I feel a chill run up my spine that has nothing to do with the cold day.

Legion is going to be full of potential defective Supes. My coming might cause them to rally, and maybe even act out against the others. My presence. It can start a revolt within the Supes, who for their entire existence have been a close-knit group. I will be hated. I will be feared. I could die even, and Athos is risking the same. He doesn't ask the others for permission to bring me, he just is.

"Alright Lily, I believe everything here is in order." I jump up, forcing a smile. He raises a brow. "You alright?"

"Yeah," I force a smile. I might consider him a close friend now, I mean, who wouldn't after all we've been through, but that didn't mean I wanted to weigh him down with my doubts and anxieties.

"Ready?" He takes my hand.

If I didn't know him as well as I do by then, I would not detect the waver in his voice. He is just as uncertain as I am. I grip his hand and look into his eyes.

"Yes." I am surprised by the steel in my voice. He straightens up, reflecting my resolve. He pulls me close to him. His extraordinary warmth hits my face before I pull my mask over it. As we slowly lift off into the sky, I can't help but think, Gaia is right in a way.

I am not enamored with Supes, but I am certainly close to one.

Chapter 25

The heart of New Hope, once called New York, is where the Supers build their headquarters, essentially their mini city, Legion.

In the beginning, Legion starts as the principal base for Supes to work out of while they rebuild the world. World leaders and humans all around feel better when they can pinpoint the Supes, back then, and they enjoy having access to them as well. Eventually, as the world needs less and less attention and assurance, Legion becomes closed off to the public. As fandom becomes rampant, they shut it down completely, claiming raging fans are a distraction.

Their underlings who work right outside of the city are reachable, or rather the Supers can reach them. The people, humans hired by the Supes, convey their messages to them and reply with the Supes response. But even that becomes too taxing for the Supes, and so, a little under a century ago, they broke Legion from the earth and suspended it above the ground.

It is popularly called Top City as it floats above the massive hole on top of a cyclone made by an unknown Supe. It spins, ever so slowly, as the cyclone turns beneath it. The hole below it is nothing but a flush field now, overgrown, but otherwise empty.

No one knows exactly how many Supes live on Legion- the last known number before they closed themselves off is nearly one hundred. The last known pictures of Legion are of vast green yards and high-rise buildings, clustered in the center.

It is very much the same today.

A floating city is easily accessible to Athos, who flies right over it. The cluster of buildings in the center of Legion is not very large in comparison to other cities. They all seem to have a maximum of seven stories, but they are all dwarfed by the large needle that rises high into the sky, right into the stratosphere. It is there at the top that Athos lands on a flat disk and holds me as we look around us.

"What a strange place," I say, clinging to him. There are no roads, only pathways that lead out of the center of the city to the surrounding fields. There are many hills in the west, and a dense forest to the east. From the south, I can see a gigantic mass of rock and a river that snakes down to the North, where it's flat. Overall, it's an enormous mass of land.

"It is silent," I say.

"Yes," Athos mutters, looking far off into the distance.

"Is it different from when you were here last?" I ask.

"Yes. They took out most of the modern buildings and roads. It almost looks like..." his voice drifts away as his eyes grow distant.

"Like what?" I prompt.

"Like they are reverting to home." He mutters.

"Oh." I lean forward to look beneath us, trusting him to hold on to me. "Why did they keep this, then? And these buildings around us?"

"It used to be the capital business of the world. I expect that they still are in a way." He explains.

"From up here?" I laugh.

"I suppose," he pulls me back a bit. "See those fields over there?" He points to the flat fields by the hills. "Those are training fields. And down there to the north is where the council will be tonight."

"Ah, well, I guess we had better get ready to go." He pulls me close to him and we lift off. Down we go, and shoot off to the east over many acres of bare land, with a home here and there, but all too fast to see well. The forest comes up, and he veers to the left, where he flies us right to the edge of Legion, to a massive home that sits on a cliff. He flies over the top of the back and lands on a balcony right at the edge.

Once on my feet, I stumble into the house. "What is it with you and extreme heights?"

"Don't you want to see the view?" He asks, laughing.

"Later!" I wave at him. He shrugs nonchalantly as he gazes over the edge to the city below.

"You couldn't have gotten a home in the middle?" I grumble.

"Briseathe built it." He replies. I lean against the balcony door, watching him as he looks across the valley.

"Oh, well, that explains it." I shake my head. "Does every Supe have a home here?"

"Most do." He turns from the view and saunters up to me. "The ones who do not want to leave, or can't stay down there. Others, like me, come and go. All homes are open, though, to those who want or need it. So they are never exactly empty."

"Should I expect unexpected company at any point?" I ask. It's a valid question, considering how many times random Supers have shown up at his home before.

"Perhaps. Not for a while, at least." Athos glances inside the house, then back toward me. "Are you sure you're comfortable staying alone here?"

I quirk a brow. "Are you staying somewhere else?" He smirks, and I realize what he means. "Alone, but with you."

His dimples pop as he smirks down at me. "Do you think you can resist me?"

I roll my eyes and step inside in room. It's very large, Roman in style, with open walkways and airy halls. All white marble, one story with no doors to speak of. The windows and halls all have sheer sheets hanging for cover, but I figure Supes weren't big on privacy so they were only there for decoration.

I take myself up some stairs to a large patio full of plants. I look around us and see we are surrounded by the forest, but no animals are in sight. We enter into a vast living room filled with numerous artifacts adorning the area that could only be Athos's memorabilia. It is spotless, with modern couches and tables, all in an off-white color. Fresh flowers bloom in pots that are built into the walls.

"Your room is down that hall." Athos points to a hallway almost obscured by the flowers. It's more of a walkway, with columns that lead down to another building, open on all sides with those sheer sheets covering it. I come to my own gossamer curtains that led into my room, separate from the main building I noticed, with nothing but the surrounding forest.

It had four solid walls, an alcove that looked over a creek that ran beneath the building, my bed right in the middle of the room, atop four steps. Everything is tones of white and gold.

"You know I am more of a blue girl, right?" I say, smiling.

Athos stands next to me. "I know. But Briseathe had this place renovated for us."

"When?" I ask, trying hard to ignore how warm his body is next to me.

"A few weeks ago." He smiles at me. "He knew I would take you here one day."

"How did he get this place like this?"

"Clones." I scoff. "Look." He shows me a switch on the wall that reveals a glass floor surrounding my bed. There's a pond beneath it, swarming with fish.

"What is it with him and fish?" I ask.

"I have no idea." Athos chuckles. He hands me a small box from one of the many bookcases that line my walls. "This is for you, and so is everything else in here. If I know my brother, he left some things for you to find and use."

"Is this place...secure?" I ask as I take the box.

"Yes. There are cameras and motion sensors everywhere. But, they can become useless if certain people choose to come here."

"My room-"

"Is not too far from mine." I nod, taking a breath and opening the box to find a bangle. "I need you to wear this, Lily, all the time. No matter where you are, or what you are doing." Athos says, his face serious.

"What is it?" I pick it up, holding it in the light. It looks like a plain gold bangle.

"I don't know how it works, but I know it uses atoms or something to create a field around you. It also can tell us where you are, and if you are…alright."

"Keeping tabs on me?" I tease.

He ignores me. "When activated, it will protect you from outside forces, but it will not make you invulnerable."

"A buffer?" I gaze back at the simple golden band of metal, admiring Briseathe's work.

"Yes. Just don't go jumping off tall buildings and not expect to get your legs crushed."

He hands me a tube full of small blue chips. "It runs on these, and they run out of power fast, so be careful."

I slip it over my wrist. It fits perfectly. "At least it doesn't constrict me," I smirk.

"Remember, wear it all the time. Just in case." He warns.

"Even in the shower?" I tease, which surprises both of us. Athos quirks a brow and I feel heat rush to my cheeks. What is wrong with me?

When I remain silent, he says, "Come on, we are going to be late."

"What? It doesn't start till dusk." I say, glancing at my clock.

"We are walking."

"Are you serious?" I ask.

"Yes. If I go around flying you everywhere, people will think you are lazy." He laughs as he walks out.

"Yeah, well, I don't need to depend on you for transportation."

"That is the idea, Lily." I scoff as I hurry after him.

The series of pathways that lead to the center of Legion stretches to every dwelling and is what we use as our means of guidance. Even though I figure Athos knows exactly where to go without them. Legion is the most verdant place I have ever seen, which I suppose has to do with Sheiba. Even in the middle of January, flowers bloom all around us, and the air is balmy.

I finger my bangle as we take the path towards the South, where the council will hold their meeting. I don't want to activate it just yet. Hopefully never. The council is composed of the most well-known Supes, and the most popular of the time. They are each given an area to cover and deal with. And if human affection goes another way, they are relieved of their position but still allowed to work under the new appointee.

Currently Sheiba holds the Southern Americas, Mathis has been charged with Australia and the Arctic's; Juno has Africa; Elsa Europe and Asia; Jace Kace the Northern Americas. Now with Mathis and Jace Kace gone there are two positions that need to be filled.

Athos called for the meeting before we met up with Korra. How I do not know, and why they agreed I can only imagine it has to do with his being the only one that can hold his own with Mathis.

"Do you know what they want to do? I know you are all very peace-loving people, but do you think they might want to fight back?" I ask.

"No, they do not want a full-out war with you humans. I do not think even Mathis wants that." Athos says.

"Really? It's not like we would stand a chance anyways if you guys-"

He spins to me, stopping me mid-sentence.

"Lily, no matter what you think about us, no matter how powerful you think we are, you humans could annihilate us on a whim. You almost did that once before, and it was to get rid of your own kind. It takes a while to get to that point. How long do you think it would take you to get to the point of total destruction just to get rid of us? We have always been concerned about preservation. You might think you do not stand a chance against us, but the reality is we do not stand a chance against a race that is alright with destroying the whole of the world to achieve their goal."

"You sound like Mathis." I say softly.

The emotion drains from his face. "Yes, Mathis thinks the same thing, but for the wrong reasons. We have never believed in waging war, and even now we do not race to arms in order to defend ourselves against you, or our own kind."

"Then why does Mathis suddenly change his mind?" I ask.

"I do not know." he shakes his head, "I have been away for far too long, and my people have changed far too much. They never used to care about the things they do now. I fear it has corrupted them."

We continue in silence. We walk past many homes of different styles and sizes and come to the center. I follow him down another path that points south.

"Athos. Killing Mathis is out of the question. Waging war is too. That leaves two options." I say.

"Detainment, or leaving him alone." He says.

"But you cannot detain him." I say.

Athos sighs, "I know Lily. This meeting is going to focus on what we as a people need to do now. I will worry about what to do with Mathis when I get him later. For now, I have to take care of this."

He gestures to around us.

"Let me run some ideas by you," I say. We follow the path, talking about possibilities, to the very end of Legion in the south. The flat land is bare of any buildings but one. It is a gazebo of sorts that sits close to the edge.

It is made of many vines and flowers, with a dirt floor that rises on steps. I immediately recognize Sheiba in her sleek outfit, standing away from a group that clusters at the opposite end of the structure. I can make out Juno and Elsa in the group, heads bowed and shoulders shrugged as they speak to each other.

So, Sheiba doesn't get along with anyone, it seems. She turns to us as we approach the steps.

"Athos." her voice is husky but loud. The other two stand straight up and part.

"Sheiba. Juno, Elsa." Athose greets them all, but the other two only sniff. Their eyes are on me.

"They did not think you would really bring her." Sheiba explains.

"We did not think you would risk it." Juno sighs. I hold my hands behind my back and take a step closer to Athos. I tap my bangle and feel a vibration rush up my arm. He glances down at me and we both exchange the same look. Hope it works.

"Risk?" he asks casually.

"We are not sure who else sides with the betrayer. Let alone who means to do humans harm," she explains.

I tried to hide a smile at Juno's name for Mathis. "I doubt anyone would try to hurt her here."

"Do you really?" Sheiba asks, looking intrigued.

"No," he smiles. Sheiba rolls her eyes as the other two look miffed,

"This is not a joking matter, Athos," Elsa hisses. "Do you think he will come here to hurt her? Or you?"

"We do not know what to think right now. Which is the only reason you may be here." Sheiba says, eyeing me.

"Right," he sighs.

"No one knows anything then," I say.

"Well, this sounds like it will be productive," Sheiba glares at me. "And you know something?"

"I have opinions. But in the end, it will be up to you." I glance up at Athos.

"Are you here to speak for humans?" Elsa smirks.

"No more than you are for the Supes," I retort.

"No indeed. I am not Briseathe," she says and they all give Athos a meaningful look.

"Perhaps you need a new Briseathe," I say, preferably a non-blue one.

Juno shoots me a look but says, "I agree."

Everyone is taken aback.

"You do?" Elsa asks.

"Why not?" Juno shrugs. "It will make everything so much easier for the rest of us."

"You mean you will have less responsibility," Sheiba sneers.

"That too. But really, it worked with Briseathe, and it will work again."

"Do you want the position?" Elsa says dryly.

"No. I think Athos will make a better candidate," he stiffens next to me.

"Well," Sheiba breathes, "he is the clear choice…."

"Wait now, we cannot just make this decision ourselves," Athos protests.

"Who else would it be, Athos?" Juno asks.

"I don't know, but I don't want to make a hasty choice now."

"We have many choices to make in haste today," I jump as Harold materializes next to me. "Hey Lillium, long time no see," he grins.

"Hey," I clear my throat.

Athos scoffs. "So they have chosen you as ambassador?"

"Yes. Taking over Jace's ward." Athos just shakes his head. "Dolf should be here soon."

"He is Mathis's replacement?" Athos asks.

"Yes," Sheiba says. "They were the only two who volunteered."

"Everyone else is too afraid," Elsa says.

"Well then, we should make our decisions fast." An unfamiliar voice comes from behind Athos. I take a step back to see a small-statured man. In the dimming light of the sun, he looks to have silver skin. He walks over to Elsa, his skin rippling with his movements. I've never heard of him before. I'm sure I would remember someone like him. What can he do?

"Let us all be seated." He says.

I raise a brow as I eye the bare ground. He raises his arms and his skin flickers. His whole body seems to vibrate as it turns into molten silver, ebbing out through his arm. It pools to the ground where it solidifies into a low table and chairs.

I try to keep my jaw from hanging as I follow the others to sit down. I tap the back of my chair first just to make sure it is solid before sitting down. Out of the corner of my eye, I can see Dolf smirking at me. I sit next between Athos and Harold, Dolf takes a head, Sheiba the other, and Elsa and Juno sit across from Athos and me.

"To begin, I think we need to address the biggest problem," Juno starts. "Ourselves."

"I agree," Sheiba sighs.

"We need to figure out who among us is on what side," Juno continues.

"And what sides are there?" I interrupt.

Juno looks miffed, exchanging glances with Elsa. "I told you," Sheiba snickers.

"Those who side with Mathis. Those who side with us," Juno says.

"I only ask because us humans are going to need specifics."

"What is there to specify?" Elsa snaps. "Those who agree with Mathis and those who do not."

"You might not agree with Mathis, but what is it you stand for?" I ask. The Supes exchange looks of surprise. Perhaps they didn't think of that.

"Specifically, why is it you side against Mathis? Just because he killed one of his own, or for something else?" I continue.

"What else would there be?" Elsa asks.

I scoff, "Peace? The world? What you all supposedly come out of hiding to protect?"

"Coexisting in peace," Athos says. "It is what we have always lived by."

"Yes, that is what we stand for," Elsa says flippantly.

"Regardless of what we think of humans." Dolf adds. Juno gives him a look like ice.

"We need to know who the enemy is," I say. The others regard me just as coolly, as if to say, of course, we do.

"By 'we' she means humans," Athos says. "Humans need to know we do not plan on taking over the world."

"Why would we do that?" Dolf asks. I can't help but laugh at his question.

"You guys really need to get off this rock more. Have you forgotten how we are?" I ask.

"Selfish, self-centered, and self-destructive?" Sheiba smirks.

"Exactly!" I say. "The second we think you pose any threat to us, we will lose our minds! No matter what you have done for the world, or for us. We fear what we do not understand or what we cannot control."

"So we have to appear to be on your side?" Dolf asks.

"Yes," Athos says.

"Based on principle, I know you all do not agree with Mathis. But it is not really just his actions we are afraid of, but what he stands for. We need to be reassured that we will not wake up tomorrow in chains. Whether or not you really think that, I know that if you stand with your age-old idea of peace, you will never act on that thought." I look around the table as everyone considers what I've said.

"So, we are all agreeing that we are choosing to separate ourselves from those who believe humans are subordinate?" Sheiba asks.

One by one, everyone nods in agreement. "Good. Now that that is settled, let us discuss what is to be done now."

"About Mathis?" I ask.

"Yes," they all say.

"Athos can get him, but then what?" Sheiba asks. "There is no place that can hold him."

"Unless we hold him forever," Elsa laughs.

"Could we knock him out with something? Put him in a coma?" I ask.

"No, his body will turn whatever we gave him into something else."

"I can't punch him in the face for the rest of my life," Athos sighs.

"Well, there is only one option we have," Dolf says. Everyone turns to him in surprise.

"There is?" Athos asks.

He smiles. "Yes. Briseathe."

Chapter 26

I feel my heart leaps into my throat as I try to empty my face. Talking about the fate of humanity is one thing - this is their issue to sort out. I can't give them an opinion if I have one now.

All eyes are on Athos now, waiting. I force myself to keep my head turned from him.

"You know that is not an option," Athos says softly.

"Says you," Dolf counters. "Does he even know what is going on?" he asks.

"Obviously. You saw the suit she is wearing," Sheiba says, gesturing to me.

"Then why can't he help us?" Dolf snaps.

"He will do what he has always done, help when he can but not directly put himself in the line," Athos retorts. "He's too vulnerable and valuable to be put in any harm right now."

"He's never just left us to die, so why would he now?" Harold says, surprising me.

By the gleam in Dolf's eye, I can tell he isn't about to let it go. He sees Briseathe as our only way, and I agree with him, but there is nothing he can do. Except make Briseathe mad. Everyone here knows Athos and I are in direct contact with Briseathe, the only people alive who can still speak to him.

"Forget about Briseathe," I say before Dolf can explode with frustration. "The bigger problem right now is my people. If they turn on you, not even Briseathe and all his intelligence can help us."

"Us?" Sheiba scoffs.

"Yes, us. We have to stop thinking in terms of you and them. Us is everyone who will die when the humans release their havoc on the world. It was only our intervention the first time that stopped them from blowing the planet up. But now we are to be considered the threat," Harold says.

"Then what shall we do now?" Elsa scoffs.

"Everything we did before, and what Lillium suggests. Humans need to be distracted and we all are still the perfect distraction." Harold pulls at his flowing shirt arms, "But we will need to step it up a bit."

"How?" I ask.

"How indeed?" Dolf rolls his eyes.

"We start with a leader," Sheiba suggests. The table hums with agreement.

"Athos has already won them by being the only one who stands up to Mathis. He will be our face now," Dolf says. I place a hand on Athos's leg before he can protest.

"I agree. He represents a strength against the threat," Juno smiles. Athos is at a loss for words. They are all agreeing to make him their poster boy, mouthpiece, leader.

"I think this should be put to some kind of vote for all," Athos stutters.

"We are enough," Sheiba waves his concern off. "The others will agree, or not, but they will do nothing. You are the only one who can do anything at this point."

"It's settled then," Harold slaps Athos on the back and winces when he pulls his hand back. I take his hand in mine and squeeze it reassuringly.

"You will need to go public, Athos," I say softly. "Let them know you are on their side, and that you are all united against them." He keeps his eyes down but I can see he has accepted his fate by the slight nod he gives me.

"His words might not be enough," Sheiba says.

Dolf scoffs, "What else can we do?"

"Move Legion," I suggest. Athos's head snaps up as everyone gapes at us.

"Move?" Elsa croaks, "Legion?"

"Where to?" laughs Harold.

"Where it came from," I say.

"You are suggesting that we just put it back down there?" Sheiba asks.

"Yes. As a show of good faith. You will be taking your places amongst us as equals, no longer above us and not accessible- which is another thing you will all have to change."

"Our accessibility?" Dolf scoffs.

"Yes. We need to see you as approachable and accessible, otherwise you are a lofty sort of deity to us that we can easily toss aside."

"We created Legion to get away from the constant attentions of humans," Sheiba says.

"I know. And you are all entitled to privacy just like any other person. I am not asking you all to invite humans to live with you." I glance at Athos, "Just, go out there. Let them see you, let them know you."

"Befriend them?" Elsa smirks.

"No, not if you don't want to. Humans like things on their level, and if they see you as a part of their community, they will identify with you and trust you. If you stay up here and claim to be on their side, they will eventually begin to distrust you. They will adapt the thoughts of, 'how do they know what it is like when they live up in the clouds? They don't know nor do they care.'"

"I understand your thoughts, Lillium, but I don't think we will gain much support from our own people if we do that," Juno says.

"Me neither." Dolf nods.

"I agree with her," Athos says. Harold nods. "And since I am the de facto leader here, I believe my decision on this is the only one that counts."

"What about those who do not agree and turn?" Sheiba sighs.

Athos stands up and places his palms on the table, "Since there is no way that we can seek out supporters of Mathis, and since there will be those who wish to remain neutral in these affairs, I will give them all a chance to leave Legion."

"Leave? Just like that!?" Dolf exclaims.

"You would let those who wish for anarchy just walk away to Mathis?" Sheiba says softly.

"It is not a choice of mine- we cannot villainize those who do not want to pick sides, and I would, no matter what, give those people the chance to find somewhere else to go. I only expect Mathis's supporters to go with them, or not. They may choose to stay here and cause trouble."

"There is no way of knowing..." I sigh.

"Right." Harold huffs.

"I will give our people a choice, and once they choose, we can move forward." Athos says.

"And when will you be executing this?" Elsa asks.

"Tonight." Everyone scoffs. "They are all expecting as much to happen anyways- we cannot waste time here. I will let them all know our intentions, and they can have until dawn to pick a side."

"How are you going to ask everyone before dawn?" I ask as I eye the night sky.

"The way we do with everything." Elsa stands. Everyone else does as well, so I get up to stand by Athos, just in time, as the table and seats start to collapse and meld back with Dolf.

"Sheiba?" Harold motions to her.

She groans and rolls her eyes. Mumbling, she bends over and slams her palms into the earth. She is still and quiet, so much so that I barely see the thick bulbous vine sprout out from between her hands. It is a dusty green with dozens of cup-like pods. Athos strides over to it, waiting until she straightens up and gives him a nod. He plucks one pod, only to have her slap it from his hand.

"You can speak directly into it. Don't mutilate it!" She cries. He rolls his eyes, his gaze falling to me. I give him a weak smile as he bends over to the closest pod.

"All are called to the gathering. All are called." His voice booms out over the valley from all directions, echoing for a good minute until dying.

"Sound-carrying plants." Harold smiles at me.

"Full of surprises, aren't you?" I say, impressed.

"At least one a day," he laughs.

"Will they come?" I ask.

"Of course. We are very into group gatherings. And those who are not

219

here will hear about it eventually." The first few to arrive pop into existence close to the gathering, but far enough so as not to be a part of our group.

Then one by one, whether by flight, foot, or transport, the Supers of Legion appear before us. As they grow, I start to question his previous statement on their numbers and his thoughts on humans beating them. Sure, we outnumber Supers, but any one of these people could take out ten of mine in a matter of minutes. Not only that, but many of them are very odd-looking.

It has never occurred to me that Sheiba, Jace, Mathis, and the like are famous for anything other than their powers - but here before me stand Supers with grotesque figures, fur, bright skin, dark eyes, and even extra limbs. Perhaps the Supes who make it to the spotlight are the ones who look like us.

I have never known that Supes can look like the crazy clones Briseathe keeps in his lab. I guess he has to model them off of something.

Once Athos seems satisfied with the turnout, he produces a small orb from his jacket. It floats above him, stopping a few feet over his head. I instantly recognize it as one of Briseathe's; he is no doubt watching what is happening. The others seem to share the same conclusion as a hushed murmur erupts among the masses.

"No introductions shall be made - we all know why we are here," he starts. His voice carries over the pod he speaks into. "The gathering has decided upon actions that must be taken now, this very minute, to ensure our safety and the safety of the world. "I have been given the title of our leader in the eyes of the humans. I shall speak for us now." Another murmur rises and dies.

"As our leader, I am officially out-casting Mathis." Sounds of approval swell. "And those who choose to follow him. He no longer holds to our sacred belief in peace and, as such, is named a traitor. He names himself our enemy, the enemy of the human race whom we share this world with, and an agent of chaos and war.

"No matter your feelings on humans, they are creatures of this world as we are. We are equals in this world." I can hear some protests, very few but strong nonetheless, which are drowned out by Athos's powerful voice.

"Mathis is an enemy of ours, of humans, and anyone who chooses to follow him or agrees with his actions is named our enemy as well. We have always been a people of peace- he breaks our most sacred law of mortality and kills one of us, he is not one of us."

That seems to settle among them. They all grow very still, and the ones who I can see in the front hang their heads at the mention of Jace's death.

"You all now have a choice to make. Either you still uphold the ideals of peace and side with Legion, or you do not and seek war with Mathis at your side. If you cannot choose between your people, you are free to remain neutral, but not here in Legion. You are all free to choose. I cannot stop you.

"But know that the moment any of you act out in any form that could be a disturbance to the peace we have with humans, you will be deemed an enemy. And I will stop you. I will seek you out.

"I do not ask that any of you fight by my side, nor your help of any kind. I only ask you to make a choice, here and now. If you choose to leave, do it before dawn. For tomorrow we are moving Legion back to its rightful place among the humans." This time I can clearly hear the uproar of protests. Athos glances at Sheiba, who approaches the plant, touching one of the pods. A high-pitched screech rings out, causing everyone to hold their ears. I grimace as it dies down, only to be replaced by Athos's booming words.

"Change is coming," he says darkly while everyone slowly pulls their heads up. "We have lived for far too long aloft from the world. Danger is imminent. Death is reachable. We are in a crisis! Have you already forgotten the war? The pain and suffering? It can and will happen again if we let it. But this time, this time, we will be fighting on one side, and the humans on the other. And we will lose. So a choice is to be made now. Do you stand with us and the humans, or do you stand with Mathis?"

His voice carries over them and disappears. Silence settles as they all look at each other.

"I take neither side, brother," a familiar face appears out of the crowd. Brogan pushes his way to Athos, his face grim. "I mean no disrespect. But I

221

cannot, even after Jace, fight one or the other."

"I do not ask you to fight," Athos says, his features tight. I see the way the sides of his eyes crinkle and wonder what history lays between the two Supes.

Brogan flicks his eyes at me, then smirks. "But you ask me to choose, and I cannot. We have always been one people, and even though some of us have chosen over the years to stray from our beliefs, we have never drawn lines."

"There was no need to then. I respect your choice to remain neutral. But you understand you cannot stay here now."

Brogan's handsome face breaks out in a rueful grin. "I understand." He tilts his head to Sheiba and the others before he turns to leave. But just before he disappears into the crowd, he looks my way and gives me a wink. I feel my heart flutter stupidly and try to hide my blush.

A small blonde Supe rushes up to Athos suddenly, startling me.

"Killing our own is forbidden, no matter the reasoning, and no one in our history has ever committed the crime. I side with you, Athos, I will fight with you." He takes her hands in his and smiles in appreciation. She pats his hands in response and turns to the crowd.

"No matter your feelings on humans, think about us. He has committed an act so heinous that he is no longer a part of us. We no longer feel him. We no longer know him." With that, she stands by Athos, confronting her fellow Supes.

Something ripples through the crowd, an unspoken feeling that I cannot identify, but that every Supe seems to feel. Her words' impact them, causing many to move to Athos, clearly taking his side.

Many Supes surround him, some voicing their approval, others taking solace within the group, as the mass that comes to hear him speak starts to move slightly together to his side. As the group moves over, it leaves a few stragglers.

They stand on the outskirts of the mass, some looking indecisive, while others are plainly agitated. One in particular stands out to me. She is hidden by the crowd, but now the Supes around her move to the growing group.

She is quite small in stature with charcoal hair that is held back from her face by a ribbon. She has alabaster skin that makes her angry expression very visible. I watch her look from Athos, to me, and back to him.

Her eyes are glowing darkly against her pale skin. I know that look, it is the same look Mathis had given me back in Paris. My heart stops when she looks back at me, her body shaking. I silently thank Briseathe for his force field before I inch closer to Harold.

"Harold? " I whisper.

"Hm? " His eyes are glued to Athos.

"There is a woman-"

"Yes." He nods.

"Alright." I croak. I have known something like this might happen, and they do too, but now that I am being stared down by an age-old Supe, I am not entirely sure I am prepared.

The woman approaches one of the bulbous flowers close to her and clears her throat loudly into it. The crowd stops moving and looks around for the person.

"I would like to address the situation of the human." She says hotly, pointing right at me. "Before I make my decision." I can feel eyes on me, and Harold moves closer.

"No," I whisper, "let it happen." Despite my fears, I know I have to appear strong, even though I really, really am not.

"What situation is that?" Athos replies.

"How do I know your words are your own?" She snaps at him. I force myself not to roll my eyes. "How do I know what you say is truly what you think is best? Or if it is in the best interest of this human and her kind?"

"We all share a common interest in the well-being of the world. What is best for them is also for-"

"No!" She cuts him off. "We tolerate this world. We tolerate these humans and their self-destructive ways." She spits.

"What else would you have us do, Anh? We have always been a part of this world. Where else would you have us go?" Athos asks, his amber eyes flicking at me.

223

She scoffs, "You tell me, Athos." He raises a brow as she smirks, "You return to us after so long, and say nothing to us of what you see. You then choose to take up with this human, and ignore us! Now you side with them. Why? Has this one seduced you?"

My face burns with embarrassment as others look at me.

"Anh, I-"

"What did you find, Athos?" She snaps. "All those years, did you even find a scrap of what we are? What we were?"

"No," he says bluntly, echoing gloomily. Anh's face falls as he says, "There is nothing out there worth seeking again."

"So this is it?" She says hoarsely.

"Yes. This is our world, our only world." The faces of the Supes reflect confusion, sadness, and hurt all around as the news settles. There is no other Source, no other home they can once again flourish in as they had before. They had a chance and lost it, their Source is gone forever.

"This world must last for us. For all of us," Athos says gently.

"Then why side with those who will turn on us and eradicate themselves?" She cries out. She turns her hateful gaze to me, her eyes glistening with pain and fear. "If it is true that we may never find it, or where it came from, we must do what we have to do to survive."

"And we have," I catch the strain in Athos's tone as he tries to calm her. "We are still here. We have been able to live among them in peace for years."

"Until now," she flicks her gaze at him and smiles ruefully. "We know the truth now. There is nothing of our old life left. There is nothing for us." I blink and she is gone.

Athos has appeared where she was, but she is quick. She now stands off to his left, her hands glowing white hot in the dying light as she aims them right at him. Molten fire pours from her palms, shooting streams of liquid fire at Athos. He dodges it in time, pulling another Supe out of the danger as well.

The next thing I know, Harold is thrown ten feet away, landing with a sickening thump. Anh now stands next to me, her face a primal mask of rage. I don't have time to react before she lifts a hand and throws all her might into her power, right at me.

Molten fire pours out of her, smothering me with its heat, sizzling around me as my force field surges to life. I can smell the hot earth and burning ozone all around me, but I am still very much alive. I hold out my arms and watch as the liquid drips right off of me into a pool on the ground. I meet Anh's eyes and we share a moment of complete shock, me with my hands held out in front of me and her with hers hanging limply by her sides.

A pop sounds as she is encased in a bubble suddenly. In the corner of my eye, I can see Juno standing over Harold, writhing on the ground, his chest smoking. She has one hand hovering over him and the other holding Anh in the bubble.

I gasp as I feel Athos grab me and yank me away from the pool of fire. "Are you alright?" he yells. It is only then that I realize everyone is running around screaming and shouting in a panic.

"Yes, I think so." I hold out my arms and look all over myself. There's no trace of the fire anymore. It has all sloughed off. I check my bangle. It still holds a glow, but much dimmer now.

"Thank you Briseathe." I breath, letting out a shaky laugh.

He forces a smile and then turns to Anh. Juno still holds her in a bubble, but her attention is mostly on Harold. Elsa's bent over him, using her healing powers to mend his chest. Sheiba holds his head in her lap, tipping a vial into his mouth. He stops moving.

"Harold-" I gasp. I run over to them, only to see his chest moving as he breathes.

"Passed out." Sheiba grunts.

"Will he be alright?" I ask.

Juno glares at me. "Briseathe didn't deem him worthy of bestowing his gifts on, but he will live."

"How!?" Anh screams behind us, "How did she do that?!"

Athos is struggling to find something to say, but Juno beats him to it. "Briseathe, of course. Can't you see that glowing bangle she has?"

"Briseathe?" someone else echoes. The chaos around us starts to settle at the mention of him.

"She lives because the half-bred helped her?!" Anh cries, "He chose her over us?!"

"Oh, no," I say as another uproar starts.

"She has seen him!" A voice cries out.

"He has chosen her!" Another screams.

"Chosen!" A chorus of Supers rises among the masses, chanting.

Anh throws herself against her prison. "He chose her!"

"For what?" I scoff at her. "Death? Because that is what it seems like."

"He has chosen her! He has sided with the humans!" The random declaration stirs the crowd into a frenzy.

"Briseathe sides with the humans!" They chant. The mass seems swayed by this, all moving together and agreeing that Briseathe had sided with humans, not Mathis.

"Briseathe has deemed her life of some value," Elsa says, surprising me. "We should trust his judgment."

"No!" Anh screams, her face a mask of fury. "We are the chosen, we can inherit this world! We can be as we were before!"

"Shut up!" Sheiba cries out. She places Harold's head on the ground and stood, holding a purple flower. She crushes it in her hand, turning it into dust, and blows it at the orb holding Anh. Juno opens a hole in it, just big enough for the pollen to travel in. Anh cries out as the poll surrounds her.

She kicks the orb and screams. But the screams grow weaker and weaker, and her legs give out. Soon she collapses and starts to snore.

Juno withdraws her hand, causing the orb to disappear. Anh's sleeping body drops to the ground with a thunk, and is soon surrounded by others. Juno gives me one last hard look before she and Elsa withdraw to calm the crowd.

I sit down next to Harold and take his hand in mine. As I wait for Athos to come for us, I stare at my bangle, wondering at the marvels Briseathe can do.

And wondering what it means to be chosen by him.

Chapter 27

"How does he do it?" I ask again.

"I tell you, I do not know," Athos sighs. I bite my lip as I look at the bangle again.

I switched out the battery when we got back to his house last night and wore it all night. Not that I expect anyone to try anything after seeing Anh's failed attempt, but you never know.

"It is like Juno's force field, isn't it?" I say. Athos groans from his couch.

We soak up the morning rays in the massive living room while he works on a list of the Supes that defected last night. By the ashed look on his face, it is not good.

When I ask him how they are all able to sever their connection, he only shakes his head. No one knows how they are doing it as it has never been done before. The only time connections are ever lost is when one of them dies.

"Juno thought so too," I mutter, trying to take his mind off the others. At first, I think the looks she gives me are because she hates humans. But now, after thinking about it, I think she recognizes the force field around me as like that of hers.

Images of Briseathe's clone cave flutter through my memory the more I think about it. He says he clones himself and a few of his friends, just to play pranks on them. Could he have cloned their abilities as well? The beeping of my pad breaks my thoughts. I twist around and grab it from the coffee table.

"Korra has accepted," I say, smiling. He grunts in response.

"She says she will be here by noon, so we should be able to start around then."

"Good," he sighs, "The sooner the better." I toss the pad on the couch as I stand to stretch.

"Are you sure you do not want to alert the others?"

"No. I do not want to give anyone time to plan something."

I nod, "Right. The second the humans figure out what is going on, many will rush down there to watch. It would be easy pickings for whoever wants to make a scene."

"So we must do this fast, and clean. Korra knows not to ask too many questions, right? It would be useless to go through all this planning just to have it ruined with an hour-long interview."

I roll my eyes. "You know she does. She's the only one we can trust with this. When has she let us down?"

"Never." He has his head bowed, but I can see his smirk.

"Right. Three hours." I sigh. "I am going to get dressed and get my things ready." He grunts again.

The warm morning breeze blows through the walkway as I make my way to my room, fidgeting with my bangle. So Briseathe can mimic a Supe's powers and make devices with it, I am sure of it. How can we use that, and why hasn't he mentioned it before?

I slip on my suit, covering it with a long-sleeved shirt and pants. Legion might be warm, but the outside world is still in winter. The Council is going to have to work out the schematics of their city on the ground by themselves; whether they should keep their warm weather, allow humans back into their city to work, selling their houses, they have to figure it all out today, and hopefully before Legion falls back to Earth.

My pad is beeping incessantly on the table where I left it. I haven't checked my messages in almost two days, so I am not surprised when I find it full.

I run the program through it to file them and see my dad has sent me a few, one from Libby, two from Max, and none from Gaia. The amount of requests for Hero for Hire is staggering.

"I need to get more Supes," I mutter. They will all have to wait, unfortunately, at least until after today. I can start on them tomorrow when we get to Briseathe's work out a few plans.

"Athos?" I call from my room.

"What?" He snaps back loudly.

"Are you done with that list yet?" I start back to the living room, only to hear him mumbling something.

"I will take that as a no," I smirk.

"This is going to take a while, Lily."

"That's fine, I just wanted to talk to you about making another list-"

"No! No more lists!" He says, looking horrified.

"Of Supes who would be willing to help us with Hero for Hire," I finish. He glances over at me, eyebrow raised.

"That's easy. No one." I roll my eyes as I take a seat next to him.

"Not if you ask them."

"I can't make anyone do anything they don't want to. Just because they made me their spokesperson doesn't make me king."

"But they will listen to you, just like they did last night." I tap a button on my pad and bring up footage from last night, of him standing in front of Sheiba's microphone plant.

"Briseathe sent this to me this morning, even though he won't answer any of my calls or messages." I say gruffly. I play him the part of the Supes coming to his side, each swayed by his words, his actions.

"You are a natural leader, Athos. Even if you don't see it, I do, and they do too." I can't see his face as he watches it, but I can see his shoulders sag a bit. He doesn't believe he can do this, be their leader and be our hero, the link between our two people.

But I have seen him do wonders not just with his powers, but with his ability to empathize with everyone. I roll my eyes and huff.

"I would know, Athos. Look at me-" he glances at me waving at my face, "I might still dislike Supes, but you managed to change my mind. Which was hard, after everything-" I trail off, shaking my head.

He quirks a brow. "You never said what happened, Lily." I never wanted to. I liked to keep that part of my life locked away, hidden beneath a sheet of scars and carefully cloaked hatred that keeps me from feeling anything.

But Athos has been digging through all that shit, even if he doesn't know it. And so, despite every warning bell and every cell in my body screaming at me to stay safely behind my cage of hate, I decide to tell him.

After all, he's been telling me the truths of his life, so I might as well remind him we are in this together.

"I had a fiancé," I start, focusing my eyes on the dust particles glittering in the sunlight. I can feel him shift next to me, but I keep my eyes forward. There is no way I can do this while looking at him.

"His name was Gabriel, but we called him Gabe. We grew up with the others, Libby, Max, and Gaia. He proposed to me right out of graduation - something I'd been expecting for years since we had been together practically since we were in diapers." I shut my eyes briefly, letting myself drift back to that day.

He waits until we are all gathered after the long ceremony under the hot summer sun. My face is drenched in sweat and my robes are crumpled, but the moment he drops to his knee and holds out the ring to me, I feel like I am glowing.

"We were going to join Gaia and run off to some wild, unknown area in need of rehabilitation. Back then, we were skeptical of Supers, but for the most part, we were just curious about you. Gabe especially. He wanted to rise in the ranks and work directly with Legion. He was on the fast track for an apprenticeship there after serving his four years."

I take a shallow, shaky breath. My mind is screaming at me to stop, that we don't have to relive this. I feel his hand encase mine, warm and heavy against my chilled skin. He gives me a slight squeeze, and I think about how I have seen this man break through concrete and wonder at how gentle he can be.

"It happened shortly after that, during the Briseathe festival. We go into the city to celebrate, something we rarely did, but we figured why not? It might be our last chance to celebrate in Sun City. We took the train home, and it was packed with people, all drunk. One drunk, stupid man and his wandering hands are all it takes. I was content enough with leaving him with a black eye, but Gabe-" I shake my head, holding back hot tears, "Gabe wouldn't let it go. He didn't see the guy had five friends with him. That's all it takes, one drunken man and his drunken friends to beat him to death."

I turn my head, so he can't see the way my lip trembles still, after all these years. "He was gone before the paramedics arrive, and so are they. There was nothing anyone can do. The train didn't have a medi pad, and no one knew first aid. But the worst part? No one tried to stop it. It isn't like we were the only people on that train. It was packed. And not one person tried to help him while they just beat him to death."

"Oh, Lily-" I can hear the pity in his voice, and I steel myself against it.

"They grew so used to letting Supers save them, they have no idea how to save themselves." I swallow the bitter, acidic pain down again, and lock it away before it gets out. I bite the inside of my cheek until I taste the metallic tang of blood. Only then do I turn back to him, ignoring the sad look in his eyes.

"No one can find them, the guys who killed him, I mean. I wrote to Legion, called them, pleaded with them to find the guys, and charge them with his murder. It takes six months, six Athos, before they send me a letter. You know what it says?" I ask, though I can see in his eyes he already knows. "It says the investigation is being handled by the local police, and that the Supers of Legion are occupied at the moment with pressing matters - but should they find the time, they will try to help." I scoff, remembering how I tore the letter to shreds and any hope I had left.

"It's been four years and those men are still free." I sniff, forcing my shoulders to relax.

Only then do I realize I have been squeezing his hand. I let go, pulling my hand back to my lap.

"And yet, despite all of that, you somehow manage to get me to follow you." I croak.

"So far I have just been doing what I think is right...." He says softly.

"So far it is." I lay my hand on his shoulder, and he turns to me. I can see his eyes softening as he takes a deep breath. It is surprising and humbling at the same time to see him so vulnerable. Athos, who can move a whole building, and circumvent the world in a second, is a man so much older than me, and he is scared right now. I slide down next to him on the floor and put my arms around him. "Athos, I am scared too."

He laughs grimly. "I would never guess it. You never show it." This time I laugh.

"I am, though, all the time, but I still face it, every day. I don't think I would be able to live with myself if I ran away. Plus, where would I go? Briseathe's clone lab?"

I think he will laugh, but when he doesn't, I pull away from him. His face goes back to stone, his eyes distant.

"I am not saying you are running away, Athos." I say, trying to get him to come back.

"No, I know. I am not this time, but I did before." My heart flutters when he says it.

"You, you ran away? From what?" I ask.

"Everything." He blinks, and turns to look at me, his face sad. "Before Briseathe exposed us, during the start of the great war, I wanted us to help. I wanted to do what he ended up doing, step into the light and help the world, to help you humans quit fighting so hard for nothing."

"Why didn't you?"

"I was scared to act on my own. No one would back me, not even Briseathe then."

"What?!" I exclaim, "Are you serious?"

"Yes. He is…different. That's the only way I can describe it. Very different from back then."

"What changed him?" His mouth drops and his eyes glaze over,

"That is not for me to say. He may tell you one day if he wants."

"So you ran away, to space, you mean?"

He smiles ruefully. "Yes. When I realized the others are perfectly happy in the dark, with the world being destroyed around them, I also realized that they were waiting for something."

"The Source?" I guess.

"Yes. They still, even now to this day, feel like it is still here, on this world, hiding in wait, but for what they don't know. They are dreamers." His voice grows harsh, "When I realized that I grew so angry. Angry and scared. So I left, in search of the place where it comes from, or another place with it, with people like us. I left to find anything anywhere that can tell me what to do, how to help my people." A silence stretches out between us, as we both know he finds nothing.

"When you came back," I start, "you came to find they are doing exactly what you wanted to do, but couldn't. Not only that, but Briseathe stepped up to do it." I snort, "The Bristeathe festival very well could be the Athos festival."

He glares at me. "Not that it matters," I say quickly. "Sorry."

He sighs and shrugs. "It doesn't. But other things might. If I step up when I want to, instead of running away, I can put a stop right then and there to the war. Many people, they will live."

I can tell by his tone he is thinking of certain people in particular, perhaps his people, but I can tell this is not a moment to push for more information. His face is already taking on stone-like features as he melts away from me to the past.

"None of that matters now, Athos. Right now, you are doing all you can to help change the world. You are at the forefront. And your people are following you like they wouldn't before. We can do this." His eyes snap back to me, his eyes boring into mine.

He places his hand on my face and smiles. "I know we can. Together, you and I can do anything. I mean, we are taking Legion down today, so who knows what we can do?" He laughs.

I laugh with him and take his hand in mine. "That's right. I never thought I would ever like a Supe, or even call one my friend, but here I am."

"I have that effect on people."

"I know." I roll my eyes, "You can be a pest."

"I think more along the lines of persuasive." His fingers trace the back of my hand and my smile falters as I feel electric heat lick up my arm. He's fucking with me, I know, but I still can't help the way the heat pools in my core or how my skin burns under his touch.

I withdraw my hand, willing my hormones to calm down. It's been a while - a long while if I am being honest, but that's no excuse.

"Pest." I correct. Clearing my throat, I move to get space between us. "Speaking of, you need to finish that list before Korra gets here."

"Right. Then we need to put up some barriers and clear the landing zone."

"And get you in some nice clothes for the cameras."

"What? These are nice." I bite my lip as he looks down at his vintage shirt and jeans.

"I have something better in mind. I will leave it in your room for when you are ready." I pat him on the head and stand to leave,

"Hey! Just because you are my PR human does not mean you can dress me!"

"Actually, it does." I snap back.

Chapter 28

"Finally!" Korra shouts, fist-bumping one of her floating cameras as she turns on her computer. "Alright, now with everything set up, we can get this over with. I want to see that floating island come crashing down!" She jumps into her chair across from us and giggles. "How do I look?"

"Better than me." Athos retorts sourly.

"You both look great." I chide, cutting him a look. Athos snorts, plucking at his new suit.

"Athos, love, you look like a real hero in that," Korra says. The sides of his lips curl a bit as he tries not to smile. Korra's wearing a very slim-fitting silver dress that pools out around her neck and down by her knees. It's a very modest outfit by her standards.

"Thank you Korra," I say, "I made it myself." I elbow him in the side. We are seated on a park bench on the top of the crater where Legion once sat. Behind us, the lush park is vacant of any people, and a barrier is up to keep wanderers from getting under the drop zone.

"I would not have picked these colors," he says.

"They are the colors from the cat's eye Jude gave us, for luck."

He stopped fidgeting with the suit and raised a brow, "The one you gave to Gaia?"

"Yes. I thought since it seemed to bring us luck, we should incorporate it into the suit. That's why you have that symbol on your back. It's the shape the Tiger's eye had in it." I explain.

Athos sits still for a moment, then smiles. "Two steps ahead as always, Lily."

He smooths out his sleeveless shirt and sat back. It's a very nice suit, in my opinion, with cobalt blue and milky white colors mixing and moving as he moved. He has a sleeveless tunic and form-fitting pants all made of the same material Briseathe made of mine. Though it makes no difference if he fights naked or in pajamas, these at least would last him longer than others. I'd let Briseathe help out with this one since I clearly have no idea what I'm doing.

"Now that we have established that we all look fabulous, let's begin." Her cameras buzz all to life, taking their places in various spots.

"Korra St. Cloud here with the illustrious Athos and boundary-hopping Lillium." I quirk a brow, *I am a what now?*

"Athos has something very important to delve into today, so I will be giving the floor to him."

The camera spins around and floats beside us. I try to keep my face pleasant, but internally I'm freaking out.

"Athos, what landmark event is going to happen today?" Korra asks.

Athos throws the camera a wide grin that makes his dimples pop. "Well Korra, today we will be placing Legion back to its rightful place."

"You mean you are returning it to the ground from where it came from?" She clarifies.

"Yes." He nods. I can hear a hushed murmur from the boundaries where people stand.

"Why now?" Korra asks.

"Because we should have never moved it to begin with." He states with a smile. The murmur grows as some onlookers gasp.

"Athos has been named the Supes spokesperson." I add. The camera tilts towards me, and I cringe.

"Spokesperson?" Korra asks.

"Yes, he now speaks for all the Supes of Legion." I can't help the tremor in my voice. The idea of so many people seeing me live makes my skin itch.

"And those not of Legion?" Korra asks.

"I will assume Mathis speaks for them. We of Legion have always stood for equality between our two peoples. And we will show that by bringing down Legion." Athos says.

"So you officially have a rift between yourselves?" Korra asks.

"We do. I do not want to alarm anyone, but there are some of us who see it fit to follow Mathis and his ideals. Those who do not will fight for our equality."

"You will fight for us? Humans?" Korra asks.

"Yes."

"Against your own people?" She gives him a pointed look, and the crowd grows silent.

Athos turns to me. "The moment they decided peace was no longer their objective, they became our enemy."

"Supers have always held peace highly," I say.

"You two have been partners for a while now, and Lillium, you have managed to do what no human has before- become a part of their world. Some say you are the one pulling the strings here to benefit us humans." Korra says.

"Some Supes think the same, but it is not true. We happened to become partners and friends at a pivotal moment in our joint history." I say, feeling slightly defensive.

"Fate?" she jokes.

"Perhaps." I force a smile.

"We are a great team," Athos says. "Lily has given us a whole new perspective on how our two species should interact. Remember, we used to live among you in secret, pretending to be human. Then we came out and became protectors. Now we are trying to be equals."

"Supers are willing to bring down their home and live among us. Work with us against a common enemy." I say, my voice growing stronger as I speak.

"And what is your plan, when you defeat our common enemy?" Korra asks.

"Mathis and his followers will be dealt with in accordance with the laws," Athos says.

She quirks a brow. "Our laws, or yours?"

"The laws we have all set for the world," I say carefully.

"Well, it seems we really are at a pivotal moment." Korra muses.

"Indeed." Athos looks down at his pad and nods. "It is just about time now."

"Alright! Let's get this show going!" Korra fist-bumps the air again and her cameras zoom into action, flying off to surround the barriers.

"Sorry if I grilled you a bit," she says as we take our places to watch.

"It's alright, it was needed," I shrug.

"There is no going back from here, Lillium." Her tone is warning but I don't need it.

"I know," I say pointedly.

"It's happening," Athos says.

Korra pulls out a screen, and a vision of the bottom of Legion descending appears.

"Look, see these numbers here? These are all the major networks and their current views. Mine is at the top right now." She says gleefully. "This will be a record, maybe even more than last year's Briseathe festival," she mutters.

It starts slowly, barely recognizable to the naked eye. But soon I can see, even from just looking up at it, that the floating city is falling. The Supe who put it up is somewhere up top, decreasing the size of the vortex she created to keep it floating.

The vines that grow over the sides sway as it gains momentum and falls faster and faster. Just before it looks like it's going to come crashing down, the vortex increases in size, stopping it, then completely disappears.

"Wow." Korra says, her mouth agape.

The people around the barriers are cheering loudly as Supes from Legion make their rounds around the city to make sure it is secure.

"Only a few hundred feet now and it will be back in place," Athos says. His eyes find mine and we share a smile. We're doing it, we're really doing it.

"Good job there, hero," I say.

"Well, not-" he stops suddenly, his face falling.

"What?" I ask.

A blood-curdling scream is my answer as someone comes tumbling down from Legion.

Chapter 29

In a microsecond, Athos is gone from my side, appearing just in time to pluck the person from the air.

Athos lands in front of us, holding a girl in his arms. She doesn't look any older than thirteen as I run over to them. A bloodstain is blooming from her chest, soaking through the light green blouse she wears. Before I get close, Harold pops out of the air next to them, blood covering his hands.

"She is fading fast," Athos says grimly.

"Anh, she got out. Someone must have helped…." Harold's voice breaks as he stares down at the bleeding girl.

"Korra-" I begin.

"On it." She pulls up her pad and begins to convey orders in an instant. The closest camera moves away from us and is replaced by a smaller bot holding a first aid kit.

"Others are defecting as we speak," Harold says.

At that moment, I realize this child-looking Supe is the one with the cyclone powers. She's responsible for lifting Legion in the air, and without her controlling it, the cyclone can collapse and bring Legion down on top of us all.

A cry from the nearest crowd causes us to look up at two more Supes free-falling. Without a word Athos pulls me down to hold the girl and then disappears.

"Harold, go back and help the others!" I say, pressing my hands to her chest. There's so much blood I can taste it as I take ragged breaths. My mind grows foggy as I recall the last time I saw so much blood. Gabe's beaten face appears before me and my pulse quickens.

His expression is grim. "Lillium, I can not do much against the others!"

"Then help me get these people out of here in case this place comes crashing down on our heads!" Korra snaps, looking fierce.

He looks from her to me and then the girl. "We will be fine." I lie. She is already so cold and her eyes look glassy. Just like Gabe, right before he took his last breath in my arms. Harold pops away and I fight back the memories rising, blood rushing in my ears as my heart pounds against my chest.

"Hold this to her chest." Korra tosses me some gauze from a first aid kit. "Do not do anything stupid." She says with a raised brow before rushing off, her cameras surrounding her like a swarm of bees.

I watch her go, dread and fear rising in my chest as I continue to hear screams and shouts from the barriers. This wasn't supposed to happen. This is chaos and bloodshed - what we are trying to avoid. I bunch up the gauze and prepare to find where all the blood is pouring from.

The girl is looking right at me. I stiffen, gazing at her pitch-black eyes and pale face.

"Uh-" I stupidly can't think of anything to say as I hold her shirt up with gauze in. Weakly, she shoves my hand away.

"You're bleeding," I say numbly.

"No shit." She croaks, grinning through the pain. It's a shock seeing her smile while dying in my arms.

"I need to apply pressure. Lay back down!" I snap, remembering I'm supposed to keep her alive as she uses me to stand up. She might look like a child, and she might be bleeding to death, but she was strong enough to push me away, pinning me with a look that said, 'I'm in charge here.'

"Hey!" I scramble to get back up as she stumbles to her feet. I catch her arm, letting her steady herself against me. I was powerless to save Gabe but I could still save her.

"I need to stabilize it before it falls," she mumbles against my shoulder.

"Or stay alive so it stays where it is," I say, grasping for anything to convince her to lie back down and live. "The others will come, and they can heal you-"

"Stupid," she coughs. "If I do nothing now, the cyclone will continue to decrease in size, like I told it to. I have to stop it." She gazes up at me and I see the resolve there. She knows she's going to die doing this, but she's going to do it, anyway.

This is what a hero looks like, I think as I tighten my hold on her. This girl is willing to die to save Legion and the humans beneath it. If she can face her death with courage, I can muster the strength to hold her through it.

It's not like Gabe at all. This is something different.

"I assume we need to get as close as possible to do this?" I ask, trying to sound braver than I feel. She nods.

"Splendid." I tilt her so she can put her weight on me, and together we trudge toward the edge of the gorge. There's a gut-wrenching plop behind us, but I force us forward, not wanting to see who is splattered behind us.

I stop just shy of the edge and glance down. The spot where we are is a slope and not a sheer cliff like other places. The girl nudges me to move forward more. I begrudgingly oblige, shuffling us to the very edge.

She huffs, but I hold on to her and say, "Hey, there is no way I am dragging you down there. I might not get us out again. I'm a weakling."

A ghost of a smile appears on her lips as she shakes her head slowly.

"I can feel it from here well enough." I help her stand straight, then take a step back as she lifts her arms above her. I hold her by her hips, ready to catch her if she falls. Legion has fallen low enough I can barely see the top of the cyclone now.

The girl makes delicate movements with her wrists until a black smoke comes from her hands. She changes her movement then, and the smoke swirls around her hands, twisting and plummeting around her arms. Suddenly, Legion drops like a rock and I almost jump to stop her until I see the cyclone beneath it growing. Gradually, the floating island begins to ascend back into the air.

"Wow." I breathe. I can clearly see the cyclone and hear the air moving around me. "At least that is-" I break off when I see someone out of the corner of my eye.

A man's standing behind us, or what looks to be a man. Large stone-like spikes jut from his body making him look more like coral than man.

"Uh-" I gasp as he tears a spike from his belly and throws it at the girl. I'm not exactly thinking when I leap in front of her. Sure, my force field's going to protect me, but what I don't think of is the force of the impact and the fact that I'm next to a damn slope.

I catch the spike with my chest, only to be knocked over the slope. I can't get a hold of anything as I slide further and further down into the gorge. A boulder stops me as my body slams against it, pushing the air from my lungs. Gasping, I force my arms and legs to move, clawing at the earth as I try to get back up. I can't leave her up there alone with that man.

I can see the girl on the edge, her hands still encased in the black smoke and I rip and claw up. I'm not far, I can make it to her if I move faster.

So close I can see her black eyes when she says, "You're too late." My heart skips thinking she's talking to me until she turns her face behind her. "Too late." She smirks. The stone man cries out in anger as she drops her arms, her work finished.

I glance behind me, Legion floating over the cyclone, back where it started. She did it. She saved them all. I turn back, reaching for the lip of the slope.

A stone spike flies into her chest, jutting from the center of her already bloody blouse. Her smirk is frozen in place as she falls.

I'm screaming incoherently as I tear up the rest of the slope, but I know I'm too late. Her eyes are completely glassy when I reach her. Sobs rip through me as I reach for her pale hand, only to pull away when a spike impales her wrist. I fall back, barely missing the ledge.

The stone man is preparing another spike, and I know my force field can only take so much. But I have nothing to protect myself with, no weapons, no strength. I can't fly away or pop around like Harold. I can only sit and hope Athos will come to save me, again.

Or not.

Anger rolls through me, giving my drained muscles the strength they need to tear the spike from the girl's chest. The stone man flings another at me, but I roll out of the way, holding the bloody spike to my chest. I'm up and running straight for him. No plan in my head, just pure rage.

Perhaps he's never had a human rush him, or maybe I'm just that intimidating, but either way, I surprise him enough to cause him to fumble for his next spike. In that second, I throw all my weight into my spike and bash it against his head. I know it won't cause too much damage, it being his own spike and all.

But it gives me a very deep sense of satisfaction to see the surprise on his ugly face when he realizes I bitch slapped him.

It's short-lived though, as he recovers quickly enough to swat me away. I danced back, clutching the spike.

"Nice try," he hisses.

"Worth it." I sneer back.

"Are you going to try and beat me with my own weapon?" He asks, laughing. "How can this end any other way but with you being dead?"

I shrug, "I suppose with you being a little uglier." A spike whizzs by my head. "And a better shot." I taunt.

"I am going to enjoy using your decaying body as a target practice." He tears a handful of small spikes out and chucks them, peppering my shield. The bangle's burning hot on my wrist with the effort of keeping it up. It doesn't have much energy left, and I don't have a replacement chip.

He takes another handful, and I get ready to roll when he throws them. This time they hit a giant root erupting in front of me. The root shoots out of the ground, extending right for him. He doesn't have much time to react before it curls itself around his whole body, lifting him off the ground.

"Sheiba." I breathe before I feel her next to me. The man is snarling, practically foaming at the mouth while the root holds in.

She's covered in grime. The smell of smoke hits me as she takes a few steps toward the girl's body. I think twice about thanking her, deciding it can wait until Harold pops next to her. I sit down hard, still clutching the bloody spike, when Athos lands next to me.

"Lily," He looks just as bad as Sheiba, his new suit covered in ash and blood but somehow still in one piece. He rushes to my side, cupping my face between his hands. "Are you alright?" His amber eyes roam my body for any wounds.

I lift my hand to meet his, and it's only then I notice it's covered in blood. My pulse quickens as tears burn my eyes. He takes my hand, holding it close to his chest and tells me to breathe.

"This wasn't supposed to happen," I whisper, trying to focus on his heartbeat beneath my fingertips.

"We can not move Legion anymore." Sheiba's voice booms behind him. Athos and I glance at the city, and I realize it's not back where it was. It's still floating above us, but lower than before.

Harold appears behind Athos, gazing at the floating island. "Can you build bridges?" He asks.

The man snarls louder and I hear something pop out of the ground followed by his muffled cries. I lean against Athos, peering over his shoulder to see Sheiba eyeing Legion. The man dangles next to her, a large leaf covering his face.

"It can be done," Sheiba sighs. I watch as she plant seeds at the lip of the edge, then coaxes thick roots from them. They climb over each other, twisting and turning as they reach out to Legion.

Bridges. After everything, she still builds bridges to Legion, connecting the Supers with the human world. I shut my eyes, suddenly too tired to watch as history is made before me.

I'm tired of history. I want it to stop.

I can hear someone approaching us, but I don't look to see who it is.

"I know this is the last thing you want to hear...." Korra starts, "You should go back on air and inform everyone that it is under control."

"Is it, though?" I whisper against Athos's chest.

He tightens his hold on me, then says, "Yes. Can you?"

"Here?" Korra asks. I open my eyes to see her gazing at the dead Super between us.

"Yes." Athos gives Harold a nod. Before Korra's cameras hum around us, Harold lifts the girl's body and disappears.

"Lily, I am going to stand by Korra now. Will you be alright?" He asks. I nod. He stands and then pulls me to my feet. I watch as he strides over to Korra, then make sure I'm out of the way of the cameras.

I'm not in the mood to be seen.

He speaks to the cameras and tells no lies. He reassures the people watching that he, and the other Supers who side with him, will keep us safe.

How easy it is for him to take control, for all of them too. I feel useless, standing there with blood caked on my hands, the girls' black eyes floating in front of me.

I couldn't save that girl and I would have died too if Sheiba hadn't intervened. I glance behind me to see the spike man has stopped struggling with the roots finally. He's glaring at Athos now, murder in his eyes as he watches.

Maybe if I had had something to help me, I might have been able to stop him, or at least slow him down. I could have protected that girl more, maybe even helped her finish her work, or heal her wounds. Something, anything.

Harold pops up next to me, watching them talk. I spot a cut on his arm, not deep but enough to draw blood and think about how he must be a mortal, like me, but at least he can move around and be useful.

And then a thought hits me. It's so crazy, so ridiculous that I laugh out loud, earning a side glance from Harold.

"Just had a thought," I explain as I move away. I pull out my pad and dial Briseathe.

Chapter 30

The clone lab is no less creepy the second time around. Something about mindless bodies suspended around me makes me uneasy. "Want to visit the one of Athos?" Briseathe snickers from his computer.

"Never again." I retort.

"You say that now." He winks as I roll my eyes.

"How about we focus on making those gadgets, yeah?"

He sighs dramatically, flopping back in his seat. "You are by far the most demanding friend ever." I ignore his comment, choosing instead to grab our list and examine it.

"Who is next?" I mutter. "I can't pronounce this name," I say, pointing to the long name.

Briseathe glances at it. "I would expect not. They go by the name given to them from the island," he says, smirking, "He is located on the twelfth row, number three."

"I will be back then." I jump into the platform pod and navigate my way through the rows. It takes a few times to get the hang of the controls, but I'm adamant about learning them since Briseathe will be too busy making my new gadgets to get the DNA needed for them.

It does not take too much convincing to have Athos take me back to Briseathe's lair. In fact, he is the one to mention it first after Sheiba is done with making the bridges out of her vines and roots. They truly are a marvel to see, twining within each other and stretching five miles out to a floating island. It naturally exhausts her so Harold has to take her home, and that is when Athos asks me if I want to spend some time with Briseathe away from everything for a few days. I agree, not to mention that I have reasons of my own for wanting to be there.

I know Athos just wants me out of the way so he can focus on our plan for bringing Legion and the humans together. He already has a few fundraisers set up for everyone to mingle at. He also has to deal with the Supes, who now want to join Hero for Hire. We have Harold to thank for that.

"I have always been seen as not entirely useful by my people, especially as of late. What can my abilities do to better their popularity or mine?" He tells me back at Athos's home on Legion. "But after what I did, saving those people, being useful, I realize I can do something. No matter how small, I would like to help."

I gladly accept his offer and set him up with a few jobs that are suited to his abilities. After that, it only takes a few hours for others to approach Athos and me before we leave for Briseathe's asking if they can join us and Hero for Hire.

The pod stops with a jolt, causing the brakes to grind loudly. I grimace, hoping Briseathe hasn't heard it; I still need to practice. The Supe I stop at is a male, or at least I think it is. The body has the appearance of being made of pearl, with a shiny and iridescent surface, lacking any distinguishable features. I tap on the container's screen and pull up the controls. I direct a small arm with a needle to the body's neck, where I take a small amount of blood and tissue.

A moment later a slim tube pops out of the control screen with my sample. I have it in my hand when Briseathe's voice booms over the room.

"Lillium! That girl keeps calling- for the love of all that is holy please come answer her!" In a fit of excitement, I accidentally make the platform rush in the wrong direction, making me hit the brakes hard again.

"STOP THAT!" He snaps. So he can hear it. I grimace.

Now that I have multiple Supes to deal with, I need more help, mainly in the area of dealing with handing out assignments and accepting jobs. Alright, so I need help to do everything. I put out a request for an assistant to help, and within an hour, I had over one hundred applications.

It takes me all morning until I land on two people in particular that I think would be good picks. I ease the platform up to the lab, then skip over to Briseathe and my ringing pad. He is squinting at me as I pick it up. She has called four times. At least I know she is persistent.

"Lillium speaking," I answer abruptly, causing her to jolt in surprise on screen. She is a little older than me according to her application, with a lot of business experience. But I am not necessarily looking for that.

"Hello!" she beams back, "I am Maureen Holt." She has short black hair and a round face speckled with dark freckles. Bright green eyes beam back at me and I can see a tiny scar above her chin.

"Nice to meet you, Maureen. I understand you are interested in joining our organization?"

"Oh yes!" she smiles, showing off a few crooked teeth. I can only see her face in the picture, and she can only see mine and none of the lab behind me. "I have two years in-"

"That is not really important," I interrupt. The smile freezes on her face, but I can see the confusion in her eyes. "How do you feel about working with Supes?"

"Supers?" she asks.

"Yes, Supes, Supers, whatever you want to call them." I hear Briseathe scoff behind me, but I ignore him.

"I have never worked with any before." *Well no duh,* I think.

"I wouldn't expect so," I say. I watch her smile fade into a tight line.

"I feel no differently about working with them versus humans," she retorts.

"Oh?" I raise my brow in displeasure.

"I would be entirely professional if that is what you are getting at." I smile at her tone, confusing her more.

"Oh, I would hope so. The hours would be long and erratic. There are no set times for you, and you would have to work from home."

"That is fine with me," she says shortly.

"I must also stress that you might have to go to Legion a few times to meet with us."

Maureen's cheeks turn pink and I can see the excitement in her eyes, but she only nods. "That's very doable."

"Good. You start in two days." I say nonchalantly.

Her eyes grow twice their size, and she gapes like a fish for a moment before hoarsely saying, "Thank you."

"I will send you directions to our home in Legion. We will expect you there at noon."

She gives me a shaky nod before I cut off the call. *Well, that had gone well.*

"You have to be the most unfriendly person I have ever met." Briseathe is twirling a slim vial in his hand, staring at me with amusement.

"The other one fainted when I said they had to go to Legion." I explain. "I need someone who isn't going to fall over themselves every time a Supe comes in contact with them. They need to have a backbone too, I can not have Supes stepping all over them."

"And you think this one has all that?" He asks, frowning.

"She wasn't afraid of me, that's for sure." I throw him a toothy grin.

"Well, dealing with someone like Harold is far different from dealing with Sheiba." He couters.

"I will deal with those ones. She will only have to work with the nice people." I say.

He laughs as he sticks the vial in his computer. "Do not go getting a big head on me, Lillium." he jokes.

"I am not the one who can genetically modify a body with that kind of a feature." I retort.

"Touche."

"Now that I can cross that off my long list of chores, how is my transporter doing?" I ask.

He grimaces. "That one is going to take me a little longer than I thought. So far I can only get it to take you to one place of your choice, just like with my own transporter here in my lab."

"That is still more useful than not being able to go anywhere at all."

"Sure, but I know I can get it to work properly, I just need to make sure it will transport your body without turning it inside out." He sulks.

"Ew. Tell me again how you can do this?" I ask, knowing it will lift his mood.

His blue face brightens a bit. "I can not dumb it down any more than I have for you." He ribs.

"Oh, do try." I give him a dismissive wave.

"It's all in their DNA. I can use it on a small scale to replicate their abilities for a brief time using a power source."

"Hmm, but you need their DNA first."

"Correct. I have to be able to read their unique codes in order to identify-"

"Yeah, yeah." I waved him off, "You are going to put me to sleep again."

He huffs, but I can see h's in a better mood now.

I lean back in my chair, gazing at the transporter belt he's working on. Athos has no idea, but Briseathe and I are going to build me an arsenal of gadgets to help me better defend myself when things go wrong.

Briseathe can replicate Juno's force field to make mine, and he can do the same with almost everyone else's powers, just on very small scales. I am most excited about the transporter that mimics Harold's abilities. The only problem with it is that I have to set my destination ahead of time, and currently, Briseathe is only able to set one.

We are using whatever clones he has in his lab to make them, which is surprisingly only a few. Apparently, he had more at one point until a sudden need to prank a bunch of Supes came over him, in which he used up almost all of them. Now when the time comes for a sample of say, Sheiba, I have to get it myself from her.

I am going to hold off on anything like that for a while and just use what we currently have, which is turning out to be a nice amount so far. Athos is supposed to be back sometime today and I want a few new gadgets before we leave for Legion again.

"Hey," Briseathe interrupts my thought, pointing at a screen, "Look at this." It is another HAS propaganda video.

"This is what, the fourth one this week?" I scoff.

"Yes, but look at this." He points to the corner of the video.

"I just watched this. Tell me if you see this too." I watch as the masked people crowd around

Supe merchandise and set it on fire, a tradition that is becoming very worn out by now. Everyone has the same outfits and masks on, only their hair and hands are uncovered. I watch the corner where Briseathe is pointing and see a masked figure come into the picture briefly, just long enough to toss an armful of shirts into the blaze.

But it is enough time for me to see the hair color. It has to have been years since I have seen that color, but I know it like I know my own. No one else has that kind of hair.

"Gaia!" I hiss, curling my hands into fists.

"So you agree? That is her?"

"I know that hair anywhere. How do you?" I snap.

"I have been keeping a close eye on her for a while now. She dropped off my radar for a few weeks after you two stopped talking." He gives me a knowing look. I haven't spoken to him about that, but Athos had.

"Then I started to see hints of her around this group. I haven't had anything substantial, and in truth, this isn't hard evidence since we cannot see her face, but all roads lead to her being a part of this group now."

"You mean she left her job?"

"Yes. Just up and disappeared one day."

"Gaia," I hiss again, my anger boiling over. This is why she isn't returning any of my calls or messages. My worst fear has come true. She has completely abandoned everything for this cult.

I stand up so fast that I almost knock over the transporter belt. "I will be back," I say through clenched teeth as I grab my pad.

Briseathe doesn't say anything as I storm over to the elevator and smash my fist into the button. This is all I need now, a cherry on top of my already toppling mountain of problems. My stupid friend, stupid, stupid! How can she do this? Has she really changed so much in the last year? Who is to blame? That stupid guy she has been with for so long, or her stupid friends there? I should have gone with her when she left, I knew I should have, this would never have happened if I had! Or perhaps if I had, I would be right where she is now, throwing figures of Supes into a bonfire, wearing a mask.

Storming into the main room, I dial Gaia, and this time she is not going to ignore me. Until now I have allowed my calls to go unanswered, but this time, I am going to use the most annoying alert option known to man.

As the last ring ends and her voice prompts me to leave a message, I choose the emergency alert message, the one that projects a live feed of my message. Knowing Gaia, I know she has her phone close by, and she can hear me.

Also, it is most likely that she is around other people.

"Gaia!" my voice is like gravel, deep and threatening. Or at least I hope it is. "You answer me RIGHT NOW! Do it, or I will start listing your most embarrassing moments in life! Starting with Heather Lien's sleepover! Oh yeah, you know what I mean- the time when you drank her mother's secret stash and invited Luke Bront over and-"

"LILLIUM!" Her frantic voice cuts me off.

"Well, look who is alive and well?" I snap.

"What the hell is wrong with you?!" she retorts. It sounds like she is out of breath.

"Oh me? I am just fine, you know. Relaxing and watching YOU ON BROADCAST BURNING SUPE MERCH!" I scream. "For the love of all that is good and holy, Gaia!"

There's a moment of silence in which I briefly think she has hung up on me and I regret not being tactful. Then I hear her take a deep breath and I know have her.

"Lillium, what I do with my time is my business." Her tone is dead, void of emotion, telling me that she must be around some cult members.

"This is not you Gaia!"

"This is more me than you have ever known!"

"Oh shut up, I know you better than that! Who has brainwashed you?" I snap.

"No one, you idiot! I have always felt this way, but never have I had people to share in my beliefs with."

"Me!?"

"You?" She laughs. "You are sleeping with a Supe." My face burns with rage as she continues to laugh at me. "You only acted like you agreed with me because of Gabriel."

"Don't you dare," I say darkly.

"It's been well over two years! Almost three now, and you still carry a torch for him!"

"Shut up Gaia!"

"No, it's your turn to shut up. I have had enough of your moods and rants about how much you hate the world and the people in it. You love to cry about it, but you do nothing. Well, I am. I am doing the right thing for the world. Oh sure, you think what you and that freak are doing is for the better good, but it is not. You are making a monster, and you don't even know it."

Hot tears burn my eyes. She knows just what to say to hurt me in the most tender of places. This isn't my friend. She would never say these things to me, even in the darkest of times.

She takes my silence as a sign of defeat. "I am through with you Lillium. You stand for everything that I fight so hard to get rid of. You are part of the cancer that has a hold of our world."

"Are you prepared to destroy the world in the process of cleansing it?" I croak. "Because that is what those people will do. It starts with a few toys on fire, and soon it turns into a town, a city, and anyone who dares to disagree."

"No, we are not Mathis!" She snaps.

"No, you are worse!" I scream. "He, at the very least, isn't disillusioned! But you, you will refuse to see the horror of what you do until the moment when you throw me into that pyre."

She is so quiet, I think she has hung up. With the deadest of voices that send a chill straight to my heart, she hisses, "So be it."

The line breaks, and I am left staring blindly out the window at the waves.

"Lilly?"

My heart sinks even further and I quickly wipe the tears off my cheeks before turning to see Athos staring wearily at me. He looks just as bad as I feel. His clothes are the same as when he dropped me off, and they look slightly scorched. His face is dirty, hair disheveled. I throw on my best smile.

"Athos, you are back." My voice cracks despite my attempt to sound happy.

"Is everything alright?" He asks.

"Yes, in fact, I just hired ourselves an assistant."

His eyes bore into me, making me feel naked. I pray he will just let this go. He has too much to worry about without having to hear about this crazy group Gaia joins.

"Lily," his voice is stern, but tired, "That is not what I am asking about."

"I am fine, Athos," I wave him off nonchalantly.

"No, you are not," he says firmly.

"Athos, really-"

"Lily, really," he mocks. "It is Gaia, right?"

"She won't be a problem, Athos. I promise."

He scoffs. "I do not care about her, Lily. I care about you."

"This won't have any impact on my work if you-" I am cut off by his arms folding me to him suddenly. I hadn't even seen him move.

"I care about you, Lillium. Not about your work, not about your friends and what they choose to do, but you. You are my dearest friend, Lillium."

The impact of his words hits me with such force that I can't think about what to do. So I cry. I let loose the tears that have built up for so long over so much. My hurt over Gaia's words, the stress of the past weeks, the guilt of not being able to help him but only making things worse, and the worse feeling of guilt over what I am doing right now, going to him for comfort.

I feel weak, and I hate feeling weak. But instead of getting angry like I usually do, I just cry more, curling up in his arms as he holds me to him.

"It will be alright, Lily," he says softly. I bury my face in his chest. I might cry on him but I will be damned before I let him actually see my face doing it.

"I know how it feels to watch the people you love turn into someone else. Someone you thought they would never be. Totally unrecognizable."

Though meant to make me feel better, it only makes me feel worse. I shouldn't be doing this, I think. He already has so much to deal with himself. I try to pull away, but he holds me to him.

"Stop trying to keep it all in. You don't need to feel guilty, Lily. You can't always be the strong one. You have nothing to prove."

I shake my head. "I am not trying to prove anything. I just feel so guilty."

"I know." he ran his hand down my hair, and a surprisingly soothing feeling came over me, "You need to let it go. None of this is your fault. Not Mathis, not the others changing, not your mother, and not Gaia."

I'm shocked. When did he learn all my fears and doubts? Did he know me that well, and I had just been too oblivious to it?

"You can always come to me Lily. I am not the delicate flower you think I am."

I chuckle ruefully, "Yes, you are."

"Hm, now tell me what happened."

"She joined Supitude."

"Ah. I see." He says.

"She has always disliked Supes, but I never thought she would go off and join a radical group. She thinks I have betrayed her by working with you."

"I got that vibe from her last time." He smiles.

"She sees me as someone who stands for everything she doesn't. She can't see that I have always agreed with her, and that I am trying to change things."

"I think she does, but she can't get past that you befriended me."

"No, she can't," I say sadly.

"Lilly," I feel him take a breath, "if this 'us' is taking a toll on your life, I will understand if you want to stop." I pull away from him, shocked.

"Athos, no, that isn't what I want. Sure, it is hard, but that is more than reason to continue what we are doing." I eye him. "Do you want to stop?" I ask.

"I personally think I am far too invested at this point to even consider it." he smirks. "But even if I wanted to, which I do not, I wouldn't because I agree with you. We have come so far, and even though there is still so much to do, I believe we will do more good than harm. No matter the cost to us."

No matter the cost? I think of Gaia, back in our school days, so insecure with herself, never comfortable in her own skin even around us. Libby,

Max, and Gabriel. My friends, my rocks, my annoyance, my love. I still have so much to lose, but yet even more to gain in the end.

If we succeed and stop Mathis, then the others who follow him will fall in line, and once they are all dealt with, Athos will be free to change the dynamic of Supes and humans.

Maybe then Gaia will see that she has been wrong.

"When we get rid of Mathis and his goons, we can focus more on fixing this," He says, surprising me.

"That was what I was just thinking." I laugh.

"Well, great minds and all."

"What?"

"Never mind. So what was this about hiring an assistant? Too much work for you?" He smirks.

"Yes, actually. I hired a girl named Maureen. She will be meeting us in Legion in a few days to go over the job. She will be working out of her own home and have very limited interaction with Supes. She will be working closely with you and I."

"Good. I already have a full time job of making sure you don't end up incinerated." I roll my eyes.

"Well, before we do any more work, you need to take a shower." He grimaces.

"Yeah, yeah. Tell my brother his suit works, but the material isn't strong enough."

I laugh. "Sure. And Athos?"

"Yes?"

"Thank you."

"Anytime." He disappears into the elevator.

I still feel the sting of Gaia's words, but I no longer feel as raw about it. I go to find Briseathe drumming his fingers on his worktable, staring thoughtfully at the picture on his wall. I still can't bring myself to ask about her.

"How goes it?" I ask.

"Swell. I am done." He says.

"Good."

"Told him?" He asks, side eyeing me.

"Nope."

Briseathe shakes his head. "Well, do what you feel is right."

"Look, he already has so much on his plate, I do not think adding that I want to carry around weapons cooked up by Supe DNA is going to make him feel any better."

"It wasn't cooked up! This took finesse, Lillium! I had to go through each sample and isolate the parts that held the abilities to do this- not an easy task!" He pouts.

I scoff. "If only you could do that to find out their weakness."

In a moment of silence, Briseathe and I stare at each other in shock.

"Can you?" I whisper.

Chapter 31

"Lillium, do we really need to go to this?"

I glare at Harold over my pad. "Do you want humans to think you don't care about all the destruction Mathis has caused?"

"No, but I don't think a fundraiser is necessary. We already have money for it- plus, this outfit!" Harold pulls at his tuxedo sleeves. "I did not wear them when they were in style, so why should I now?"

"So that you fit in with the other elites there? And, because I said so." I drop my eyes back to my pad, ending the conversation.

Harold grumbles a bit before stomping back into Athos's room. To think a little thing like a tux could cause such drama with these guys.

"I think I look just fine in normal clothes Lily," Athos says.

"Don't care." I sigh.

"I would rather wear that suit over this penguin outfit."

I raise a brow. "Didn't men wear them back before you skipped out on Earth?"

"Yes, but like Harold said, it doesn't mean I wore them!" Athos huffs.

"I don't understand why you two are so childish about this. Back in the day, when fundraisers were a thing, they were an event. Everyone wore expensive clothes, ate expensive food, and threw money around, so the masses thought they were being generous." I say.

"It was an excuse for the rich to gather." He counters. "I know, I went to some."

"Right. And this one is much the same, except for the rich people part. You will mingle with normal, everyday humans."

Athos snorts. "I thought I did that already? Or are you not a normal human?" I roll my eyes.

"You are all going, and you will all be dressed nicely in those tuxedos. They were not easy to come by." I say.

"But why a tux?!" Harold yells from the back.

"Because I said so!" I retort. "I have to get dressed up too, so quit crying about it!"

Athos quirks a brow, a slow smile growing over his lips. I shoot him a look that means 'quit thinking about it' and he chuckles. Athos cocks his head to the door suddenly.

"I think Maureen is here." He says, and I drop my pad on the couch and jump up. I'm trying to contain my excitement, but so far am failing. Athos smiles at my eagerness.

"It will be nice to have someone take some of this away from me." I explain, reigning in my emotions.

"Right." He says, nodding in such a way I know he doesn't entirely believe me. "It has nothing to do with having another human to work with."

The most timid of knocks comes from the front door. I try hard not to smile like an idiot, but once I open the door and see her standing there, I can't contain it anymore.

"Maureen!" I grab her by the arm and pull her inside. The poor girl is so startled all she can do is gape at me. I shut the door and size her up. She's my height, slimmer build, and a darker complexion.

"Uh, Lillium, nice to meet you." She holds out a slender hand, her voice unsteady.

"You as well." I take her hand. "Don't be nervous. I am sorry about the interview call- I had to make sure you weren't some kind of fanatic only in for the opportunity to see some Supes."

She raises a brow. "So you were testing me?"

"Yes. Others either freaked out by the idea of coming here or responded with an attitude." I explain.

"Don't be fooled, though." Athos saunters over to us. "She acts like that normally. You will get used to it."

Maureen's eyes grow twice in size, but she keeps her composure. Athos takes her limp hand in his and laughs. "Lillium is all bark though."

"What?" I ask, confused. "I don't bark."

Maureen chuckles. "He means you act tough but are soft."

I shoot him a look. "Well, looks like I finally have someone who understands your little idioms. That is in itself a job." She chuckles again.

"I went through a phase in school where I studied pop culture before the war. I picked up a few of the phrases." She says.

"You will need them with this one." I sigh. "Maureen, this is Athos, obviously."

"I just wanted to say, how much I loved watching your interviews with St. Cloud. I don't normally what her shows, but the ones with you, were fantastic."

He smiles, looking bashful, which causes me to raise my brows. "Thank you. Korra is wonderful to work with. Lily made a great choice when she picked her to do them."

Maureen turns to me, impressed. "You chose her?"

"Yes. She seemed to be the perfect choice. Seems like I was right. Which will be much of what you will be doing." I explain.

"Oh, right." Maureen produces a pad from her handbag and pulls up a program. "This is what you sent me, right?"

"Yes." I motion to the couch. "We can sit down and discuss it. Athos needs to go get ready."

He blanches. "I thought you might forget."

"No." I point to the back room and raise a brow.

He pouts. "I hope Maureen won't work me like a dog." She laughs as he turns to walk away. I frown at his back, slightly offended.

"Make sure Harold and the others are ready in the next hour!" I call to him as he disappears.

"He sure is fast." She comments.

"Don't be fooled. This is much more of a babysitting job than anything. They can all act like such kids." I sigh as I take my seat.

"I understand from this program that much of what I will do is assign

261

various jobs?" She asks.

"Yes. The program is set up to do a lot of the legwork, and everything has to go through my approval before being set in motion, but in the end, you will give out jobs to Supes to do." I say.

"Wow. I never thought I would see the day when a human told a Super what to do." She smiles. "I can see why you had such an intense application."

A sense of pride glides through me. I'm glad she sees and appreciates my work. Not that the others don't, it's just nice to have it acknowledged. "So you understand the importance of giving out these jobs?" I ask.

"Your goal is to build a bridge between our people, and the best way is to bring Supers into the everyday life of humans, and make them seem as helpful as possible instead of as celebrities." She says.

I smile and nod. "Exactly. But, another part of your job will include sifting through messages, and managing our sites."

"I can do that." She says, jotting down notes.

"Good. You will work from home, mostly. Every now and then we will have you come here, or we will come see you to go over plans. This is mainly to make sure you have very minimal contact with Supes."

"Right," she says. "So I don't become a target for the ones who are following Mathis."

"Yes. Right now we have many humans coming and going from Legion, so your visit won't be seen as important. But from now on our contact will remain limited. You are free to contact myself or Athos at any point, for help or questions. But as for the others, you won't be seeing too much of them other than cases you assign to them." I explain.

"So I won't be able to contact any of these Supers here on this program?" She asks.

"Not directly, no. You will be able to send them messages and notes in accordance to their jobs, but other than that, no."

She notes something, then asks, "So if I have a question about a job, I would take it to you or Athos?"

"Yes."

"Is there a preference for who?" She asks.

"No, not at all. It may come down to who is available at the time, though."

"Right." She taps through her pad again, making notes. "This is all very exciting." She says, smiling.

"That's good. I am thrilled to have someone to help with this. I have been a little overwhelmed lately, and it will be nice to have another human who understands what is going on." I grab my pad. "Speaking of, there is a disclosure agreement you need to sign before we continue. This ensures that you understand that whatever information you see or hear is not to be shared with anyone other than myself or Athos."

"Right." She says.

"Once you sign this, the program I sent you will activate and you will be ready to begin." Maureen takes my pad and signs.

"Good. Thank you so much, Maureen, you do not know how much this will help us!"

"I should thank you, Lillium. I never thought I'd have such a cool job, even if I can't tell anyone about it." She laughs.

"Well, hold off on thanking me. You might end up hating it."

"I doubt that." She shakes her head.

I smile. "I will schedule another meeting in a week or so, just to see how you are doing. But from here on, you are free to work. Again, if you need us, we are just a click away. I hate to cut this short, but I have to get ready for this fundraiser."

"Oh, I heard about that! It's being held here in Legion, right?"

"Yes, in what used to be the inner city. We hope to get many people together tonight with nothing happening." I say, a tone of warning in my voice. I do hope she understands the risks involved in this job.

"Oh, well, it is a good thing you will be with Athos then." She smiles as she stands. "It was great to meet you. Please tell Athos as well."

"I will, thank you again, Maureen."

I feel a weight lift once she's gone. I have one less thing to worry about tonight.

Sheiba truly outdoes herself in the decorations. The event is held in the streets of what used to be the city's main hub. Nowadays, Legion has no use for the buildings, so they are left empty and allowed to deteriorate.

But tonight, Sheiba uses her powers to build bridges between buildings, create flowery canopies, light the night up with glowing flowers, and even create seats and tables. The inner part of the city has only been seven blocks before Legion was created, but it is jam-packed tonight with Supes and humans.

Music plays from buildings, rooftops now held in place by Sheiba's plants provide dance floors or lounges. Athos and I aren't entirely sure where to start or even to stand. There are so many people.

"I suppose we should check the donation area?" Athos suggests. I nod as we weave our way through the crowd. We find the donation table teeming with people who are watching Korra St. Cloud broadcasting her show as humans and Supes alike put their donations in a giant plant that resembles a flytrap.

"And the movie star Chelsea Haze just adds her generous donation to the pile!" Korra titters.

"Well, it looks like a success so far," Athos comments.

"So far, yes." I nod.

Supes mingle with humans all around us, drinking and eating, or dancing and laughing. I have seen nothing like it, and I have never thought I would.

"You should go make an appearance," I say, motioning to Korra.

"So should you." Athos places his hand on the small of my back, sending shivers up my spine as he steers me toward Korra. I try to hide the heat that settles in my cheeks as my mind focuses on how warm his touch is.

Before I can protest, Korra spots us and beams. "At last! Athos and Lillium have arrived!" She stands up, giving me a good view of her ruffled dress. I cock my head to the side as I try to figure out just what it is, or where it begins. Honestly, it looks like a bunch of lace wrapped around her.

"Korra," Athos says just as her cameras swing to meet us.

"This event is a hit, my dear, a hit! I have never seen so many stars and politicians in one place. I have already interviewed six of our world leaders. Can you believe that?" She gushes.

"Well, this is the first time anyone has been allowed inside Legion. And it is for a good cause," I say.

"And everyone gets the chance to meet a real live Super," Korra points out.

"So, you two, what are your plans for the night?" She wiggles her brows suggestively.

"Just mingling." Athos smiles at the camera while I stand there, mouth slightly open. Did she just suggest to the entire world we were together?

"Just?" Korra winks at him. *She is!*

I cock a brow. "What else would we be doing?" I ask nervously.

"Oh, I don't know. Dancing?" She swishes around in her dress.

Athos smiles, his dimples popping as he glances down at me. "Maybe."

"Together?" She asks, smirking.

"Korra." I warn, plastering a smile on my face. "You know it isn't like that."

"Oh, I know. You two just work together." She winks at him. I feel Athos stiffen next to me.

"No really, we do," I explain.

"Right, but what a grand story that would be if you two were together! The fans do so want it." She says, smiling at the camera.

They what now?

Athos and I share a look of astonishment. People out there want us to get together romantically?

"You are, after all, the first human Super relationship ever to exist. Openly that is." She points out.

"Just as coworkers," I say. "That's all this is."

Athos nods. "We argue enough as it is. Imagine us married." He shakes his head, earning a hearty chuckle from Korra. I frown, suddenly feeling offended.

"It was nice seeing you, Korra, but I have to go find Sheiba. She did a wonderful job with the decorations, no?" I smirk, moving from Athos's arm, and walk away. I hear Athos saying goodbye and suddenly feel him next to me.

265

"That was…." He starts then falters.

"Unexpected." I snap. "What in the world got into her?"

"The drinks." He laughs. I crack a smile. "She didn't mean anything by it."

"I know. But we don't need people focusing on us as a couple. We need them focusing on this." I gesture to the surrounding people.

"Everyone getting together." He says.

"Right. People making us into some kind of couple fantasy only diminishes our work."

"I get it, Lily. The very idea of us together makes you sweat bullets." He says, a strange gleam in his eyes. I pause, looking up at him.

"What?" I ask.

"Nevermind. How about dancing? That sounded fun." He says.

"No, thank you," I say.

"I thought you liked dancing with me?" He sounds wounded.

"It's not a matter of liking it or not, I just don't want to right now." Athos shakes his head.

"Alright then, I am going to go find someone who does."

"Have fun," I smirk, waving him off.

I find a quiet corner where no one is and take a seat on a stump. The music from the rooftops flits down to me, calming me. I know I shouldn't get so worked up over anything so small. But it catches me off guard, to have Korra, of all people, ask me about it. I feel betrayed in a way. And I can't help but remember Gaia's cold accusation of sleeping with him.

Maybe it was more obvious than I thought.

"This seat taken?" My body flushes. I look up to see a finely dressed Brogan smiling down at me.

"Do you want it?" I counter, smirking.

"Always." He took the stump next to me, looking as graceful as ever. "Here I was thinking I would find you dancing with everyone else." He gives me a knowing look and I blush.

"That's only on special occasions."

"This isn't one?" He leans back and looks up at the canopy.

"I thought you weren't going to participate in this kind of thing?" I say.

He chuckles. "That was, until my home nearly crushed you." He meets my eyes, and I blush again. *Dammit*, I think, *he was one step ahead of me.*

"That is a nice dress." He says.

I pluck at it suddenly. "Thank you."

He narrows his eyes. "It looks familiar though." I raise a brow, it had been sent to me by Briseathe when I told him I didn't have anything fancy to wear.

"Oh?" I clear my throat. "Well, I just found it at some old store."

"Hmm. Nice." He sits up, locking eyes with me, "Come dance."

I feel my body go cold, then hot. The last time we danced, I ended up kissing him. Even though it was only to make my cousin jealous, I still feel awkward about it now.

He holds his hand out to me, and I find myself taking it.

"No mind games," I say.

"I can't get into yours, remember?" He smiles. I follow him up to the nearest rooftop, and in his arms once again. Unlike Athos he's cooler to the touch, but not in an unpleasant way. As we sway to the music, his curls fall around his face. I feel calm in his arms as he led me around the floor, just as calm as I had been back in Rio, dancing in front of my mother and cousin.

As if he reads my mind he asks. "So how did that night end?"

"Very well. My cousin was very jealous that I got to dance solo with you, and my mother even noticed me for once." I smile as he laughs.

"I am glad I could help. After you left, your cousin had a fit and nearly went into hysterics." He leans closer, his lips touching my ear. "It looks like we get to dance solo again." I glance around and notice everyone has left the floor to watch us.

I feel my cheeks burn, but I smile. "You do know how to impress a girl."

"Oh, I had nothing to do with it, this time." I shake my head, smiling.

"Right. They all just want to see us dance."

"Do they? Well, let us give them a show," he spins me around, and I nearly fall but for him catching me. I laugh as he leads me around the floor, spinning and dipping as the music swells. I know he's the cause of all of it, but I don't care at that moment. It's too much fun. I even find myself halfway believing the crowd when they clap at the end. Almost.

We stopped dancing, but he's still holding me, and once again I find myself gazing up at him, thinking about his lips. But this time Brogan's the one who broke our eye contact and moves away just as I see Athos approach us.

"Change your mind about dancing?" Athos asks with a smirk, but there's something in his eyes.

"I have that effect," Brogan says smoothly.

Sheiba appears behind Athos, clearly amused. "Only on some, Brogan." She retorts.

"I didn't expect to see you here," Athos says.

"Well, I do not get many opportunities to dance with Lillium." he smiles at me, "So I take the ones I get." I clear my throat as I try not to blush again.

"That display will squash any rumors of you two," Sheiba says, nodding at Athos.

Brogan shrugs. "Whatever I can do to help." He takes my hand and kisses the back of it, brushing his lips across it as he holds my gaze. "Always a pleasure, Lillium. I have to take my leave now."

"Thank you for the dance," I murmur as he leaves.

Sheiba and Harold are exchanging looks as Athos approaches me.

"Think he will want to join us?" He asks.

"No. I think he enjoys making a scene too much." I say shaking my head.

He raises a brow. "That is true…." the sudden beep of his pad startles both of us.

"What is it now?" I sigh.

"Mathis." I glare up at him.

"He hasn't shown up for a while now," I say cautiously.

"Yes. He is apparently in Sun City causing havoc." My heart skips a beat as I think of Libby and Max.

"I have to go." Athos says.

"Athos, wait-" but he takes off too fast.

Mathis hasn't shown his face for some time now, and who knows when he will or how long he will be out in the open in Sun City? This might be my only chance to try Briseathe's idea out. Even though Athos has no idea about it, I still have to try.

I run over to Harold and take his hand, "Come with me, now."

Chapter 32

"I don't think this is a good idea Lillium." Harold says.

"I don't care Harold. I have to do this."

Harold shuffles nervously in the doorway. I look up from my dresser and sigh. "You can wait outside if you want. But don't you dare leave," I warn.

He huffs but stays put, a sour look on his face.

I grab my things and run over to my closet, throwing my dress unceremoniously to the floor.

I know Harold's afraid of making Athos mad by doing what I ask, but his fear of Mathis far out weighs that. All I have to do is tell him that I have a way of stopping him, but that it's risky and I haven't even told Athos of it.

He protests a bit but gives in when I tell him Briseathe came up with the idea. He knows better than to question me further, and as much as he doesn't like to do it, we were going to.

I come back out wearing my suit but with a new belt and a few gadgets attached.

"Ready?" I ask.

He takes a deep breath and nods.

"Are you sure you want me to leave right after? I would feel a lot better if I were around to get you out quickly."

"I told you I would be fine." I pat my belt. "Briseathe made these for me, specifically for this."

Not entirely a lie, but enough to smooth over his nerves. The gadgets aren't all finished. They are for defensive purposes only, not what I'm about to do. The ones that Briseathe is designing for that are still being tested and fine-tuned.

"Alright. Now, this won't be disorientating at all. Most people think it will cause you to get dizzy and sick, and that you won't be able to think straight, but that's not true. So when I drop you off, you will be fully aware of yourself, just not your surroundings." He explains.

"As long as you place me where I told you to, I will be fine."

He rolls his eyes and takes my arm. "Let's get this over with."

"I-" The air whooshes around us suddenly, and in a second I hear sirens screaming. My quiet room is replaced by a city street, the early morning sun in my eyes. I can hear the sounds of a titanic struggle taking place somewhere nearby.

"Still want me to leave?" He asks ruefully.

I take in the smoky sky and rubble on the streets, then nod. "I will be fine." I place my hand over the belt again.

Harold looks me up and down, then shakes his head. "I would almost say you have a death wish if I didn't already know you."

I give him an encouraging smile as he vanishes. The second he is gone, I bend over and take a deep breath. *Keep it together,* I think, *you can do this.*

The street vibrates beneath me as a loud boom echoes overhead. *You have to do this.* I bring up my pad and find a visual of the fight being broadcast. Just as I thought, they have stayed close to the main part of the city, where Mathis can do the most damage.

I'm off a few streets to the North, just far enough out so they can't see me right away, but close enough so I can get Mathis's attention when the time comes. So far, Mathis has followed the same routine each time he met with Athos. He will engage him for a while, then another defected Supe will pop up and take over, and that's when I will take my turn.

I jog down the street while watching the broadcast. I have to time this perfectly or I will miss my chance.

Mathis is still able to evade Athos, who is now trying to stop the destruction of the city's main shopping district.

I can make out Athos swooping in and out of a building, taking people to safety, all the while Mathis is busy turning the building's walls into glass.

Athos grabs a few people, then goes after Mathis, who disappears for a while, letting Athos grab a few more, only to return to continue his work. Those walls are going to come down any moment now, and Athos can only make sure he gets everyone out before it does.

This looks like the perfect opportunity. I come upon the corner of the street they are on, and look down to see a perfect view of Athos rushing in and out of the building. It is a few blocks down from me, but I know Briseathe's gadget has enough power to get Mathis's attention.

Just in time, Mathis appears in front of the building, getting ready to turn another part into glass. Without a second thought, I grab the first gadget, an orb, and throw it with all my might down the street. It bounces once, then rolls and stops suddenly. I take a breath and cover my eyes just before a blast of energy erupts from it, breaking all the windows nearby and causing such a noise. I know he will look.

Uncovering my eyes, I see him through the wisps of blue smoke from the gadget. I have only a second to wonder why it is blue before I tear another from my belt and toss it as well.

This time, I turn and take off back down the street before it erupts. We make eye contact just before, so he knows it is me. It is only a matter of him following me. And me staying out of his grasp.

I take a second to look behind me and see him right where I had just been, looking perplexed. I stop running and place my hand on my belt.

"Well, fancy seeing you here," I say. Mathis looks from the blue smoke to me, anger in his eyes, but he isn't seething just yet.

"Wondering about these?" I hold a ball in my hand and smirk.

"Those are very powerful toys for such a child to have," he retorts.

"Jealous?"

"Curious mostly." He takes a step towards me, and I cock my arm. He stops, and tilts his head. "Those won't hurt me."

"They aren't meant to."

"They won't stop me either." I shrug.

The confusion is wearing off now, and he is getting annoyed. "I must say, I do not expect us to meet again like this."

"Let me guess, it was a little more like me begging for my life?"

"Something like that." he smirks. "I will so enjoy tearing you apart. It's incredibly stupid of you to face me with Athos."

"Oh, I could never dream of that."

"What are you doing?" he asks, looking back to where the building is.

For a second, I fear he is going to go back, and that I am wasting my chance. But instead, he surprises me and appears next to me. He takes me by the arm, and our eyes meet. I know he means to kill me right then and there.

If it wasn't for the barrier, he would. I can feel the bangle burning against my wrist in an effort to keep it up. He is far more powerful than Anne. I throw the ball at him, hitting him in the chest.

It explodes like the other, but instead of a white hot light, ice comes erupting from it. Blue ice. It encases his whole torso and part of the arm that holds me. In a moment of shock, he lets his grip loosen enough for me to get free.

Mathis touches the blue ice gingerly with his free hand, then studies the ice on his encased arm. He no longer looks angry or confused. In fact, he seems to know what the ice is in the way he touches it, like he has seen it once before.

"How?" he whispers to himself. I prepare another ball as he looks at me, "How?"

I am not sure how to respond, and in that moment of silence, he regains his usual rage and breaks free of the ice.

"How?" he asks more forcefully. I take a step back, realizing it is now or never.

"How do you think?" I spit.

He glares at me, at my belt and ball, and I know what he is going to do. In an instant, he turns into a wisp of smoke, then reemerges behind me.

He has a hold of my neck, but I have already dropped the ball. This one isn't like the others, it is specially made to ensure not only my escape but that he will seek me out from now on. It is the only gadget that is completed with this exact intent.

The ball opens to reveal a halo-project of a busty-looking woman. She is wearing a type of clothing I have never seen before, and when she speaks, it is a language I don't recognize. But Mathis does.

As she speaks, he drops his arm from my neck and stares at her, in disbelief. I only have a few seconds left, the ball isn't going to last long.

I unsheathe a small knife from my belt and stab him in the arm. Mathis cries out, shoving me to the ground. I drop the knife, stupidly, when I fall, and just as I do, the ball ends the halo-project, and the woman disappears to be replaced by maniacal laughter.

Mathis cries out again, this time with such a note of pain that it scares me. I scramble to my knees and grasp the knife just as he turns his attention to me.

"You!" He screams. "You bitch! I don't know how- but you will die!" tears are streaming down his cheeks as he rages. I have never seen such hatred before, and it rocks me to the core.

I kneel there in the street, frozen in shock as he comes at me. I can't will myself to move until I hear my name screamed out loud.

"Lillium!" it echoes down the street, even drowning out the feral cries from Mathis.

It's enough to force me into action. Mathis throws his body onto me with such force that we both fall backward, but I have already placed my hand on my belt. I tap the gadget just before I hit the ground, and instead of seeing his face when I open my eyes, I see the night sky above me.

The sirens and smoke are gone, and in their place, I can hear the crashing waves below me. The belt will one day be able to take me anywhere I want to go, but for now, it only brings me here, to the cliff above Briseathe's cave.

I let out a heavy sob of relief. I have made it, I am alive. I have the knife. I clutch it to my chest and rock back and forth on the ground. I have it, the key to beating Mathis and ending this chaos.

I will be able to stop all of them, and then the Supes can finally focus on helping heal the world and working with humans. And Gaia, she will be able to see she is wrong, and she will come back to us, and maybe, maybe even work with us.

My romantic thoughts are marred suddenly by the image of Mathis, screaming at me. I shudder. There is still the matter of actually stopping that lunatic.

I sit up, feeling weary. It is going to be a hard road, but at least we now have the upper hand. I rub my face with my clean hand and find the hidden halo-screen to call Briseathe.

He is going to have to send up the elevator to come get me because there is no way I am going to scale his cliff tonight.

"Lillium!" he exclaims on the screen, "You are entirely crazy, you know that!? I told you NOT to use those gadgets like that, and what is the first thing you do with them!?"

"I have it, Briseathe." I say, breathless.

"That is a relief. Here I was thinking, well, maybe she will be dead with it still, or just dead. For no reason." He snaps.

I roll my eyes. "Briseathe, could we finish this argument inside, please? I am a mess, and I am very tired."

He scoffs. "I expect so."

A little ways away, the earth opens up, and the elevator appears. I drag myself up and stumbled over to it. By the time I get down to the living area, I'm bone tired. All the adrenaline is gone from my body, and in its place are sore muscles and blooming bruises. Briseathe is waiting, arms crossed and pissed off, as I get off.

"Look at you. You look like you got struck by lightning." he curls his nose. "Smell like it too."

I hold the knife out to him, and his expression changes.

"Well, look at that." his lips twitch as he fights back a smile.

"We will see if this idea works now. Or if I made the most bloodthirsty Supe ever make me his number one target for no reason." I say.

Briseathe takes the knife from me, shaking his head, "Just go take a shower, please. And you might want to call Athos and tell him you are alive."

"Athos?" I ask.

"My brother, yes. The guy who just watched Mathis tackle you to the ground like a sack of potatoes, yes."

"I didn't think he saw...." Then I remember hearing my name echoing down the street. He had seen it then? My stomach churns with guilt. I search for my pad, but can't find it.

"I must have lost my pad, Briseathe, could you?" I ask.

Briseathe sighs. "Yeah, and I will get you another pad." I smile and thank him. "Don't thank me, just please go take a shower Lillium!"

Chapter 33

A rumbling wakes me up. I fight it as best as I can, but in the end my eyes open and I become aware of my surroundings. It is dark now. I can see the moonlight on the waves. I had passed out on the couch listening to them.

As I blink myself to existence, I start to make out the rumblings. They are words. More so, I know it is Athos. I sit up to see a very fuzzy image of him stumbling around the kitchen.

"What are you doing?" I croak.

He turns to me, and that is when I notice how beat up he looks. His clothes are tattered, his hair a mess, and his skin is so dirty it looks black.

"Lily?" He whispers.

"Yeah, what are you doing?" I repeat. He is making such a ruckus.

"You… are alive?" Now I am getting mad. Here I am sleeping, and he dares to come in and make such a fuss.

"Athos, really. I was sleeping, so what do you think you are doing?"

"I…I saw him kill you." Only now does it dawn on me that he might have not gotten Briseathe's message.

"Oh, Athos, no. I use Briseathe's belt." He stumbles over to the couch, hanging on the back of it.

"Belt?" He whispers.

"I had him make one. We were going to tell you about it when he had finished all the gadgets, but that didn't happen."

"Belt?" He repeats.

"Yes, just like the force field, he built me a belt using the same technology. It just so happens that Mathis shows himself, and I don't think I am going

277

to get another chance to try out our plan-"

"What are you talking about!?" He snaps suddenly. "Lilly, I thought you were dead!"

My groggy mind is clearing now as I focus more on his face. He looks so distraught. He thought I was dead. I can see the tear streaks in the dirt on his cheeks, the stress lines under his eyes. What has he done to be in such a state?

"Athos." I say softly, "What happened?"

"I saw you and him, in that street, and he jumped on you," I recall Mathis's face, in pure rage. "And then you were gone, and he was screaming." As he speaks, I see it from his perspective. Of course, he had no idea I had the belt, so the only answer would be that Mathis had turned me into something and killed me.

"Oh, Athos." I grab his hand. "I am so sorry, I did not think about that at all. We were so occupied with the sample that we must have forgotten. I honestly didn't even know you saw it at all."

Athos stares into my face, his features twisting as he says "Lilly, I have no idea what you are talking about!"

"Briseathe and I came up with an idea," I blurt. "We thought that if we could get a sample of his DNA we could find his weakness and use it against him." Athos narrows his eyes in confusion, "We came up with the idea when I realized he was using the DNA of other Supes to make his gadgets mimic their powers….." I trail off as I notice his eyes glaze over.

"You two made plans to get a DNA sample from Mathis, without me." He says bluntly.

"No, no." This isn't going well. "We meant to tell you, but we wanted to wait until we had the gadgets all ready."

"So, you went ahead with it without the right gadgets?" He asks.

I bite my lip and say, "Yes."

"So you put yourself in danger with the high chance of nothing coming of it?"

"Athos!" I protest.

"No!" He yells. "I understand what you are telling me Lillium, even if you want it to sound another way."

"I had a chance, a tiny chance! Mathis hasn't been coming out very often and I needed to try at the least! I owe the world that!"

"You don't owe anyone anything, Lillium! You could have died!" He says. "But I didn't!" I scoff.

"This time!" He grabs me by the face, surprising me as he holds me closer to him. "Lilly, you don't owe anyone anything and you don't need to prove anything!"

"I am very aware of that, Athos." I snap, trying hard not to breath in his scent. His hands are so warm against my skin and I feel myself drifting in memories. They've been getting harder and harder to ignore lately.

"No, you aren't! I should have been the one to get the sample, not you! You could have DIED!" He's shaking, shaking all over. The thought of me dead has affected him that badly.

I reach out, cupping his hands in mine as he holds my face. "Athos, I didn't mean to hurt you. I am sorry."

"I thought you were dead," he says weakly. "I couldn't bear it."

"I am so sorry." He leans in close to me and places his forehead against mine. His breath coasts over my face, making me shiver. It's dangerous to be this close to him. Alarm bells are ringing in my mind.

I've been keeping my distance, trying hard not to acknowledge the hold he has on me. But, there's a reason I approached him in that bar and went home with him. It's the same reason I'm helpless now, unable to put distance between us even though I know I should.

"I panicked." He says. "I was so angry at him. I thought he turned you into the air or a microorganism. I went into a rage and we ended up destroying half the city."

"I lost my pad, I didn't think you saw." I explain.

"I felt so lost then, Lilly. I thought I lost you forever. I died on the inside. Don't, ever do anything like that again Lillium."

I'm so shocked I can't respond.

"I am serious. You are never to engage my kind again like that. That is not your place." He says. I snap my head back, holding his gaze.

Anger wells inside me. He has no right to tell me what to do. What's more, he dares to tell me what my place is.

"Shut the fuck up." I snap back, earning a look of shock from him. "You have some audacity if you think you can speak to me like that." I stab his chest with my finger, though I doubt he can barely feel it.

"I did what I thought was right, Athos. I'm sorry you thought I was hurt, but that doesn't give you the right to boss me around. I am not your subordinate."

With a speed I cannot detect, he grasps my hand, pulling me closer to him. His scent surrounds me, the heat from his body instantly making my skin slick with sweat. I try to pull away, knowing this is a thin line we've been dancing on for months.

I'd promised - no, we'd promised, this would never happen again.

"Athos-" my tone is a warning, but my words turn to ash in my mouth the moment he presses his lips to mine. Heat explodes inside me, threatening to melt my bones under his touch. My mind screams to pull away, to tell him no, but this has been a long time coming.

My body felt his touch once before, and it's been starving for him ever since. I'd been playing with fire, acting like I couldn't get burnt for too long, and now I knew I was about to be consumed by him.

I melt into him, letting his arms pull me to him, letting his lips claim my mouth with such hunger I have no choice but to let him devour me.

I forget how mad I am at him the moment I feel his hands beneath my shirt, his fingers crawling towards my erect nipples. I whimper into his mouth when he pinches one, rolling it between his fingers until I arch my back, pressing my chest into him.

"That's right, Lily," he breathes into my hair, "Make those sweet noises for me."

I moan when he slides his hand down my pants, his fingertips pressing against my already soaked underwear.

"Fuck, Lily. I've been dreaming about this wet pussy. I missed how you taste." He teases my clit through my underwear, and my knees nearly buckle under the feeling. I want to tell him how much I've craved this, too, but I'm still pissed about his attitude.

"Tell me you want it," he whispers, caressing my neck with his free hand.

"No," I whimper, defiant. "You can't tell me what to do," I say, but deep down I know I'm ready to shatter myself against him.

He chuckles, and I am instantly transported back to our first night together. His dark laughter is a promise of things to come, and I find myself whimpering again in anticipation.

Before I know it, he's behind me, his hard cock pressed into my ass while he pins me against him with one arm. His other is between my legs again, his fingers pushing my underwear away.

I try to swallow the noise that erupts from me the moment his naked fingers find my clit, but the wanton cry escapes my lips.

"You like to disobey me?" He asks, his fingers rolling against my clit while his free hand kneads my breasts. I throw my head back against his chest, letting him place gentle kisses down my neck. "Tell me you want it, Lily." He says again.

I shake my head, as I suddenly am at a loss for words. "I won't," I say, defiant, stubborn - the wanton part of me wants him to rip the words from my mouth. He sees it in my eyes, the challenge I'm declaring.

I can feel his lips stretching into a smile against my neck. "Fine, we will do this the hard way, then."

A finger finds its way to my pussy, slipping in and out as his thumb rolls over my clit with a sudden speed that I have no way of preparing myself for the orgasm that rocks me. I cry out, my hips bucking as the orgasm rolls over me.

But before I have a second to think about how fast he'd made me come, I'm on my back. He has me on the couch, and in one swift motion, he's pulled off my pants and underwear.

His amber eyes are molten in the dim moonlight as he leans over me.

"Tell me you want it." He says, but I remain silent. He sees the defiance in my eyes and smirks, gently pushing my knees apart. My legs fall away as I realize what he's about to do.

His tongue hits my clit, and I am transported back to that night, when he ate me out three times in the span of an hour and left me a shaky, puddle of a woman.

I shut my eyes, trying hard not to let myself come undone so quickly again, but the man is an expert. I'm coming on his tongue after a few strokes, my legs shaking with the quaking orgasm.

I gasp through it, but he doesn't stop. Just as I feel my waves of ecstasy rolling away, I feel him slip two fingers inside me, hitting my G spot instantly. My lungs scream for air as I feel my core turn into liquid fire, the heat spreading across my body as I cry out.

Three. He's made me come three times already, and he's barely broken in a sweat.

"Tell me you want it." He repeats, licking his lips like he's savoring my come.

I gape like a fish, knowing he's close to breaking me. And he knows it too.

But I relent and shake my head. Stubborn.

My legs are shaking, and my skin is slick with sweat, but he refuses to give up. Athos is between my legs again, but this time he's taking his time. His tongue is making slow, torturous circles around my clit while his fingers are making their way in and out of me.

This time the build is gradual, the fire inside me stoking with each touch, each breath against my skin. This time I think I can hold out, that I won't give in. But then a finger is wandering down, slick with my come, pressing into my ass. My hips betray me as they buck and push into the finger, needing it inside me too.

I want to feel full, to feel stretched out.

"Tell me you want it," he says quickly, his tongue lashing out like a viper.

I whimper, still bucking into him as I feel the building orgasm about to break. *Fuck it.*

"Yes," I cry, "Fuck yes, Athos. I want you to fuck me." There is a slight shift in his movements and I shatter against him again. I scream out. My body is consumed in flames, but his mouth silences me. I can taste myself on his lips as he devours my cries of pleasure.

"Come for me, Lily," he whispers against my mouth as I feel him bury his cock inside me. "Come for me."

"I can't," I say, my voice hoarse. "There's no way-"

"You will," he moans into my hair as he begins to move. His motions are quick and hard as his cock stretches me. I shake my head, sure I can't come again, but I know it's not true.

He managed to break me and build me up multiple times that first night.

"You're going to come for me, Lily." His tone is gentle, but demanding.

"Fuck," I grind out as he picks up his speed. My pussy is clenching his cock as I feel another orgasm rip through me.

"That's it," he praises as I cry out again, "Come on my cock like a good girl."

I scream, my nails raking down his back as I ride out my orgasm. He groans and I feel him spilling out inside me until my thighs are slick with both our come.

We lay there for a moment while I catch my breath, my heart slamming against my chest in time with the waves outside.

Athos sits up, and I roll away from him, too spent to sit up.

I'm so dazed from all the orgasms, I barely notice him getting dressed. It isn't until he turns from me, his back to me, that I realize he's gone into his statue mode.

"Stay here, like a good girl, Lily." Before I have a chance to respond, he's gone.

Chapter 34

Things change after that.

I find him in the kitchen with Briseathe the next morning and by their tones, I know they're plotting something. I approach them, keeping my eyes downcast.

I don't regret last night, but I regret how it happened. I mostly regret what it might mean for us now. We are not just coworkers or friends anymore. We are something more, but what? I'm not sure if I want to know the answer just yet.

"Lily." Athos says. His tone is serious. *Fuck, this is going to be bad.*

"Am I in trouble?" I ask, forcing a smile. "Should I be sent to my room?"

"We need to talk to you," he says, ignoring my attempt at humor.

I eye them both, then sigh. "Athos, I know you are upset, but-"

"No!" He snaps, surprising me. "I am livid Lillium. You both went behind my back and plotted- even if it was for a good cause, it was still sneaky. And then you went and put yourself in danger for something that *might* have worked."

"Of course it will!" I scoff. Does he have such little faith in me?

"I do not care!" He yells.

"But it will! Mathis will want to find me now- he won't stay in hiding anymore, and it will give us the chance we need to capture and stop him!" I say stubbornly.

"You think just because you threw a few bombs at him that it will make him want to seek you out?" He almost laughs.

"They weren't just bombs," Briseathe says ominously.

Athos glares at him, then back at me. I shrug.

"I mimicked the powers of Simone." Athos's face falls.

"You did what?" He croaks. I quirk a brow seeing how he pales.

"And then I made a hologram of her…." Briseathe says, sinking into his chair the moment Athos explodes.

"YOU DID WHAT!?"

"I meant it for you to use, but Lillium had an opening-" He waivers.

"And I took it." I finish for him, my chin held high. It might have been stupid and reckless, but it was worth it.

"Lillium you have stepped outside of your role!" Athos says.

I gape at him. "Athos, I only did it to help you! To help us!"

"That was not your job! You are my publicist! Not my sidekick!" He roars.

Angry tears well up, but I refuse to give in. "You think because I am a human that I can't help?" I spit back.

"I think that because you can *die* you should do nothing to speed up that process!" He counters.

I scoff. "Athos, you are being ridiculous-"

"No! What is ridiculous is you two making plans alone, without consulting me or anyone else! And I am putting a stop to it right now!" I knew he'd be upset when he found out, but he's livid.

"Athos, we can help-" I try to reason with him, but he won't hear it.

"Yes, you can. From a safe distance. And that is where both of you will be from now on. Lillium, you are to stay here until Mathis is caught."

"That will not happen." I laugh bitterly.

"Yes, it is. Briseathe is going to make sure of that." He shoots him a withering look.

"I will not be put under house arrest. And you do not have the authority to do so!" I say.

"When someone is needlessly putting themselves in harm's way, then yes, I do!" Athos snaps.

"I am capable of making my own life choices!" I scream back.

"YOU ARE NOT LEAVING HERE!" He bellows. "You have become

reckless, and you are a threat now to all that we accomplished! You are to stay here until either Mathis is captured, or you come to your senses!"

I'm unable to muster a retort. He's so angry, it shocks me. I watch numbly as he throws Briseathe a bag and storms out.

The second the door shuts, I regain my senses and blurt. "Where is he going?!"

"Back to Legion to rally the others, I suppose," Briseathe says, slumped in his chair gloomily.

"Who does he think he is!? He can not tell me what to do!" I stomp around the room. "If he thinks I am just going to sit here-"

"Well, you kind of are," Briseathe mutters and I cut him a cold glare. "I had to reset all the doors, so the only people who can get them to open are him or I."

"WHAT?!" I scream. My pulse quickens as I the realization sinks in - I am trapped here.

"If you need to punch something, please do it in the gym!" Briseathe says.

"That self-serving, good-for-nothing idiot!" I shout.

"I am surprised you had the restraint not to hit him right then," Briseathe muttered.

"I thought I could leave then!" I cry.

"Well, I said you couldn't use the doors."

"The belt is still not working!" I snap.

"For now. It will take me a few days, but I know I can get it to where we need it. In the meantime, how about you hold off ripping my couch to shreds and use the gym to practice with those element balls?"

I stop kicking the couch just in time to see him toss my belt with the element balls. I grip it tightly and decide he is right. I am going to channel my rage at Athos in the gym and do something useful with my time as a prisoner.

Athos is right to be upset with me. I should have told him what we are doing. I shouldn't have allowed him to believe I was dead. But that does not mean he has the right to stop me from continuing to help. He believes that I am trying to take over the whole thing, that I want glory and fame, and that I will turn my back on him like the others have. I should have thought about that before, but it is too late now. I just need to tell him that I do not want any of that to show him. I only want to stop Mathis from continuing his destructive path. That is all I care about now. If he can't see that, then he is blind. His erratic behavior is the threat, not me.

As I make my way to the gym, I decide that I will not stop going after Mathis. He wants me dead now. He is looking for me. I have the advantage, and Athos is too stubborn to see that. I know no matter what happens now, Athos won't let me near Mathis, won't let me help directly. That is a mistake, and I have to make sure we don't make any more mistakes. I am going to take my chance again when I get it. With, or without Athos.

Chapter 35

A week later and there is no word from Athos- at least to me. I am certain he is in contact with Briseathe, checking to make sure I am still jailed up, but he still hasn't asked for me. And I am not going to be the one to break the silence.

So I spend the week angrily throwing Briseathe's inventions around the gym, blowing up walls, freezing weights, burning the mats. Anything to keep me occupied really.

It doesn't help that I see him on the news every so often conducting an interview, or cleaning up a devastated area, which there are a lot of now that Mathis is on a raging rampage. So far he has appeared in three major cities wreaking havoc for as long as he can before disappearing.

I know he is calling me out, trying to make me appear again, and the longer that I don't the worse he will get. I fear how much damage he will be able to do before Athos can get to him, but the upside is that he is getting sloppy now.

A few times he pops up in small towns just long enough for Athos to swoop in, and each time he is getting closer to Mathis. Perhaps we won't even need Briseathe's invention just yet, Athos might just be able to hold him for a while. I can only hope.

Partway through my week I realize that I have no way of getting into contact with Maureen to check in on her, and when I ask Briseathe to help me, he tells me Athos is taking care of it. I spend an extra hour in the gym that night, using the last of my supplies.

The next morning Briseathe balefully agrees to show me how to make them. He is busy with his own projects.

So the better part of my days are spent making my own element balls, and throwing them at inanimate objects, until the day our theory comes to life.

A week and a half and still no word from Athos has me rethinking my actions, and considering contacting him, while I tweak one of my elemental balls. I have designed one that mimics air by pressurizing the contents inside. When released, it has the effect of a punch and throws anyone off their feet.

The trick is to make the range far enough so that it doesn't hit me, but powerful enough to stun the person I throw it at.

So far, I have only managed to knock myself over and blow off the gym door. I am adjusting the pressure when Briseathe tears into my makeshift workshop, grabbing me by the elbow and tearing me up off my chair.

"What are you doing!?" I yell as he drags me out of the room before the ball explodes and all my work goes to waste. "THAT TOOK ME THREE HOURS!" I cry, but at least the range is within what I want.

"I did it!" He laughs, "I finally did it!"

"You mean you got it to work?" I gasp.

"Yes! After all this time, I finally got the program working!"

"Well, what is his weakness?" I ask.

Briseathe grins, his blue eyes gleaming. "Come look." We enter his part of the lab and come up to the brand new computer he made just for his program.

"Before I show you, I want you to take a moment to realize what we created." He says, placing a hand on the computer. "This program will be able to tell us my people's greatest weakness and aid us in our mission for peace. But, it could also be used in a time of war against us."

"In the wrong hands, it would be the extinction of the Supes." I nod. "I understand." It's another historic event, and I am honored he trusts me with it.

Briseathe rubs his hands together, looking excited. "As much damage as it can do, I understand the importance of it. That is why I mean to destroy it once we have no need for it."

"I agree," I say flippantly. "Now, can I please see what we are going to use against Mathis? Garlic? Poppies? Bee venom?"

"Even better-" Briseathe taps the computer, and it pulls up a data page full of information. I scan the page until my eyes fall on the lower left corner where the print is bright green.

"Gallium?" I ask, confused.

Briseathe squeals. "Yes! It makes perfect sense!" I raise a brow.

"Does it? I don't even know what that is."

"Of course, you don't. Gallium was phased out many years ago. It's a man-made metal that has unique properties- such as it will melt in your hand." He holds his hand open and wiggles his fingers.

"A metal that melts in your hand?" I ask, unsure.

"It also is known to cause structural failure in other metals." He says, waving his hand.

"Now that is interesting," I smirk. "So, what do we need to do with it? Injected him?"

He shakes his head. "No, I think a nice coating of it would do the trick. It would stop the natural process of being able to transform."

I bite my lip. "So we either need to lure him to a giant vat of this stuff, or make a bomb of sorts to make sure he is covered."

"Well, first off, I need to make this stuff," he sighs.

"Right. How long will that take?" I ask.

"That depends. I am not sure how pure it has to be to useful, and then there is the problem of making it too pure and possibly killing him."

I stare at him. "Well, we both know I have no problem with that. But Athos and the others don't want that."

"Yes, so a few more tests and dry runs must be done in order to make sure this is right." He says.

"Have you told him?" I ask slyly.

Briseathe shakes his head. "No, not yet."

"He hasn't said anything yet?" I ask, trying to look nonchalant.

He side-eyes me. "Nope."

I groan. "Look, if I am going to be stuck in here for another week or more, I need a way to contact my dad and my friends. I haven't spoken to them since before Mathis, and I want to make sure they are alright."

He smiles. "I was wondering when you were going to bring that up." I roll my eyes. "I have one here for you." He tosses some books off his desk and picks up a tiny pad.

"This is for family calls only. It won't connect you to anything else."

"So I can't work from it," I state bluntly.

"That is the idea." I take it from him. At least it's something.

"Thank you." He waves me off.

Another week at the least, I think, I might go mad. Sure I have my tinkering to do, and now I can talk to the outside world, but the need I have to do something useful, it is eating me up now. Briseathe is making the very substance that will be the downfall of Mathis, and Athos is out there still working, even if he is being a huge infant about it.

I speak to my dad first, fearing he will be the most worried. To my surprise, he isn't.

"Lillium, how are you, dear?" He asks, surprisingly cheery.

"Uh, fine," I say, confused. I haven't spoken to him in weeks, why is he so calm?

"Athos told me you lost your pad, and that you were staying with a friend." He explains once he notices my furrow brow.

"Oh, yeah. I lost it. Shouldn't have left my wristpad at home. So, Athos has been in contact with you?" I ask.

"Yes, he has. He has been doing very well with this whole mess." He says.

"Hmm." I hum.

"You both have. I am glad to see that you are getting some rest, though. The last time I saw you, you looked so tired. It was a good move hiring Maureen." He gives me a wide dad grin.

I jolt up, shocked. "How do you know about her?" I certainly didn't tell him.

"Lillium, they were on the news last night, with the others from your group, Hero to Hire, helping clean up the towns that Mathis attacked." He

291

raises a brow. "You didn't know?"

"I wasn't aware she went with them," I admit. He sees how confused I am, but in true dad fashion doesn't pry.

"It was a good move to hire her to help you out. You were working too much." I crack a smile. Only my dad can focus on how much I work instead of the possibility of being attacked while working. I let him go shortly after that and give Libby a call.

After a few minutes of listening to her yell at me for not telling her I'm alive, and also yelling about Gaia, who isn't speaking to anyone so far, I learn that she and Max are finally done with their internship at the store and are moving.

"Some town in England, we haven't been told where yet." She says.

"I am so happy for you two!" I say, and truly I am.

"Thanks. It is weird though, if you had stayed with us you would be going too." She muses.

"Hmm, that actually sounds a lot better than what I am currently doing. Maybe I shouldn't have quit." I laugh.

Later that night, while I pull up the news footage of Athos and Maureen, I keep thinking about it. If I hadn't quit, if I hadn't met Athos, I would be getting ready to move to England, or maybe some place else. I would be going through with the plans I have had all my life. Plans Gabriel has too.

The news shows a town marred by destruction. Though it is by far, the least amount of damage he could have done, there are many homes in rubble and a few businesses totaled. I can make out Sheiba cleaning up the streets by hand, with a group of volunteers. Logan, a new member of the group with the ability to melt objects, can be seen rebuilding homes with Harold, who is popping in and out with materials.

Athos is busy doing some heavy lifting, flying in and out of view with rubble in his arms. He stops long enough to speak to the camera crew, and he pulls Maureen over with him. Apparently, she is the new face of Hero for Hire.

"Our group is working around the clock to get this place back to what it was. Just like with the other towns, we will have it cleaned up by tomorrow night." He says to the camera, smiling.

"And if Mathis attacks another town?" The announcer asks.

"I will be right there, just like I have been. We have such a dedicated group of people that they will be there too." He says.

"There you have it." The announcer says as they walk back to the others. "Athos and the group Hero for Hire, headed by Maureen, will be there to help whenever we need them."

I let the screen go black as the recording ends. Anger is rising, and hurt, but mostly anger.

"So that is the one you hired, huh?" Briseathe startles me as he appears behind the couch.

"Yeah." I mutter darkly.

"Oh Lillium, don't take it too personally. Don't think of it as him replacing you, or thinking you can't do your job."

"He just wants to protect me, right?" I say hotly. My pulse is quickening, I can feel the heat rushing through my limbs. Even without my wristpad I recognize the signs of an anxiety attack are building.

"Yes." He replies, as if it's obvious. Which, to some extent it is, but I feel like he doesn't trust me. Maybe after all I have done, sneaking around behind his back and putting myself in danger, he's right to, but still. It hurts that it feels like he's replaced me already.

Gaia's words still echo in my mind, fueling the tension in my heart.

I shake my head. "He doesn't trust me anymore. I have become unpredictable in his eyes." I jut my chin at the screen. "She is more controllable."

"You think this is about control?" Briseathe asks, looking flabbergasted.

"It always is. We started this with the mission to make Supes more relatable, and he had the upper hand being a Supe. Then Mathis happened, and I had the upper hand because I knew how humans would react. Now he feels like he is out of control, and that I am taking advantage of it."

He's quiet for a while, letting me seethe in my anger.

"Can I show you something?" he asks softly. It takes me by surprise. I'd expected an argument.

"I really don't have anything else to do." I say, shrugging.

I follow him back down to his lab, where we stop by his desk.

He picks up the picture of the girl. "You have seen this?"

"Yes." I say.

"Athos hasn't told you about her?" I shake my head slowly.

"No, he hasn't." I assumed she was a Supe, but because of their complicated history, I chose not to pry.

"Her name was Claire. She was my wife." He says, a ghost of a smile on his lips.

I gape at him. He had had a wife?

"Don't look so surprised. I wasn't always blue, you know." He snickers. "Claire was born before me, to a human and a Super. We found each other when we were young, or rather, she found me. Claire was a Seer."

"A clairvoyant?" I ask.

"Not entirely, no. She could see the past, the present, and the future all at once. Seers have been our people's history keepers, and like me and my kind, they have been held in high regard. So Claire was special, to begin with, and so was I, but we were also part human."

"And you fell in love," I say, grinning as I imagine a young, not blue, version of him falling in love.

"Not at first. Claire was the first Seer to be part human, and though it did not affect her abilities, it could affect her personality at times. There would be times when she wasn't at all here, in the present. She would act like a robot, and go through the motions, but she would be somewhere else, at another time. It creeped me out at first, and when she told me she couldn't tell me where she had been, it only made it worse. You see, a part of being a Seer is the fact that they see everything that was, is, and will be. They cannot change the course of history. According to Claire, if she had ever told me what would happen, it would still happen that way." He explains.

"Because she was meant to tell you from the start." I say. He nods. "That sounds like a horrible way to live, to know everything but not be able to say anything about it. What is the point in having that kind of power?"

He gives me a sad look. "For starters, it only applies to Supes. Claire could not see the past or future for you, but for her kind, she could. Secondly, even though she couldn't tell us what was to happen, she would give advice. Do you think that everyone just left her alone? Just like me, they were on her from day one to give them answers about the Source. She was the first Seer born in hundreds of years, and they weren't going to just leave her alone.

"So we both ran off together, seeing the world, trying to get away from the others. It was during this that I started to fall for her. She was amazingly kind, and generous, and had an appetite for life that I had never seen from our kind. Even though she could see everything in her head, she would tell me it was different from feeling the experience for herself."

I lean against his desk, impressed. "She sounds like a very special kind of person."

"Entirely opposite of you." He says, smirking. I roll my eyes but smile. He's right, of course. She sounds like my exact opposite.

"Of course, she knew from the beginning that I would fall in love with her. She let it happen naturally, and we ended up getting married a few decades later." He winks at me. "Back then I didn't alter my clones, I didn't have to."

I can picture him, looking like a normal person, living out his life with this sweet girl.

"What happened?" I ask, though I have a feeling it didn't end well.

Briseathe rolls his eyes. "I am getting there. Jeez, let me tell it how I want to." I hold up my hands and back off.

"Claire and I lived a long life full of love and happiness, with the occasional annoyance in the form of the others. There were a few that we enjoyed time with, Athos being one of them. Claire loved him like a brother, and I knew then that she could see his future held something important in it.

"They had many discussions on the state of the world as we neared the beginning of the War. Most of it I didn't pay attention too. I was far more interested in my projects then. It wasn't until the war started that Athos started to become more vocal about what he felt we needed to do.

"He was the first person to suggest that we come out of hiding." I smiled,"You don't look surprised."

"He's told me a bit about it," I say.

"Trying to sway his people, or expressing his views openly?"

I nod. "Both, but the Athos I know have always doubted himself a little."

He nods. "He has been that way as long as I have known him. His talks with Claire, however, spurred him into action." he smiles. "She had that way with people."

"Then he was turned down." I say, recalling how the others dismissed his ideas.

"Oh yes, very harshly too." I wince. Athos isn't very good at being turned down. Just look at how we met.

"Leading to his little excursion into space," I muse.

"Yes," he nods. "He didn't take it too well, and decided that he would go searching for where the Source came from, or possibly another one."

I sigh, leaning against the desk. "Why does he have such little faith in himself?" I wonder aloud.

"Besides the obvious rejection? Our father was a natural leader, and when our home was destroyed, he held us all together. Athos has always felt that he, as his son, should be able to do the same. When he died, Athos tried to keep leading us down the same path, but he failed."

I take a deep breath and then say, "And here we are now." Briseathe bops me on the nose with his index finger, causing me to glare at him.

"Right, you are." He wags his finger in my face.

"What was your point?" I grumble.

"Athos has never been about control. He has only wanted the best for people." He says.

"He also has never been able to inspire them to follow him until now," I say pointedly.

"True. But that has never been his goal to lead. Lillium, Athos only wants to make sure you stay alive, nothing more. You have to admit, you running after Mathis like that was a stupid thing to do."

"That is your opinion. The way I see it," I motion to his newest computer, "I helped make it possible to put a stop to him."

"And if you had died during it?" He asks, cocking his head.

I look away, trying to hide the way I wince. I'm being stubborn, I know, but right now, it's all I have. "That is my choice. Just because Athos doesn't have the luxury of choosing when to die doesn't mean he can butt in on mine."

"Even if I think it is an incredible waste of life?" I spin around to see Athos glaring at me from the elevator.

"Especially then." I spit back.

Chapter 36

"Then you are as pigheaded as the rest of your kind." *Pig headed?* I think. "That kind of thinking is what started the War."

"Right as always, Athos," I saunter towards him, my face a mask of indifference. "We humans just love to cause strife, especially when needless deaths are involved."

"Alright you two, not in my lab, thank you." Briseathe holds up his hands, but we ignore him. The weeks apart have done nothing for his attitude, and it only fuels my own.

"It is alright Briseathe, I only came to check on you. I am not staying." He says.

"It must be nice to just come and go." I shoot at him.

"It's a privilege for adults only." He says, leaning closer.

"Or a way to maintain control of someone you think of as a threat." Color rises to his cheeks, and I take his moment of silence to ask, "What happened to Claire?"

Briseathe knows I', asking him, but still looks at me in confusion.

"She must have died in the war, right?" I ask.

"Yes. She did." He answers slowly.

"That is why you came out, isn't it?" I watch Athos's face go dark, and know I'm right.

"I took her death very hard," Briseathe says softly. "The others did too, so I knew it would be easy rallying them together. I had always agreed with Athos about showing ourselves to the humans, but…." he trails off.

"But he didn't have what it took to get them on his side." I tsk. "But hey, he now has the cause and," I pat him on the chest, "what it takes to get everyone to listen to him. And once he takes care of Mathis," I shrug, "there will be no limit to what he can do." My words are burning jabs meant to get a rise from him, but instead of responding with an equally piercing comment, he just stares at me.

At first, I glare back with the same intensity, waiting for him to act. After a while though, I start to think he's going to go into statue mode and ignore me.

"What, are you out of things to say?" I ask snidely.

"Oh no, I have comments." He retorts. "I know what you are trying to do, and I am not playing into it." He smirks at my surprise. "No matter what you say right now, I know it is out of anger, and meant to make me mad, so it will be easier for you to stay mad at me."

"That isn't-" I take a step back as he comes closer.

"Yes, it is. You are upset that you cannot leave here, that you cannot continue to do your work, and you are blaming me for it all. It is easier for you to say that I am afraid of you taking the limelight away from me, and that that is why I won't let you leave here, instead of the truth." I have to back up into the desk, nowhere else to go while he comes closer. His amber eyes dig into me with their gaze. He has me right where he wants me, with nothing to say.

"What you did was brave." My heart skips d a beat when he says it. "You took a risk that could kill you to help save your kind and end a war before it gets too bloody. It was brave and incredibly stupid. Sure, this gadget of my brothers will help us in the end, but if you had died, it would have been an incredible waste of talent, skills, and personality." He's inches from my face, the heat of his body coming off in waves as I fight the blood rising to my cheeks.

"You would have become a martyr, but Lily, you are far more valuable alive than dead. Are you so keen to follow Gabriel to the grave?"

I can't move. I'm paralyzed, transported back in time to that terrible night. My heart is slamming against my lungs, pressing the air from them and making it hard to breathe. Shallow, quick breaths are all I can manage as I gaze back at him, silently drowning.

"Once you realize that, and promise never to do such a thing again, you can come back to Legion. I can't have you running straight at danger, Lilly, I can't protect the world while looking over my shoulder for you."

Just like that, the moment is gone, and my anger rises again.

"I am not some demur underling that you can control." I seethe. I glare up at him, fuming, pushing back against him. "You do not have to 'look after me', and I will *not* promise you anything! And don't you dare bring Gabe into this. He has nothing to do with us!"

"Then you will stay here," Athos says, his face deadpan.

"As a prisoner, forever!?" I screech.

"If that is what it takes to keep you alive, yes!"

"Ugh, you are such an egotistical misogynist!" I scoff.

His eyes widen. "I am not!"

"And a whiner!" I snap back.

"I am *not*!" He protests, looking from me to Briseathe, who takes a step back.

"You are telling me to stay in my place, or you will make me!" I say.

"I- no, that isn't what I am doing! Mathis is out there right now, tearing up the world because he can't tear you to pieces!" He shakes his head.

"I want him to find me, dammit! Then we can use this gallium stuff to stop him!" I point at the new machine.

"Good!" He yells looking at Briseathe. "That's wonderful news!" Briseathe nods quickly. "But you won't be anywhere near us when we do!"

"Well, being held prisoner like I am, I highly doubt that happening!" I say.

"Damn right! You let me know when that gadget is ready!" He says as he turns back to the elevator.

"Where are you going!?" I snap.

"Back to work!" He yells.

I gape back at him. My pulse quickens when I realize he's going to leave me again. "Well fine! Go on then, I bet Maureen is doing a wonderful job!"

He stops short. "Maureen?" He asks, incredulous.

"Yeah, the girl I hired? The 'head' of Hero for Hire?" I say in a mocking tone.

"Are...are you jealous?" he asks, looking me up and down.

I freeze for a moment under his gaze. Jealous? Me? Even as I shake my head slowly I can feel the way my cheeks burn. *Liar.* "I would like my job back." I hiss.

"And you will get it when you decide to stop putting your life in danger." With that he takes the elevator up, leaving me to seethe next to a nervous Briseathe.

Chapter 37

"It has been five days since the last attack," Korra's neon yellow hair bounces around her as she speaks. "Hero for Hire has been working around the clock in various parts of the world, not only cleaning up what destruction Mathis and his followers have done but also areas that have been left untouched after the War."

I groan as I flip the channel. Two weeks full of watching Athos and Maureen rebuilding homes and businesses while smiling for the cameras has put me in a foul mood. I no longer find comfort in blowing up parts of the gym. I have had enough of gadgets and gizmos, and find myself camping out on the couch, watching the world go by without me. Watching him go on without me.

It pisses me off.

"Tonight's gala event will be the biggest fundraiser to date." Korra looks pretty good tonight. She has toned down her attire a bit for a more formal dress.

"I will have exclusive interviews with Athos, and Maureen," I boo loudly while throwing a handful of chips at Korra's face, "Also a few of their associates, so make sure to watch!" I switch the channel while shoving more chips into my mouth. Everyone's covering the gala tonight.

Athos and Maureen decide to host this gala as a way to raise even more money for their work with Hero for Hire, which becomes a real organization overnight. Using the funds donated to them, they rebuild towns, cities, homes, and anything that Mathis and his minions destroy while also providing families of the chaos with food and shelter. Supes become tired of using their own funds.

Absolutely everyone goes tonight, well, everyone important, that is. Far more bodies than when we open Legion. Of course, being under house arrest, I can't go.

Not that I am invited. It would be nice to turn it down, though. The swoosh of the elevator opening declares one of Briseathe's short visits. He stops just short of the couch, eyeing the chips strewn about.

"You know, when I built this place as my hideaway, I never envisioned being holed up with a slob like you." Briseathe grumbles.

"When I met your brother, I never thought I would be held prisoner by an indigo colored man- yet here you are," I mumble around my chips.

"I am not indigo, I am azure thank you." I roll my eyes. "Are you trying to be a pest, or is this really how you are?"

I shrug. "You could always toss me out."

"Not a chance." He fumbles with his pad, tapping a few keys until a mini robot pops out of a nook somewhere, promptly vacuuming my mess.

"Do not get any ideas," he says when he sees me eye the robot. "I am the only one who can control it."

"How is the gallium coming along, oh Lord of the Fortress?" I ask, flicking a chip at the robot.

He narrows his eyes at the chip. "It will be done, not soon enough, though. Have you left this couch at all in the last week?"

"Where do you think I got the chips from?" I say, shaking the bag.

He sniffs the air, grimacing. "Have you... showered at all?"

"Does it matter?" I deadpan.

"Kind of, yes." He says.

I shrugs. "I think I did the other day." I flop to my side as I flip back to the coverage of the gala's venue, a large property in Italy supposedly owned by one of the Supes. People are already arriving in droves.

"Lillium, whose shirt is that?" Briseathe asks, his tone panicked.

I pluck at the light green shirt I'm wearing, "Yours." He twitches, which makes me smile.

"Lillium." He says tensely.

303

"Briseathe." I mimick.

"Take that off. How did you even get it?!" He scoffs.

I frown. "You left it in the laundry room. It's not like I have much clothing of my own here! Athos didn't exactly pack for me."

"Please take it off." He begs.

"No." I curl up on the couch, glaring back at him.

"It's one of my favorites and you haven't showered in days!"

"No! I am being held prisoner by you people. You want me to be naked too?" I snap.

"Argh!" He yells. He stomps off to the elevator, cursing.

It has been liked this all week. He rarely comes up from his lab, so I pretty much own the living room and kitchen now. Soon I will spread my dirty depression out to the other rooms.

A roar from the crowd causes the cameras to swerve, revealing Athos, smartly dressed, coming up the stairs to the building. At his arm is none other than Maureen, dressed just as nicely. She looks so at ease, like it's second nature for her to be in front of all the cameras a people. Something I never could accomplish.

As they near the top, a reporter stops them briefly, and in that moment Athos does something so strange. He takes her hand in his and then continues on their way. I am so shocked by this simple gesture that I can't hear the news anymore. I feel sick suddenly, and it has nothing to do with the chips.

Why would he take her hand like that? What was going on between them? Sure, he'd taken my hand in front of the cameras, even held the small of my back before, but that is... us.

This is Maureen. She isn't us.

Or is she? We haven't spoken about that night, what it makes us, which is clearly more than friends. But maybe not? Maybe it was a one-time thing for him.

I'm spiraling now, my hands clenching the chip bag so tightly I can feel them crumbling beneath my fingers. The thoughts are swirling and my breath is becoming erratic.

She is taking over everything I have started and getting all the credit for my hard work while I am here, alone. In all this coverage of the gala, not a word has been said about me.

It isn't like I've been mentioned all the time before, but I'm at least referred to. Not even Korra mentions anything now that I think about it. I could be dead and no one would be the wiser. Or care. In a way, it is like I have. In an instant, the mess I have been sitting in disgusts me.

I jump up, throwing everything off the table and couch. I turn to the elevator only to be stopped by Briseathe getting off.

We both speak at the same time, "You need to finish the gallium-" I start.

"I've completed the gallium-" He says.

"It's done?" I ask.

"Yes, now I need to get a hold of Athos and get your messy self out of here." he sniffs.

"Well, he is a little busy with the gala." *And Maureen,* I think.

"It might have to wait." He says.

"Mathis is still in hiding. We don't have a plan on getting him out in the open." I grumble.

"Agreed, but I need you gone. I am this close to shoving you in the chamber I built for him." He warns.

I pat his shoulder. "I deserve it."

He raised a brow. "Really? Why the sudden change of attitude?"

"It doesn't matter. We have what we need to stop Mathis now."

"Oh, no." He pushes my arm away. "Lillium, I might want you gone, but I am not stupid. I am not sending you out there."

"I was not suggesting that I go out. But maybe just the rumor of me being out in the open will be enough." I smile slyly.

"A rumor?" he looks thoughtful.

"There hasn't been anything said about me for a month now. Maybe a little rumor that I am in a town will make him want to come check it out."

"It could work. But we would have to make sure he thinks the information is legitimate." He muses.

"I know just the person. It will give you enough time to get the gallium ready to transport."

He nods. "It could work. I already have a place in mind."

"Just give me an hour to set it up." I say.

He smirks. "Korra?"

She takes my call pretty fast, considering the fact that she is at the gala. Thankfully, she does not ask too many questions, so we keep it brief and she agrees to report that I am in a dinky little town ravaged by the war working on rebuilding it. By the time I shower and change into my own clothes, Briseathe already has the gallium ready to go. He has crates full of sheets of it stacked on a transport pad in his lab. The plan is to get Athos to ambush Mathis with just enough time to break a crate of sheets over him. The heat from his body will melt them instantly, coating him with the gallium, and hopefully leaving him powerless.

"Alright, so once Athos is done dancing to his heart's content, Korra will send out a report on my whereabouts. Then we will have Athos slip out of his party and lie in wait." Briseathe says as he gives me an approving look over the controls to the transport pad. "You showered."

I pat my wet hair. "I even washed my hair."

"Hm, well, all we have to do now is wait for Korra to make her announcement. Then it is all up to Athos."

"If he comes at all." I retort.

"He will. This is a good plan. I am sure it will work."

"How sure?" I ask.

He pats my arm. "I am certain. Mathis will take the bait. He wants you dead, Lillium. He wants your blood."

"Good." And with all my strength, I shove him into the transport controls. The weight of his body hits the activation screen, and if it worked like my belt, I only have seconds. I lunge onto one of the crates just as he starts to yell my name.

Then there's silence.

Chapter 38

It feels fabulous ramming Briseathe like this after living with him for a month. It is exhilarating catching him by surprise, but short-lived as the lab disappears and I find myself surrounded by darkness. I am surprised by how quiet it is until my eyes adjust and I realize Briseathe's perfect location for Mathis's take down is a pre-war factory of sorts.

I jump down from the crates, looking up to see half of the ceiling is gone, allowing moonlight to stream in. I can make out objects that could have been machines at one point, but the effects of years have rendered them indistinguishable. Foliage grows out of them, the walls, the rafters, and all over the floor. The spot I am in is the only empty patch in the area; the rest is overgrown up to my shoulders.

A warm breeze comes through, reminding me it is almost summer, and with it my birthday and the holiday Briseathe. It is almost a year since I met Athos. I shake my head. There will be time to think about that once Mathis is taken care of.

I pull off my clothes, which are just bagging enough to cover the sight of my belt and suit. I have just enough time to slip into them while talking with Korra. Briseathe is right in that my plan is enough to bring Mathis out of hiding.

But only if I am really where Korra says I will be. Mathis isn't stupid, he will breeze in here, literally, and once he realizes I am not around, he will leave. That or he will have one of his goons check it out beforehand. That is a risk I can't take. So I lie, and Korra actually makes her report on me right after we talk.

Now all I have to do is sit around and hope Mathis takes the bait, and also that Athos shows up. I realize when I see him take Maureen's hand that I have lost him to the light of the cameras. Maureen can stand with him in the light, but I still stand for what we have originally set out to accomplish, which he no longer needs. He has lost sight of what is important, and in doing so, I have lost my confidence in him. I know Briseathe will do whatever he has to do to get Athos to come, since my transporter gadget no longer works and I cannot flee.

This is near suicide, but at least it's better than laying on a couch and watching my life pass by, while Mathis continues to destroy the world.

Gaia is right, Athos is just like the rest, so it is up to me now to force his hand and make him finish what we started. It can't be me to do it. That would just be fodder for HAS, a human overtaking a Supe. It needs to be Athos, to show the world he is on their side, and will do whatever it takes to protect them. We need peace.

So I fix my suit and belt, getting my gadgets in place in case I need to use them, and walk outside the building. It would be too suspicious if I just sit there. Mathis needs to see that he has a chance to get to me.

And he will take it, no matter the cost. As I near a collapsed wall, I hear someone behind me. I turn expecting to see Athos, instead it is Mathis.

My surprise must be evident- I really didn't expect to see him so soon.

A smile creeps at the sides of his mouth ever so slowly as he says coldly, "Lillium."

His emotionless tone makes my skin crawl. Rage is burning in his eyes, and for the first time, I start to doubt my choice. Maybe the isolation made me a little unhinged and over confident.

"Mathis," I try to sound calmer than I feel.

"I half expected this to be a hoax," he looks tense, ready to spring, "I was not sure you were stupid enough to go out on your own."

I need to buy time until Athos comes, and the best way is to annoy the hell out of him.

"How do you know I am not alone?" I scoff.

"I know." He says it so assuredly that I have a hard time not believing him.

"Hmm, so Athos is still at the party? Figures, he really likes to-" He lunges so quickly I almost don't roll away in time. I bounce back up, an elemental orb in my hand ready.

"I suppose we are done with the formalities, then?" I grunt.

He glares back at me in response. Even though he's a good five feet away, my force field is still humming with the intensity of his power. If he gets his hands on me even for a moment, he will burn it out and leave me bare. I curse myself silently. *I need to be more careful, dammit.*

"Do you think those toys can help you?" He sneers.

"No, they can only delay the inevitable." There's no need to lie now.

He paces in front of me, his cat-like eyes glowing in the moonlight, never leaving my face.

"Will you disappear like last time?" He taunts.

I shrug. "Wait and see."

He doesn't, instead turning into vapor. I activate the orb just before his hand materializes to take hold of my raised arm. The rest of his body solidifies.

"Old tricks," he hisses in my face. My bangle burns against my wrist.

"Or new," I grunt. The orb expels a burst of sand in both our faces, but I have my eyes shut. He growls, still holding tight, so I jab him in the crotch with a knee. He lets go, one hand on his face, the other holding himself in pain. I toss a smoke bomb just before running into the dense growth to find a place to hide.

Athos should be here by now, the jerk. Mathis howls while I pick my way through the thick growth.

"Such a human thing to do!" He coughs. "Go ahead and drag out your death! I know I will!"

Oh, I know you will, I think. My foot catches on something nearly tripping me, so I bend down feeling around. My fingers find the opening of something, something I can fit into. I climb in to find it's a tube of sorts with an opening at the end. I can just make out the light.

A rustle behind me alerts me that he's now trying to find me in the foliage. Taking an orb out, I tuck myself in the tube and wait.

"Did you use your little disappearing act again, you filthy animal?" He growls.

By all that is holy, this guy sure loves to throw insults. Then again, I had brought him an image of his dead wife to taunt him with; I think as I just started to make him out.

With a smile, I chuck the orb, then dive further into the tube before it explodes into a fireball.

"SON OF A-" I pop out the other end just in time to see the whole area on fire with him in the middle, flapping his arms around him. He has turned himself into stone to battle the flames.

"Where are you!?" He screams. *Why not turn it all into water, idiot,* I think. Half the place is catching on fire now, but I can still see the crates from where I am, untouched so far. I pray that Athos will show up. I only have a few more orbs and very few places to hide now.

As if reading my thoughts, Mathis starts to taunt me. "No one is coming for you! Athos rather take photos, then come and save your pathetic hide." My heart skips a beat, knowing it's a possibility. But a part of me still believes in him enough to have me jump on that crate and come here, risking my life just to put a stop to this psycho.

The force field hums a warning, but I'm too slow to react before Mathis takes a hold of my hair. He drags me out of my hiding spot into the clearing, shocking me with his strength. I fail to grab an orb as he takes both my hands and forces me to stand up. The bangle is searing my wrist with the effort to keep the force field up.

"Is that flesh I smell burning?" I can see the firelight in his eyes he's so close, "That looks like it hurts."

A grunt is my only response. *Hell yes it hurt!*

"I wonder," he rubs his cheek against it. "If I try harder to turn you into ash, would it hurt more?" I bite my lip, glaring at him. The bangle grows hotter in a second, then explodes. He laughs manically at my screams.

"Oops, I meant to make that last a little longer." He turns my blistered skin around as he examined it. "No bother, now that that is done with, let us have some real fun, huh?"

I kick at him, only to have him block it.

"You might be more comfortable if you-" he kicks my knee out so hard I fall over into him, "kneel." He positions me next to him on my knees, facing the crates. "Which one will we start with? This one?" He digs his nails into the burned flesh, making me scream with the pain.

"Hmm, the other than." Clutching my bleeding arm to his chest, he stretches the other out in front of me. "Now this, this will hurt."

At first, all I feel is the searing pain of my left arm and can't fathom what kind of pain will replace it. Then the very tips of my right hand begin to tingle as if they have fallen asleep. In a matter of seconds the tingle ignites into the worst pain I have ever felt. I'm so stupefied I can't cry out until the sensation shoots down straight to my shoulder.

The primal wail that erupts from me makes him sneer with pure joy. I twist my body around with all my strength, managing to get one leg out from under me, only to have him stomp on the other, pinning me to the ground. I can't escape him, escape the pain, but that doesn't stop me from flailing in desperation.

"I am going to make this slow," he hisses in my ear. "There will be no release from this."

I feel like the life is being sucked from me, my limbs begin to shake from the shock, and just when my vision starts to blur and I think I am going to pass out, it all stops.

I let out a shaky sob of relief. Instinctively I go to flex my finger, only to find I can't.

I look up at him weakly, seeing the leer in his face. "Now, watch." I don't want to, but I also don't have the strength to resist.

My skin is turning a different shade at the tips of my fingers, and the pain is spreading down. I am watching in frozen terror as my fingers are turning into sand, falling apart as they do. I can't tear myself away from seeing my fingers fall away into nothing, right up to the knuckles. When it stops, I realize he is cackling.

"I have waited so long to see that look in your eyes, you stupid human. And all it took was losing your fingers." Numbly, I glance at his face, blinking.

I didn't realize it, but I'm crying. He bends down smoothly, and with one motion, licks the tears off my cheek. "I will admit, I expected more of a fight from you." He searches my eyes for something, and when he doesn't see it he says, "So easily broken. Humans really are so weak."

His words pierce me like daggers. He is right; I am weak. Slumping against him, one arm blistered and bloody, and another missing finger in a matter of minutes. How do I think I can hold my own against him, even for a moment? Well, I don't. I put my faith in Athos, thinking he will drop everything and come to help me. They are both right. I am a stupid, stupid human.

I am defeated; I am weak. I am going to die. My body sags with the weight of that knowledge.

"Oh no, I won't have you doing that just yet." He yanks me back up, stepping in front of me to hold me up. "You will watch this, little flower."

He places the hand right in my face just as it starts to turn again, only this time it doesn't fall apart right away. Instead, it changes up to the wrist, with him leaning down smiling. He takes a deep breath and blows the rest of my hand away.

When I don't react, he scoffs. "Are you really giving up so soon? Perhaps, dear flower, I should bring someone in here and let you watch." He smirks. "Remember Paris?"

I twist my remaining hand around until the palm is on his chest. Weakly, I press it against him.

"Is that all you have left?" I press again, a little harder. "Really? Are you trying to feel me up now? Let me help." He slaps himself on his chest with my hand, and it sends him flying backwards into the crates. I fall over, surprised that he actually activated the gadget on my glove.

The range is been better than I thought, and he lands right into the crates, breaking a few. I can see him struggling to get up, cursing.

Get up, get up NOW! I scream at myself. Summoning my strength, I force myself to get up and limp over to him. He's rolling around in a broken crate, the sheets of gallium falling all around him. But they aren't melting over him.

"BITCH!" He spits as he finds his footing. Without thinking, I tackle him back to the ground, causing the other crates to fall on us. One hits me in the back, knocking the air out of my lungs. I lay there, spent under the crates, as Mathis roars in rage, fighting his way back up.

I don't struggle when he grabs me by the hair again.

"I am going to turn you into slug, you little-"

"MATHIS!" We meet each other's eyes, surprised. Then he swings me up, holding me in front of him to see Athos, still in his party clothes, hair disheveled, eyes burning.

"I was not expecting you." I can hear the chagrin in his voice.

"I am sure." Athos says coolly.

"Did you beat Siv to a bloody pulp that fast, or did you come running once you heard she was here?" He pulls my hair back, making me cringe.

Athos doesn't respond. I can tell he's weighing his options now, and none of them are looking that great.

"You didn't really think you could keep her safe, did you?" Mathis taunts. "She is a human, prone to self destruction. She would have found her way to me one way or another. It is in her nature to seek out chaos." He holds out my stub of an arm, and I watch horror run across Athos's face. "This is her fate, Athos. The fate of all her kind. I will not stop until they are all our slaves, or dead. And this little flower is too weak to be a slave. Say goodbye."

"No!" Athos screams. But nothing happens. Mathis tenses as Athos gives me a questioning look. I glance at his hand holding my arm and see the gallium melted on him. I begin to say something but Athos is too fast. He swoops in, punching Mathis in the face. I fall into his arms.

"Gallium," I gasp weakly.

"I can see." He snaps.

"Briseathe's, cell. You have to get him there." I say.

"What is this shit?" Mathis growls.

"Briseathe says hello," Athos retorts.

"That meddling ass!" Mathis screams.

In the distanced I can hear the hum of mobile cameras hovering. Apparently, the fire has caught the attention of the media.

313

"Well, you can tell him yourself." Athos lets me lean against a crate as he approaches Mathis. "He will be the last person you see in a long time."

"Oh yes, plan on putting me in a cell for the rest of eternity?" He scoffs. "Are you sure you can contain me?"

Athos responds by taking him by his shoulder, "Are you sure they will trust you to contain me?" Athos glares back at him.

"Oh yes, parade me out there like a trophy for your humans to see. Let them see their murderer go with his fellow man. I am sure they will trust you and your justice. Right Athos? People trust your judgement, they follow you and your word."

"Shut up." I croak. "Athos, just take him, please." I can't stand to look at him anymore, let alone actually stand. "Athos!" I groan when he doesn't move. He's gone into his statue mode. We don't have time for this. The gallium can wear off, the cameras will be in here any second, we don't need them filming Mathis screwing with his head.

"Are you sure I can be held? Are you sure they will follow you? I have killed, well, hundreds of them. They thirst for my blood. Do you think they will really let you get away with just throwing me in a cell?" Mathis taunts.

"Shut up Mathis!" I snap louder as panic creeps up my spine. Mathis is starting to get to me. My heart is pulsing with his words as dread fills my heart.

Maybe he's right.

"If they don't get my blood, they will thirst for yours, turning on you, and all that fame will go away in an instant. They're fickle like that." He hisses.

"He's trying to get under your skin Athos, just take him to Briseathe!" I push myself upright only to fall back again. My strength's gone. "The best thing for everyone is to put him away, you know that."

"Are you sure she is right? Will her word be enough for them?" Mathis sneers back at me, hissing. "Or is it really her that we need to thank for all of this?"

I gape at him. Me? He's really going to try and pin this all on me?

"Oh, so it's true. I knew you couldn't have gotten this far without some help. Everyone knows it. So she's the one will all the power, or she thinks she is-"

"Shut up!" I scream.

"She wants the spotlight just as much as you. Why do you think she came here by herself?" Blood is pounding in my ears. He needs to shut up. He needs to be stopped. Why isn't Athos stopping him?

There isn't anymore time the cameras are almost inside, and if they see Athos and Mathis talking like this, it will all be over. No one will trust that the Supes are acting with the best intentions for everyone. Athos has to take him now or never. Fueled by panic and fear and I push myself upright, reaching out for them. If I have to, I will slap some sense into Athos.

A slow smile creeps onto Mathis's face as he says. "Well, what will it be, hero?"

"Mathis-" Athos starts but falters.

"I'm going to kill them all, hero. Every last one will be turned into dust." Mathis hisses, then laughs. He laughs in Athos's face when he sees the doubt there - the doubt that they will be able to hold him, and the others. To what end?

I barely feel the way the knife slips into his chest. Or hear the way he gasps, gurgling on his own blood as it fills his throat.

"Shut up," I ground out between my teeth, driving the knife deeper into his heart. "Just shut up." Tears burn my eyes as the dead rise behind them.

Gabe, broken a bloody while I hold him. The boy from Paris, his face white with terror. The poor little Super girl, who with her last breath saved us all from the falling Legion. Their deaths won't be in vain.

I won't let them.

Athos is screaming in my ear, but I don't hear him. I'm watching the shock and terror play across Mathis's face when he realizes a human, a lowly creature like myself, has killed him.

I savor the way the light dies in his eyes.

Athos pulls me away, grabbing for the knife just as a camera comes barreling in.

Chapter 39

Looks like rain, I think bemusedly while drumming my fingers on the table. Outside my dad's home, clouds gather. I have a feeling it has nothing to do with the storm-inducing Supe, Vander.

I might just have to give him a call tonight.

"Lillium?" I cock my head to see dad and Libby both giving me the same look. Apparently, I have missed a conversation I am a part of.

"Sorry," I sit forward. "I am thinking it might rain tonight."

Libby looks from me to the window, sneering, "Who cares?"

"Well, it's Briseathe. You know, the award tonight?" I say.

"We know," my dad says, "That is what we were just talking about."

"Well, if it rains, it might, you know, mess up the stage or something." I mutter.

"That is Maureen's problem then, right? Why should you care?" Libby scoffs.

"She only handles Hero for Hire," I say tersely. "I still handle Athos."

Well, if that is what you call it these days. They exchange looks, then my dad says, "Well, we were both just saying that it is a sure thing, him winning this year."

"Of course," I wave nonchalantly, "I am just worried about image. It should be perfect since he is the first one to win it who actually deserves to."

"You still think so?" Libby asks. I raise a brow. "Even after a good amount of his people call for his excommunication because he killed one of their own?"

316

"Sadly, some of his people still think what he did is unforgivable and refuse to follow him or anyone associated with him. And yes, some end up joining the defectors, but…." But what? Athos kills Mathis, in front of cameras no less, even though we have a way to stop him for good. Officially, he claims that Mathis is too dangerous to let live. *I will do whatever it takes to keep the peace,* he says to a reporter.

But only he and I know it's a lie. I killed him. I drove a knife into his heart and watched the life leech from his eyes.

And I have no remorse for it.

But it would have been a fiasco if the world knew the truth. We might have grown accustomed to the fact that Supes could kill each other, but a human?

A month later and we still haven't spoken to each other face to face. Maureen relays all his messages to me, and I through her, figuring he needs time.

I suppose I do too. I am still upset over being held prisoner with Briseathe.

"But," my dad finishes, "it is what is good for the people. He puts a stop to the mayhem, and he still helps everyday humans with mundane tasks." He laughs. "I heard he built a track for a new tram system out in Greenland for HAS."

"Yeah, he built it in one day. They were pretty sour about it." I grumble.

"That is what they get for publicly announcing anyone can come help." He points out.

Libby fidgets with her braid, and I give her a bemused look. "No, Gaia still has not contacted me." I say.

She shrugs like she doesn't know what I am talking about. "Is Korra doing the interview tonight?" My dad asks.

"Yes." I say. He looks at me expectantly. "What?"

"Well, are you going to be there for it?"

"Duh. I am not going to miss him getting his award and showing it off." I laugh.

"No, I mean, are you going to be a part of the interview?"

I look from him to Libby confused, then realize what he means. "We talked about this." I sigh.

"I know Lillium, but you really don't think the public should know you had a part in the whole thing? It would be empowering to the rest of us to know that a human came up with the idea to use gallium against Mathis and weaken him!"

I have told them half truths about that night. Mostly that I have a crazy idea I think could work after too much research into minerals and metals.

"It is a stupid thing for me to." I hold my right hand up, flexing my fingers. "I could have lost more than this hand." I could have died.

Briseathe might be able to clone me with a new hand, but not a new me. No matter how many times he is able to do it himself. I glance down at my left wrist, the scar still a pale pink. I decide to keep it as a reminder of how fragile I really am. But also how strong I can be.

Also, it looks pretty epic.

"But don't you think showing how our two people can work together like that-"

"No, I do not." I cut Libby off. "It would only be fodder for HAS to know that we can actually find ways to kill them. Let the public think Athos is the only one who can. As long as he continues to be their hero they will be fine." With that, my pad beeps, reminding me to get moving, or I will be late.

"Do you have to go?" Libby asks sadly.

"Sorry." I give her a weak smile.

"I still think you work too hard." Dad says smiling.

"Well, I had to find some way to buy my house, didn't I?" I smirk.

"Oh, I can not wait to come to Flossom and see it!" Libby squeals.

"Me neither." I stand up, gathering my gifts. "Thank you for the birthday cake, and gifts!" Libby gives me a quick hug, and my dad walks me to the door.

"I can't believe you are twenty-six now," he says, shaking his head.

"Sorry I couldn't come in on my birthday. Moving was such a hassle."

"Well, I have heard of this really great company that employees Supers who help with jobs like that for free. It's called Hiring Heroes or something.

You should look into it." He snorts at his own joke.

"Oh, ha ha." I roll my eyes. "Thank you dad, I will see you next week for dinner."

He gives me a hug, then pats my head. "You really have changed a lot in the last year, kid. I was worried about you for a while there, after Gabriel. You seemed lost, so unhappy. But now when I see you, you are motivated and sure of yourself. You seem at peace." He laughs, "I know that sounds ridiculous after all that has been happening, but you really do."

I struggle to come up with a sarcastic remark, knowing he is right. "I really am, dad. I have made myself a place, become my own person. I am happy."

He kisses my forehead as I walk out. "See you next week! Try not to get too busy!" I wave back, smiling.

The truth is tonight is going to be the first time I actually do work since Mathis. I haven't handled anything to do with Hero for Hire, or really anything huge with Athos. I have mostly been suggesting what jobs he should take to keep up his image, and I have been in contact with a few of the other Supes to check on them.

Other than that, I have been locked up in my room at Briseathe's until he is finished with my new hand. With Mathis dead, his followers have stopped wreaking havoc and went into hiding.

HAS can't claim that Supes serve their own agendas anymore, the public opinion has shifted again, and they have lost their momentum. Not that they will go away by any means, either of them. They are just licking their wounds until another opportunity arises.

While I wait for my train, I look down at the spot where I fell a year to this day, when Athos pulled me out, thinking that the train won't stop. I smile, remembering how he is so hell-bent on me thanking him that he followed me around.

I think about our together before that, and the one at Briseathe's after he found me alive. I'd wanted to talk with him about it, but after Mathis, I knew things have changed.

"Excuse me." I jump, startled by the sudden appearance of a maintenance person popping out from the tracks.

I step back and let them climb up. "Sorry, I was daydreaming." I say.

"Ah, don't worry. Now that this is finally fixed, there is no way I could be hit." He says.

"I am sorry, what?" I ask.

"Oh, the censors on this track have been faulty for the last year. They haven't been detecting lifeforms and alerting the train." My mouth hangs open as she speaks. "These trains took out two deer, and ran over a maintenance worker's leg while he was trying to find the problem. Finally, we figured out it was a family of raccoons getting inside and chewing up the wires. Little critters, had to build them a replacement home and put up mesh."

She lifts a cage holding a raccoon that looks suspiciously like the one who stole my dad's cake last year. "It was a good thing no one decided to cross them, they could have been killed, thinking it would detect them."

She walks away, leaving me gaping like a fish.

I really would have died then back then when I was crossing the tracks. If Athos hadn't come along, I would have been crushed. The thought that I'd been wrong is so profound I find myself choking back tears.

Athos is right about a lot of things, despite me being nothing but stubborn and rude to him. He saved my life numerous times, all for the sake of saving me with nothing to gain for himself. He didn't need to pull me off those tracks.

He could have just let me face Mathis and die- I certainly acted like I wanted it that way.

I've been so blind, thinking all he wants is the fame like the rest of the Supes. He is nothing but kind to me since we meet. He shows me a secret side to his people few ever get to see. I am so privileged I let it all go to my head.

My prejudice blinds me to his true nature. He is someone I trust with my life, my secrets. He is my best friend. No, he's more, and I fucked it all up being a stubborn bitch.

It is because of all this that I felt so hurt when he stuck me with Briseathe.

He injured my pride, but mostly, he hurt my feelings. I like him more than just a friend, and I am just too stubborn to see it until now.

I hurry back to my new home, bought with funds given to me by Athos for being his PR manager. I never think I will actually use the money for anything, but once I find myself not wanting to move back in with dad and without a real place to call home, I decide to put it to good use and buy one.

I change quickly for the festival, putting extra care into my appearance. I am going to tell him how sorry I am, how he is right, and maybe even how I feel.

I know Athos almost better than I know myself. His pride is hurt, and he is just as angry with me as I am with him. Neither of us wants to be the first to admit it, but I am going to.

I am going to put my own ego aside for once and try to be a better person than I am. I live too long in the past, obsessing over what happens to Gabriel, of missed opportunities and dreams that I am letting current ones slip through my fingers.

I can't be consumed by my anger anymore. I have to let it all go and move on. I need to start with Athos.

The Hero of the Year award is being handed out in Sun City this year, since it is the first city to give him any recognition putting him on the map of Supes.

The streets are crowded with bodies and food stalls. Kids run around wearing shirts with his name or face on it. I see one girl wearing an exact replica of the suit Briseathe and I design for him. I almost go into my old store to see what they have on sale, but decide against it when I remember the last time I was in there.

Showing my credentials to security, I am led into a nearby building where I see Korra and Harold conversing closely in the lobby. When Korra spots me, she screams so loud everyone in the room stops what they are doing to watch her run to me.

I almost double back, thinking she is going to tackle me to the ground. Instead, she wraps her arms around me and tries to squeeze the air out of my body.

"Lillium!" she has tears in her eyes. "I have missed you SO much!"

Really? I don't think we are close at all. Oh, stop it, I think. *You are trying to not be so cynical anymore, remember?* I return her hug with as much enthusiasm.

"I missed you too, Korra." It isn't a lie. I really have missed this eccentric ball of energy.

"Hey there," Harold says from behind her hair.

"Harold!" I take a hold of him too, surprising him. "I really have missed you guys."

"Well, stop going off the grid then," Korra laughs.

"I plan to," I nod. I spot Sheiba in the background, watching us. She doesn't smile, but she doesn't have her usual scowl either.

I take that as a good sign.

"I am so excited," Korra says. I nod back at her. "This will be the first time I get to interview a Hero of the Year!"

"He could still lose, you know," Harold says, smiling coyly.

"Sure he could, but he won't," I say.

"She would know," Athos says behind me. I stiffen a bit. There is a sour tone when he says it, but I put a genuine smile on before turning around to face him.

He is wearing modern clothing instead of his beloved vintage clothes. He gives me a tight smile before shaking Korra's hand.

"Are you nervous?" Korra asks.

"Is this off the record?" I retort before he can say anything. She and Harold laugh, Athos doesn't react at all.

"I am optimistic," he says dryly. So, he's still mad at me.

"Would you excuse us? I need to discuss something with Lillium," *Alright, very mad then.*

"I will catch up with you guys later." I say as I follow Athos out of the lobby.

I figured he would want to talk, since we really hadn't in months, but I had thought it would be after the award ceremony. Well, better sooner than later.

Athos leads me in silence to the outside gardens, where we stop at a lilac covered arch. It smells fantastic. Everything is in full bloom.

Then I notice all the tables set up and realize this is where the after party is going to be held. Sheiba probably did the gardens just that morning.

"Athos," I start, hating silences.

"I am letting you go," He says coolly.

For a moment, I think I mishear him, or just imagine he says it because he does it so fast.

When I don't respond, he continues, "This partnership is not working out. You have been incapable of doing your job for some time now, and thankfully Maureen has been here to pick up your slack, but I cannot justify keeping you both when you refuse to do the work."

"W-what?" I stammer.

"These past few months, you have deemed yourself unfit for your position as my manager. You have taken unnecessary risks that could have resulted in huge losses, and I just cannot have that kind of person working for me. I will give you a settlement payment, and I am sure you will be able to find work somewhere else quickly. How many humans can say they manage a Hero of the Year?" He won't look at me. He's saying all this, stabbing me in the heart, and he won't look at me.

"Athos, what…I don't understand! You are firing me? "

"Yes." His amber eyes are cold as he speaks.

"Because I went after Mathis?" I whisper.

"Because you disobeyed an order. You are insubordinate, clear, and cut. You put everything at risk for your own pride. I have a business to run. I cannot have that kind of employee around." He's dancing around it, but I can feel it between us. This void that started when he trapped me with Briseathe and ripped open when I plunged that knife into Mathis's heart.

"Employee?" I snap, "Athos, look, I know I make a mistake, and you are right-" He holds his hand up, stopping me.

"I don't care. This partnership is over. You are welcome to stay for the ceremony, but you are not invited to the after party."

"I know you are mad, Athos, but seriously! This is a bit overboard, don't you think?"

"Firing an employee for-"

"I AM NOT JUST AN EMPLOYEE!" I yell. Tears are building up. My chest feels like someone is squeezing it. This can't be happening. He can't do this. We are more than partners.

"I am your friend." I sob.

Athos looks me up and down coolly. "I am sorry if you got that impression. You knew what this was from the beginning. Remember? No personal questions? That was your rule. This has never been about friendship. We both needed something from the other. Now we have it, and there is no genuine reason to-"

"WHY!?" I cry. "Why are you being so cruel? This is not you!" I wipe the tears from my face. "The Athos I know wouldn't do this. Not like this."

"Then perhaps you never really knew me." He raises a brow, "Please do not create a scene, Lillium."

"A *scene?*" I growl. "Is that all you care about? Athos! There is more to this than me making one mistake. I was mad. I was hurt by you abandoning me. I thought you were trying to get rid of me. I thought...I thought I'd lost you."

"You have," he says hotly. "You did a terrible thing, Lillium. A terrible, awful thing that cannot be fixed. My people think I'm a murder now, do you realize that? They look at me the same way they looked at him."

I gape at him, shocked. Then my age old anger starts to boil. Sure, I had made a mistake. Sure I might deserve to get fired. But not like this, not so coldly.

"Then you truly have become like them." I snap. He glares back at me. "You only care about the cameras and the fame. Well, congratulations Athos. You got it all, and you will go down in history, just like your brother."

"Do *not* dare insinuate that's what I want!"

"Oh, don't you? Why the hell else would you take the blame for killing one of your own people!?"

He yells, "Because it would ruin everything we worked for! They would all turn on me, each and every one of my people, if they knew the truth. Then where would we be, Lillium?"

I shake my head. "I wasn't thinking, Athos. I just wanted him to stop. He was right. How could we know for sure we'd be able to hold him? Or the others? I wasn't willing to risk it."

"It's not just that you killed him. I saw the look in your eyes when you did it. You enjoyed it." I gape back at him.

"No. No, that's a lie," I say, shaking my head.

"You enjoyed it, Lillium. And that is why we can't work together anymore. You are a danger to yourself and my people. I was a fool to trust you." Athos turns to leave, but I refuse to let this go.

"So you trust Maureen? Just like that? I'm nothing to you now?" I cry. Tears are pouring down my cheeks as my heart breaks. There is a chasm between us, growing with each heated word, but I cannot stop myself. I'm dying, drowning as my entire heart shatters.

He stops but doesn't turn to look at me. "You were my everything. I was willing to defy my people, my entire world, just to be by your side. But you changed. What would Gabe think of you now?"

A hole breaks open where my heart was. A gaping, bleeding gorge that aches with every breath. This isn't my Athos - he's sweet, and caring and believes in me even when he shouldn't.

I don't know who this person is before me, but it's not him.

The hole fills with venom, pumping the poison through my veins. I've grown weak around him. I let him get to me.

Never again.

"You will never be able to say you get where you are without me. That is a fact, Athos. You are nothing before I come along. You are nothing without me. I make you. I do not need your filthy Supe money. Go spend it on a fabulous party. Or someone to hold your hand and tell you you are worth something." I pull my pad out of my purse, take my bangle off and throw it at his feet.

"Enjoy tonight. This time next year, another one of you will be right here, waiting to get their name called, and you will be forgotten by everyone."

He goes in to statue mode, his back still to me.

I force myself to walk away without looking back, without crying anymore. I know I cannot go back to the others.

I need to leave, to go home. No, not there. I buy that place with his money. I walk back into the building and find an exit on the other side of the lobby, far from everyone else.

I rush to it without glancing at any of them. It does not matter anyway, I am never going to see any of them ever again. I am leaving all this behind me.

As I walk out into the streets, a little girl recognizes me. She points me out to her parents.

"That is Athos's wife!" *Wrong on so many counts*, I think as I rush away from them.

I need to go somewhere far away, where no one knows who I am. Somewhere without Supes.

I need to find the one person who is right all along. I am stupid to think that Supes and humans can coexist on the same level.

They are selfish creatures with otherworldly ways that I will never understand, and if I had listened to her, I would never be here, running through this crowd of people, holding back tears of heartbreak.

I need to find Gaia.

Made in the USA
Columbia, SC
31 October 2024

45408663R00200